Patricia Wendorf was born in Somerset but, just before the Second World War, her parents moved to Loughborough, which is where she still lives. *The Patteran Trilogy*, of which BYE BYE, BLACKBIRD is the final volume, is based largely on her own family history.

PATRICIA WENDORF
Bye Bye, Blackbird

Futura

A **Futura** Book

ISBN 0 7088 3676 3

Reproduced, printed and bound in Great Britain by
Mackays of Chatham plc, Chatham, Kent

Futura Publications
A Division of
Little, Brown and Company (UK)
Brettenham House
Lancaster Place
London WC2E 7EN

Glossary of gypsy words

atrashed	frightened
bebee	grandmother
chavvie	child
chie	gypsy girl or young woman
chor	steal
chovihanis	clairvoyant
diddecoi	derogatory term for gypsy. Half-breed gypsy
dinilo	fool
drom	road
engro	master
gavmush	policeman
gorgio gorgie	non-gypsy
kipsie	basket
mush	man
rai	young man
Rom	gypsy
vardo	caravan

Greypaull Family Tree

Elizabeth m. John Greypaull (cousins) — Daniel Greypaull m. Rachel (cousins)

Elizabeth m. John Greypaull (cousins):
- 4 sons
- Eliza m. Philip 1829–81

Daniel Greypaull m. Rachel (cousins):
- Samuel
- 2 sisters and a brother

Children of Eliza m. Philip 1829–81:
- Candace b. 1858 m. McGregor
- Madelna (Mina) b. 1860 m. David Lambert
- Jack (James John Daniel) 1862–90
- Blanche b. 1865 m. The Hon. Hugh Deveraux Fitzgerald
- Annis b. 1867 m. Frank Nevill
- Simeon b. 1872
- Louis 1875–92

Children:
- William (Billy) b. 1883 (Candace)
- Laura b. 1884 (Madelna)
- Nicholas b. c. 1889 (Jack)
- Abigail b. 1894 (Annis)
- Eve 1901 (Annis)

Carew Family Tree

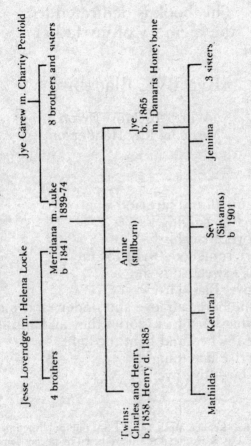

Jesse Loveridge m. Helena Locke

Jye Carew m. Charity Penfold

4 brothers

Meridiana m. Luke
b 1841   1839-74

8 brothers and sisters

Twins:
Charles and Henry
b. 1858, Henry d. 1885

Annie
(stillborn)

Jye
b. 1865
m. Damaris Honeybone

Mathilda

Keturah

Sey
(Silvanus)
b 1901

Jemima

3 sisters

This book is dedicated to
the memory of my father

Bye Bye, Blackbird

Words by Mort Dixon
Music by Ray Henderson

Pack up all my care and woe
Here I go singing low
Bye bye, Blackbird —
Where somebody waits for me
Sugar's sweet so is she
Bye bye, Blackbird —
No one here can love and understand me
Oh what hard luck stories they all hand me
Make my bed and light the light
I'll arrive late tonight
Blackbird, bye bye.

T HEY came round the side of the Hill, moving slowly in the early twilight of April. The tall green caravan with the stovepipe chimney led the main procession; followed closely by smaller vardos of red and yellow. The flat-carts, loaded with poles, and the blankets that would cover bender tents, also carried weary children and sleeping babies. In the rear, tethered and restless, stepped the company's wealth; a string of rough-coated, long-tailed Exmoor ponies. The lurcher dogs, also tethered, would be running underneath the flat-carts. There would, she knew, be a goat or two, song-birds in wicker cages, a child's pet dove in a little covered basket.

Meridiana crouched low in the lea of the hedge, and watched the coming of her people. So long had she lived in a house, between stone walls and beneath thatch, that she was no longer certain of the styles and colours favoured by separate tribes. The Penfolds had once possessed a vardo of apple-green; but then, so had the Lockes. She peeped between the leafless boughs of blackthorn, and caught a flash of silver harness. It might be the wealthy Boswells, on their way from the Bridgwater Fair? Good business had clearly been done with horseflesh; the grais were still mettlesome even after their long journey. Meri rocked back on her heels, wrapped the folds of woollen skirts about her bare feet, pulled the shawl tight about her head and shoulders, and settled down to watch.

There had, she recalled, been a morning long ago, when a company of travellers, similar to this one, had crossed the border from Dorset into Somerset. They had come from the Packe Monday Fair in Sherbourne, and were anxious to be across the border, and camped safely in Yeovil, before nightfall. Meri remembered the long and dangerous descent of Babylon Hill; the braked wheels, the restraining dragshoes that clattered against the flints and stones of the uneven surface; and herself at the age of seventeen, walking alone behind her father's bow-top. It must, she thought, be all of forty years ago, since she had halted on that summit and looked down into Yeovil. She closed her eyes and saw again the steep banks of Windham and the blue rise of Nine Springs. They had pitched overnight in Fever Hospital Lane, and moved out from that place early the next morning. She had worn her best Scotch plaid and starched white pinna'; the red, blue and yellow ribbons plaited in her hair and flying loose about her head and shoulders. The morning road had been sweet with promise. In Montacute there had lived a gorgio who was the beauty of all the western counties, and she would have him. At the memory of Luke a sharp pain clawed behind her breastbone; and who would have dreamed on a long-ago morning that the golden village was to be her trap, and he the precious bait? She opened her eyes and leaned forward. The company had halted in the dingle known as Tinkers' Bottom. Three men removed the tinkling harness, headed-up the many horses and led them silently away. Meridiana chuckled deep in her throat. Farmer Drayton would not sleep so sound in his bed that night, did he but know of the hungry grais which were feeding in his pasture field. With a speed and dexterity that she had almost forgotten Meri saw brushwood grabbed from the hedges, by a young woman, a fire of willow and then green ash-sticks kindled into a quick blaze, and a kettle hung upon a tripod. The vardos, set in a semi-circle within the dell, bloomed one by one with yellow lamplight. Bender-tents were arched in the lee of each waggon, and Meri saw the weary children creep inside them. Conversation was brief among the men and women who gathered to eat and drink around the fire. A few words of pure Romanes, mingled with the drawls of Somerset and Dorset, confirmed for Meridiana that these were indeed her people, although she no longer recognised a single face.

The watcher rose from the hedgeside with one lithe and silent movement. She began to back away, keeping carefully downwind of the dingle, lest the lurcher dogs should sense her presence.

*

Meridiana Carew came back, full of thoughts, towards the village. The darkness was total now in hollow and field. At night, the Hill was a magical place of treacherous quarries and leaping hares; down here in Montacute yellow light spilled from oil-lamps and candles set in cottage windows. In their Rectory the Reverend Powys and his family would be dining at a mahogany table. Ploughmen and drovers, stone-masons and glovers were occupied at this hour with a bread-and-scrape supper. No dog or cat moved upon the road. She came into Middle Street and halted before the house of Jye, her son. Shadows passed rapidly across the close-drawn curtains of the upper windows. Meri stood quite still, shawl about her head, one bare brown foot lapped across the other. She knew how it must be in that room; the midwife fat and self-important with her scissors and bag of boiled rags, her cans of scalding water and knotted rope of towels. The whole business was taking far too long! Jye's two little girls, Mathilda and Keturah, had been hurried to a neighbour's house at noon, the midwife had been summoned soon after, and the broad shadow on the curtain confirmed that she was still there. Jye had come down from the quarry towards evening time; Meri had spied him from her kitchen window, noted his swift step and troubled face. She smiled into the darkness. Her son would have wished that the troublesome birth had been already accomplished in his absence. Meri, of course, had known from the very outset that this child would be born alive and complete, singular and perfect. All through that winter and early springtime she had watched the gorgio girl turn pale and sickly as her thin body swelled with the growing child. This Damaris had already born two daughters, easily and in fine health; but on this occasion she carried awkwardly, very high and forward. Meri had proffered to Jye a bottle of her raspberry-leaf tea, a concoction of rare, water-violet flowers, and a distillation of the wild tansy; all those remedies for easy childbirth, long known and trusted among the old wives of her people. He had been embarrassed by his mother's offer.

''Tis like this see,' he had mumbled, 'be much better all round if us leaves the care of Maris to her own ma, what do understand her.'

Pride would not permit Meri to admit hurt, but her spine had grown rigid, her gaze more penetrating. She had reached up to the high shelf and replaced the green glass bottles.

'Plenty of women in this village,' she had said, ''ull pay good silver for my potions.' In the months that followed, Damaris Carew had sickened and looked fit to die. Meridiana had waited and watched, knowing all too well the cause of this peculiar affliction. The sight of the ailing Maris had given her mother-in-law a certain satisfaction. Meri had said as much to the Reverend Powys.

''Twill be a boy this time, Reverend, just you mark my words. 'Twas just like that Chapel-happy Maris to keep me waiting while she birthed two maidens, but I shall have my grandson soon; my Silvanus what was promised to me.'

The shadows had ceased to move across the upper

window, and all at once the little house was turned to black and silver as the moon swung above the Hill. The silence was total. Meridiana's head grew light from her held breath; it was as though the whole earth turned upon that moment. Then came the thin, indescribable wail of the newborn, and her pent-breath escaped in a long sigh. He was here, and all the reluctance of Damaris Carew had not been sufficient to prevent his coming. Meri held out her arms towards the moon. She rocked her body back and forth in an ecstasy of wonder. She knew, in a way that Jye her son could never know, that the child born in Montacute this night was one of her own kind.

Meri returned to her stone cottage, opened the door of ironbound oak and closed it, regretfully, behind her. Village propriety required that all windows and doors should remain fast between eventide and daybreak, and this she thought was all of a piece with the gorgio false-front of whitened doorstep and thick lace window curtains. She moved towards the fire's glow, lit a willow spill from the embers and touched it to a stump of candle. The crowded room leapt up and closed in upon her; she remembered with pain the atchin-tan in Tinkers' Bottom, the bender-tents and painted waggons seen in the April twilight. On this special night she could wish to be roaming underneath the moon, treading the white clover that lay thick up in Drayton's meadow; but she must wait now for Jye. It would not be right to deprive him of the pleasure of announcing to her the birth of her first grandson.

She settled down to wait, and within the hour came his light tap on her window and his footfall in the porch. Jye came in, head bent and shoulders bowed against the low beams of the ceiling, and she looked with pride, as she always did at the dark beauty of him, the head of black curls, the gentle eyes. He sat down in the carver chair beside the fire.

"Tis a boy, a liddle scrap of a thing. Whoever would

have thought that something so small cud make so much trouble.' Jye spoke in the toneless voice of the totally deaf, it was not possible to tell if he was pleased or disappointed. He touched both hands to his ears.

'I've never heard the two girls cry, only saw their mouths stretched wide and know'd that they must be wailing. But this one!' His eyes were wide with a kind of shock. 'I can seem to hear him, he screamed the minute he was born, and he have never stopped yet. 'Tis like a high-pitched pain what fills my whole head; it do almost drive me crazy. Whyfor should I hear this one? Whatever do it mean, Mother?'

He so rarely called her 'Mother', that the word, when it came, had all the power of an unaccustomed endearment. She leaned towards him, touched his fingers and formed her lips with care so that he might read the words. 'Thass a powerful pair of lungs what he got there.' She looked into the fire, and then back at Jye. 'That'll be a dark child, o'course,' she said firmly. 'Bound to be. They two maidens is your livin' image. No grandson o' mine 'ud dare to be born with anything but black hair and brown skin.' Jye stared at the fingers that still lay upon his own. 'Maris is in a bad way,' he muttered, 'I better be getting on home. I on'y come to tell'ee – '

'Her'll be right as rain,' said Meridiana, 'with that old Jemima Honeybone fussing round her.' As Jye rose from the chair, she clutched at his elbow. 'Mind now!' she warned him. 'That mother-in-law o' yours is more'n welcome to they two maidens – but this boy is to be all mine. Let there be no mistake about that. You understand me, Jye? The Honeybones can have your Mathilda and Keturah.' She looked up into his eyes, knowing too well that he could never outface her. 'That Maris have made me wait over-long already. I want him here, Jye. In my arms. As quick as you can bring him.'

'I can't! You knows very well that no infant ever goes outside the front door for the first six weeks. Mrs

6

Honeybone 'ud kill me stonedead if I even asked her.'

Meri laughed. 'Then don't ask her, you gurt ninny! Why you was riding on my hipbone, wrapped up in a blanket, when you was only days old, and you never came to no harm!' As he turned to leave she swung him back to face her. ''Tis an omen,' she said, 'that even you can hear his crying. He already got a mind to be heard – an' thass no bad thing. Let him shout back at this wicked world, Jye. They good lungs'll be the making of him, one day.'

*

Jye stood at the end of the bed, and thought how ill Maris still looked. He spoke in what he hoped was an intelligible whisper. 'I got to take him to her, and soon. There's no help for it, Maris. Her waylays me on my way to work, and when I comes back every evening.' He gestured towards the sleeping child. 'What with his wailin' and my mother's pesterin' to see him, I cud wish that he had never see'd the daylight.'

Maris said, 'He don't leave this bedroom! He idden strong enough for one thing.' Her too-high forehead wrinkled all the way up to her scraped back hairline. 'I knows what went on with Mathilda and Keturah. Six weeks old they was when you took 'em to your mother – and what did she do? She stripped 'em bare and sorted 'em out like they was piglets going to market. Tested their arm and legs, fingered their liddle backbones to see if they was growed crooked. Clapped her hands loud beside their ears to find out if they had caught your deafness.'

She paused to draw breath. 'Oh I've heard the talk around the village! 'Tis said that she've been waiting for this baby. She told the Reverend Powys that this child would be "very special".' She turned wearily towards the basket-cradle. 'He'm special all right. He don't never sleep for ten minutes put together.'

'I got to take him, Maris.' He paused. ''Tis a funny

thing, but you been lying there these three weeks and you don't seem to get no stronger do you?'

She knew at once what was in his mind.

'You don't never think that your mother have put – ? Ah no, her wudden never dare to do that – '

Jye shook his head. 'I never see'd her so dead-set on anything, Maris!' He smiled, persuasively. 'We be into Maytime, and the sun so warm; I could swaddle him in shawls. 'Tis on'y a short step down the street.'

She was still unwilling. 'May is a treacherous month, Jye'. She attempted to pull herself up onto the pillows. 'He'm frailer and smaller than the girls was – ' Tears of weakness filled her eyes. 'Don't look at me like that!' she cried, and then, 'oh, very well, take him then! But straight away, mind. All the people is in Church and Chapel at the minute. I'd die of shame if you was to be seen out in the street with a babe of only three weeks.' Jye lifted the child and began to wind shawls around him; he knew that the scolding note was in his wife's voice by the way her thin lips twisted. 'And don't you dare let her lay a finger on him; and while you're about it you can make it clear what his given name is. David John is what I've called him, for my father.' She leaned forward and beckoned him towards her. She looked anxiously at the swaddled bundle. 'Now you keep his face covered with the shawl, mind. He'm too young to take the full strength of the spring air.'

Meri saw Jye coming down deserted Middle Street, and grinned. With her respectable neighbours tucked safely away at their Sunday morning worship, Maris had obviously relented. Meridiana sat down on her low stool and waited. Jye came in and without a word handed over the tiny woollen bundle. The child's face was covered with a thin layer of shawl and she allowed it to remain so. Part of the pleasure was anticipation, and for that moment just to hold him was enough. She sat quite still, and gradually the warmth of the tiny body seeped into her sad heart. She knew again the exultation of the blood that had seized her long ago at Jye's birth. There was, she thought, a kind of golden glory that comes only with the birth of a longed-for child. She glanced sideways at her son, and caught the sudden apprehension on his features; she lifted the layer of wispy shawl and understood his terror.

Meri gazed on the face of Silvanus for a long time; she touched her brown fingers to his pale hand and struggled towards some understanding of what had come to pass. At last she said, 'Ah, dordi dordi! So 'tis a liddle Honeybone boy what you have brought me. She have managed to spite me after all – he'm the livin' image of her. Skin as white as skim-milk.' She pulled the shawl all the way back and gasped, 'an' look at his hair, Jye! So much of it, and of a colour hot enough to burn the hand what touches.' Reluctantly, she took the child's head into her palm. 'Long and narrow,' she muttered, 'ah, you's'll be too clever for your own peace o' mind. An' what else have the gorgie mother foisted on 'ee, my poor dearie? What colour be your eyes, then?'

As if he had heard and understood, the infant's sandy lashes swept upwards; but the gaze that met hers was not that of a baby. He looked back at her with an equal fierceness; and that strange compulsive stare confirmed for Meridiana his instant recognition of her.

'Blue,' she cried, 'blue as eyebright – as cornflowers – an' such eyes'll never turn to brown!' She spoke to Jye and there was triumph in her face. 'Go back,' she said, 'and say my pretty thank-you to your wife. Tell her I be not at all put-out by her liddle trick.'

Meri stretched out an arm and snapped her fingers close to Jye's frightened face. 'So he'm the colour of whey, wi' hair as red as a new-pulled carrot? That don't signify nothing.' She lifted the child and held him out towards his father. 'Take him – baptise him in your Chapel – call him any name you fancy.' She spoke to the child. 'You knows me an' I knows you, my heart's joy! You's'll learn all my secrets, one day. Us'll walk the

9

drom together.' She stared hard at Jye. 'Know you what I be saying? This boy is pure Rom, wi'out taint, an' more gypsy than the ribs o'God.'

*

Jye went away; the baby clutched tight into his shoulder. Meri stood at her door and watched him turn into Middle Street, his head slewed anxiously towards the Church gates as the Reverend Powys and his flock began to emerge. She grinned briefly, and then grew sober; she returned to her fireside, reached for the clay pipe, cut a plug of thick-twist tobacco, and began to roll it, thoughtfully, between her fingers. Meri filled the pipe, lit it with a spill of willow and drew smoke deep into her lungs. The company of travellers was still pitched in Tinkers' Bottom. She had watched them, secretly, from a vantage point above the dingle; the birth of a child had delayed their departure. A separate tent had been erected for the woman's confinement. The gypsy child had been born, according to tradition, not in the vardo, but on straw and down upon the good earth. It had pleased her to see the old rule of mokardi still observed, even into this year of 1901, in what Jye had told her was the twentieth century. No male Rom had entered the tent of this mother and her new-born; special crockery had been used, food cooked separately, and their washing hung well away from that of all other families. The woman's labour had been long, in the end a doctor had been brought out from Martock; it was almost a month now since their arrival. Meri tapped out the cold ashes of her pipe and prepared to relight it. Her curiosity as to the ultimate destination of this tribe had grown stronger since the birth of Jye's son. She had crouched behind a furze bush, caught at the few short phrases of their conversation that came to her upon the wind. The name of Buckland St Mary had been mentioned frequently among them in latter days. Meri remembered the Councils held in the Blackdowns, in the times of her father, and his father. She also remembered a red-haired woman called Eliza Greypaull, and despite the warmth of May, Meridiana Carew moved closer to the fire. Dwelling upon the past, she had always believed, could hold very little profit for her. A belief that she would never make old bones had caused her to live each day as if it was her last. But the earth had continued to turn, and here she was, still walking upright, and above ground. Meri closed her eyes and saw Eliza as she had been on the day of her wedding to Philip Greypaull, neat-boned and tiny, clothed in gold and stepping high. A conviction that momentous events were about to take place down in Taunton made her cry aloud, 'Wait for me, 'Liza! The time have come now for one last meeting betweeen us. Wait by your father's gate, where the blackthorns lean inwards. There's words to be said, secrets to be told, Eliza! I got to know what have happened to the coral pendant. The peace of my very soul do depend upon it.' Meri turned towards the dresser which held cups and plates of old Crown Derby. 'I still got your blue bowl,' she whispered, 'hid in a cupboard and never used for fear that I might break 'un. I's'll bring it back to 'ee, Eliza. Time is running close for thee an' me, and I must have all wrongs put right, and lies must be chopped for truth.'

Meri sighed and looked away towards the ındow; she tried to hold on to the memory of Eliza Greypaull, but her mind came at last to the thought that could no longer be denied. Once again she refilled the clay pipe, applied flame and drew smoke deep into her lungs. Silvanus! Her breath expelled on a long moan and the blue smoke of tobacco wreathed about her head. She relived those moments when he first lay in her arms, his face still hidden by the shawl, the warmth of his tiny body seeping into her sad heart. For the sake of Jye, and her own pride, she had, to begin with, stayed silent, had not allowed disappointment full voice; but at sight of that white skin and red hair the very heart had withered

11

in her. The boy was all gorgio in his looks, a Honeybone child from the soles of his feet to the last carrot-coloured lock of hair. Despair had seized her in that moment. Ah dordi! but she had never doubted that Jye's son would be a dark child. Even now, with heart and mind braced against it, the memory of that small white face laid against the walnut sheen of her own arm, caused her to draw hard on the lit tobacco.

Meri laid aside the pipe and clasped her hands together. She sat very still, willed herself to recall exactly how it had been between them. The eyes had betrayed him to her! Blue; blue as eyebright, like a drop of ocean, a patch of sky; but old! That deep look, every bit as fierce and penetrating as her own, had locked them together into lifelong understanding. The child had recognised her, and not with pleasure! Oh, he had known her, but only as old protagonists acknowledge one another. She smiled. The long knives had been drawn this day, and Meridiana Carew was not the one to retreat from battle.

The day would come when Silvanus Carew would halt before a mirror, and the features reflected in the glass would be those of Damaris, his mother. But the eyes! Meridiana laughed aloud. She had gazed that May morning into his soul's window; and what she had seen there could never be denied. 'Pure Rom, wi'out taint,' she had told Jye, 'and more gypsy than the ribs o' God!' So the future was settled; the patteran laid down; the drom still stretched out, long and white before her. The time had come for the making of her last journey from this village. 'Tomorrow, Eliza,' she promised, 'tomorrow is when I set my foot to find you.'

Her bed was positioned underneath a low rear window, and against all Jye's urgent pleading, Meri slept in all seasons with the casement thrown wide. She lay awake on that special night, watched the moon climb the Hill, and considered many things. She remembered the journey from Buckland St Mary, made long ago with

Luke, her husband; the deep coombes, the steep hills, the wild and flinty places. Age, and the long and sheltered life lived in the village, had weakened the old conviction that all things were possible to her, and Meri knew now that she could never return to that place by her ownself. She drifted into sleep on the comforting thought that the company pitched in Tinkers' Bottom were preparing to move on; but her dreams were all of red-haired, blue-eyed children, she saw them ranked down the generations, those descendants of Silvanus – ! She awoke at the sound of her own voice, crying out 'Eliza, Eliza!' and Meridiana knew then what she must do. Even while the dawn was still streaked red and pearl above Ham Hill, she snatched up her old plaid blanket, fastened it at the shoulder with her best gold-crown brooch, considered the detested boots worn only for Jye's sake, and kicked them away into a chimney corner. Her need to see the first stirring of the tan in Tinkers' Bottom had now become urgent. Time was, when she could have gone to them openly and without fear. Take me with you, she would have said, let us travel together to Buckland St Mary. But that was before Jye; before his strange avoidance of all contact with her people, and the years had also seen a thinning-out of the familiar faces. Taiso and Lavinia had not been seen in Montacute in an age of harvests; the faces in the dingle were those of strangers. Driven by need, and that instinct which had never failed her, Meri found her sheltered spot of the previous days, wrapped woollen skirts around her bare feet, and settled down to wait until the company should waken.

The first stirrings came from the apple-green vardo. The half-door opened and a head appeared; Meri caught a gleam of the hooped gold that swung beneath black braids. The girl gazed cautiously about her; she sniffed at the morning air like a vole or a rabbit that emerges from its night-hole. The wide, dark gaze roved across the dingle, turned upwards and rested briefly on the hedge where Meridiana sat concealed. The lower section of the vardo door came open, and a tall girl was revealed, dressed in plaid, with yellow ribbons threaded in her hair; she stood for a moment upon the top step. Meri caught her breath at the beauty of the rackli who might, she thought, have been her ownself at the age of sixteen. The girl dipped one brown foot into the wet grass, and then withdrew it. Suddenly she plunged and ran the short distance that brought her to the banked-up embers of last evening's fire. A handful of brushwood, a few sticks of green willow, and a blaze was kindled. A copper water jug stood beneath the vardo; the girl bent to lift it, and finding it empty, began to walk up the sloping sides of the dingle to the place where Meri sat.

The move was so unexpected that Meridiana could only shrink within her plaid. She should have remembered that the girl's first action would be to mend the fire, and then seek water! Too late to run, now! Meri willed her tongue to find the old words; but the girl was already looming above her.

'Awve adray the yog dudee,' she commanded. Meridiana obeyed, and came slowly down to stand in the firelight.

'You can rokra Romanes?' the girl asked.

Meri grinned. 'When I be of a mind.' The rosy brown face crumpled into laughter.

'I knows you now! You be that one what wed wi' the gorgio.'

'I be that one. I goes by the name of Carew, but I was born Loveridge.'

'Sarishan!' the girl whispered. 'Sarishan!'

Meri sighed.

'Ah, but that do fall kindly on my ears. 'Tis many years since I was bid Sarishan. What is your own name?'

'Now that depends. Oftimes I be know'd as Boswell; somedays I be called by the name of Stanley.'

She waved away the intrusive surname, 'Elvira,' she said, 'thass what everybody shouts when there's water to be fetched.' She snatched up the copper jug. 'Bide you here, put they sticks on the yog, keep it burning until I gets back. Us'll rokra some more Romanis together.'

Meridiana faced-to beside the gypsy fire, she fed the blaze with sticks and felt unusually content. The lurcher dogs, which lay untethered beneath the flat-carts and vardos, had not stirred at her approach; they lay, heads on paws, studying her with soft, melancholy eyes. Elvira came back, and at once the tan was all commotion and confusion. Tousled heads emerged from bender-tent and vardo. Children were sent to fetch wood and water; smoke from many fires rose up in the dingle and mingled among the leafless boughs of tall trees. Elvira fetched a large iron pan from the box beneath the waggon, into it she placed thick slices of fat, rancid bacon which had, she said, been the gift of a farmer's daughter who had begged a love-potion from her. The bread, hard as rock, and at least a week old, had been pushed into her basket by a baker's wife who feared the 'evil eye'. Elvira's rose-brown face curved with laughter at the recollection.

'Proper trashed she were, when her see'd I coming, but not frightened enough to give I her fresh bread. Never mind!' She sliced the loaf with a wickedly curved knife, and laid the slices to fry in the fat from the sizzling bacon.

'Awve avree,' she shouted at the apple-green vardo, 'brekfus is ready, an' we got a caller!' A peep of fear showed in Meri's eyes, and Elvira reached out a hand of comfort. ''Twill be alright. They's'll be so glad to see thee. But better you tell me quick what's your given name.'

'Meridiana.'

'A-ah!' The word was spoken on a long sigh. 'So that's who you be. Then 'twill surely be a welcome. They have spoke oft of you around the fire, when many families come together. There can't be a gypsy in all the western country what don't know the sad tale cf Meridiana.'

The door of the apple-green vardo swung open, and the man was first to emerge, followed by his wife. 'Cousin!' cried Jubilia Boswell, but Meri held back, still unsure.

'Us played together as chavvies,' said Jubilia, 'us hid under Granny's waggon on the day of Sinty Loveridge's wedding! Us "took" roses out of Parson's garden – and sold 'em back to the Missus Vicar! You can't have forgot me, Meridiana! I never did forget you.'

Meri held out hands that were cold and shaking.

''Tiv bin so long Jubi, and I gone so far from all the old ways and places.' There were tears in Jubilia's eyes. She turned back towards the apple-green vardo.

'Don't you recognise your waggon? The one your father had built for you, down to Bridgwater? My father brought it from you when you wed wi' your gorgio man. 'Twas for a wedding-gift to me and Amal.' She grinned at the man by her side, whose skin was so dark it was almost black.

'I birthed many children underneath that vardo, 'twas a lucky chop my father made an' no mistake.'

'How many chavvies?' Meri's voice was gruff with chagrin.

Jubilia held up the five fingers of her right hand, and the thumb and forefinger of her left.

'Five and two,' she said.

'That makes seven,' said Meridiana, who had learned long ago from the gorgio how to count up to ten.

'All living?' she enquired.

'All living, an' most of 'em wed, 'cepting my Elvira.' She paused. ''Tis a shame that your son have took to himself a maid from the village. Elvira have spied him many-a-time across the Hill an' down the quarry. She have remarked on his looks – '

'Jye was hitched in the Baptist Chapel,' said Meri, sourly, 'and you can't be no surer wed than by the Baptist parson. You know'd that Jye was deaf?'

'Us know'd that he never spoke with any gypsy. I met wi' him, full-faced, one time along the Tintinhull drom. That was not the eyes of a satisfied man, cousin. Though he is the most beautiful Romminichal I ever did see!'

Meri shivered. 'He'm a deep Romani – deep as I ever

was – but he 'ont allow it. There's danger in that, Jubilia! A man can't deny his nature wi'out harm coming from it. I fear for him. There's confusion in his hand and head. He bain't neither the one thing, nor yet another.'

Jubilia put an arm about her cousin's shoulders.

'Come you to the yog an' warm yourself. You's'll take some brekfus wi' us, and tonight us'll sit around the fire. Us'll tell about the old times.'

Meridiana sat down beside the fire and accepted a bone-china plate heaped with fried bread and bacon. She began to eat, absentmindedly, with her fingers, as she had done long ago, at her father's fireside. Her gaze was fixed on the apple-green vardo.

'I disremembers that colour o' green', she said abruptly. Jubilia nodded. 'Amal have took good care of him,' she looked lovingly at the waggon. 'A fresh lick o' paint every springtime, and his wheels kep' in good trim. He'll see us out for our lifetime, but you'm right cousin. He was done up in a much darker green when I first see'd un.'

Jubilia wiped the fat from her plate with the last piece of bread, and chewed, vigorously.

'Bide alongside I, Meridiana,' she urged, 'the men got business to see to, hereabouts. Us'll bide in this dingle one more night, at least. You is welcome to look inside your first home, if that be of your mind?'

Meridiana was reluctant. 'I got a new grandchild,' she murmured, 'born just three weeks ago.'

'And will the gorgie daughter-in-law want you over her doorstep?'

'I always bides in my own house until Jye sees fit to bring his chavvie to me.'

'There you be, then!' cried Jubilia. 'Fancy-free an' footloose!'

Breakfast over, and there was movement again in the tan. The men went away, climbing from the dingle, their arms draped with ropes, and flash, silver-trimmed harness. Meri looked upwards to see a string of long-tailed Exmoor ponies being led away across the hill by the path that led to Stoke-sub-Hamdon. On the far side of the dingle, horses were being harnessed, backed-up to flat carts, and driven smartly away. Meanwhile, the young women of the tribe were preparing themselves and their hawking baskets for a day's work in the surrounding villages.

Elvira had changed her plaid for a long skirt of crimson velvet, and a blouse of yellow silk; over which she draped crossways a Paisley shawl of many colours, fastened at the left shoulder with a fine silver brooch. Her necklaces and bracelets were of deep-rose coral, her earrings of coral and silver almost reached down to her shoulders. Her black braided hair was looped above each ear and held in position with silver-and-tortoiseshell combs. Her basket was square and deep; Meri watched as the girl hung her bits of hand worked lace temptingly across its rim. The clothes-pegs, carefully counted out into bundles of five-and-one, were packed into the bottom of the basket. A few cheap trinkets, bought at Bridgwater Fair, were added to her wares.

Meri felt the old pain that came with remembrance; every Romani chie had her own bits of treasured jewellery; with her it had been amber. She had loved it in all its colours; yellow as a cat's eye, tawny as a chestnut –

Jubilia broke in upon her thoughts.

'You had some rare beads at one time, Meridiana. You was give your grandmother Loveridge's very best pieces. My Elvira is powerful fond of the coral and silver.' She paused. 'There was a pendant, a very old piece, a gurt heavy thing, like enough to bow the head on your shoulders. I don't reckon as how you wears that one anymore?'

Meri made no answer, and her cousin went on, 'Us could never make out why your chavvies was born so hindered. That pendant had once belonged to a chovihanis. 'Twas said that any woman who wore it would bear strong and healthy children.'

'I chopped it. I chopped it with a bori-rye in exchange for a blue bowl.' Meri stared at Jubilia. 'Ah, you needn't look so wild at me. I've paid the price, four times over. My twins was borned with crooked backs, my liddle Annie never drawed breath – as for Jye.' Her features twisted with an agonised spasm. 'Jye is tall and strong, but he is stone-deaf, and that deafness have cut him off from gorgio and Romani, alike. I was wilful, Jubi. Surely you remembers that much. I always done exactly what I wanted, but there's a price to pay at the end, and I've paid mine.'

'Where's the pendant now?' whispered Jubilia.

''Tis like I said, I chopped wi' a farmer's wife, name of 'Liza Greypaull. They lived in a place called Larksleve, high up in the Blackdowns. Minds you Dommett Wood?'

'I minds it.'

'Thass where we was pitched that summer, and me so proud and sure at seventeen that I was the fairest rakli in all the Western Counties – '

'And so you was, Meri. I can see you now in your plaid and amber. Us danced at your wedding, me and Amal, but you only had eyes for your gorgio man; though I must say he looked more gypsy than the ribs o' God!'

'Luke was my heart's joy,' Meri's voice became gruff, 'I lived most of my days in a stone house for love of him.'

'Can't be no better proof nor that,' nodded Jubilia, 'but surely you lived first together in yonder vardo?'

Meri looked fearfully towards the apple-green waggon.

'Aye, and I'm glad that your time in it has been good, for I past some of the worst days o' my life inside they walls. My twins was born there, in Dommett Wood, in a bitter winter, with snow as high as the trees, and me sending Luke out to chor eggs and tiddies.'

'But you was still unharnessed, Meri. No man had put a tether on you.'

'And you think that I be tethered now, do you?'

19

'Word is, among the Loveridges,' said Jubilia, 'that you bides in Montacute only for the sake of Jye, who have took him a gorgio wife when he could have had his pick among our racklis.'

Meridiana smiled. 'Then you'se can tell they Loveridges that I bain't tethered no more, altho' I was, once. Aye, dordi, dordi!' she sighed. 'I bides in Montacute, 'tis true; but I bides there of my own will, these days.' She hesitated. 'I got a favour to ask – I need to travel the Chard road. If mayhap you'se is going in that part of the country – ?'

Jubilia grinned. ''Tis Buckland St Mary what you wants, now idden that the truth, cousin?'

'I can't deny it.'

'Then rest easy, Meri, for 'tis Dommett Wood what us is bound for.'

*

Whenever she thought about age, which was not very often, Eliza Greypull calculated that she must, almost certainly, still be on the sunny-side of seventy. She did not feel old. The sight in her remaining eye was poor, but then it always had been. The fierce tint of her red hair had faded to a pale marmalade shade, which amused her greatly. She was as thin and active as she had been on her wedding day, her mind as clear and sharp, her will still iron-clad. The only sign of advancing years to be found in Eliza was as yet unsuspected by her children. More and more, her thoughts had a tendency to slip away into the past. This ability to recall what was gone had always been hers, but until now such memories had been safely linked to an inevitable future. Now, she had only to sit in her old rocking chair before the fire, for all of those days lived in the Blackdown Hills to come back to her mind; but no longer with the immediacy she had once known. Those years seemed to haunt her lately in a strange and retrospective manner, like a story told and already completed upon a printed page. Some names came back gently to her. There was Samuel, the cousin whom she had once loved, and who now farmed, unmarried up on Larksleve; Loveday Hayes, the servant who had been closer and more faithful than a sister; her cousin Rhoda, who had sailed to America, and who farmed in Suamico, Wisconsin. The Reverend Soames, who had performed the ceremony of marriage between herself and Philip Greypaull.

But there was another name, one that hovered reluctantly on the edge of conscious memory; and now, on this May evening, it returned, swift as an arrow, powerful as a revelation. Meridiana Carew! Eliza leaned back in her chair, closed her eyes, and allowed the name to bring Meri to her; a tall woman, dark of skin and eyes, her black hair in a coronet of braids, hoops of gold in her earlobes, amber and coral necklaces at her throat. That Meridiana still strode the earth, Eliza had no doubt! Out there, beyond factory chimneys and paved streets, away from the tiled roofs and chimneypots of Taunton, walked a gypsy woman who had always possessed strange powers. Eliza recalled, with a chill of fear, the last meeting between herself and Meridiana. Threats had been uttered, predictions made that remained, as yet, unfulfilled.

The telegram arrived late that evening. 'Cousin Samuel dead. Funeral on Tuesday. Your attendance urgent.' The address was that of Larksleve Farm in Buckland St Mary. The sender of the bad news had been her oldest brother, Francis.

Eliza, dressed in her best black cloak and bonnet, sat up beside the Buckland carter, and regretted the impulse that had allowed her to even consider taking such a journey.

'But you must go, mother,' Madelina had said. 'There's bound to be a Will, and your name listed in it. Why else would they miserable Greypaulls have bothered to inform you?'

Madelina was, as usual, absolutely right. What Mina

21

could not have known was the scope of the pain that filled Eliza's heart on learning of the death of Samuel. She had loved him. Easy to admit it now, when he lay dead, and she so old that it scarcely mattered. She remembered his kind eyes, the ploughlines of worry in his thin face; it was to Sam she had looked for reassurance on the morning of her marriage to his older brother. All it had needed then was her straight refusal to marry Philip Greypaull, but she had lacked the courage. Almost thirty years had passed since she last travelled this road, and yet Eliza ignored the beauty of hedges and fields, of villages and hamlets. The thoughts rolled and tumbled in her head with every turn of the cart's wheels, and suddenly they were passing the schoolhouse, the Church, the Post Office. Nothing had changed in this place except the faces of people; Eliza rode through Buckland St Mary unacknowledged, and she in her turn, recognised no one. The long climb began up to Larksleve Farm, and if at that point she could have turned the horses back towards Taunton, Eliza would have done so. They drove slowly between high-banked lanes, the steep sides of which were bright with all the wild flowers of her childhood. She remembered the bad years lived in Hunter's Court, the colourless quality of her present life in Greenbrook Terrace and she was finally touched by the beauty around her. She had told tales of Larksleve to all her seven children, but no words could convey the long blue line of distant hills, the shapes of fields, the dark coombes; the sight of corn in August, the bitter-sweet October.

The blue and white house came into view, smaller, less imposing than she had remembered, its reeded thatch no longer golden, but dulled and brown with years. The sight of the ageing thatch was to be her undoing. The pent-up tears could no longer be held back. Eliza wept.

'You have a good cry, Missus.' The young carter, his face brick-red with embarrassed emotion, had heard the story of the Philip Greypaulls at his mother's knee. ''Tis a wonder to me that you cud stand to come back here, after all what happened to 'ee!'

''Tis a strain,' confessed Eliza, 'there's so many things I had forgotten.'

The carter helped her down and placed her bag beside her. She stood before the gate of Larksleve and waited, like a visitor, to be invited in. An old, stooped man came towards her; he spoke from a pinched mouth. 'Don't you recognise me, Eliza?'

'Francis?' She smiled. 'The last time we met I flung five sovereigns at you.' The pursed lips grew tighter. 'Best if we forget the old days,' he said. 'We are gathered here on solemn business.'

For the past ten years Samuel Greypaull had lived and farmed on Larksleve with Mary his unmarried sister. It was Mary who now kissed Eliza, led her through the blue-flagged hallway and up the little spiral staircase.

'I've put 'ee in the middle bedroom, cousin,' she said gently, 'I thought you'd be more – more at your ease, in there.' She indicated the wash-basin and ewer. 'I brought up hot water when I see'd the carter coming. There's soap and clean towels, and a pot of fresh tea in the kitchen just as soon as you be ready for it.'

Mary went away; Eliza took one step towards the window, and then halted. It would only prove painful, she told herself, if she was to be too self-indulgent; the inglenook fireplace, the cold blue parlour, the sunlit porch where she had sat with Loveday, the view from the window, had all existed in another life. A life that had died with the passing of her cousin Samuel. It was this resolve that took her dry-eyed through the funeral service, the interment, and the uncomfortable meeting with her cousins and brothers. The Will was read by a solicitor from Chard. 'To my dear cousin Eliza Greypaull, widow of my brother Philip, I leave the sum of seven hundred pounds.' The farm itself, according to custom, would revert to other, more affluent Greypaulls. Cousin Mary was a wealthy woman in her own right;

she intended, so she told Eliza, to retire to a little cottage in the village and keep bees. Meanwhile, Eliza was welcome to spend a few days on Larksleve, if she so wished.

*

Her resolve to remain unaffected by this return to Larksleve had taken Eliza through that day and evening, and into a deep sleep of exhaustion. In the morning she awoke to birdsong, the lowing of cows, the smells of mown grass and hawthorn blossom. She sat up in bed, disorientated by sunlight, and just for a moment she thought that the years had played a trick upon her, and that she was still a young wife, awakening on Larksleve to a new day. Then she saw the black gown and cloak draped across a chair, and her sad hands lying on the bedspread, their knuckles swollen huge with age, their skin liver-spotted. It was then that Eliza truly knew herself to be seventy years old, and Samuel, whom she had loved, to be dead and lying at peace in the Buckland churchyard. It was then that all the heartbreak and joys of those seventy years came back to her mind, and she could not deny them. She had returned to this place to bury Samuel Greypaull; had stood at the open grave among the family mourners, and thrown a rosebud on his coffin for a remembrance of a love that had never been spoken between them; and how strange that on this May morning her unwilling thoughts should turn back towards the weak man she had married. Girls of Eliza's generation had rarely spoken of love, and never of passion. They confessed, shyly to feelings of warmth, to affection, respect, and admiration; but she had not even liked her cousin Philip. Eliza had tried to feel as a good wife should towards a husband, but in those nights when he had lain drunk beside her, it was always Sam of whom she dreamed. Samuel, who in her imagination, had run with her through darkened meadows, danced with her, reckless and abandoned, underneath the moon.

24

Eliza recalled herself as a young wife, self-righteous and determined in her blue dress, the red curling hair escaping from beneath a white cap; she sighed and eased herself more comfortably against the pillows. Today she could find the courage to look towards the window, and gaze out across the woods and fields that had once been in her sole possession. Larksleve had never belonged to Philip Greypaull! She could admit the truth from a space of years. On that very first morning of their life together, she had sat in the window embrasure of the master-bedroom and looked out on the drilled green of the growing crops. It was then that the rich red earth of Larksleve had reached out and claimed her. From that hour her husband Philip had been no more than a hind, a servant to be paid-off with her dowry money; the pair of hands that she intended should guide her plough, sow her corn, reap her harvest.

Poor Philip! He had craved the love she could not give him, had pleaded for a sign of kindness from her. But she, young and confident in her own judgement, had lavished all her love on Philip's children, and the good husbanding of Larksleve. The bitterness of truth distressed her now, and she tried to close her mind against it; but the resolute will that had shaped her past life would not allow her to renege. She remembered her mother, but unwillingly; called up Elizabeth of the dark hair and high colour, the proud and domineering farm wife, who had driven her dog-cart like a chariot around the lanes of Buckland. How desperately the young Eliza had tried to emulate her mother, and how strong had been the pressures to galvanise her husband Philip to similar ambition.

Eliza paused, and reminded herself that this was her day of truth. She forced her mind to a less comfortable conclusion. The fault could not all be set at her mother's door. In those days Eliza herself had felt a dangerous pride rise in her; had longed to see her shelves lined with cheeses, her foldyards filled with livestock, her cart houses, barns and stables crammed with waggons, grain and horses; and Philip? He had never been the strong man she demanded; all he had wanted was to be happy, to sing among his friends, to be footloose and carefree. Those elegant shoulders had been meant for the wearing of fine clothes, the slim hands never equal to the drawing of wood, the tending of livestock. She sighed, and the pain in her heart settled down to a gentle aching; her life was coming to an end, quite soon it would cease altogether, and when that day came she would go to join them, the fair-haired man she had so misunderstood and the dark-haired one whom she had loved. There remained one window through which she must look, one other land that must still be walked down; and this was to be her day of discovery, for Eliza Greypaull would never pass this way again.

*

Eliza watched the gypsies' ascent of Buckland Hill, always a dangerous business with the sweating horses pulling on the heavy waggons. She recognised the inevitability of their arrival. A strange, fatalistic mood had lain across these past days; there had been so many signs and events that contained a quality of revelation for her, and she was grateful for it. Only a very favoured few, thought Eliza, were granted these special times at the close of a long life, in which to say their goodbyes.

The lane into Dommett Wood was still green and dim, narrowed in its beginnings by hedges of untrimmed blackthorn which grew inwards and shut out the daylight. Further in, the pathway, she knew, would widen into a clearing, a secretive shuttered place, rarely visited by Buckland people. The high gate, hung all those years ago by Eliza's father to prevent his cattle straying, hung loosely now on rusted hinges. No one had ever dared to lean upon it, and it was only the superstitious legend of the gate's propensity for ill-luck that had saved it from total decay. The gypsy waggons swayed and creaked into the lane, and Eliza, concealed behind the blackthorn thicket, watched closely this company of travellers, and searched for the significant face that instinct had told her must be among the number.

Time passed. The warm May evening drifted into twilight; smoke rose up between the elm trees, a dog barked, she heard the jingle of harness, words spoken in an unfamiliar language, and still Eliza waited. She felt no surprise at the sight of Meridiana Carew, walking slowly through the trees towards her. They met as if it were only yesterday that they had last spoken together.

'You'se have come then.'

'I've come,' confirmed Eliza.

They gazed unsmilingly at one another.

'I'd have know'd you anywhere, 'Liza.'

'You never altered much either, Meri.'

The words of their greeting were unimportant, a flimsy link across the years, inconsequential and without edge. The initiative, as always, was to come from the gypsy.

'Tomorrow,' she said briefly. 'Us'll take a step or two together. Time have come, Eliza, for thee and me to talk of many matters.'

Eliza nodded. 'Wait for me, straight after breakfast, in our old spot down by Home Meadow.'

*

The sky was overcast, the air still and heavy. Eliza, impatient to be gone from the breakfast table, drank tea but refused food.

'A last look around the fields,' she excused herself to Mary. Her return to Taunton was to be made at noon, in the company of a neighbouring farmer who had business in the town.

Eliza went down, very slowly, to Home Meadow, to the old place where Meridiana had so often waited for her, beside the blackthorn. But this was to be no moment snatched from allotted tasks, no quick word exchanged above hedgetops. Eliza could just make out the blue of faded plaid, the faint glint of earrings beneath black braids. Confrontation would require that they sit facing one another. Without a word they began to walk up to Pickett's Copse. Cut logs lay in the woodland clearing; a fortuitous arrangement of dead elm made it possible for them to sit comfortably, and eye-to-eye. Eliza smoothed the folds of her black skirt, and then raised a hand to the curling hair that had strayed from beneath her white cap.

Meri grinned. 'You didden never go greyhaired, Eliza?' She touched a finger to the coronet of black braids. 'Mine kep' its colour too, as you can see, what is a marvel considering all our lifelong troubles.' She scuffed her bare feet among the dead leaves. 'I see as how you still goes well-shod.'

Eliza looked down at the smart black boots that had been a gift from her son-in-law in London.

'Things idden always what they appear to be,' she murmured, 'take this dress for instance. I cudden afford to buy silk, 'twas a present from my daughter, Blanche. She said that I should wear proper mourning for the old Queen.'

'Looks after you, does she, this one what lives in London?'

'She's very good.'

'What about your other children?'

'I lost two of my sons. Jackie took a fall while steeplechasing, Louis – he was the youngest one and backward – he died of influenza. Simeon have gone for a soldier, and we don't never see him.'

Meri nodded. 'So that,' she said softly, 'do leave you wi' your four maidens.' She leaned towards Eliza. 'I well remembers your girls, from our last meeting.' Her voice was sharp with envy. 'Like a bunch of pretty flowers they was, perched up on that farmcart.' She paused. 'You is not surprised to see me, 'Liza?'

'The Lord works in mysterious ways – '

Meri laughed. 'Still the same idden you!' She sobered.

'For myself, well I know'd as you 'ud be here. Certain things is meant to happen.'

Eliza said quietly, 'What is it that you want with me, Meri?'

'You knows what I want – what I always wanted. This matter of my coral pendant, it got to be settled, Eliza. We be both gettin' older. I won't rest easy in my grave until I know that the necklace is back where it belongs.'

'And where do it belong?'

'In the tents of my people.'

Eliza said sharply, 'Then why did you chop it all they years ago for something so cheap as my china bowl?' Head tilted, she studied the taut features of Meridiana.

'I wondered about it then, Meri. I've been years working out the answer. Ah, but I knows you now!'

'You read my mind? Why you be so simple I could offer you Buckland Church and you 'ud buy it from me!'

Eliza said quietly, 'You dreaded the carrying and birthing, didden you? Oh you wanted children – but full-grown and independent of you. You've always envied me my daughters, but I paid a price for them – and that debt is far from settled-up.' Eliza paused and sought for the words that would explain her conclusions. ''Tis like this, see Meri – a mother is ever the prisoner of her child. Something binds the two together. You can't have the glory and escape the burden. You wanted babies – but you also wanted to be free. You cudden bear to be trammelled, could you? And you were so beautiful at seventeen!' Eliza nodded. 'Oh I can see now how your young girl's mind had worked it out. Get rid of the pendant you thought; for 'tis the necklace what do make certain sure of the babies! Chop the coral for a blue bowl, and let Eliza bear the chavvies!'

A long look passed between the two women; an even longer silence. Meri said at last, 'You be quite right, Eliza. I cudden stand the thought of carrying and birthing. I was proud of my looks – I wanted it to be jus'

29

Luke and me, and no child to come between us. Remember, 'Liza, how I sickened fit to die afore the twins' birth? Ah dordi, dordi, I might as well tell 'ee the truth now. Yes, I wanted rid of that coral, but I was jus' seventeen and foolish. The minute I looked on my Charles and Henry – then I know'd what a bad thing I had done. I came back to see you afore Jye's birth. I begged you to give back the necklace – '

'A bargain is a bargain,' broke in Eliza, 'and my need was greater than yours.'

Reluctant admiration warmed Meri's voice.

'You was never 'trashed of me, was you, 'Liza?'

'Frightened? No, I was never frightened of you. But you made me believe that you'd got magic powers – and that goes against the grain for a Christian woman.' Eliza paused. 'There's another matter what do stand between us. My Blanche got to know your Jye when he was up in London.' The brown fists unclenched; Meri leaned across to grip Eliza's fingers. 'There's two sorts o' women in this world,' she said grimly. 'There's the givers and the takers. Your maid do take all and give nothing back. I warned 'ee long ago that she was a bad 'un. Her have ruined my son's whole life.'

'But you said he was married – you mentioned children – '

'He got that harlot Blanche still in his blood!' Meri's penetrating gaze sliced through Eliza. 'She worked magic on him; hammered six iron nails across a threshold and watched him step across 'em. That spell have bound his heart and soul forever to her!'

'I don't believe you.'

'You shud see him, 'Liza Greypaull.' Meri's smile was grim. 'But I have settled Miss Blanche – '

'What have you done?'

'Turned her own witchcraft back against her. Don't look so wild, Eliza. 'Tis done, and it can't be undone.' She gripped Eliza's trembling fingers.

'My Jye won't ever forget her – but she shall never

forget Jye. Twin souls they be, locked together until the day she dies!'

Eliza released her fingers from Meridiana's grip. 'You're mad,' she whispered, 'you've lived too long by your ownself.'

'I idden mad, Eliza.' The quiet statement held a note of absolute conviction. 'I told 'ee once about patteran. I sees which way the signs is pointing; things what the gorgie can never know.' Meri wagged her head and glanced slyly at Eliza. Her voice took on the flat and singsong chant of the prophetic gypsy, her eyes closed. 'You got another daughter. A fairhaired one name of Annis. Your Annis already got one child, what was not fathered by her husband. Your daughter is again with child. Her lawful wedded husband is the father, this time.'

The closed lids swept upwards. 'Know'd you all that, 'Liza Greypaull?'

'Not all of it.'

'But you believes me! Never mind your Parson, you can't deny what I have told 'ee. I'll tell thee more! Your maid do wear a pendant, a pretty piece wi' coral petals set in silver. You lied to me, 'Liza. The Taunton bailiffs never took my pendant.' She grinned, unexpectedly. 'Well, I don't blame 'ee.' The unwilling admiration was back in her voice. 'Rom do sometimes lie to Rom, not often mind you; but we do always lie to gorgios.' All at once her voice changed, became gruff and demanding; her face was rapt, her eyes wild. 'No more lies! Admit that your Annis do wear a piece of coral and silver, and that my necklace was never lost! I got to know the truth, Eliza!'

Eliza studied the taut face, the crazed eyes, the miserable and desperate aspect of Meridiana. She looked deliberately away towards a bush of holly. 'I didden understand before,' she said gently, 'I never know'd it meant so much to 'ee. Yes,' she lied, ''tis your coral beads what my Annis do wear. But you shall have 'em back, I promise. If I can't bring your necklace myself, it shall be brought to 'ee by another!'

Meri spoke on a long sigh. 'Ah dordi! You have give me a quiet heart this day.' All at once the tension left her face and body, and she grinned. 'I meant to bring back your blue bowl,' she confessed, 'but I was feared o' breaking 'un.'

Eliza smiled. ''Tis no matter. You can hand 'un over when you gets your pendant back. That'll make our chop a fair one.'

They regarded one another with deep satisfaction.

'I cud tell 'ee such a lot – ' began Meridiana, 'give me your left hand – '

'No! I don't want to know the future – '

They rose, stiffly and slowly from their long sitting. They faced one another, the tiny woman in her black silk, the tall gypsy in her faded plaids.

'Makes small diff'rence to me, 'Liza Greypaull, whether you wants to know or not know the future.' Meri's tone was hard and certain. 'My grandson, Sev, was borned some weeks back. Your daughter Annis is bound to bear a girl-child before this year is out.' She paused and bent her black and terrifying gaze upon Eliza. 'Know you this! 'Tis to be they two grandchildren of ours what shall put right all wrongs betwixt you and me.' She laughed. 'You won't live to see that day – ah, but I shall, 'Liza! You spoke truer than you know'd a few minutes back. You said that if you cudden bring my pendant back, then it sh'ud be brought to me by another.' Meri nodded. Eliza's gaze was caught and held by the slow, hypnotic sway of the great, gold earrings. 'I see a meeting – between a red-haired man and a maid wi' a gentle face and brown curls. That maid is not yet born, but 'tis she what shall bring my pendant to me. Ah, dordi, that might take many-a-long-year, but I's'll be waiting for her.'

✻

Annis Nevill felt the child within her quicken; she leaned upon the kitchen table, and breathed deeply in an effort to control her anger. The cheese dish, aimed at Madelina, had failed to find its target. Annis stooped to pick up the pieces; she tested a sharp edge against her palm and fought a desire to bury the shard in her sister's throat. She picked up the broken china and threw it into a bucket underneath the sink. The composed voice of Madelina continued to reason with her as if nothing had happened.

'You shudden work yourself up into such a temper Annis, that baby'll be born afore December if you idden careful!' She glanced at the shards lying in the bucket. 'Poor Frank! I don't know how he stands it. By the time this child is here you won't have a decent cup left to drink from.'

'Then you shudden goad me,' muttered Annis, 'after all, Abigail is mine. 'Tis for me to decide if Blanche and Hugh should take her out for a birthday treat.'

Mina said, 'Late dinner at the Castle Hotel – and her only seven years old! Tidden fair on the child, our Annis, to put her through such an ordeal.'

Annis's hand strayed towards her teacup. She eyed the shards lying in the bucket, thought better of it and continued knitting. She spoke in a tight voice and on a safer subject.

'Something happened to Mama when she was up in Buckland St Mary. She talks as if she knows for absolute certain that I shall have another girl. I be worried about her, Mina, she've gone very quiet just lately.'

'Thinking about that seven hundred pounds no doubt, what Uncle Samuel left her!' said Madelina. 'That'll take a year I expect, before 'tis in her hand. You know how 'tis with lawyers.'

'She don't never mention the money. 'Tis always my pendant that she talks of.'

Mina laughed. 'That old thing? First of all 'twas you and our Blanche fighting for it. Now Mama do go rambling on about it. Superstitious clap-trap! Best place for rubbish o' that sort is the ashbin!' She frowned. 'To get back to the subject of your Abi – now if you wants my opinion – '

*

Abi stood beside the front door of her parents' cottage; through the archway, between the shopfronts, she could see the waggons and horses pass by, out in North Street. Father grew fuchsias in the tiny garden; great pink-and-purple flowers like bells, that swayed beneath the weight of bees. Abi flung her rag doll in among the fuchsia bushes, disturbing the feeding bees, and breaking several blossoms. She looked around for other means of showing her distress. Sitting on the doorstep was strictly forbidden to her, so Abi sat down, quite deliberately, in the hollowed centre of the worn step. She began to inspect the new, button-sided boots, and the starched white petticoats and dress which chafed her knees. She scraped the toe of one boot experimentally across the shiny toecap of the other, and smiled at the resultant damage. She pressed her palms against the dusty path, then bunched both fists around her skirts until the birthday gift of broderie-anglais was crumpled and dirty. It was kind of Aunty Blanche and Uncle Hugh to ask her to dinner; everybody said so. Granny Greypaull had warned her about the strange knives and forks that would be set out in two long rows beside the plates; and the napkin to wipe her mouth, and the finger bowl to rinse her fingers. Abigail leaned back against the warm wood of the front door, and her slight weight caused the latch to give a little. The sound of Aunt Mina's voice, low and persuasive, came clearly now from the kitchen; Abi crouched low upon the doorstep and felt the familiar contractions of terror in her chest and stomach. The argument, as always, was about herself. She heard her name spoken, several times, among words like disgrace and shame. She reached for the blue-satin ribbon that

34

secured her hair, dragged loose the bow, and then kicked it away among the fuchsia bushes.

The lady had come so quietly along the garden path that Abigail was unaware of her presence until she chuckled. 'That's quite a display of temper from one so young, and on your birthday, too!'

The lady was old, older even than Granny Greypaull. She always wore black, but never wool or cotton; her gowns and capes were made of silk and velvet. Her carriage and horses would be waiting with her groom, beyond the archway, out in the main street. Although she had never said so, Abi knew that this lady loved her. Today her eyes were filled with tears; she touched the child's face and hair, and kissed her on the forehead. 'Seven years old, my little one?'

Abigail nodded. They always played the same game, in exactly the same way. The child held out her hands, and a coin was placed in each grubby palm, and the little fingers pressed closed around it.

'Take the money straight to your mother – tell her to be careful of you.'

Once, Abigail had asked her mother why the lady came. Mother had peeped at Father with that funny look that meant she was afraid.

'She's your – your fairy godmother. She'll always look after you, no matter what happens. Don't you never forget that all your life!'

*

The argument, as usual, had reached no positive conclusion. Madelina had just declared that she was about to return to her own house when the kitchen door swung open and Abi stood before them.

'Oh, my heavens! Just look at her, Annis, see the state she's in.'

Mina bent to the child and wagged a finger at her. 'Have you been playing with they rough boys? Oh, you bad girl! Just look at your nice new frock, and where's

35

your ribbon?'

Abigail edged to where Annis now sat knitting in the chimney corner. She held out both fists and uncurled her fingers.

'The lady came to see me. The one in the carriage. She said you must be careful of me.'

Madelina stared at the newly minted gold on each grubby palm.

'So 'tis sovereigns this time. She usually brings silver.'

''Tiv always been gold in the month of September; for her birthday you see. When Abi was a baby the money was put in an envelope, and the footman pushed it underneath the front door.'

All at once they became aware of the child who was listening and watching.

'Little pitchers got big ears,' warned Madelina. She reached out a hand towards the creased and dirty broderie-anglais. 'Whyever did you dress her up so early in the day? Blanche won't be fetching her till seven this evening. You must have known how she'd finish up – she's always playing with the boys – always getting dirty – '

Abigail began to scream. She threw the gold across the kitchen, beat her fists in her mother's lap, and shook her long hair into wild disorder.

'Now you see what you've done, our Mina,' cried Annis, 'why don't you – ?'

A voice from the doorway cut across the commotion.

'Whatever's going on?' asked Eliza Greypaull. 'No wonder this child is so nervous, with the pair of you screaming over her like fishwives.'

She held out her arms to Abigail. 'Now come you here to your granny, my lovely, and tell me all about it.'

Abi pushed the hair back from her face, and smiled triumphantly at her Aunt Mina. 'My frock got dirty,' she whispered, 'and I scratched my boot on a stone. My ribbon fell out somewhere in the garden.'

'Us'll soon put all that to rights, my baby,' said Eliza. 'Let Granny take that dirty frock off.'

To Annis she snapped, 'Well, don't stand there, maid. There's hot water in the kettle. Wash the dress and starch it.'

'That'll never dry by seven o'clock,' stated Madelina.

'Oh yes it will,' said her mother, 'and if you got nothing better else to do, our Mina, you can bide till then, and iron it for us.'

Madelina moved towards the door.

'Well, all I got to say is this. You be all making a big mistake with this child. Dinner at the Castle, indeed! I can foretell now what'll come to pass! She'll shame them, that's what she'll do. There'll be soup and cabbage down her frock, gravy on the tablecloth – and if she gets into one of her temper-tantrums she'll be down on the floor, kicking on the carpet!'

'No I won't,' cried Abi, 'me and Granny have practised, so there! I knows what knife to use, and how to rinse my fingers in that little bath what they gives you. Granny knows lots of things what you don't know, Aunt Mina! Granny have showed me all my manners – '

Eliza stroked the child's hair.

'There now,' she said, 'don't take on so, Abi. You'll do very well, tonight. Your Aunty Blanche will be proud of you.'

She turned a grim face towards her daughter. 'Now get this frock washed, Annis, and on the clothes-line, and make up the fire to heat the flat-iron.'

To Abi she said, 'Us'll rub soot from the chimney on that scratched boot, and then put some polish on it. Now go you outside and find your pretty ribbon, and Granny'll brush your hair and wash your face.'

*

Frank Nevill left French's Tanyard as the first stroke of six rang out from St James's Church steeple. He hurried along Tancred Street, ahead of his workmates, anxious to be home on Abigail's special day. Strange how his thoughts shuttled backwards at this certain time. It was always the same in this month of September. In his mind he relived the dramas of seven years ago. His footsteps slowed as he turned into East Reach, and he recalled himself, coming home from India on the troopship *Euphrates*, remembered the infected neck gland, his fever and weakness. Then had come the journey to Netley, the Military Hospital, and the operation. The Army had a uniform to fit every condition; convalescent soldiers were kitted-out in bright blue cotton. His sisters had visited him that summer; Jane, her plump face serious, had said, 'That girl – that Annis, is no better than she should be, never mind all her fancy airs and graces. Carrying-on, she was behind your back, with some officer up the Barracks. Dressed up in their Blanche's London outfits, with earrings dangling from her earlobes, and her hair frizzled up in curls. Oh, our Frank, you should just have seen her!' His sister had blushed and looked away. 'I don't want to tell 'ee, Frank, but somebody got to. Her's in the family way, and no wonder! You had best forget all about her. We don't speak to her, and no more should you.'

For the rest of that day he had sat beneath a beech tree, remembering Annis as she had been at the age of sixteen. That first day, in Gliddon's collar factory, himself a boy in the packing department, and she, with all her haughty ways, still blushing hotly at the loose talk of the collar-makers. He had tried to protect her then; she was the sort who would always need a strong arm on which to lean. Long before his acceptance of Queen Victoria's shilling, Frank had known that he loved this girl; would always love her. 'Come to terms with it, soldier!' Serjeant Bath had roared, when they fought the Infidel in Burma, and Frank had made his adjustment to the fall of Annis, right there at Netley, on a morning in late June. It had been the hardest blow he would ever suffer; he wept bitter tears. He came back to Taunton; waited for her beside the Silver Street standpipe; in an agony of mind and spirit he had offered her marriage, and she accepted. The baby Abigail was born two weeks later, delicate and tiny, but determined to have life. Frank had, straightaway, recognised a fighter. He loved the child at once, just as if she were his own. At the thought of Abigail waiting for him now, his footsteps quickened.

*

The blue satin bow, retrieved from between the fuchsia bushes, had been washed and ironed, as had the birthday dress of white broderie-anglais. Annis had, in fact, overdone the starch; the skirts now stood out like windmill-sails above the child's skinny knees. The button-sided boots had been rubbed with soot, and polished to a high gloss by Granny Greypaull. The straight brown hair had been tortured in a hundred tiny plaits in an attempt to make it wave. Annis brushed it out, and tied the ribbon with only seconds to spare. Abigail held thin arms up to Frank.

'I don't want to go, Father.'

'Yes you do, maid! You been looking forward to it for weeks – why just look at you – all dressed up like a proper Princess!'

A small, black-shod toe began to tap ominously on the kitchen floor.

'Look' he said hurriedly. 'I cudden buy your birthday present today, my pension don't come till the first of October. When it arrives, tell 'ee what we'll do, maid! We'll go down to the toy shop, the big one by the Tone Bridge. You shall have the red fire-engine with the silver bell.'

Abigail thought about it.

'Can I take it out in the street to play with?' she bargained.

''Course you can,' Frank said. 'But don't let the boys ride on it.'

Abi grinned. 'They knows better'n to try.' She ran towards the front door. 'I can hear horses,' she shouted.

'It must be Uncle Hugh and Aunty Blanche, come to fetch me.'

Frank stood with Annis on the hollowed step of worn stone. They watched as Abi ran towards the brougham. They saw her change pace as she approached the archway; in a froth of white petticoats and blue ribbons, her brown hair shining in the evening sunlight, Abigail Greypaull stepped sedately up into the waiting carriage, without a backward glance.

*

Small children rarely took late dinner at the Castle Hotel. The head waiter gazed doubtfully at Abigail as she sat on the low gilt chair, her forehead level with the table's edge.

'Cushions, my man!' commanded Hugh Fitzgerald. 'Two or three, at the very least!' Cushions were brought, and Abi, her windmill petticoats standing stiffly around her, was able, finally, to survey the dinner-table and its strange appointments. She felt insecure and nervous upon the velvet cushions; she gripped the folds of damask cloth, and thought that she might scream; but then she remembered her Aunt Madelina's prediction, that she would disgrace the Fitzgeralds. Her attention was trapped just in time by the pink carnations in a silver vase, the tall pink candles in their silver holders, and the cutlery, laid out in long rows, exactly as her Granny Greypaull had said it would be.

She studied the man and woman who had brought her to this place; now he must be a Prince, at least, and she a Princess. He wore strange clothes, and sometimes he carried a stick and a tall hat. His hands were white, and undamaged. Father's hands were always sore and bleeding from using the big knife. Just to look at poor Father's hands gave Abi a pain in her chest and stomach. The lady they called Aunty Blanche was staring hard at Abi. How pretty she was, with those red curls on her forehead, and the blue satin gown that left her shoulders bare. Abigail had never seen bare shoulders; Mother undressed in the dark, and washed herself behind a long dark curtain in the corner of the kitchen; so much exposed flesh made the little girl uneasy.

'My mother,' she said primly, 'always wears a pinny when her's eating dinner.' Aunty Blanche began to twist the sparkling rings, very fast, around her fingers.

'What presents have you received, so far?' she asked. 'What did your father and mother give you?'

'None yet,' said Abi, ''tis like this, see,' she became confidential, 'Father's pension don't get paid till Monday, and Mother's best boots was in pawn already, but Father don't know that.' She paused to consider. 'Granny gave me a comb and a hair-tidy. Cousin Laura sewed a hanky for me. You sent me this dress and boots, and thank you very much! Aunt Mina made me a cake, but I cudden eat it today in case it spoiled my dinner. My fairy-grandmother brought some money, but Mother used some of that to buy tea and sugar. She got Frank some prawns for his tea, too! Father do love prawns, but usually us can't run to stuff like that – not on a weekday!'

The silence lasted quite a long time; Aunty Blanche said at last, 'I think you mean your fairy *godmother*, don't you, Abi?'

'Oh no. She's my other grandma. I got three, you know. There's Granny Nevill – she's Frank's mother, but us don't never see her. Then there's Granny Greypaull – she looks after me when Mother's earning a crust of bread in Cooks's factory. I don't know what the other one's called, nobody ever told me. But she's my granny alright! Aunt Mina's always saying so, to Mother.'

Abi saw how the Prince and Princess gazed helplessly at one another.

'Too much of her time is spent among the adults,' he said. 'Does she never play with other children?'

'I only like the boys' games,' Abigail informed him, 'and Granny don't like it when I sit on the doorstep, or play marbles.'

Aunty Blanche nodded slowly, and smiled. 'That sounds exactly like Mama,' she said. 'Does she want you to be a little lady, too, Abi?'

'Oh, I am, already. We practised with the knives and forks. I shan't bring no shame on you and Uncle Hugh.' Abigail sniffed, but delicately. 'That dinner do smell good,' she whispered. 'I be terrible hungry, Aunty.'

She was never to recall the journey home. Abigail awakened briefly to hear her mother's urgent question.

'How did she behave, Hugh?'

'Impeccably, my dear. I simply can't imagine why you were so worried about her. A very sweet child, and such exquisite manners. You are to be congratulated, Annis!'

It was dark inside the carriage; Abi smelled perfume, felt the softness of silk and fur against her cheek. She heard her mother's anxious voice, 'I'll take her from you now, Blanche.'

All at once, the supporting arms gripped so tightly that Abi came fully awake. She could see her mother's face, white and angry in the gaslight. 'Give her to me, Blanche, give her back, this instant!' Something wet splashed onto Abigail's hands; she looked up at the beautiful face so close to her own. The Princess was crying. Uncle Hugh said, 'Don't alarm the child. Give her back, Blanche. She isn't ours, you know. We only borrowed her for an hour or two. She belongs to Annis.'

The thrust, when it came, from one pair of arms to another, was so swift and unexpected that Abi whimpered. So tightly was she clutched against her mother's shoulder, that breathing became painful. As Mother ran with her towards the cottage, the Princess began to scream.

'I want that child, Hugh! Oh, I do! I just want and want her – '

*

The disability pension, awarded by a grateful State to

Frank Nevill, was paid to him quarterly, by money order. Annis touched the scar that ran from chin to earlobe, his legacy from dirty water drunk in the campaigns of Burma, and considered this four pounds hard-earned.

'You shudden spend your money on Abi,' she said, gently. 'You need boots, and new working trousers.' She pointed at the wooden fire-engine, which stood on the hearth.

'That's a boy's toy, Frank. Whatever possessed you to buy that!'

'It was what she liked best,' he said. 'In that whole damned shop, that red fire-engine with the silver bell was the only toy she wanted.'

Annis sighed. 'I be so worried about her, Frank. Perhaps our Mina is right after all. Abi do get very wilful. Everybody spoils her.' She leaned across the supper table and touched his damaged hands. 'You work so hard for us in the tanyard. 'Tidden fair, the way I be always putting all my family's troubles on you.'

He smiled. 'You was ever a worrier, Anni. But my shoulders is broad enough to stand it.' He pushed his plate away and reached for his briar pipe and tin of twist tobacco. 'Come on now. Better tell me all about your problems, you'll get no sleep, else.'

Annis moved her chair closer to the fire. 'Well,' she said, 'there's Blanche, of course. Now she 'ud love to tempt Abigail away from us, her being so rich, and no prospect of a child of her own.'

Frank said, 'You know very well that I 'ud never let that happen.'

'Then there's Madelina!' Annis frowned. 'She's a good soul, and she means well. Oh but she do meddle so in everybody's business.'

'Then have a word with her about it.'

'Oh I could never do that, Frank!' She hesitated. 'Truth to tell, I always been a bit frightened of our Madelina. She's always so sure that she's right – and she usually is. I could never go against her.' Frank touched a flame to the tobacco; when the pipe was drawing well he said quietly, 'Come on then – let's have it all, Anni!' Annis twisted her hands together. ''Tis to do with Mama – but you'll laugh at me if I tell it to you.' She glanced sideways at him. 'It got to do with witchcraft, Frank.' She paused. 'Mama should never have gone back to Buckland St Mary. For her to hear that Uncle Samuel was dead was upset enough! But to stay three days on Larksleve farm – and meet up again with that gypsy woman – well, I can tell 'ee, Frank, my blood do run cold at the very thought'.

Frank looked bemused. 'I never heard tell of no gypsy woman, Anni?'

She touched a hand to the silver and coral pendant at her throat. 'Well no,' she said slowly, ''tis an old tale and a very strange one. Things have come to pass up in Buckland St Mary what you Taunton folk 'ud scarcely credit. Why, there's a book could be writ about my family's stories! an' every word of it true!'

'So what about this gypsy?'

'When mama was a young girl she had a friend, a gypsy, name of Meridiana. There was some argument between them what never got settled.' Annis shivered and seemed unable to continue.

'Well go on then, maid. How do this concern you?'

'I was six years old when we was turned off Larksleve. Oh, I remember that day, Frank! We came into Taunton riding on a farmcart, with us children all perched a-top our feather beds. We met the gypsy on the Taunton road. Her son was with her, a deaf boy name of Jye. She talked about a pendant. She put a curse on Blanche and then she looked at me. I've never forgot that look, Frank. Nor the words she spoke. She asked my name, and when I told her it was Annis, she said, "So, Annis Greypaull! Remember this day when you met up wi' a gypsy, for 'tis you what'll put this matter right betwixt me an' your mother." '

Frank moved uneasily in his chair. 'You can't set no value on what gypsies say. 'Tis always money they be after!'

'No' said Annis, 'she never wanted money. When she looked at me, why it was as if she was bending me to do her will – she was a powerful woman, Frank. You had to see her to really understand what I mean.'

'Look Anni – tell the truth now. 'Tis they old beads round your neck what is causing all the worry. Is it the gypsy woman's pendant? If it is, then give it back to her –'

'No Frank. The gypsy's pendant got lost, years ago, by my Mama. The necklace I wear now is very like it. It was brought from London by our Blanche. But it got magic powers too!'

Frank laughed. 'So that's what 'tis all about. You got no cause to worry, maid. I've see'd pieces like that in the bazaars of India and Burma. They calls 'em fertility beads – and to judge by the size of the native families – 'tis a powerful magic! Just forget all about the gypsy woman. In any case, 'twas your Blanche that she cursed.' He grinned. 'But 'tis you alone what must put matters right – eh Annis?'

'Don't laugh at me, Frank. I haven't yet come to the end of the story. When Mama was up to Larksleve, for Uncle Samuel's funeral, she met the gypsy again – 'twas as if, Mama said, that this Meridiana had already knowed that she would be there.'

'So where's the harm in that?'

'She talked about me. According to Mama, that woman knowed all sorts of private things about me. I find that frightening, Frank, don't you?'

'Not if she means you no harm! Sounds to me as if this gypsy took quite a fancy to you! Anyway, 'tis just a lot of old woman's stories. It got nothing at all to do with you and me, and our liddle family.'

*

Frank Nevill was a good man. Some people said that he was too good. His mother and sisters prayed regularly for him in the Wesleyan Chapel that he might be forgiven his unwise alliance with Annis Greypaull and her base-born daughter. For seven years they had watched the pretty cottage in the rear of North Street, anticipating a second fall of the flighty Annis. Frank's family nodded coolly whenever they met him, walking hand-in-hand with Abigail on a Sunday morning. The child, they observed, had the same haughty air and condescending manner as the rest of the Greypaulls; even worse, she was said to be encouraged in her naughtiness and temper by Frank, who would not allow a corrective hand to be laid upon her.

Even among the Greypaulls, Frank's goodness was recognised and remarked upon.

'You don't deserve that man,' was Madelina's constant cry. 'How he keeps his patience with you, our Annis, I shall never fathom!' The qualities of Frank were a source of comfort to Eliza. His forebearance seemed to complement the foolishness of Annis; he was, she thought, the ballast to her daughter's lightness, and even more important, whatever would become of Abigail without his loving guidance?

*

The failure of Annis to conceive had been seen as a blessing by Frank in the first years of their marriage. His wage of twelve shillings a week earned at French's Tannery in Tancred Street, was barely enough to keep a wife and one child; and Annis, after all, was no ordinary woman. She had been born a Greypaull; had spent her first years on Larksleve Farm in the Parish of Buckland St Mary. The streets of Taunton were still made busy on a Friday by farmcarts and waggons inscribed with the name of Greypaull. Frank was aware of the honour done to him by Annis; why even Abigail, her child, had not been fathered by some low-born fellow from the stews of East Reach, but by a high-born officer from Jellalabad Barracks.

The passage of years had convinced Frank Nevill that he was not meant to father a child of his own. He remembered the long and difficult birth of Abigail and was gentle and considerate of Annis. She had, he concluded, probably suffered irreparable damage both in body and spirit.

'Come to terms with it, soldier!' had been Frank's watchword since those terrible days of the Burma campaign. Easier, he thought now, to grin and bear with things than to waste time on regrets and recriminations. Whole months could pass by and not once would he ever recall that Abigail was not flesh of his flesh. Stoicism of the spirit brought its own compensations. He asked no more than a tankard of cider in the Half Moon Inn, a pipeful of 'baccy when he could afford it; an occasional visit to the Circus and Music-Hall with Abigail and Annis. When Annis first voiced the suspicion that she might be with child, he had simply not believed her. Knowing little about women's matters he had said awkwardly, 'You've no doubt took a chill – or something?' It had taken the wise nods and smiles of Madelina to convince him.

'A child of your own, Frank, and no man do deserve it more than you do! Our Anni don't know whether to laugh or cry – her's that pleased about it.' Mina had looked thoughtful. ''Tis our Blanche we shall have to look out for, the greedy grasping creature! She've got everything in this world what Hugh Fitzgerald's gold could buy her – but he can't give her a child, and 'tis my opinion that he never will, now.' Madelina patted Frank's shoulder. 'You be advised by me, Frank. I knows our Blanche and all her trickery. She once tried to lure away my Laura with fancy presents. She've started now on Abigail. You mark my words – that dinner at the Castle is only the thin end of the wedge! Let me be your guide, Frank, in the case of the Greypaulls,' she paused, 'most of us is decent, upright people, but there's others what'll stop at nothing to serve their own ends.'

Frank Nevill's daughter was born on a day in late December. He came back from the Tannery on that winter's evening to find the cottage filled with women. Eliza met him on the doorstep, her scarred face joyful.

'Oh Frank, such good news! You got a lovely liddle maiden.' Her voice lowered to a whisper. 'A child of your own after all these years. I be so happy for 'ee.'

'How's Anni?'

Madelina, tiny and important in her role of nurse, said, 'Tired – but grateful 'tis safe-over. 'Tis a lovely child, Frank. Fat as butter and so content.'

As Frank moved towards the staircase Mina shook her head.

'No,' she said, 'you can't go up there yet. Annis is asleep. Wash your hands and face, and eat your tea. You can see her later.'

Frank ate the food they set before him; obedient, and quiet in his ways, he gave no sign of the deep joy in his heart. Other men fathered many children. His brother George, once widowed, and swiftly remarried, had already a total of seventeen offspring from two wives, and another child expected. But some pleasures were lessened by repetition, and no man, thought Frank, could ever feel as he now felt about this birth; and because he was not a vindictive man, and harboured no grudges, his first thought was for his wife, but his second thoughts were for his estranged parents.

Later on that evening, when permitted by Madelina, Frank held his own daughter for the first time, and wept for the comfort of it; Annis, drifting in and out of sleep said, with satisfaction, 'Her's the living image of you, Frank. A proper liddle Nevill.'

*

Except for a sharp five minutes in which Aunt Madelina had dared to threaten a beating with the back of a hairbrush, and had in fact slapped her, no one that day had bothered to notice Abi. Accustomed as she was to the undivided attention of those around her, Abigail had demanded entry to her mother's bedroom, and been refused. She returned from school that afternoon to be told by Aunt Mina, 'What a lucky liddle girl you are! You got a beautiful new baby sister!'

Abigail held her breath for temper, as she had when an infant. Her heart began to pound and her head felt light.

'I don't want a rotten sister,' she screamed at last. 'Send it back where it came from! If us got to have a baby, then get me a boy one. You knows that I don't like girls.'

Abi had waited, unnoticed in the chimney corner, for the return of Father. Granny had taken her hand and offered to take her upstairs to see Mother and the new baby sister, but Abigail had refused.

'I be waiting for Father,' she wailed. 'Father'll know what to do about all this!'

But Father, when he came home, had also failed her.

'A child of your own, after all these years,' Aunt Mina had whispered. But surely, thought Abigail, she too was his child? He called her his Princess. When the demon was in her and she could not sleep it was Father and not Mother who came to comfort her in the darkness; Father who sat with her on the stairs and brushed her hair until she grew calm again, and quiet. She went now to where he sat, eating bread and cheese and drinking tea. She slipped her fingers into his free hand, 'I be still your Princess, idden I, Father?' Abi murmured. He noddded; but absent-mindedly, as if he had not really heard her question.

*

Blanche had ordered that a telegram be sent to her in London just as soon as Annis gave birth. Within two days of the confinement, the fashionable Fitzgeralds arrived at the London Hotel, their many trunks wheeled up on a handcart from the railway station. Poised and beautiful in dark green velvet with a cape and matching toque of fox-furs, Blanche brought the mingled odours of fine old brandy and eau-de-cologne into her sister's bedroom. She went straight to the cradle and stood beside it for a long time. As always, in the presence of this sister, Annis became anxious.

'Well,' she asked, 'do she come up to expectations?'

The face that turned back towards her was strained and suddenly much older.

'She looks exactly like Frank,' said the dulled voice.

'She's a good baby. Don't never cry 'cepting when she's hungry.'

'How long have you waited for her?'

'Nearly seven years – give or take a month or two.'

Annis laughed, a small deprecating sound that deceived neither of them.

'I'd begun to fear that poor old Frank 'ud never set eyes upon his own child.'

Blanche said quietly, but with infinite menace, 'No you didn't you little liar! You've got the lucky pendant! You knew that it would happen for you, sooner or later!'

She pointed to the silver and coral, outlined beneath the thick pink flannel of her sister's nightgown.

'Give it back to me, Annis! I'll make it worth your while.' Blanche gazed around the tiny bedroom, and all at once Annis saw the iron bedstead, the cheap torn lino, the shabby cupboards, through her sister's eyes. She hesitated, but only for a moment.

'No, Blanche. You had the coral once but you didden want it. Remember what you said? Blanche'll make her own luck, that's what you boasted, and so you have, in one way. You got more of this world's goods than the rest of us have dreamed of. Why can't you be satisfied, eh?'

'Give it to me, Annis!'

An uneasy smile stretched the lips of Annis. 'Don't think that I idden tempted,' she assured Blanche. She looked towards the sleeping infant. 'I shall have to go back to the factory, or take in some outwork, before much longer. With two children to feed and clothe, us won't never manage on what Frank earns. But I don't forget what happened to Mama on Lárksleve when her parted with her necklace – '

'But this is a different pendant – ' Blanche interrupted.

'I don't care. 'Tis the self same pattern of coral and silver. 'Tis a – a fertility symbol according to Frank. He knows about such things, having lived in the East. Anyway, if you don't believe in the magic of the necklace, whyfor be you so desperate to wear it?' She raised herself from the pillows. 'No!' she cried. 'I dursent part with it, Blanche! All I got in my life is Frank and these two children. You got no right to ask it of me, 'specially when you and Hugh goes about the world so rich and haughty.'

Blanche returned to the cottage every morning, but on subsequent occasions Hugh Fitzgerald came with her. On their final visit the elegant couple stood, one on either side of the iron bedstead, and gazed fiercely at one another.

Blanche said in a tight voice. 'May I hold her, Anni?'

Annis handed the child, reluctantly, to her sister. She watched dismayed as the long, beringed fingers reached out to clutch and curl around the white-shawled bundle.

Hugh cried, 'Gently now, do be careful of her! She's like a bit of Dresden china!'

Blanche said, 'You're to call her after me. Now you hear this Annis! The child is to be named for me.' Blanche leaned over, thrust the baby unexpectedly back into her mother's arms, and ran from the room. Her high-heeled boots clattered down the uncarpeted stairs, and her high-pitched voice could be heard from the kitchen in a sudden fierce exchange with Madelina.

Annis touched the downy head, and looked up at Hugh.

'Whatever will I do?' she pleaded. 'I be already in bad

books with her because I won't give up the pendant.'

'You don't wish to name your baby Blanche?'

'No,' whispered Annis, 'truth to tell, 'tis a name I don't much care for.'

'Then don't do it,' said Hugh Fitzgerald. He sat down on a hard chair beside the bed. 'She's a pretty thing,' he said softly. He reached out a finger to touch the infant's dark hair. 'She reminds me of a girl I knew, long ago; before Blanche.'

'You were fond of her?'

'Very fond,' he hesitated, 'if the name of Blanche is distasteful to you, and you have no other preference, it would please me very much if this child was to be called Claire.'

'That was *her* name?'

He nodded, and pulled his chair closer to the bed. He spoke with a rueful tenderness that touched Annis. 'I'm the sort of fellow who is predestined to be treated badly by women. My mother abandoned me at the age of ten days, I was jilted by Claire on the eve of our wedding –'

'Blanche bides with you.'

He shrugged, and gazed at the child in Annis's arms. 'For how much longer? I ask myself. My first waking thought is always that this may be the day she will desert me.'

Annis, uneasy yet flattered that a gentleman like Hugh should confide in her, said brightly, 'There was talk that you might come down to live in Dawlish?' He sighed. 'Another bone of contention between us. There's a house called Summerlands, it stands on the cliff-edge. It's been on the market for quite some time now, but Blanche refuses to leave London.'

'Why don't you take her to Dawlish? Show her the house – and then tell her she can't have it. You know what she's like, Hugh. Her can't bear to be thwarted.'

He looked thoughtful. 'You could be right. By the Lord Harry, I do believe you've solved it!' He stood up and began to move towards the door. 'Claire,' he whispered, 'now don't disappoint me will you Annis? The baby is to be named Claire.'

Hugh went away, and almost at once Blanche came back into the bedroom. She twitched aside the thick lace curtain, and looked out through the archway that gave onto North Street.

'I hate this town, Anni. I've got nothing but bad memories of it.'

'You keeps on coming back here, Blanche. I wonder why you does that?'

'I don't know! Something seems to draw me. I feel this urge to see Mama, and all of you. But when I get here – well nothing is ever quite the way I expect it to be.' Blanche came back to the bedside and sat down on the hard chair. Annis, conscious of her old flannel nightgown and work-stained hands, felt a pang of envy at her sister's beauty. How well the dark-green velvet gown set off that auburn hair and white skin! The hour-glass figure, unchanged by pregnancy or ill-health, was as voluptuous now as it had been when Blanche was sixteen years old and setting out for London. The brooch, said to be a parting gift from the Prince of Wales, glittered in the firelight. Frank, who could read and write, had confirmed for Annis that the diamond-set bar of gold, pinned at her sister's throat, did indeed spell out the name of 'Persimmon', the Prince's Derby winner. Annis tried to imagine the intrigue and scope of her sister's life in London, and could not. Her arms tightened, involuntarily, around the sleeping baby. Blanche leaned close and the scent of her eau-de-cologne quite failed to mask the smell of Martell's Four-Star brandy.

'What was my husband saying to you, Anni?'

There was menace in the question and Annis shrank inside the flannel nightgown. Experience had made her timid of aggressive people, and yet it would not do to lie to Blanche.

'He wants me to call the baby Claire,' she murmured. Blanche nodded, unsurprised. 'I know'd as he was up to no good. That sneaky bastard! Go behind my back would he? Try to get my niece named for his fancy trollop! God rot the lyin' toad! God help him when I get him back to London.'

The curse, uttered in the broad vowels of Buckland St Mary, alarmed and yet intrigued Annis. 'Do your curses really work?'

Blanche smiled. In a high, unnatural voice she said, 'Oh yes, Annis, they work! But I don't bother no more with candle wax and pins – all you need is a photograph of the one you hate, and a good sharp darning-needle. Much less risky than stealing candle-ends from churches, and the results are just as satisfying.' The baby began to stir and waken, and Blanche turned a speculative eye upon mother and child.

Annis cried in a nervous voice. ''Tis alright, Blanche! I won't never call her Claire, I promise I won't. She shall be named for you and nobody else! You'll always be good to her, I know you will.' Blanche smiled her satisfaction; she pulled the chair closer to the bed, and began to speak in a low and confidential tone. 'I have something to tell you about my husband. That fine gentleman you all admire has turned out to be no better than our Papa. He drinks heavily, and leaves me to take the consequences of it. He tells lies about me. I should have heeded my first instincts. I knew at first sight that he was not to be trusted.' Suddenly the strength of her emotion overlaid the careful Mayfair accents, and Blanche again lapsed into broad speech.

'Oh, our Anni, you can't think how I do detest that Hugh! You don't know what they've made me suffer – him and his bloody Aunty. There've been times jus' lately when I've felt black murder in my heart towards him!' She laughed into Annis's shocked face. 'You lives all quiet here with Frank, but I've see'd your face when you looks in my direction. Don't never envy me, Annis.' She paused. 'You don't believe me do you? He got you all bamboozled.' She halted dramatically. 'You heard me telling last night about the old Queen's funeral? I told it very well didden I, maid? All about the freezing weather, the tiny liddle coffin pulled by sailors on a gun-carriage. How she had never liked black drapes, and so left orders that when she died the city was to be done up all tasteful in white and purple.' All at once the hushed tones of Blanche became loud and triumphant. 'Well, 'twas all a bloody spoof! I was never there, maid!'

Annis said, bewildered, 'But where was you then?'

'In the Inebriates Home, where my devoted husband and his aunty had shoved me!'

'In the what?'

'A place where they puts hopeless drunkards.'

'But Blanche, you surely don't drink that much?'

'No I don't, Anni. But he does.'

'So why –?'

'To fool his aunty o' course! 'Tis that old bitch what do hold the purse-strings. I've never found out exactly how matters financial do stand between them two. But Hugh and me got debts all over London, and he won't own up 'tis any of his fault. He tells her that 'tis all down to my extravagance and heavy drinking. So what did she do? She had me locked up in a Home for Boozers.' Blanche grinned briefly. 'Oh, 'twas all very posh, mind you. Only the very richest of sozzlers gets put into that place.' Her face grew bitter. 'No, I never saw the Royal Funeral. I was on a diet of milk-pudding, and bloody Vichy water!' She reached for Annis's hand and gripped it. 'Aunt Porteous came down to visit me in that place. She brought me a Bible, and a black frock, the ugliest gown you ever did see. Wear it, she said, out of respect for your deceased Monarch!' Blanche grinned. 'Well, she don't never frighten me, drunk or sober. "You better look out," I told her, "your days is numbered. Us got good old Bertie on the Throne of England now. He'll bankrupt us all in six months." ' Blanche dabbed at her eyes with a wisp of hanky, and Annis said gently,

'I don't like to see 'ee in such a state, Blanche.' She

hesitated. 'Why don't you get away from London? P'raps if 'twas just you and Hugh, by yourselves – well, you never know?'

Blanche grinned and blew her nose. 'You mean well my dear, but it would never work, you see.' She spoke once again in her Mayfair voice, which, thought Annis, must prove that she was feeling better.

'Hugh and I have not a single common interest, except the spending of his money; and even that begins to pall just lately.'

*

It was on a Sunday evening when the three weeks of her lying-in were almost at an end, that the unexpected visitors arrived at Annis's bedside. They stood side by side, a white-bearded, rosy-cheeked man and his tiny wife. Annis recognised the Silver Street shoemaker who was Frank's father, and the mother-in-law, who had never, until now, acknowledged the existence of Annis.

She saw Frank's vulnerable face and pleading eyes, and willed herself to be pleasant to them. They admired their grandchild, who, they said, was every inch a Nevill and the image of Frank.

It was as they were about to leave the bedroom that the request was made. Frank's mother turned back to her son. ''Twould please me very much,' she told him, 'if you would call the babe Evangeline – after me.'

*

'Coming to terms' with the Greypaull family had proved more difficult and taken longer than any of his previous adjustments. Frank had tried at first to maintain a stance of uninvolved spectator, but in this cabal of formidable women he found outright neutrality was not allowed. Slowly and inevitably Frank had accepted the daily, often hourly presence of one or another of Annis's relatives. Eliza, his mother-in-law, accustomed to a lifetime of early rising, would walk through the summer dawn from Greenbrook Terrace to his cottage at the rear of North Street. He would find her with Annis, raking cold ashes from the range and lighting the fire to boil his breakfast kettle. He would return at midday to find Madelina entrenched. All too often it was Mina who ladled stew into his bowl, cut bread and filled his teacup. The evenings brought Laura, Mina's shy and pretty daughter. There were also the visiting sisters, Candace and Blanche, one or other of whom seemed always to be just arriving or departing. Frank respected Candace. He admired the independent spirit of this tiny widow; was amused by the stories she told about Billy her actor son. There were times when all six women gathered around his kitchen table, and those were the Sunday evenings when Frank would withdraw to his carver chair in the chimney corner, draw steadily upon his briar pipe, and hope to be overlooked. Their requests for his opinion were made out of courtesy; they rarely spared him time to reply. They called him Uncle Frank, as if he was already an old man. Some men would have taken exception, showed anger; but not Frank. Bolstered by her family, his Annis was easier to live with, less fearful and anxious. Their physical presence reassured her, and so he had willed himself to be understanding and tolerant, to close his mind to all the arguments and tantrums. Until the arrival of his own daughter.

The birth of this child, no matter how hard he tried to conceal it, had roused the first watchfulness in Frank. From his place in the chimney corner he observed, eyes open, his mind receptive. Nothing, he now saw, was straightforward between the sisters. Discord and argument, vindictiveness and grudge-bearing went oddly hand-in-hand with devotion and partisanship. There was a childishness in all their dealings with one another; each relationship dependent for strength on the giving and acceptance of secrets. Madelina would make a confidante of Annis, insistent that Blanche and Candace were never to be told. Annis would murmur to Candace her resentment of Mina's domineering ways. Even Abigail, barely eight years old, would wind her arms about her grandmother's neck and pour out her childish rantings against all three aunts, and her own mother.

His vigilance had begun on the day Frank registered his daughter's birth. So long had the arguments raged about her name, that the legal time of registration had passed and he was now forced to lie about the true date.

'She should have been registered within six weeks,' he told Annis.

'You don't have to say she was born in December.' Blanche, on an extended new year visit to Taunton and determined that the child should be named for her said, 'Tell them she was born in January – say the fourteenth – they won't ask any questions.'

So he had told the lie, and it was not the falsehood that disturbed Frank but the foolish need for its invention. Opinions among the Greypaulls had been divided. When it came to currying favour with the Fitzgeralds, the merits of naming the baby Blanche or Claire were thought about equal. On the other hand, said Laura, who was young and romantic, the two names linked together had a pretty ring about them.

'So what about *my* mother's wishes?' he had dared to asked Annis.

'Your mother never showed her face in my house these many-a-years, so why should I bend to her will in the matter of a name?'

'Evangeline,' he had murmured. ''Tis easy on the tongue –?'

'Blanche!' Annis had cried. 'Don't you make no mistake, now!'

Frank had studied the form in the Registrar's office. The space headed Forenames was wide and tempting. He wrote BLANCHE, and then CLAIRE, and still the line was only half-full. He hesitated, dipped the pen into the inkwell and frowned. Annis would never know what he had done, so great was her fear of the written word. As for the rest of them, if they asked to see the Certificate of Birth he would say that he had lost it. Frank took a deep breath, squared his shoulders, and grinned. In the space remaining, and with a flourish, he had spelled out the name EVANGELINE.

*

From her window Damaris Carew could see the Borough, that triangle of rough grass around which were grouped the village shops, the Phelip's Arms, and just out of her sight, but very much in her mind, the high stone pillars and iron gates which guarded the entrance to Montacute House.

Since her marriage to Jye, Maris hardly ever left the cottage. Except for a brief visit to her mother, and her regular Sunday attendance at the Baptist Chapel, the small square window was her only link with the world beyond babies and glove-making. Her gloving-table stood beneath that window. It held the machine, the reels of thread, the scissors, the flat tin box which contained her assortment of sewing needles, and the round-ended gloving-stick, polished from much use, which she used to push through and shape-out the completed thumbs and fingers. On a separate bench stood the half-dozen bundles of cut-out, but still unstitched gloves. She picked up several of these bundles and began to untie them; she assessed the state of the room, content with the fire banked-up with damp potato-peelings, the fresh depth of dry rushes on the earthen floor, and Mathilda and Keturah playing happily with the scraps of leather used to tie the gloves together. Maris sat down, her head and shoulders bent to the first tasks of needle-threading. Her foot, of its own accord, reached for the rim of the wooden rocking-cradle in which her son slept; her girls were fine and fat, they thrived and were content, she smiled her satisfaction at their round, rose-brown faces and black curls.

As to her own state of health, well, she tried not to

dwell upon it. Childbirth, she had observed, caused a comfortable plumpness in most women. Girls who had once been thin, scrawny even, became desirably well-endowed as to hip and bosom after the delivery of a first born. In the case of Maris, the carrying and birthing of a son and two daughters had brought her to a state of near emaciation. She was always weary now, and with exhaustion had come a shrewishness of temper, an irritability with those around her, and a distinct disinclination for the bedtime attentions of her husband. The very thought of Jye wrinkled up her forehead. Maris lifted her head as a passing shadow dimmed the morning sunlight; the waxed thread wavered around the eye of the sewing needle, and then fell to lie unheeded on the table. Meridiana Carew paused momentarily beside the window of her son's cottage, shifted the hawking basket to her left arm, and then strode on with that long, barefoot lope, across the Borough, and towards the lane which led to Yeovil. Maris knew the winter contents of that basket; the bunches of mock chrysanthemums whittled from elder wood, a few late blooming asters, their stems enfolded in damp moss; the bundles of newly-made clothes-pegs, and underneath, tucked wisely out of sight, the love-potions and the cures for indigestion and fluxes. There would be a few cheap pedlar's trinkets, necklaces endowed with so-called 'magic' powers; bits of dried-up snakeskin, the 'lucky' feet of white hares and rabbits. The housewives of the Town, at sight of the gypsy, would call their children home, would draw their curtains close and bar their homes against her. But when her knock came at their door, resolution would weaken, and fear of her curse would persuade them to open up.

Maris allowed the dropped thread to lie; she watched the tall figure draped in plaid, disappear across the Borough. Her last view was of black, looped braids and the flash of sunlight on earrings of hooped gold. She rose abruptly, leaned across the machine and the heaped-up gloves, and pushed open her window. Cold fresh air overcame the stench of leather and her breath caught on a sob. Ah, she thought, what pleasure it must be to walk in the sunlit winter lanes on such a morning! Tears of weakness and frustration filled her eyes. She looked down at the thinness of her body, acknowledged her own need to eat so that she might feed the baby; remembered the constant hunger of the growing Keturah and Mathilda, and the appetite Jye brought home from the quarry each night. Food, and the getting of it, had become her main preoccupation. He grew roses where potatoes should have flourished; but he could not, she had learned, be persuaded to do anything against his will. The silence of the deaf was unarguable, all her clever words, carefully rehearsed throughout the day, could be blotted out by the simple closing of his eyelids. Jye, she had recently discovered, had the gift of instant sleep, his facility to elude her was one source of her frustration; another was the sight of his mother, walking proud and free in the winter morning. She leaned once more across the gloving table and slid-to the window; she looked around for comfort to her healthy babies, her scoured and tidy cottage, the suety-pudding tied up in a cloth and steaming gently for Jye's supper. Young she might be, thought Damaris, but she knew where her duty lay.

She glanced once at the long row of books that gathered dust upon a high shelf, retrieved the dropped thread and began to aim it, purposefully at the eye of the gloving needle. She sat down at the low wide table set close beside the window; counted the piles of doeskin gloves waiting to be stitched, and knew that she could no longer afford to waste a single minute of the precious sunlight. The hand sewn gloves were a special order, and paid well; she placed the two halves of a doeskin thumb very carefully together, and began to stitch, plying her needle with the regular rhythm that encouraged thought. The problems between herself and Jye had multiplied, just lately. Much of the trouble could be put down to the difference in their ages. Jye was already thirty-six while she was still in her mid-twenties. He had warned her, right at the beginning. 'I be set in my ways,' he had said, 'nothing much ever going to change me now.' She had listened but she had not heard him. Instead she had looked at the height and the breadth of him, the great shoulders, the fine head of black curls, the walnut-coloured skin and soft brown eyes. She had known that other girls desired him; observed the side-long glances that came his way in Chapel on a Sunday evening, and never dared to dream that he would notice her. She smiled above the doeskin thumb, remembering her own artfulness on that evening when her father had first brought the stonemason home from the Hill to share their supper. Damaris Honeybone, tiny and thin, with a nose that was over-long for her small face, and a forehead that was broad and too high, possessed, nevertheless, one striking and remarkable feature of beauty. Her hair, which had never been cut, hung down past her knees, and was of a colour that matched mint-new sovereigns. She had timed the washing and drying of that hair to coincide with Jye Carew's arrival in her father's garden. She had positioned herself underneath the pear tree, had turned her face away, so that his first sight of her would take in that glorious hair, brushed out to its full length, and drying in the evening sunshine. After that, her conquest of him had been simple.

Maris laid down the glove; she was finding him a strange and difficult man with whom to live; his long silences unnerved her. There was a hint of something 'other' in him, dark places of the soul that put her in mind of that first woman in his life, Meridiana Carew. There was also the second woman, the 'clever baggage' who had once deceived him, up in London. Maris picked up the glove and began to push the needle, with force, through the amber-coloured leather. She had questioned Jye about London; had begged him to describe it to her; but every request had set off such a mood of depression in him that she had let the matter lie. His old mother, she suspected, knew all there was to be known upon the subject. The half-completed glove again lay idle in her fingers. There were, she was certain, no secrets between those two. The baby stirred and at once her foot found the ledge at the base of the rocking-cradle. Maris sighed. Let him sleep, she prayed, if only for a few hours! She looked down upon the infant's thin, pinched features, the tight red curls, the knowing eyes over which his tear-swollen eyelids hardly ever closed; eight months old and still he did not thrive. She had called him David John, against Jye's wishes. She remembered Mathilda and Keturah at the age of eight months; their contented rose-brown faces and dimpled bodies. This boy slept briefly, awakening to scream with an intensity that reached the stone-deaf ears of Jye; even in sleep, that small fiery head twisted restlessly upon the pillow. The argument about his given name had not yet been settled. In the Baptist Chapel he had been baptised David John; but by Meridiana Carew and her son, Jye, the child was called Silvanus; a heathen name which they had already shortened to Sev.

*

Jemima Honeybone had seen the trouble coming. Daily visits to the dark little cottage in Middle Street had warned her long since that all was not well between Damaris and Jye. Had she and David, Jemima asked herself, been mistaken in allowing the girl to marry at such a young age? The fact must be admitted that their daughter was not at all like the other village maidens. She was argumentative and quick in her mind; Maris came over-easy to both laughter and tears. If truth should be told, thought Jemima, David Honeybone's daughter was that most feared and undesirable of females – a long-headed woman!

As for Jye Carew, well he was no longer anything like the simple biddable giant to whom she had first been introduced. Jemima had thought, on that long-ago evening when he had shared their supper of rabbit-stew, that the dark and handsome face, the fine tall body, explained the whole man. He had seemed so open, in those early days of his courtship of Maris; so pitiable in the prison of his deafness, so needy of comfort and affection. But Jemima had watched her son-in-law through the ensuing years, and now she suspected a secretive turn of mind, a deep dissatisfaction of spirit, a division of the soul that was beyond the comprehension of herself and David. To understand all, the Baptist minister had assured her, was to forgive all. She looked down at the scrawny, tear-stained scrap of life that lay in her arms, and knew that all her insight of his troubled parents would never permit her the complete forgiveness of what they had done.

He had been brought to her in the small hours of that Sunday morning. Damaris, terrified and white-faced had wakened them from sleep, demanding entry to the cottage, the baby clutched tight against her shoulder.

That something bad had come to pass Jemima had no doubt. The child was blue and stiff and scarcely breathing. She had set a bowl of water on the hearth-stone, before a fire of re-kindled wood. She had taken the baby from his mother, removed the many layers of clothing and lowered him gently into the warm water. The spasm of his skinny limbs had gradually eased; she had felt his trust in her steady hands, saw normal colour creep back into the small face. All at once, the awful rigidity had left his body and his eyes closed in sleep. She had dried him on a cloth, warm from the clothes line above the range, and wrapped him in a piece of blanket.

'Is he dead, Ma?' Damaris had whispered.

'Not dead, maid. O'ny sleeping. He must have took a very bad shock to get hisself in that state?'

The face of Maris that until recently had always been so clear and open, now took on that exact closed look of Jye.

''Twas only temper,' she said briefly.

'Whose temper, maid? His own, or that of some other party?'

Her silent refusal to be drawn could no longer be maintained; Maris had covered her face with both hands, and all at once the guilty words had come tumbling from between her fingers.

'I be at my wits-end! This boy don't sleep for ten minutes put together. 'Tis like he got a devil in him. The girls was never like this!'

Jemima had said, 'Some babies need more cossetting than others.'

'But I got no time to fuss wi' him, Ma. There's always so much to do, and me so weary from no sleep.' She paused. 'He do cry more than ever since I was forced to wean him.'

'And what do Jye say?'

The defensive note came back, 'Jye's so wore-out he can hardly drag hisself from bed every morning. He do work so hard, Ma! Twelve hours a day at his banker, and every spare minute he got is spent in mending our boots and digging in the garden – and then no sleep at night – 'tis hard on the man – no wonder that he do grow edgy – '

''Tis just as hard on you, maid. You never was too strong in your body. Father always said as how that goodness all went upwards into your brainy head.' Jemima had hesitated then, but only briefly.

'Go home, Maris. Leave the boy with me and Father. Get some sleep, maid, and in the morning us'll fetch his cradle and clothes – '

'I dunno, Ma? Whatever will people – '

'Never mind people! Some liddle 'uns do need more looking-at than others. I got the time, Maris. I got plenty of time to cuddle and love him.'

'I dursent think what Jye'll say.'

'Jye Carew 'ull do and think exactly what you tell him to! Ah, Damaris, 'tis high time you learned how to manage that man. However do 'ee think I've put-up with your father for so many years!'

*

Jye visited his mother every Sunday morning in the brief time between the ending of Chapel Meeting, and the exact stroke of twelve when Damaris set his dinner on the kitchen table. On this particular Sunday his mood of deep depression tempted him to linger. He gazed around the single room of his mother's occupation; studied the hawking basket, the dried snakeskin which hung on a line above the fireplace, at the high shelves lined with green-glass jars and bottles which held ointments and potions; at the bed, set widthways beneath the rear window.

'I don't know why you bides in this one room?' he cried, irritably. 'Not when you got a whole house all to yourself.'

'Don't 'ee boy?' Meri's voice was soft but full of scorn. 'I was born on the straw, underneath a vardo. I growed up in that vardo, what is, as you well knows, no more than one room on wheels.' She paused, leaned forward, and fixed him with that compelling gaze. 'Have 'ee ever tried living by yourself in a whole house? Roamin' from the downstairs to the upstairs, mooning out of the windows, and never finding rest in any corner? I likes to have my treasures close about me, where I can turn my head and see 'em.'

She waved her fingers at the fine Crown Derby china on the dresser; at the bed with its clean white coverlet and draped scarlet shawl with silken fringes; at the faded velvet of the yellow cushions.

'Close about me,' she repeated, 'where I can see 'em.'

The signs of her unholy indulgence in alcohol and tobacco were displayed for anyone to see. The keg of cider stood in a corner; Jye wished that she would, at least, make some effort to conceal the clay pipe and thick-twist tobacco which lay openly upon the mantleshelf.

66

'I gets comfort from a smoke,' she remarked, 'as for the cider, why, 'tis no more than nature's own cure for sadness. After all, 'twas God hisself what made they apples.' Meri smiled, revealing teeth, which despite her age, were still strong and white. Jye studied the thick braids of hair looped above her ears, and could find no streak of grey in the blackness. A strong woman, he thought, in every way, even though she had always denied that she would ever make old bones. Her humour was of the dry kind; the sly amusement of the Romani rawny for the antics of the gorgio.

'Day might yet come,' Jye's mother told him, 'when you too needs to find a bit of ease in a pipeful of 'baccy and a drop o' cider.'

She paused to consider him and her scrutiny was even more clairvoyant than usual. 'Church clock is striking the noon hour,' she said drily, 'time you was off home to your dinner idden it?'

He twisted his grey woollen muffler between fingers that betrayed his state of mind. She pointed towards his father's chair.

'Sit down,' she commanded, 'you got something you needs to tell – so tell it!'

Jye surveyed his mother and the strange room, and admitted finally that the one belonged inside the other. Meridiana had never been a motherly mother. She was, he thought, as unlike Jemima Honeybone as the kestrel is unlike the sparrow. It was only the press of his desperation that tempted him to confide in her now; he sat down, the scarf bunched-up between his hands, his gaze fixed upon the fire's glow.

'Last night I done a bad thing,' he began; he risked a glance in her direction. 'I done a bad thing,' he repeated, 'I thought to lose my shame in the morning Chapel but 'tiv bided with me.'

'Then tell I, boy,' his mother's tone was gruff, 'tell I what you'se hev' done what is so shameful.'

'The boy,' he began, 'the baby – Sev. He don't never

stop crying. 'Tis like a saw-cut screaming through my head. Us gets no rest. There's days when I all but falls asleep across my banker.'

His dulled tone rose to a pitch of panic.

'I had thought myself a patient feller – slow to anger – peaceable on all counts – '

'What is it you'se hev' done, Jye?'

'Last night, end of a hard week – and me so dogtired – only wanting sleep – '

'Go on!'

'He cried and cried. Maris tried all she knowed to stop him. 'Twas getting light towards the morning – she was sitting up in bed beside me – child screaming in her arms. That awful pain was going through my head, Ma! I snatched him off her – I throwed him from me in temper, as hard as I cud – 'twas only the iron footrails on the end of the bed what saved him from landing on the floor.'

'And then?'

'He went quiet. Too quiet. I rushed to pick him up. Maris lit the candle. He was dark-blue in the face. 'Un had quite stopped breathing. I was sure I'd killed him, or broke his bones!'

All at once Jye began to weep the agonised tears of an inarticulate man. 'I can't never trust myself to touch him again, Ma!'

'Was there any harm done?'

'Maris said not. He was swaddled thick wi' shawls against the cold night, even his head was covered over. 'Twas mos'ly temper and shock what turned him blue, according to Maris.' Jye knuckled the tears from his cheeks with a defiant gesture. 'Her was pretty put-out with me – I never see'd her so angry – she said some very hard things – threatened to take steps – '

'So what hev' the gorgie wife done, Jye?'

'She've – she've took Sev away. She've give him to her mother to look after.' Jye's look was beseeching. 'I told her as how you wudden allow it!'

Meridiana stood up. She walked towards the window

and gazed in the direction of the Honeybones' cottage.

''Tis alright Jye,' she said quietly. 'No need for 'ee to be atrashed. Old Jemima Honeybone'll serve our purpose very well – for the time being.' A rare thread of hesitation came into her voice. 'I idden myself all that partial to very young chavvies. My Sev shall come to me on his own two feet, just as soon as he can walk here.'

'Then you don't mind?'

Meridiana grinned. 'That do make small difference to me whether he be brought-up under your roof or Jemima's. Jus' you wait till he hev' growed a bit. That chal is pure Rom, he 'ont bide under any gorgio rooftree!' She moved from the window, back towards the fireplace. She reached up for her clay pipe and packet of thick-twist tobacco, cut a plug of the pungent black stuff, and began to roll it, slowly, between her fingers. She sat down on her low stool. 'I don't like to see 'ee so upset, boy.' She sighed. 'Well I tried to warn 'ee that marriage wi' the gorgie wudden be easy. There's times when a man is sore-tired and needs a bit o' comfort.' She tamped the tobacco hard into the clay bowl, lit it with a long spill, placed the stem of the pipe between her lips and drew upon it. Meri breathed the fragrant smoke towards Jye. 'How old be you now?'

'I lost count. Reckon I must be pushin' forty.'

'Then 'tis time you considered yourself a bit, boy!' She leaned towards him, and thrust the pipe-stem between his lips.

'Draw on it!' she commanded.

Jye took the tobacco smoke deep into his lungs and began to choke. He coughed for a full three minutes. When the spasm had passed Meri said, ''Tis always like that, first time. You'll get used to it quick enough. That'll quiet your head, Jye – '

''Tis a habit I can't afford,' he interrupted. 'I got three children to feed and clothe – rent and coal to pay for – '

Meri rose and went towards an oaken chest. From it she pulled a new clay-pipe and a packet of thick-twist tobacco. She pushed the items into Jye's jacket pocket.

'Come back when that lot's finished.' She grinned. 'I be always well-supplied. As for my Sev – that trouble with your son wudden never hev' happened if you had been a smoker. Try it, Jye. See how it do soothe the temper. You'll be a better husband and father for a pipe o' baccy, now and again.'

*

Damaris had failed, and conviction of that failure seeped now into her voice and gestures, slowing her quick words and movements, dragging at her step, fumbling at her fingers, until all her nimbleness was lost.

To begin with she had run night and morning to her parents' cottage, held the baby close, assured herself that he still breathed and moved. As he thrived and his crying quietened, her fears for him had lessened. Her visits had become infrequent. Sometimes a whole week would pass and Maris not find a single minute in which she might cross the village street.

It was not uncommon in a crowded household for a weakly baby to be taken from its overburdened mother, and reared by a grandmother or aunt, until it had grown strong enough to take its place beside brothers and sisters. In the case of Jye and Damaris Carew, tongues had wagged. Their cottage was not overfull by village standards; the continuing frailty of Sev was made much of by Jemima to her neighbours, but still the condemnation had been made.

'Her can't manage,' was the dreaded assessment that every young wife and mother feared to hear, and Damaris had her pride. The day had come when Sev, newly-shy and aware of strangers, had tucked his face into Jemima's neck and refused to come to his mother's arms. Maris knew then what she had done. A tiny fear had touched her, but still she made no effort to reclaim her child. There was plenty of time, she told herself, to set matters right in that direction. Her preoccupation was all with Jye, whom she had also failed to manage.

The easy way would have been to accept her mother's explanation of the trouble. It could all be put down, according to Jemima, to the sly, insidious undermining of Meridiana. The evidence was there for anyone to see. There was those regular Sunday morning visits of Jye to his mother, and the two of them closeted together. She had found shreds of thick-twist tobacco in his jacket pockets, smelled cider on his breath. There was money, locked away for the first time in their marriage, in the middle drawer of the oaken dresser; silver that he insisted was to be kept for his sole use.

Long hours spent alone at her gloving-table gave her time for introspection. Mind kept pace with fingers as she stitched doe-skin and chamois, as she threaded needles and snipped at loose ends. Damaris remembered her young girl's plan to make a merry fellow of the melancholy Jye. A house filled with laughter had been her intention; chuckling babies who would delight him.

Well, the babies had come. Two plump, contented maidens, as gentle as Jye himself. As for the boy who had been baptised David John, it was as if his birth had never come to pass. He seemed no part of either of them. Long before the child's arrival, the predictions of Meridiana had reached Damaris. A boy would be born she had said, and his name was to be Silvanus. He was to be the sole property of Meri. So great had been the arrogance and the pride of the woman that she had laid claim to an infant just conceived. That fearsome expression 'more gypsy than the ribs o' God' had been used by Jye's mother, and its implications laid a strange reluctance upon Damaris. Once born not even his Honeybone looks could endear the baby to her. Red hair and blue eyes notwithstanding, there was something 'other' in him; an old look, knowing and fierce.

There was her own weariness of course, an exhaustion of her very bones, severe enough to stun mother-love at source. Most women, said Jemima, suffered lowness of spirit after childbirth. At the thought of her cast-down state, tears blurred Maris's vision. Her fingers stumbled among the piles of cut-out, unstitched gloves, sending the neat heaps slithering towards the floor. She leaned back in her chair and gave herself up to misery. How could it be, that she who had read many books, who knew words seldom used among village people; she, who could argue religion with the clever John Powys and best him, had failed to make of Jye Carew the man she would have him be?

There were many ways of failing. Her natural inclination was to use the gift bestowed on her by nature. Words were her weapon. Her soft voice and sharp tongue had gained respect and a certain awe among Chapel members. But what use her reasoned arguments and unanswerable logic in the face of Jye's deafness? And there was defeat of another kind, one she could hardly bear to dwell on.

Was it something in his dark, closed looks, some deep and alien quality in him, that made her miserly with love? She had never confessed the wild sweet passion he aroused in her, never shown him by touch or gesture the extent of her enslavement. What would he do with her love, entombed as he was in his world of silence? He would read the words upon her lips, mouthed carefully to aid comprehension, but without the cadences of voice surely there could be no meaning for him?

She was jealous, and her jealousy was a bad thing, an animal that lived inside her, biting at her heart, the pain of it so severe that she would turn on Jye in her frustration to chide him for faults he did not possess. Certain rivals had been faced and measured long ago. The threat of Meridiana was strong and likely to be lifelong; as for that other woman in Jye's life, the clever baggage up in London, well, distance and time were taking care of her.

It was his abstraction that aroused the demon in Damaris, his withdrawal into a place where she could not go. It was possible for her to gauge his mood by the progress of the work which stood presently upon his banker.

In the first experimental days of wedlock, when they still had energy enough, and inclination to reach for understanding, she had complained about his strange abstraction, and he had tried to make clear the quality of his mind. Jye's tongue had stumbled among unfamiliar words. She had wanted to ease his hindrance, to put words into his mouth. But a shake of his head had shown up her mistake. Jye's words might be few and rare, but they were very much his own. Restoration, he told her, was his main occupation; he made good the ravages that time and weather had wrought upon the carvings of medieval masons, and monks, long-dead. It was, he said, a secret thing, his feeling for the Ham stone; like a dowser's knack of finding hidden springs; like those miners who were said to be able to smell gold. Sometimes, Jye told her, when the piece to be restored was particularly fine, and he was nervous of it, he would sense the presence of a spirit that was not his own. For those days and weeks in which he struggled to repeat another man's glory, Jye would *be* that medieval mason, that long-dead monk. He had told her about Ham stone. He carried a small piece in his jacket pocket, as if he could not bear to be parted from it. Living gold, he told her solemnly; and make no mistake, that stone still grows underneath the Hill. The Romans were using it in their time, and then the Saxons! The supply was neverending. He described for her the block of uncut Ham stone on his banker; how he could eye it, walk around it, size-up its strengths and flaws, see in his mind's eye the finished carving that was concealed inside it.

She had wanted to understand but could not. She had laughed, because there was nothing else that she could do. He had looked at her then with the eyes of a kicked dog, and Maris had known, too late, that her laughter had been a mistake. He never talked to her again about his work.

The tears had dried, stiff and salty on her face. Maris rubbed them away, and then stooped down to retrieve the fallen gloves. Even a single dropped glove, according to Jemima's superstition, was sure to bring a disappointment. Maris snatched up the dozens of unstitched doe-skins and chamois, and set them back in neat piles on the gloving table. It was later that evening, while Jye dozed by the fire, and she washed up the supper dishes, that a note was brought from the quarry-master. The presence of Jye Carew was required in the Abbey of Westminster. A contract had been won by Adge and Joby Stagg, who had lately set up in business together in London. The work was to be completed by early June in time for the new King's Coronation. Jye must travel to London on the following Sunday.

*

Jye laid his mason's tools between folds of clean sackcloth, and placed them, with his leather-strop and razor in the shabby carpetbag which had served him on so many trips to London. Damaris had washed and ironed his spare shirt and trousers. Between the shirt and the pairs of darned socks she had packed his Bible. He glanced at her now, removed the book, lifted it briefly in his right hand and returned it to the dresser drawer. He waited for her censure, but she passed no judgement on his action. Her finger pointed towards a low stool. He sat down, and she placed a towel around his shoulders. With her bluntest gloving-scissors Jye's wife clipped the black curls that grew onto his coat-collar. He polished his boots, trimmed his moustaches, and took a last look at his garden. All their tasks were performed in a curious silence; after that first reading of Adge Stagg's letter no reference had been made to Jye's destination.

They parted awkwardly on that Sunday morning. She standing on the doorstep, hands clasped, body stiff, as if in prayer. Jye, shy of showing affection before his watching neighbours, did not kiss her, but stooped to whisper. 'Don't worry! 'Tis work what pays well! I'll send a Postal Order every Monday. You'll be alright. You got your mother and father to rely on!'

The West-Country train was almost empty. Jye stared at the changing landscape, and all he could see was the thin, taut face of Damaris, her anxious eyes and clasped fingers. He was met at Paddington by Adge Stagg. They drove first to a chop-house in the Borough of Westminster. Jye was conscious of the master mason's raised eyebrows when his former apprentice ordered porter, and filled-up and lit a briar pipe. Jye was surprised by Adge Stagg's confident manner and affluent appearance.

'You find me altered, eh boy? You should have stayed in London!'

Jye nodded towards the tankard, removed the pipe from his clenched teeth. 'Reckon we be both changed, Adge.'

The mason grinned. 'They tell me that you got married?'

'I wed wi' Shepherd Honeybone's daughter. Us got two girls and a baby boy.'

'A son, eh? Another mason to work beside you in a few years.'

Jye looked uneasy. 'Dunno about that. It do take a certain kind o' man to be a mason. Carving do need patience and a quiet head.'

'How old is the boy?'

'He'll be a year come April.'

Adge laughed. 'Then 'tis early days yet!'

'No Adge.' Jye's face was grave. 'He's all Honeybone from head to toe. The very image of his mother.' He paused. 'Honeybones is, in the main, long-headed and full o' words. Even their women is smarter than most men.'

The master mason nodded. 'Got yourself a clever wife, is that it?'

'Her's argumentative and won't be bested. She got a sharp wit and the tongue to match.'

Adge Stagg said, 'There was a girl, when you first came to London. Prettiest piece I ever did see.'

'You know'd about that?'

'Couldn't hardly miss it, could I, the way she chased you? You were very young and shy with women. I was worried about you.'

Adge grinned. 'Well I needn't have fretted. In the end 'twas your own good sense that sent her packing.' He signed. 'Ah, but she was a beauty! I wonder what happened to her?'

Jye spoke slowly and in a dull tone. 'She found a man who had plenty of money. All she thought about was clothes and jewellery.'

Adge said, reflectively, 'Devout Chapel members, the Honeybone family. You'll have no problems with their daughter.' He hesitated. 'I'm grateful that you came, boy. It was due to you that I got this contract. You was asked for by name, down to the Abbey.' He stood up. 'I'll walk down with you to your lodgings. I found you a room in Great Smith Street. Don't look so took aback – you won't be staying with the Widow Murphy!' He looked keenly at Jye. 'There's much work to be got through, and not too much time allowed us. The Coronation is set for less than three months – '

'I won't let 'ee down, Adge.' Jye sighed. 'I got a wife and a family to keep, these days,' his lips twisted wryly beneath the black moustaches, 'and nothing else on my mind but hard work.'

*

Jye took possession of the small, clean room in Great Smith Street. He unpacked his few possessions, and laid the packets of thick-twist tobacco on a shelf where in other days his Bible would have rested. He walked out into the chill twilight of late March, and found his way into the Dean's Yard to gaze at the miracle of the South Face. Nothing had changed. Even in the dim light, and he weary from the unaccustomed travelling, that old constriction was in his throat, that warmth in his chest. Tomorrow he would sit in King Henry's Chapel, he would walk in the Cloisters; he would touch with his mind's finger the work of his masters – the medieval masons. He stood for a long time, concealed in the shadows, and a strange thought came to his head. Jye knew and truly understood for the first time what his mother had meant by her talk of patteran. The understanding came to him unbidden, as if a voice spoke. Her people, Meridiana had said, came centuries ago out of Egypt and India. Among them there had been musicians, silver- and copper-smiths, artists and carvers. Jye lifted his hands, spread them wide, peered through the cold spring twilight at their great size, the knotted knuckles, the splayed tips of the fingers. Until this moment he had seen himself as belonging to that company of masons who had raised this Abbey. Less talented, less skilled than they, but coming down in their direct line. Now he recalled the coloured pictures in his illustrated Bible; the Temples of Egypt, their great pillars and elaborate carvings. From 'gyptian to gypsy, his mother had said, was but a short step. The conviction, slight at first, quickened and spread until it filled his whole being.

Patteran, he now saw, must mean more than his father's tools and the damask rosebush. It was something of the blood, a sign, a gift, undeniable and certain, straight from some ancient Egyptian temple-carver to Jye Carew. He strode out of the Dean's Yard and back to Great Smith Street. He fell asleep, weary but elated with the simplicity of his new thought; and all Jye's dreams, that night, were of Blanche Fitzgerald.

*

A friendship with Bertie, Prince of Wales, it was said, no matter how brief, had a way of marking a woman forever. One could not, it seemed, accept the Royal favour without retaining some aura of its splendour. In the case of Blanche Fitzgerald, association with the

Prince had developed an almost regal quality in her; for Bertie had declared, many times, that every drawback could be turned into an advantage, given the correct state of mind. Her hoydenish behaviour, retained for so long deliberately to annoy Hugh, had been abandoned for a quieter more effective style. She no longer slammed doors to express her displeasure, or kicked carpets and furniture to show annoyance. Her natural ability to cut down an adversary with a few choice words, had been encouraged by the Prince to a point when it had become her most valuable weapon. Those days were over when she lingered in the hallway in order to intercept her morning post, so that it might be read privately to her, by a housemaid in a pantry. Blanche no longer attempted to defend her illiteracy, but spoke openly and proudly of her inability to read and write. The defect had lost its power to embarrass, and become an advantage which set her above and apart from those unfortunate enough to be forced into grappling with the written word.

In times of doubt Blanche would open the red leather case and gaze at the brooch which had been her farewell gift from the Prince. Bertie had once asked her what memento she would like of their afternoon meetings, and she had answered, 'Anything that will pawn well, your Highness!' Blanche touched the jewels, which formed each separate letter of the word 'PERSIMMON'. The promise, that if in the year of 1894 his horse should win the Derby, the Prince would present Blanche with the name of the winner made up in diamonds, had been fulfilled. But the brooch was so much more than a farewell gift or a promise kept. It was her personal insurance against disaster. That seemingly light and outrageous remark, which had so delighted the Prince of Wales, had been made with a good deal of forethought. She had heard that the offer of a Royal gift meant goodbye; some of Bertie's ladies received a fine carriage and a pair of horses; others settled for a 'little place' in the country. But diamonds were negotiable and transportable; and they were forever.

The trips to Taunton had, as always, been successful in some ways and a failure in others. To return to her mother's house, in Greenbrook Terrace, to observe her sisters in their little homes, always gave Blanche satisfaction of a kind. She had a need, periodically, for the reassurance of their drab lives. It salved old hurts and slights to bestow her gracious charity upon them, and know that their need was so great that they dared not refuse. Blanche dressed as carefully in Taunton as she would for any Mayfair function. The resultant gasps and envious glances of Annis and Madelina made the transportation of a large trunk and several hat-boxes a necessity, and worth all of Hugh's complaints. At the thought of Hugh she at once put a rein on her mind. She replaced the brooch on its bed of crimson velvet, snapped shut the case, and thrust it into a drawer. Her fingers moved clumsily among the dressing-table silver, she experienced her usual irritation at the sight of the ugly unmatched hair brush and hand mirror, the cut-glass perfume bottles, and silver knick-knacks passed on to her by Hugh's aunt. Almost everything in the apartment was the property of Mrs Porteous: the furniture, the carpets and curtains, the ornaments and bedlinen, the very brush and comb with which she dressed her hair. 'Nothing more than lodgers, that's what we are!' she had said, repeatedly, to Hugh. She had described the exquisite dressing-table silver to be found at Penhaligon's of Bond Street; the powder bowl with the floral silver lid, the heart-shaped jewel box, the seventeen-piece set of mirror, combs, brushes and perfume bottles, made up in tortoiseshell, cut-glass and sliver. 'I want my own things around me,' she had cried, 'I want –!'

'Your wants,' he had interrupted, 'no longer keep pace with my income.' He had waved a hand at the paintings on the walls, the leather-bound books shelved from floor to ceiling; at the violin beside the music stand.

'We have our own essential things around us, and you

must understand this, Blanche. Russell Square is a good address. We live here entirely at my aunt's expense. There would be no two hundred-guinea gowns for you, no trips to Taunton, no flutters at the gaming-tables, if I should be forced to maintain an establishment of my own.'

'You have *your* own things,' she cried, 'you never begrudge the money spent at Christie's auctions. You've got cupboards full of figurines, drawers full of coins. As for the paintings!' She had turned away from the sight of herself, repeated in almost every framed canvas. 'I want a child, Hugh, and it'll never come to pass in this – this mausoleum.'

He had moved towards the table which held bottles and decanters; she heard the chink of glass on glass, and knew that he sought his usual solution.

Such confrontations had become more frequent and bitter since September. Blanche wore her 'Persimmon' brooch on every possible occasion, knowing how much it distressed Hugh. She leaned now towards her triple-mirrored image, sought imperfections and found none. She was, at the age of thirty-seven, as beautiful as she had even been; her hair as auburn and glossy, her violet eyes still clear; her skin white and unlined, except for the tiny vertical crease that had lately appeared between her eyebrows. Hugh Deveraux Fitzgerald had better be careful. She had other admirers, only slightly less wealthy and important than the Prince himself. For a moment she allowed herself to think about them; the raddled, the effete, the seekers after partners who were willing to indulge in strange erotic practices; and knew that she would never leave the safety of her husband's protective love. But did he love her? Had anybody, ever, in all her life, loved Blanche? She had always aroused resentment and animosity in women; even her mother. In the case of men, she had never known affection, the kind of rough and easy camaraderie that she had witnessed between Frank and Annis. Even the Prince had admitted to a certain fear; a dangerous filly, was how he had described her, the kind of woman who could become an unbreakable habit. He had given her the diamond brooch, and let her go. Her mind skimmed back across the mild flirtations, carried on with decorum, and from a judicious distance, among her husband's friends. Then there had been Mr Solomon, the artist met in her St Martin's Lane days. Now he had almost certainly loved her, but as a parent might care for a precocious child; and he was not, after all, quite a proper man.

She smiled, remembering how he had quoted the Song of Solomon to her. 'Who is she that looketh forth as the morning, fair as the moon, clear as the sun, and terrible as an army with banners.' The recollection was a sweet one, it bolstered her courage, so that she found it possible to think, finally, of Jye. She clenched her fists until the pointed finger-nails pierced her palms. She did not so much remember Jye Carew, as admit to his constant presence beneath conscious thought. She, who had hammered six iron nails across a threshold, and made sure that he was bound to step across them, had been caught just as surely as Jye in that dangerous magic. He was always with her now, straight and tall in his Baptist black, or wearing his mason's apron, his dark face rapt as he bent to carve the Ham stone She always knew when he was thinking of her, for at that precise moment, no matter where she was, or with whom, the image of Jye would come back to her mind. She supposed that the spell must work in reverse, and in fact so strong was her sense of communication with him lately, that she had no doubt of her own frequent presence in his thoughts. The irony of her situation had not escaped Blanche. Money and status had been her aim, she had made certain sacrifices in order to achieve this. Men existed to be used by women, and in view of their cruel and unpleasant natures they deserved to be so used. These were the truths she had learned as a child on Larksleve Farm; she had only to recall her father's treatment of her mother, to reinforce conviction. This single-mindedness had been her great strength, until she had come upon Jye Carew. She picked up the hairbrush, gazed absently at it, and set it down. There must be a way to lift the spell, to claim back her independent soul; but Loveday Hayes, her mother's servant, who had taught Blanche the magic practised in the Blackdowns, had concerned herself only with overlooking and illwishing. No mention had ever been made of how these invocations to the devil might be countermanded. Blanche considered a visit to Mrs Gimball in St Martin's Lane, and was bound to smile at the thought of herself, on bended knees, silken gown hitched up around her waist armed with pinchers and crowbar, and about to prise loose the six iron nails from the pawnshop's threshold. It was all too late. The damage had been done on that summer Sunday. She stood up, abruptly, and moved to the window that overlooked the Square; she pushed aside the heavy lace and velvet which Mrs Porteous considered necessary to shut out air and sunlight.

The April day was cold and still; a carriage rumbled past, a maid set down a bucket noisily upon a top step, and began to scrub half-heartedly, her reddened fingers swollen and painful-looking around the brush. Blanche shivered, unwilling to be reminded of her own brief time spent as a skivvy in Berkeley Square. She watched as the girl pushed a lock of straying hair underneath her cap with a sudsy hand; there was such irritation and hopelessness in the gesture that Blanche felt a curious kinship with her. Dead leaves, brown and dusty, lay underneath the plane trees' branches; scabrous yellow patches had appeared on their bark, causing it to flake. London, she thought, was the spoiler; perhaps Hugh was right, after all? She began to think about the fishing-village in Devon; the place called Dawlish. There was a house, he had said, which stood high on the very edge of red cliffs. With a little help from his aunt they might just be able to afford it. In the quiet of the country, in the clean sea air, the miracle they both hoped for might eventually happen. The conviction that she would never conceive while living in Aunt Porteous's house, had grown stronger since their return from Taunton.

A nursemaid was leading a small girl through the Gardens. The child looked a lot like Abigail. Blanche gripped the folds of dark-red velvet, pulled the curtains wider; she had only to whisper the little girl's name to feel the slight body in her arms, to see her perched high on cushions in the Castle Hotel. Blanche had coveted many things in her life, but nothing so much as this child of her sister, Annis. How far, she had asked Hugh, is Dawlish from Taunton? Oh, not far, he had said, just a short ride on the train.

*

The Monarchy of Victoria, Queen of Commonwealth and Empire, had never failed to provide its loyal subjects with regular melodramas and scandals. The Victorian appetite for pathos and sensation had been tantalised by the tiny majestic lady and her volatile children. Even in death the ancient Queen had given good value for money. With the income-tax standing at one shilling in the pound her funeral had been memorable; her marble mausoleum at Frogmore a prime example of what money could buy.

The old century had turned on a note of satisfying sadness, but now there was an excitement in the air, endearing stories were told about the new King. He was said to be superstitious; would not permit his mattress to be turned on a Friday, or his finger and toenails to be trimmed on a Sunday. On the eve of his Coronation, Edward Albert had developed severe peritonitis, and was operated upon at great risk. Prayers were said, the populace agonised and suffered with him. His swift recovery was seen as a sign from heaven. On August 9th 1902, only six weeks after major surgery upon their King, Blanche and Hugh Fitzgerald stood in Westminster

Abbey and awaited the postponed event. Blanche finally wore the ivory satin gown, embroidered all over with tiny seed-pearls; that expensive creation from Worth which had once been intended for a very different purpose and occasion. She allowed herself a brief smile. Across the aisle, in a separate pew which people were openly calling the 'King's Loose Box', sat Mrs Paget, Lady Kilmorly, Sarah Bernhardt, and Mrs Keppel; Blanche had never aspired to such notoriety. She touched the Persimmon diamonds pinned at her breast, remembered her secret afternoons spent with him in Park Lane, and was content. She had loved the intrigue of it all, the jealousy of Hugh, the embarrassment caused to his Aunt Porteous. Poor Bertie. All his life he had waited for this day when he would be crowned King. They had sat together beside a laden tea-table; she had told him about her West Country magic, the powers of ill-wishing and overlooking. She had read his future in the cards and teacups. 'A coffin and a crown, very close together', she had said.

Blanche had also waited all her life for something wonderful to happen. There was a sudden stir among the people, a great blast of sound from the massed trumpets; Hugh pressed her elbow and murmured, 'The King – the King!' She twisted white-gloved fingers restlessly together, and wondered how and when her own day would come. Blanche had also dared to hope that the century's turn would see a fulfilment of her dreams. The longed-for child had not been born to the Fitzgeralds, but to Annis Nevill and her husband, Frank. Miracles happened; but to other people. Her mind leapt across the years to Jye Carew; she glanced sideways at the ermine-clad shoulders, the tiaras and jewels of the assembled nobles, and grinned, hugely. How surprised they would be to learn that Blanche Fitzgerald, wife of the Honourable Hugh, had once long ago, courted and attempted the seduction of a stone-mason right here in the Abbey of Westminster.

With a sudden and absolute conviction she looked towards the gloomy recesses of the Poets' Corner. Her vision blurred at the sight of a dark head and face, a man who stood taller and prouder than all the other Abbey servants. She should have guessed that he would be here on this of all days. Refurbishment of the Abbey was to be expected before the Coronation of a King; and Jye Carew was an acknowledged master of his craft.

He stood among a group of Abbey workers, behind a width of fretted ironwork. But Jye's great height had placed him head and shoulders above the screen. He was, she now realised, so close that she could almost touch him. She at first felt cold and sick at the nearness of him; she stood, head bowed, fingers clasped together and thought that she might faint. It came to her then that even as she was trapped among this close-packed congregation, so was Jye hemmed-in by his fellow stone-masons. Every eye was strained towards the drama of the crowning. She was free to examine the impassive features at her leisure. No other man had ever roused Blanche to such a pitch of longing; that old temptation to reach out and touch him was as keen as it had ever been. The curls still clustered black and thick about the fine head; the walnut sheen of his skin, his brown eyes were just as she had remembered. Ah, but Jye was altered! There was a hard line to his lips beneath the black moustaches. Below the high-set cheekbones his once rounded face had thinned and hollowed, giving him an older, more mature aspect. She examined the dark planes of his chin and jawline, the splendid column of neck that rose from his white shirt, his great breadth of shoulder. She looked up into his eyes, and found that Jye's gaze was upon her own lips and throat, and moving downwards into the cleavage revealed by the low-cut of her satin gown. In the stifling heat of the close-packed Abbey, Blanche shivered at the revelation of carnal knowledge in that gaze. It came to her then that Jye Carew was no longer a young and inexperienced boy, but a husband, probably a father. The knowledge was sufficient to transfuse her body beneath the ivory-satin and seed-pearls. She raised her head, looked straight into his eyes, and saw the skin drawn suddenly across his cheekbones, a crease of pain pull his brows together, and Blanche knew then, that Jye's desire was equal finally to her own.

There was singing and movement all around her. Silken banners, carried high, passed along the aisle between herself and Jye. She moaned, deep in her throat, and leaned out towards the fretted screen, to the place where he was standing. The procession passed, the aisle was cleared, but he was no longer there. Blanche became aware of Hugh's restraining hand on her forearm, the curious glances of his Aunt Letitia. Her mouth twisted up in a wry grin; she knew what they must be thinking. All her desperate peering and forward leaning for a last glimpse, must, they imagined, be all for the sake of King Edward Albert!

*

They travelled to Dawlish in late November on a mild day of low cloud and soft rain. The journey from London had been made in silence, she in her corner seat and he in his. Blanche noted, absentmindedly, the familiar railway stations; Reading, Westbury, Castle Cary, and then Taunton. The next important stop, Hugh told her, would be Exeter. Had she ever, he enquired, travelled this far south? She shook her head, and glanced curiously at him. Since leaving Taunton station, Hugh had undergone a sure and subtle change. The hip-flask, which contained neat Scotch whisky, remained in his pocket. He became animated, as he never was in London. She studied him, closely, for the first time in years. Hugh had aged. The fine fair skin was lined heavily, around the eyes and across the forehead; there were streaks of grey in his yellow hair. His body was still slim, but no longer upright; even when seated his shoulders bowed in a dispirited fashion.

They changed trains with the help of several porters. The hatboxes and trunks without which Blanche refused to make the shortest journey, were transferred to the little local train that ran to Dawlish. The difference in Hugh became more marked; even Blanche could no longer ignore the new note in his voice as he pointed out landmarks that were familiar to him. Determined to remain unimpressed, she stared wearily at yet more green fields and white farmhouses, and then, suddenly, she looked down from her window, and realised that the wheels of the train were running through water. A swift glance upwards confirmed that she had not imagined the vast expanse of ocean that stretched away to the horizon. Instinctively, Blanche lifted her feet from the carriage floor.

'You never warned me about the sea! Oh it can't be safe, Hugh – '

'It's only high-tide,' he reassured her. 'The railway track runs close beside the shore and sometimes, if the tide is especially high, a wave or two will lap the lines. It's perfectly safe, Blanche.' She had never seen the ocean, not even on that disastrous honeymoon in Dover, when they had been snowed-in and fog-bound. He gazed at it now, silvery and calm beneath low skies. The carefully cultivated accents of Mayfair were abandoned for her native speech.

'Why, thass beautiful,' she whispered, 'oh, I never see'd nothin' in all my born days what could match that!'

Tears burned behind her eyelids; there was awe in her face and voice. 'I once give my Mama a length of silk that exact same colour. How far do the waters reach, Hugh?'

'All the way to America.'

'And to think I've lived all these years and never knowed about it! 'Tiv been here all this time just a-waiting for me.'

She turned back to Hugh. 'I was meant to come here,' her voice was fierce with suppressed emotion. 'Some old gypsy woman once made a prediction about me. I – I don't recall the exact words at the minute – 'twas something about me only finding peace beside the ocean.'

'And so you shall, my darling!' The unaccustomed warmth in his voice endeared him unexpectedly to her; the coldness of many months fell away, and Blanche reached out her hand towards him.

'Will it be alright, Hugh? I don't like changes. I've lived in London since I was sixteen, I get nervous in lonely places – ' she hesitated, unused to confessing her deepest fears, '– in the country, well, there's no distractions. You come face to face with your own self. My Papa, I think, must have had the same feelings. He cudden abide the sight of his own soul.'

*

The Royal Hotel stood close beside the railway station; it catered for people of distinction, but now, in late November, the summer guests had gone and it was almost empty. Hugh, who was known to the management from previous visits, was greeted effusively. Two footmen were despatched to collect the trunk and hat-boxes from the station platform, while Blanche and Hugh were shown to a pleasant room that overlooked the ocean, and brought tea and biscuits on a tray. Blanche scarcely noticed the admiring gasps of the maids as they lifted her beautiful gowns from the trunk, and hung them in the wardrobes. She was drawn irresistibly to the window. Even with the sashes closed she could still hear the susurration of the waves as the tide turned towards the ebb. The maids went away; Hugh sat down in a comfortable wing-chair beside a blazing fire, and began to drink tea. She could hear his voice, explaining how the oceans were ruled by the moon, about high and low tides; and all at once her thoughts were back with

Jye Carew and her last meeting with him. Significant things, thought Blanche, always happened to her in winter, it had been a day of yellow fog in London when she had gone to Westminster Abbey, convinced that she would find him there. Jye had stood engrossed beside an old carved pulpit, and the unwilling admiration in his eyes as he turned to face her had aroused hope. With no pretence at modesty she had said, 'I want you, Jye . . . Take pity on me, for God's sake!' 'I don't want you,' he told her, 'not now, not never. There's something unholy in you . . . my mother don't often foretell the future . . . but she knows all about you.'

Blanche had demanded to know the gypsy's prophecy of her, but it was always at this moment of recollection that memory failed her. Words had been spoken about the ocean. She could hear Jye's voice, made toneless by his deafness.

'No peace shall come to her,' he had quoted ' . . . until she rests with her face towards the sea, the sound of the ocean beating in her . . . ears.'

Blanche stirred uneasily beside the hotel window; she had not, she suspected, recalled that prophecy quite correctly. There had been more; certain dreadful words that had made her cry aloud, 'Sweet Jesus, help me!' She held on to the gold brocade of the hotel's curtains, and her mind closed down abruptly as it always did at this point. A violent shudder swung her away from the view of darkening sky and ocean, and back towards Hugh and the safety of the firelit room. He observed her pallor and was all concern. 'Oh my darling! You must be tired and hungry. Here I am, thoughtless as ever, drinking tea and talking, while you're still in your cloak.' He rose and came towards her, lifted the heavy sables from her shoulders and pulled at the ribbons that secured her bonnet.

'You're very pale, Blanche. Does the sight of so much water alarm you? I recall your disinclination to cross the Channel – we never did have that honeymoon in Paris.'

'No,' she murmured. 'In fact I find it – well, it seems to draw me. I just want to look and look – I can't explain it.'

He smiled. 'It was bound to come as something of a revelation to you, after thirty-seven land-locked years.' He removed her bonnet and threw it into a chair. For a moment he hesitated, and then pulled at the pins that secured her hair. Gently but firmly, he led her towards the fire. 'Take off your gown. Let me fetch your robe.' He grinned, 'What does this remind you of?' She grinned back, one eyebrow raised, 'That awful honeymoon night in Dover?'

He looked away. 'I've never apologised properly, Blanche. I behaved like an animal – ' She placed a hand across his lips. 'It was mainly my fault. I've cheated you, Hugh. I'm an evil woman – I've done wicked things – I don't deserve to be loved by anybody, least of all by you.' He drew her closer and began to unfasten the tiny buttons of her gown. 'Things will be different here in Dawlish. We shall have our own house, just the two of us, together.'

' – and the sea,' she interrupted, 'always there, just outside the windows.' Her arms crept up around his neck. 'Tell me it will be alright,' she said, 'tell me that you care about me. Those others – the Prince of Wales – they never meant anything to me, really.'

'Do you think I don't know that? I know you better than you know yourself, Blanche. I couldn't go on living unless I believed that you loved me.'

Her clasped hands tightened about his neck, she pulled his head down towards her lips. 'I want a child. I want a child of my own so badly that I can hardly bear the pain of waiting.' The clasped hands loosened about Hugh's neck, and flexed in a grasping motion.

'You know how it is with me,' she cried. 'I can't stand disappointment. I just want and want – I can't endure to see my happy sisters with their children – why should it happen to them and not to me.' She grew thoughtful. 'If I could only persuade our Annis to part with the silver and coral pendant −?'

Hugh unfastened the final button, and the gown fell around her ankles. He lifted her from the mound of velvet and carried her to the bed.

'You don't need witchcraft,' he whispered. 'All you need is your love for me, and we shall soon make a child together. All the sorcery you could ever need is right here in Dawlish.'

*

Just to think about the house called Summerlands, standing high upon the red cliffs, made Blanche impatient to go out and view it. As soon as they had breakfasted that morning, a horse-cab was summoned from the rank beside the railway station. They rode out along the Exeter Road in a pale and wintry sunshine. Such excitement in Blanche was rare; Hugh noted her animated face, the tight clasp of her hand in his; the inevitable swing of her gaze towards the shoreline whenever the ocean came into view. She was, he knew, of an intractable nature, her loyalties were of the unconventional kind, her obsessions terrifying. But that first sight of the sea, from the train, had seemed to quieten and soothe her extravagant nature. He looked back across their years of unhappy marriage lived in Russell Square beneath his aunt's roof; the flirtations of Blanche, his own heavy drinking. There were times when his inability to command her obedience and respect proved so shaming that he could only find manhood in the whisky bottle. Ridicule was her favourite weapon. She laughed at his books, his paintings, the efforts he made to play the violin. But she had not laughed at the ocean!

The hand in his tightened suddenly until the grip was fierce. She lapsed once again into the speech of her childhood.

'Thass the house, idden it, Hugh? That big white place with the four tall chimneys?'

They drove in between stone pillars which supported a wide double-gate. The house-agent, a Mr Angel from Dawlish, had arrived before them. He began to explain that the house was surrounded mainly by a high wall; that on the seaward side lawns and flowerbeds sloped down to the very cliff edge.

'I am no stranger to this property, I know it well,' Hugh informed him. 'The previous owner was a friend of mine. I've spent many holidays in Dawlish and in Dawlish Warren.'

Blanche rounded upon him. 'Well I haven't,' she cried. 'I've never set foot in the place!' She linked an arm through that of the astonished agent.

'Come, Mr Angel. You and I shall view this desirable residence together. You shall tell me all about it. Now let us begin with the – ' The sound of her animated voice grew fainter and then loud again, as she proceeded through the house. Window sashes were thrown up, doors opened and closed. Hugh looked upwards to see her standing, rapt, upon the white wooden balcony that ran directly beneath the windows of the upper rooms.

'Oh Hugh!' she cried. 'There's nothing but ocean to be seen from this side of the house. It's so wonderful. I can scarce believe it!' Even as she spoke a cloud came across the sun. Hugh began to tremble. The balcony, which had appeared so substantial in sunshine, looked suddenly frail and unsafe. 'Go back inside at once, Blanche,' he shouted. 'It's a dangerous fall into the garden. Be careful, I do implore you!' She waved at him and laughed, but stepped obediently backwards across the low sill of the open window. Hugh reached for his hip-flask, unscrewed the silver top and drank deeply of the whisky. Gradually, the trembling in his legs ceased; he began to walk down the garden path that led to the sea. The sun reappeared but he did not look back towards the house. The falling figure that he had envisaged across the balcony rails had, after all, not been Blanche, his wife, but himself.

The purchase of Summerlands was in the end to be resolved without too much argument. Hugh Fitzgerald, on his wife's insistence, made an offer of precisely half the current price of asking. The owner of the house, already poised in London to board a liner bound for New York, and weary of the tiresome negotiations between himself and Dawlish, had settled finally for a figure of £400.

'What did I tell you,' Blanche crowed, 'never pay more for anything than you absolutely have to. I learned that much in Mrs Gimball's pawnshop.'

The matter of repairs was put in hand right away with a firm of local builders. Blanche instructed Hugh, and he conveyed her wishes as if they were his own. A new roof, replacement of many timbers, new floors in most rooms. A bathroom in the new style of mahogany and flowered porcelain. Two water-closets. A completely remodelled kitchen with water piped to a tap above the sink, and the very latest thing in blue-tiled cooking-ranges. Last, and most important of all, the installation of gas. Anticipating Hugh's question as to how the money was to be found, she said simply, 'The brooch will pawn for several hundreds of pounds. I've already made enquiries. Tell the workmen that we shall be down again, immediately after Christmas. It won't do to leave them unsupervised for too long. Say that we shall expect to see all of the work underway, most especially that roof!'

As the little local train pulled away from Dawlish station, Blanche began to watch for that section of red cliff, above which the white gables of Summerlands were just visible.

'I can hardly bear to leave this place,' she told Hugh, 'but to stay on at the "Royal" and pay their ridiculous prices would be a waste of money. We shall need every penny we can lay our hands on, in the future –'

He smiled at this new, parsimonious Blanche, but he also gazed upwards at the gable-ends of Summerlands and remembered his own addition to the builders' last instructions. 'A thorough examination of the wooden balcony' he had ordered, 'and a renewal of any suspect timbers.'

'It looks safe and sound enough to me,' the honest fellow had said.

'Never mind,' Hugh had insisted. 'I want that balcony attended to, most particularly. It's a feature of the house that troubles me greatly.'

*

Meridiana had been unusually patient. She had twice watched the winter floods rise over Sedgemoor, seen wallflowers spring from the Vicarage walls; roamed whole summers long in the white lanes around Odcombe and Tintinhull; heard acorns fall to earth in the mild Novembers. But still the child called Silvanus had not been returned to his father's house.

'Makes small difference to me whether he be brought up under your roof or Jemima's,' she had once told Jye, and believed those words to be the truth. One year later and she was uneasy; two years on and she was restless, unable to settle in any place but the vantage point above the village, from which she could view the Honeybones' cottage.

The boy had walked before his first birthday. She had witnessed his first faltering steps away from Jemima's hand. He had spoken early. Sometimes, towards evening, Meri would just happen to be passing David's garden gate as the shepherd returned from the Hill. She would glimpse the child, hear his ecstatic shout of 'granfer's comin'!' and feel the black rage stir within her. Sev was never left unattended. He was taken to Chapel every Sunday morning, he skipped beside Jemima as she went about the village. Just lately, on these fine summer mornings, Meri had spied him, perched high on David Honeybone's shoulders, riding the Hill path that led to the grazing flock.

To a woman like Meridiana Carew, love was a weakness of the mind, a soft word never to be uttered. It would not have occurred to her on their first encounter, and it had not come to her yet that this agony of longing, this yearning to touch and hold him, could be anything but a grandmother's need to assert her prior rights over Jye's son.

She watched him now from behind the shepherd's shelter, so silent in her approach that even the black and white dog failed to sense her presence. David had whittled a tiny crook for Sev's second birthday, and the little boy, imitative in his devotion to the shepherd, stood watchful, head tilted and crook in hand, among the sheep. Meri studied every aspect of him. The crest of red hair rose bright and curling above his thin face. He was small for his age, but all his movements were quick and agile, and the colour in his cheeks was fresh. The blue gaze, directed now towards unruly lambs, was fierce and angry – and all Rom! In all her life she had never experienced such a poignancy of longing, such a need to know, and to be known. She took one step forward, almost cried out, but did not. Instead Meri lifted her hands to the golden earrings, touched her amber necklets, smoothed the plaid skirts. To beg was for diddicois and mumpers. Pride would only allow her to accept what was freely given. The boy must come to her at his own wish, and in his own time.

She turned away, and chagrin and disappointment took her clear across the Hill, towards the deepest quarries. Meri came to the place where Luke, her husband, had died from a fall of stone. To the place where Jye still laboured. She paced the outer limits of the workings, heard the chug of the steam-engine, and the voices of men rising clearly on the still air. She halted, backed away from the dangerous edge, and sat down in the lee of a furze bush. Ah dordi, dordi! This was not what she had meant when she had sanctioned Sev's removal from Jye's house. A few weeks she had thought; a month, a year at the very most. The child filled every corner of her heart and mind. She closed her eyes against the sunlight, and at once the vision came that was to haunt her lifelong. Again, she heard the muffled clink of copper sheepbells, saw the white flock move slowly across green turf, and there was the tiny shepherd boy, crook in hand, his gaze trained upon his charges in faithful imitation of the man he called 'Granfer'.

Meri opened her eyes. She rose up and began to walk, swiftly and without direction. Her thoughts were equally haphazard. Jye had returned from his recent time in London. He looked strained and weary, smoked tobacco and drank cider from a needy desperation that she could only guess at. Maris was again with child. The return of Sev to his father's house seemed less likely than it had ever been.

*

Summer passed and the days grew short. The tiny boy, muffled now against the cold of winter still rode the hillpath daily on David Honeybone's shoulder. In November the gales brought apple boughs crashing in Mr Coles' orchard. Meri filched logs in the windy darkness, concealed and then burned them on the midnight hour of New Year. She stared into a fire of blue flame and glowing heart, sought a message for the future, a picture of Sev walking at her side. Meri looked for confirmation that one day soon she would possess him, but the image which came was unexpected in its clarity, and told her nothing of the boy Silvanus.

The applewood fire still burned red and blue about its edges, but now the heart of it had sunk down into valleys and plains of white ash. Meri sat, immobile, and willed the child to stand before her, but the figures that rose from the white ash were fully grown – and female; one red-haired, one fair, and one with hair of nut-brown. Even as she watched the vision blurred and shifted; the image of Eliza faded quite suddenly, and was gone. The figure of Annis Nevill retreated and grew pale; it was the nut-brown girl who came smiling towards Meri, both hands outstretched. Neat hands they were, square-fingered and compact. Those fingers advanced until they filled all of Meri's vision. Her heartbeat slowed so that her breath was almost stilled; linked between those hands, and glowing like a live thing in the firelight, swung a necklace of heavy silver and carved coral.

*

Frank called his daughter Eve. His quiet insistence upon the name had brought curious glances from the Greypaull sisters, and high-tempered words from Annis, who feared the vengeance of her sister, Blanche. Eve had grown into her name, until now, at the age of two years, she responded to no other. She had taken so much from Frank; his fine and regular features; his brown softly curling hair; the firm mouth which despite her gentle aspect, was hinting already at Eve's determination. Only her eyes were a direct inheritance from Eliza; as green as deepest jade without a single fleck of hazel.

Abigail, since her sister's birth, had quietened and grown thoughtful. She watched and listened, alert to every shift in her altered status of beloved only child. She was also, at the age of ten years, aware that Frank's wage of twelve shillings weekly was no longer sufficient to feed a family of four. His Disability Pension, used once for the purchase of Abi's toys, now saved them from the level of poverty experienced by their neighbours. Mother, since the birth of Eve, had grown listless and irritable. The story of Philip Greypaull's bankruptcy and his banishment from Buckland St Mary, was repeated endlessly by Mother, who always finished her tale with the words 'and so Abigail, that is why I fear debt more than death itself!'

The realisation that life was lived differently among the Greypaulls had come early to Abi. The knowledge that her mother's family were a 'better class of person' was enforced by the attitudes and manners of Granny Greypaull, the obvious gentility of Aunt Madelina and cousin Laura; and the possession of an aunt called Blanche who had been a close friend of the King of England.

There were other aspects of her situation that puzzled Abi. New babies arrived in other households as regularly and as often as Easter or Christmas. She had counted the numbers on her fingers, and discovered a lapse of seven years between her own birth and that of Eve. There was also the strange behaviour of her aunts and Mother. The admonitory finger raised for silence, the sudden hush that fell when Abi intruded unexpectedly on murmured conversations. The conviction that Abi herself was superior in some ways, and blameful in others, had grown stronger since the arrival of Eve. Most of Abi's troubles could in fact be put down to what Mother still referred to as 'our dear little stranger'.

For Abigail there was never to be the comfortable compromise of liking or disliking. She either loved or hated. Her hatred of Eve was single-minded, and verged on the destructive; she loathed the nut-brown curls, the dimpled smile, the strange green gaze that monitored her every action. When unobserved she would pinch the rounded arms and plump knees; watch with satisfaction the slow tears fall from the puzzled eyes, and deny all knowledge of the resultant wails and bruises. Because of Eve, mother had been forced to take-in gloving; a demanding job which occupied all her day and most of every evening. It was Abigail who, on her return from school, must run the errands, wash the dishes, mend the fire, and set the table; while Eve sat warm and safe on mother's lap. Even Aunty Blanche, who knew nothing about children, had noticed and commented upon the affection that was lavished on the little sister.

'I don't know how you manage to do that,' she was saying, 'hold the child on your lap, and stitch gloves at the same time.'

Abigail hitched her stool closer to the fire, and composed herself into an attitude of stillness.

Mother said, 'Oh – 'tis surprising what a woman can manage when there's no choice.'

'I could hold her for you, Annis.'

'No Blanche! Well – she's nervous with strangers. When she's a bit older – when she knows you better –'

'How much do they pay you for doing that job?'

'Two shillings and fourpence in a good week.' Mother held up the large glove of tough-skinned leather. 'It's not the sort of stitching I've been used to. These are gloves for farmhands. Hedgers' gloves is what they calls 'em. Frank brings the work from French's tanyard, on a Saturday, and takes it back the next Friday morning.' Mother's voice changed. 'I don't suppose that two and fourpence sounds much to you. You probably spend that much on gloves for your ownself! But let me tell you, Blanche. That money buys all our groceries for a whole week.'

Aunty Blanche stretched out her long white fingers, she fluttered them towards the firelight so that the big square ring on her left hand glittered green and gold. She laughed. 'Oh Anni, you have no notion of prices and values. I buy my gloves from Derry and Toms, at ten shillings and sixpence for the half-dozen pairs.' She paused. 'When we move to Dawlish there will be gowns and hats I no longer need. Quite a lot of things, in fact! You've kept your trim waist, Anni. My clothes will still fit you. But of course,' and now the light tone sharpened, 'I shall need a favour or two from you.'

Abi sat so still that all her bones ached, and yet to move would be bound to alert Mother to her presence. Her gaze moved from Mother's pale and weary features to the beautiful face of Aunty Blanche.

'If 'tis my coral beads –?'

'No Annis. Not the beads. You need them to protect your children.'

The understanding in the quiet voice brought tears to

Abi's eyes.

'But you have two daughters now, and you said yourself that times are hard. Hugh and I have discussed the matter, and he is concerned for Abigail's health. Poor little soul, she's grown so white and peaky-looking. She needs a holiday, Annis; we would like to take her back to London with us, and then down to Dawlish for the rest of the summer.'

'But there's her schooling, Blanche. As for Frank – well I can't imagine what he'll say –?'

'Hugh is an educated man. Abi can have lessons with him. As for Frank, let him look to the welfare of his own child. Abigail is your concern, surely you would never deprive her of all that Hugh and I can offer –?'

'I don't know, Blanche. I'll have to talk it over with Frank – '

Mother became agitated. She turned towards the gloving-table, took the ball of hemp in her right hand, the piece of black wax in her left. She allowed the wax to grow warm in her palm and then drew the hempen thread across it. The motion was repeated until the pale hemp shone blackly, then she picked up the long, three-sided gloving needle and pointed the waxed thread towards the eye. The sleeping child stirred and whimpered.

Aunty Blanche said sharply, 'That's dangerous, Annis! You should never be working with the little one in your arms. That needle is murderous, why, one false move and you could put her eye out! As for that wax – why it's falling on her face and hair –!'

Mother's voice was very quiet. 'She's alright. I have to keep her in my arms – she's cutting back teeth.'

Aunty Blanche stood up; she put an arm about mother's shoulders and said in a kind voice, 'It's too much for you, Anni. Let me at least take Abi off your hands for a few weeks.' She turned to where Abigail sat in the chimney corner. 'What says you, my sweetheart?' Abi's throat was dry. She nodded and smiled, and finally croaked. 'Oh, yes please, Aunty!'

The lovely face bent towards her, the white fingers gripped her arms. 'You shall ride in a carriage, Abi. I'll buy you pretty dresses. Anything you want, my sweetheart! Only tell Frank Nevill that you want to come with me!'

*

The vaccination of young children against smallpox was not obligatory, and Annis, indecisive and fearful as ever, had not yet allowed what she called 'the use of needles' on Abigail or Eve. Frank's answer to Abi's plea to be allowed to visit London was to read aloud the newspaper reports of the smallpox epidemic at present raging in that city. His fears were confirmed by Madelina, who also read the papers.

'Eight hundred and ninety one cases, up to date,' said Mina, 'and more reported every day.' She glanced briefly at Abi. 'A delicate child wudden stand a chance against such a fever. According to what I read, the London victims get took by ambulance to a hospital ship that is moored in the Thames. Just imagine a sick child – dragged away to die – among strangers – and on the river –'

Annis imagined, and was convinced. In matters medical there was no doctor living who knew half as much as Madelina.

'There's smallpox in Taunton, too,' argued Abigail. 'Only last week a girl in standard five was took off to the Fever Hospital!'

'Then that settles it,' cried Madelina. 'You'll have to give in to the vaccination, Anni!' She turned her gaze on the child who slept in Frank's arms. 'And there's liddle Blanche to think about now. You wudden like anything to happen to her, would you Frank?'

'Eve,' murmured Frank, 'her name is Eve.' He looked down on his own daughter's gentle face, 'No London trip this time, maid,' he told Abi. 'Even if you escaped the

101

fever, you might bring it home to your baby sister.'

Two weeks later, with money provided by Hugh Fitzgerald, both children were vaccinated, privately at home. Eve sustained no more than a raised temperature and swollen arm. Abigail sickened and came closer to death than if she had in fact contracted smallpox. A bad reaction to a normally safe injection, was the doctor's explanation, but Annis was not convinced. It was Mina who sat with Abi through nights of delirium and fever, and Mina who persuaded Frank that a convalescence in Dawlish was essential if the child's life was to be saved.

Abi had reached a state of convalescence that was almost enjoyable. Pallor earned sympathy, and physical weakness, she discovered, could be a positive advantage. She came to Dawlish on a day in April, carried to the train as if she were a baby, in Hugh Fitzgerald's arms. Cousin Laura, who was clever with her needle, had cut down a cream serge dress of her own, to make an outfit smart and warm enough for Abi's journey to Devon. She was placed in a corner seat of the compartment, a plaid rug tucked around her legs, a casket of handmade chocolates set on the seat between herself and Aunty Blanche. Abi, fearful of soiling the new cream dress, nibbled carefully upon a chocolate. She sat, shoulders stiff and eyes wide open, determined not to miss a moment of the journey. But even as the train pulled away from Taunton station, her eyelids closed, and Abi slept. She awoke as the train pulled into Dawlish station; wrapped in a travelling rug, Abi was carried by Uncle Hugh to a horsecab. They drove out along the coast road, and she was never to remember exactly what it was that gave her the most delight on that journey. There was a blue sky, with clouds so low that she could almost touch them. There was the sea, so fast that she, overawed and a little frightened, could only bring herself to take quick sideways glances at it. There was her Aunt and Uncle who moved and spoke with such authority among important people like horsecab drivers and railway porters.

They turned a corner and Uncle Hugh indicated a large white house that seemed to hang directly above the sea. The cabby slowed, and Abi read the word Summerlands engraved upon stone pillars which supported wide double gates. Two young women who wore blue dresses and white caps and aprons, were waiting at the open front door. Abi glimpsed a staircase, crimson carpet, a bannister rail of polished wood. She was lifted from the cab by Uncle Hugh and placed in the arms of the girl called Florrie. Against her will, Abi's eyelids began to close. She heard the maidservant say, 'Oh, the poor liddle soul! Her's quite worn out, sir! I'll put her straight to bed.'

She awoke to a world so beautiful and strange that she lay quite still, believing herself to have died and been transported, overnight, to Heaven. Such a fate, she had learned from her Sunday-school teacher, was quite common among the children of the poor.

Abi had not, until this moment, known herself to be the child of needy parents. Poverty in Taunton was to live in a Court down in East Reach, to go barefoot in winter; to be unable to redeem the family treasures from Jeremiah's pawnshop. Slowly she became aware of the soft bed beneath her body, of the lace-edged pillows that supported her shoulders, of the coverlet ruched and frilled in palest pink; of the rosebud wallpaper, the deep-rose carpet. There was a dressing-table with a wide swing mirror and many tiny drawers. There were wardrobes of satiny wood, so large that if Abi wished, she could walk about inside them. There was a pretty armchair covered in a pale silky stuff, so delicate that she would never dare to sit upon it.

Gradually she became aware of the sounds and smells that lay beyond the bedroom. There was a murmuring of women's voices, the scents of frying bacon, flowers and toast. Above all was the regular, insistent booming noise like the guns at Jellalabad Barracks on a Sunday morning. Abi slid out from beneath the bedclothes; she

103

stood for a moment, giddy and unbalanced upon the carpet. Supported, at first by the armchair, and then by the dressing-table, she made her way towards the long sash window. No heavy lace impeded the view in this household. The curtains were light, rose-sprigged and made from some filmy silk stuff. Abigail stood, her forehead leaned against the windowpane, her hands upon the white frame.

The sea stretched away in all directions. It was as if the very house was afloat, and Abi riding on those pale blue ripples. The booming sound, she now realised, was made by the sea as it flung itself against the sea wall.

The bedroom door opened and Florrie, a can of steaming water in her hand, called out, "Morning Miss Abigail. There's just time for you to have your bath before breakfast.' Abi had never seen a bathroom. She gazed about her, sought the familiar yellow enamel of her mother's hip-bath, a glowing fire, and towels warming on a brassrailed fireguard. In their place she found a group of porcelain, flower-embellished objects that appeared far too delicate for her intended use. Seeing the child's hesitation, Florrie pointed to a forget-me-not spattered bowl of white china, with a hinged seat and lid of polished wood.

'That's the lav,' she explained, 'now you do all what you got to, and I'll come back to bath you in about ten minutes.'

Abi remembered the thunder-box at the bottom of her parents' garden. She peered into the flowered bowl and considered briefly the indignities she was about to inflict on so delicate an object. She hoisted herself up onto the wooden seat and pondered on the wonders of her Aunty Blanche's bathroom. Florrie came back; she pointed upwards to a fine silvery chain from which hung a pendant of painted china.

'You pulls on that when you'm finished,' she told Abi. ' Abi gazed down into the flushing bowl. 'But what about the nightsoil men?'

Florrie laughed. 'We don't have nothing like that in this house. Everything is done London-fashion by your Aunty and Uncle.'

Breakfast reminded Abigail of that long-ago birthday dinner at the Castle Hotel in Taunton. There was the same damask cloth and table napkins; the same heavy cutlery and silver dishes. Her appetite was tempted only slightly by the array of dishes set before her. She was overwhelmed when given a whole egg.

'I sometimes get soldiers dipped in the yolk of father's egg,' she explained. 'We can only afford to keep but the one fowl, and she don't lay reg'lar.'

*

She was too frail at first to venture into the garden. There were many rooms in the house, each one remarkable for colour and style. Aunty Blanche told Abi about the grand house in Berkeley Square, London, where she had worked as a servant, long ago.

'Oh but that house was beautiful, Abi! I made up my mind at the age of sixteen that I would also, one day, be the mistress of a fine house.'

Together they moved through the rooms of Summerlands and Abi who had only known brown paint, linoleum, dark curtains and heavy overmantels, was bewildered by the light and luxurious aspect of all she encountered. It all had to do, said Aunty Blanche, with a great emporium in London called Liberty's, where she had once worked as a fashion model. From Liberty's had come the pale damask wall-hangings, the filmy curtains, the delicate brocades and satins. It was there that she had also acquired her exquisite teagowns of Chinese silk, her chiffon nightgowns and undergarments, her flowered and feathered hats, her embroidered slippers.

As the days grew warmer and her strength returned, Abi was permitted to stroll and then play, at first in the garden, and then on the beach. She was taken to Page's of Exeter and measured for several new dresses.

It was late September when Abigail came back to Taunton. She walked into the cottage at the rear of North Street on a sad day of rain and racing clouds. Her tilted chin and jaunty air had been intended to conceal her reluctance to return home; but consternation dragged her feet as she approached the open front door.

The house was even smaller than she had remembered, the furniture scant and shabbier, the adjacent streets so crowded and noisy that already she felt stifled. Father kissed her and stroked her hair. Mother hugged and then held her at arms' length. Her guilt was compounded by the awe and shock in their familiar faces. She at once felt compelled to remove the smart blue velvet dress and doeskin boots, and put on her old starched pinafore and pattens.

Abi wept, but not as they assumed from her joy at this reunion with her parents. Father and Mother had not changed at all. But she had.

*

Attempts had been made to return Sev to his father's house; painful episodes which always resulted in the baffled anger of Damaris, and the mute, unhappy child creeping back to the box-bed in his grandmother's kitchen. On this Sunday afternoon Sev felt the wrenching in his stomach, the agony that came whenever he must part from Granfer. He submitted to the swipe of the soapy wash cloth around the face and neck, the scratchy nit-comb through his thick hair, and the need for care imposed by the wearing of clean shirt and breeches.

Granny said, 'Straight to Sunday school, mind! Now don't forget to call in on your mother on the way home. Her looks forward to seeing 'ee on a Sunday.'

Sev twisted away from Jemima's hand; he turned to where David sat dozing in his high-backed chair. 'Don't let Granfer go up in ground wi'out me, will 'ee, Gran?' Tears stood unshed in the boy's eyes. His grandmother pushed Sev gently through the open doorway. 'You knows very well,' she murmured, 'that man won't stir a blessed step 'cepting he got you and Ruff beside him.'

The certainties that lodge in a child's mind will sometimes form the creed by which the man will live his whole life. Already, at the age of four years, Sev's ability to learn was swift and selective; he was passionate in his devotions, and implacable in his hatreds.

Sev believed that he belonged to Granfer.

In the Sunday school for the Montacute Baptist Chapel, an earnest young woman taught her class of forty souls about the ways of the Lord. Sev absorbed only those words which held significance for him. The first lines of the Twenty-third Psalm had gone straight to his heart. 'The Lord is my Shepherd; I shall not want, he maketh me to lie down in green pastures; he leadeth me beside the still waters.'

Sev would wait, mind closed against subsequent verses until the teacher intoned the final words. '. . . and I will dwell in the House of the Lord forever.'

From the first time of hearing, these words had held a special meaning for him. The adjustment had been made several months later, on a morning in high summer when Sev and Granfer walked together in the high pastures of the Hill. The boy walked a little apart from the old man. Sev glanced sideways and saw the fine head, the beaked and jutting nose, the deep-set blue eyes; the clean white flannel shirt and the moleskin trousers bound from knee to ankle with strips of amber-coloured doeskin.

Granfer halted, leaned heavily upon the crook in his right hand, and surveyed the grazing sheep. Sev also paused and leaned upon his small crook. Something in the child's mind, and all at once those words were transposed, their meaning clear. 'The Shepherd is my Lord.' That was how it should be! Wasn't it Granfer who walked with Sev in green pastures, who stood with him beside the still waters of Vagg's Pond? Sev dwelt in Granfer's house; he had every intention of dwelling there forever. He recalled a picture of the Lord in his grandmother's illustrated Bible, a lost lamb across His shoulder, a shepherd's crook in His right hand.

Reality and coloured picture fused together in the child's mind, and Sev knew, without any doubt, that God was Granfer.

*

Damaris stood beside the open window; through the lacework of the curtain she saw Sev turn the corner from South Street into Middle Street. He paused briefly at the entrance to Montacute House, looked up at the great gates of iron and kicked a stone in their direction, even though the day was Sunday. Already his head hung low, and his features were set in the mutinous cast that he always presented when obliged to visit. The boy's resentment was like a red coal that seared and scarred. He never once smiled in her direction, or uttered a voluntary word when in her presence. Out of desperation on his last visit she had said, 'Do 'ee know boy, who I am?' The question was twice repeated before he had answered, 'They says you be my mother.'

She would tell him about the doings of Mathilda and Keturah, about the antics of his new baby sister. But her words caused the mutinous lower lip to jut even further; he would shuffle his feet, twitch his shoulders, in an agony to be gone. In the end he would mutter, 'I got to be off now. Granfer might go up in ground wi'out me.'

'Up in ground' was where Sev spent his days. Damaris saw him take the Hill path in the early mornings, trotting alongside her father as closely and faithfully as the dog, Ruff. They returned late on these summer evenings, the sleeping boy slung across the shepherd's shoulder in the manner of a lost lamb, found.

Something fierce and anguished would twist inside Maris at the sight of these two, bound so irretrievably together. But when Sunday came she would stifle her need to hold the boy close, to touch his bright hair and fair skin. She would study her three hungry daughters, look at Jye, stoop-shouldered and exhausted from heavy toil.

"'Tis better so,' she persuaded herself. 'He'll be better off wi' my mother and father.'

*

Granfer's winter hut was a dry warm cave which reached back for several feet into the hillside. Here it was that he kept his medicines and ointments, the lambing oils and the tailing-irons, the buckets and hurdles. Preparations for the shepherd's occupation were begun early in October. Straw was brought up to line the earthen floor; parafin lamps were cleaned and new wicks fitted. A supply of oil was laid by and a wood stack built.

Sev remembered, dimly, the bad days of last winter when Granfer had been absent both night and day throughout the time of lambing. Sev had fretted then and refused food, eating only at those times when Granfer came back to the cottage for a change of clothing and supplies. It was not until early spring that some consolation had been found for the bereft child. Granfer had brought home a bundle of freshly-docked lambs-tails, tied together to form a white, woolly ball.

'Here boy!' he had said.

'I've brought 'ee a liddle lost lamb to look after. You bide yer wi' Granny, close beside the fire, and keep 'un warm, eh?'

Sev had known that the fleecy bundle was not a real lamb, but he found it easy to pretend. He carried the little fleece inside his buttoned-up jacket, slept with his arms tight about it; fed it with scraps from his plate. When the smell became too rank for Jemima's toleration, the 'lamb' was replaced while Sev slept, and the tails of later-born lambs substituted. The ruse had taken the child contentedly into the April days when he could go, once again, 'up in ground' with Granfer.

*

The caravans appeared in late October; a great concourse of coloured waggons, their approach visible for many miles. They were coming up from the Vale of Taunton; Sev and Granfer saw them first as they skirted Windwhistle. It was several days later that the travellers came into Norton-sub-Hamden. A few latecomers moved on into Little Norton and pitched beside the Covert. Sev, who believed the Hill to be the sole property of Granfer, protested at the presence of the strangers who were settled within sight of the winter hut.

'Tell 'em to go away! They got dogs an' funny-looking horses. They be like the pedlar-man what comes out from Yeovil. The one what sleeps underneath the hedge because 'un got no house to live in.'

Granfer grinned. 'No, boy. Not like the pedlar. There'll be no mumpers nor diddecois amongst this lot! They be true Romani; you can always tell 'em by their looks, 'specially their women.'

'What's Romani?'

'Gypsies, Sev. Travelling people. They does no real harm, save when they be drink-proud. Then 'tis mostly the young gypsy bloods what do give the trouble.'

'But where have 'em come from? Where be 'em goin' to?'

Granfer shook his head. 'Thass what you calls an everlasting wonder. Not even the gypsy-man hisself do know the answer to that one!'

The child walked away to the far rim of the Hill. He looked down onto Little Norton, studied the line of waggons, their colours made brilliant by the October sunshine. He liked the reds and yellows and the sharp apple-green one with the row of caged birds suspended from its roof; the little brown tents and the painted flat-carts. He crouched in the lee of a furze bush and settled down to watch. His nostrils flared at the acid tang of so many open fires; his stomach contracted at the rich aroma of roasting rabbit. A woman called, and at once a pack of children came running from the covert to the fireside. The men came slowly to their meal, pacing several steps away from the fire and looking keenly in all directions before sitting down to eat.

Gypsies! Sev's mind had fastened upon and retained that lone word. He repeated it several times, quietly at first, and then loudly. The name excited and yet frightened him. He jumped up and began to run towards Granfer. He tugged at the thick drabbet of the shepherd's smock.

'What do gypsy mean?' he demanded. 'What do it mean?'

Between Sunday-school and supper Sev visited his mother. Intrigued and still disturbed by the arrival of strangers, he uttered the first voluntary words ever spoken in her presence.

'Gypsies is stopping down by Norton! They got liddle wood houses what goes about on wheels! They lives out in the open all year round!'

Even as he spoke the bright colour rose in the child's face. Already, and in spite of the mild autumn weather, he waited for the dreaded winter order that he should 'bide safe in house alongside o' Granny, till the warm days come back'. Sev's natural habitat was the Hill. He could only tolerate the cottage on those rare occasions when Granfer dwelt in it. At his mention of the gypsies, Damaris spoke sharply.

'You never went close to 'em did you?'

'I never goes far from Granfer.'

'Well mind you don't, then!'

His mother glanced quickly at his father and then away. In a softer tone she said, 'You mustn't never talk to strangers, now you hear me David! You must always bide close to Granfer and Ruff.' She beckoned him closer, and Sev went, reluctantly, to stand at her knee. 'There's danger on the Hill. There's adders in the summer, and poison berries. Then there's the deep quarries, where your father worked – '

Sev looked towards his father. Even seated, the size of

the man brought a kind of awe to the child's heart. Father sat with the iron boot-last clamped between his knees; he picked up a boot, fitted it onto the last and measured a square of new leather against the sole. He scored marks on the leather with a sharp knife, and then began to pare away the square until it was the exact shape of the boot sole. Sev had rarely heard his father speak. The sound of the deep slow voice was as shocking as the words it uttered.

'How old is the boy, Maris?'

'He'm four, coming five next April.'

'Time he went to school.' Father put down the sharp knife and picked up the hammer. 'Time he came home to live wi' us – for good.'

Mother smiled. 'Oh Jye,' she said, 'I've waited such a long time to hear you say they words.'

Sev returned to his father's house early in December. He went quietly this time, heeding the advice of Granfer.

''Tis not a bit o' good we making a fuss, boy! After all, they be your natural mother and father. You've see'd it many a time, how the ewe do bleat and cry for her lost lamb.'

Sev did not feel like a lost lamb. He turned back to Granny.

'Granfer's right, Sev. Your mother is grieving for you. 'Tis nearly Christmas, an' she wants all her childer close around her. 'Twill be alright, you'll see! You can come round and see we whenever you wants to.'

*

His parents' house was very much like Granfer's; it had the same black-leaded cooking range and earthen floor, the same low ceilings and tiny windows. Even the smell, a pungent odour of simmering food and newly cured leather, was familiar and homely. The differences between the two households were too subtle for the child's immediate evaluation. On that first night Sev was aware only of his deep mistrust of these people; there were too many of them, and but for his mother who talked in a strange jerky fashion, they all watched him but said not one word.

He ate nothing at that first Sunday evening supper. Two bowls had been set upon the clean scrubbed table; one contained boiled cabbage, the other held mashed potato. The single strip of fried bacon was given to his father. The fat from the bacon was divided equally between the three children. Sev did not like bacon fat poured over his cabbage; but did not dare to say so. When it became clear that he would not eat the food provided, his plate was removed and the food shared out carefully, between his two sisters.

The bedtime routine was the same in his father's house as in Jemima's. A bowl of warm water was set down on the hearth, beside it a piece of carbolic soap and a washcloth. Three flannel nightgowns were put to air on the brass rail of the fireguard. His mother washed the face, neck and ears of each child, beginning with Mathilda who was the oldest. Then she scrubbed in turn the arms of each child from fingertip to elbow, and the legs and feet from big toe to kneecap. He had, his mother told him, just missed their regular bath night, which was on a Friday.

Sev took off his woolly jumper, aware of his grandmother's careful darning at elbows and wristbands. His lower garments were removed, for decency's sake from beneath the folds of his flannel nightgown. It was when he stood in line awaiting his turn with the nit-comb, that he became aware, for the first time, of his own distinctive shade of hair and skin. He watched the fine teeth of the metal comb flash in among the coal-black curls of Mathilda and Keturah. He studied the pretty rose-brown of their dimpled hands and faces. Sev examined the white skin of his own hands, the thin pale feet that peeped from beneath his nightgown. When his turn came for the ordeal by comb, he noted the fall of red hairs loosened by his mother's zeal. He spoke for the first time that evening. He pointed at Mathilda and Keturah, and the baby, Jemima, asleep in her cradle. 'I don't look like them,' he cried. 'Why don't I?'

His mother smiled as if he had pleased her. She spoke to the watchful girls. 'Now idden he a bright liddle feller! See how quick and sharp he do take notice.' To Sev she said, 'Your sisters takes after your father's side. They was all dark and tall, and very handsome. Now you and me, why we two is Honeybone, through and through. Just you look careful at your Granfer next time you sees him, and you'll know what I mean. Honeybones is thin as willow-wands, wi' pale skin, blue eyes, and reddish hair.' She took his hand and led him towards the stairs. 'No more box-bed for you,' she told him, 'you'll sleep in a proper bed from this night on!'

The iron bedstead was so large it almost filled the room. Two pillows were set, side by side, at the head of the bed, one single pillow at the foot. Sev climbed up onto a mattress filled with lumpy flock, laid his head upon the single pillow, and pulled the thin blankets close about him. The room was chilly, the coverings inadequate, the pillow iron hard. His mother said, 'Straight to sleep now.' As she closed the door he heard her murmur, 'God bless you.'

Sev had hoped that his mother might leave the candlelight. In his granny's kitchen he had fallen asleep in the safety of the fire's glow. The moon shone in at this uncurtained bedroom window; by its light he could see, at the top of the bed, the dark heads of his sisters outlined against the whiteness of their pillows. He moved uneasily and flinched as his toes touched the cold feet of Mathilda. Her whisper held all the menace of a shouted threat.

'Bide still down there! Us don't want you kicking about at the bottom of our bed. Us don't like you! Why'n't you go back to where you come from?'

Keturah murmured, 'Us don't like your nasty red hair.' She began to chant, very softly, 'Sev the fair – wi' carroty hair. Get back to your Granfer – where you come from!'

He went back to his grandparents' house early the next morning. Anger was to be his safeguard this time against tears; not even to Jemima could Sev admit his deep distress.

'There was no gravy on my supper,' he protested, 'and they made me sleep at the bottom end of an upstairs bed.'

''Twill be Christmas next week, boy. After that you'll be starting to school.'

'I sooner bide wi' you and Granfer.'

'I know.' Jemima held him close and stroked his rough curls.

'Old people do grow selfish, what makes life hard for you young 'uns. Me and Granfer have kep' you wi' us for too long already.'

'I don't like her dinners.'

Jemima sighed, knowing it was love he craved. 'Then you shall come and eat supper wi' me and Granfer. But that's all mind! I made a promise to your mother.'

*

The penny whistle lay in Miss Sparkes's shop window, between the pink and white sugar mice, the brown striped humbugs and the liquorice sticks. Damaris had stitched gloves far into the night to earn the extra pennies that would provide a few luxuries for her children's Christmas stockings. She chose four rosy apples, four oranges, four sugar-mice; three pink and one white. The whistle was painted red and green. She gazed at it for a long time, put the penny back into her purse, hesitated and then said, 'I'll have that whistle, Miss Sparkes, the one in your window.'

The gift was given secretly, on the eve of Christmas. She pushed it into the boy's hands, embarrassed and yet gratified at her own impulsive action.

''Tis somethin' a bit special – just for you. Don't let

your sisters see it – keep in in Granfer's house – don't never bring it back here.'

'What is it?'

''Tis a penny whistle. You puts your fingers on they liddle holes, and then you blow down the mouthpiece. You'll be able to play tunes on it, but never take it near your father. 'Tis the kind of sound what'll drive him mad!'

The woolly ball, made of lambstails, and given by Granfer, had until now been Sev's first toy, his singular and fleeting possession. A Christmas gift from his mother, shop-bought and to be concealed from his father and sisters, was so significant that he could hardly bear to think about it. To begin with he could not even bring himself to show the gift to Granfer. After supper that evening, when Granny had gone to the Carol Service and Granfer dozed beside the fire, he hid the penny-whistle among the blankets in the box-bed.

On Christmas morning, in company with his sisters, Sev thanked his mother for the sugar mouse, the apple and the orange. He remembered the secret toy, its bright red and green colours; the tunes it would play for him; and he smiled at Damaris for the first time.

That hesitant three-cornered smile was of a peculiar sweetness. She would carry the memory of it all her life long.

*

There was never to be a good time for Sev Carew to begin school; but to start in January, with lambing underway and Granfer absent from the supper-table, was more than he could bear.

His time spent with the shepherd had alienated him from his sisters, and the children of the village; he came among them now as a stranger, mutinous and silent. They pushed and pinched him; called him ginger-nob, formed a ring around him in the playground and chanted Keturah's rhymed insult. 'Sev the fair, wi' carroty hair.' He was, he now discovered, very small for his age;

vulnerable and thin-skinned. He wept, so he told Jemima, from the pain of the chilblains on his hands and feet.

Easter brought his first reprieve. All at once, the days were longer, the sun came back, his chilblains almost disappeared. There was no more school. His birthday came; his mother said he was five years old, and hugged him. When unobserved, he had visited the penny whistle in its concealment among the blankets of the box-bed, he had stroked it, turned it around to catch the firelight, so that its colours glowed. On an April morning, while his sisters slept and mother was busy with the baby, he left the Middle Street cottage and ran to his grandmother's house. He went straight to the box-bed, fumbled for the penny whistle, found it and was gone before Jemima could question or detain him.

Sev had never walked the Hill path by himself. He took the familiar route to the winter hut, and it seemed much longer than he had remembered; his legs ached and he grew breathless. He sat down on the springy turf, pulled the whistle from inside his jacket and examined it in daylight. It was, he thought, the prettiest thing he had ever seen. He placed his fingers upon the holes, raised the whistle to his lips, and blew. He lifted one finger and then another, he raised three fingertips at once, and then four.

The whistle was clever. It made different sounds. He became excited at the sounds; his stomach muscles tensed, his face became animated. His mother had said that he would be able to play tunes. The only one he could remember was the Christmas carol 'When Shepherds Watched Their Flocks'. He found the first true note, and then the second. He lifted too many fingers, knew the sound to be false, and began again. The sun was high in the heavens when Sev came back to the world, realised that he was alone, and on the path to Jack o' Beards. He stood up, played his tune right through without one single wrong note, and began to run towards his Granfer.

*

Eliza had placed her chair close beside the kitchen doorstep. To sit alone and idle in the morning sunshine was her keenest pleasure. As the day progressed she would follow that patch of sunlight, moving her chair to the daffodil border, to the newly-leafed privet, to the tiny lawn. There she would doze and dream until the golden warmth was withdrawn across the rooftops. Old age had brought compensations. It no longer mattered that she would freckle at the first touch of the sun's rays, or that inactivity might set a bad example to her daughters. Her chair, a recent gift from Blanche, was made of lightweight bamboo with curved arms and an adjustable headrest. The very latest style, Blanche had informed her, from Liberty's of Regent Street, London. The chair had become important to Eliza; it ran on small wheels which made it easily transportable from house to garden, from fireside to sunshine. It had become her haven, her place of prayer and recollection.

Strange, how most things in this garden held a power to remind her of days past. Perhaps she had so planned it? She could not remember. The sun rolled around to the daffodil border, and Eliza moved with it. She adjusted her cushions, her many shawls, her warm bonnet. She linked her fingers deceptively among crochet hook and tangled yarn in case strangers should call upon her. Eliza gazed towards the golden flowers, and was at once returned to Larksleve.

The daffodils had bloomed free in Buckland St Mary; wild and yellow they had swayed in her father's fields, a paler shade than her wedding gown; almost the colour of Philip's curling hair. She had raised a bank of earth in the Larksleve garden, had written upon that earth the name of her home in white and yellow flowers. There it was that she had stood with the tiny Annis when the bailiff's men had come back for the last time to dispossess her.

Larksleve. All so long ago and far away, and she too old and frail ever to return there. But she had spoken about it. Eliza recalled Abigail's bright face, her frequent pleading to have told and retold all the old stories. Abi would never forget the name of Larksleve, or allow it to be forgotten. The story of Philip and herself would live on, down the generations.

Autumn came to Eliza's garden; the days grew cool, the shadows lengthened, but still she set her chair beneath the trees and watched the leaves turn colour in the quiet October.

Her affairs were in order, her Will legally witnessed; provision made for all her children. She dreamed and dozed through days of gold, observed the dying of the year, and was each time surprised at her own persistent awakening. She dreamed of Samuel and Philip. It was said that in Heaven there would be no giving and accepting in marriage. The Lord had, no doubt, by this time come to some more sensible arrangement. They were waiting for her. She could sense the nearness of them in the pale October skies.

Eliza remembered Meridiana; that final meeting up in Buckland St Mary. She said to Annis, 'Your coral beads, maid! You must pass them on to Eve. Now remember that Annis, when I'm gone! The coral is for Eve.'

*

It was Annis who found her on that Sunday evening. Annis who ran sobbing from Greenbrook Terrrace up to Holway.

"Tis Mama!' she cried to Madelina. 'She's in her chair, in the garden. She's so sound asleep that I can't wake her!'

They buried Eliza one week later in St James's cemetery, beside Jack and Louis. They replanted the white rose bush, and told one another that life could never again be the same, without her.

*

Meridiana sensed great grief and loss and she could not

comprehend why, without strong cause, the heart should weigh so heavily in her. She had always been disturbed by the dying season, but never so keenly as in this year of 1906. She walked many miles in those October days, and part of her mind that was tuned to those sounds and portents seldom heard by other people, caught a sobbing on the wind that was an echo of the name Eliza; a great sadness in the white mists of evening that was, at the same time, like a great peace. Far back in her soul Meri knew what had come to pass, but to acknowledge the mortality of Eliza would be to anticipate her own death. There seemed no end to her capacity for mindless grieving, and then, overnight the world was altered. Meri woke to a great frost and brilliant sunshine, the final leaves had fallen from the oak trees, there was a crust of ice over Vagg's pond. The shock of change turned her heart away from things past; Sev was new life, new direction. Sev was patteran! A great anger rose up inside her, an impatience directed solely towards her own self. Was it pride, or some delicacy of feeling, that impelled her to tiptoe past him, instead of declaring out loud just who and what was their relationship, one to the other. She began to take a daily tally of his movements, all his hours of school, the supper eaten regularly at Jemima's table, his unwilling return each night to the house of Damaris and Jye. His thinness and increasing pallor. It needed all of Meri's strength of will to hold back from the questioning of Jye in those precious minutes when he came to visit on a Sunday morning. Jye had the look of a man who carried a great burden. She filled his pockets with a week's supply of thick-twist tobacco, pressed cider money into his palm, and took comfort from his obvious dependence on her. No word of the boy they had named Silvanus ever passed between them.

*

The sight of Shepherd Honeybone, down from the Hill when lambing was near, and up behind the butcher's dray horse, was so unique that Meridiana was drawn out, irresistibly, into the bitter morning. The cart halted in Middle Street, before the house of Jye. She saw Sev lifted up onto straw, saw him driven away towards the Yeovil road.

Meri ran back into her house, snatched up the distinctive plaid, considered, and then exchanged it for the anonymity of her black shawl. She banked her fire against a late return, and hurried towards the rumble of cart wheels upon the ice-hard road.

The miles to Yeovil were covered by her wild conjectures; distance counted nothing against Meri's urgency to know the purpose of this extraordinary journey. She moved cautiously behind screening hedges, took short cuts through copse and covert, and arrived on the outskirts of Yeovil with time to spare. She watched the passing of the cart from behind a thorn bush, saw the pull on the reins that directed the horse into a side road, and knew at once that Sev was Hospital bound.

The Yeovil Hospital was a place into which many people entered, but few emerged walking upright. Meri's instinct was to run forward, to grab the child, to save him. But even from a distance she could see the concern in the shepherd's face, the tender way he took the child's hand and led him forward through the wide door. Reinforced as it was from their constant closeness, David Honeybone's love of the boy would never allow any act that might hinder or harm Sev.

Meri moved towards the Hospital gates; she waited for a long time, one bare brown foot lapped across the other, as she had stood on the night of Sev's birth. The aching cold dulled her mind; she was startled by the shepherd's words, his sudden presence close beside her.

'There was no need for 'ee to walk all this way, Missus Carew. You cud have ridden with us if you had so minded. I spied you right from the end of Middle Street. There's no woman in the village as upright and tall as you be.'

Meri said, 'What goes on, shepherd?'

"'Tis what doctor calls an operation. Something gone bad in the boy's throat. He can't swallow proper. He don't eat nor thrive.'

Meri straightened her bowed shoulders, she looked down upon the little shepherd, and spat hard and accurately, just missing the polish of his Sunday boots. She said in a low tone, "'Tis your daughter what do stick in that child's throat, shepherd! Boy needs to know where his proper place is. He'm like a parcel, shoved about from one house to another.'

"'Tidden all the fault of my Maris. Your Jye – '

Meri gripped David Honeybone's shoulders, she shook him so hard that his cap fell to the ground.

'Not one word about my Jyė,' she warned him.

She released the man, retrieved his cap and handed it to him. A voice from the Hospital doorway turned them both around. David Honeybone began to run; he went into the Hospital. He was gone for a long time.

The horse, restless from cold, would not stand quiet. Meri stroked and soothed him. The shepherd emerged from the green-tiled entrance, in his arms he carried a scarlet-wrapped bundle. He laid the boy down upon the straw, climbed up onto the cart and motioned Meri to do likewise.

'They've cut out his tonsils,' he said briefly. 'Told me to get him home quick, and let Dr Brown keep an eye on him.'

Meri looked down on the white-faced child; already the straw was stained bright with his blood and vomit. A sickly, sweetish smell hung about him.

'Oh my dear Jesus,' she cried. 'They've slit his throat and killed him.'

'Thass not death,' the shepherd said, gruffly. 'Thass the ether what they puts on a rag underneath your nose to take away the pain.'

It began to snow. Meri cradled the boy in her arms, she pulled the shawl across his face, dragged loose straw around his trembling body.

'He shud have been brought to me in the first place. I got potions what'll cure every kind of sickness.'

David twitched at the reins. 'You holds yourself well away from me and my family, Missus Carew. There's many a time when I have see'd you on the Hill, but never a word have passed between us.'

Meri wiped blood from the child's mouth. 'Your Maris don't like me, shepherd. She wants my son all to herself. She'll allow him but ten minutes with me on a Sunday morning. Yes, I holds back from this chavvie, though it breaks my heart so to do. My Jye got troubles enough wi'out his old mother adding to 'em.'

'Seems to me,' said David, 'that there have been mistakes made on both sides.'

'Mostly by your Maris. She made her mind very plain, right from the outset.'

They came back into Montacute in late afternoon; a covering of snow hid the scarlet of the child's blood, and the hospital's loaned blanket.

Meri found the words difficult to utter. 'What happens to him now? Do he go home to be looked after by his mother?'

The shepherd's voice was firm, his features grim. 'No. No, he don't go home, not this time. He'll bide wi' me and Granny now, until he'm fit and strong.'

*

Sev lay in the box-bed, secure and drowsy in the fire's glow. The sickness had ceased; his throat ached and blood still seeped from the corners of his mouth, but he was dwelling once more in the House of the Lord; very soon, they would walk together in green pastures, and stand beside the still waters. His memories of the day, still clouded by ether, were of pain and vomiting, and the horror of his spilt blood. At the very edge of thought and almost in a dream, he felt the shadow of a stranger bend across him. His mind cleared. He remembered the dark woman, her arms hard about his body, her fierce eyes and harsh voice. Her face was familiar, he had seen her many times, watching him from behind hedges, walking on the Hill, standing beside the School door.

He grew hot and thirsty. He threw aside the coverings, and at once his Gran was there beside him, her hand on his forehead, a cup of water to his lips. To drink was painful. He tried to speak.

'The dark woman,' he croaked, 'don't let the dark woman take me!'

'Nobody ever goin' to take 'ee, boy. You be safe home again wi' Granny. You got a touch of fever and no wonder! Go back to sleep now. 'Twill all be better in the morning.'

The morning came and he was so restless and wild that he fell from the box-bed and begged to be left to lie on the cold floor. The doctor came. He said, 'This child should never have been brought home, Mr Honeybone, especially in such inclement weather.'

Granfer said, 'I cudden leave 'un in that wicked place, Doctor. I wudden never have left one of my flock there! He looked fit to die when they showed 'un me. Caught a-hold of my hands, he did! Never let me go until I vowed that I 'ud take 'un with me.'

The medicine was bitter. Sev moaned and bleated like a lost lamb. His mother came. He heard Granny say, 'The doctor's physic have on'y made things worse. 'Tis no sooner down his throat – than up it comes again. Oh, what ever shall us do, maid?'

It was late in the evening when Sev woke. He could see many windows, all of them blocked by snow. He counted four lamps, six tables and, most worrying of all, two separate and distinct Granfers. A great scream ripped from his throat. Warm blood filled his mouth, and he closed his eyes. When he opened them again it was to further terror. A man's black bulk stood between himself and Granfer. A deep voice said, 'You must get my mother round yer right away. Go, shepherd! Go!'

Hands took him up from the bed; Sev felt a blanket wind about him. His head was cradled on a broad chest, the man's strong arms controlled his violent trembling. That same harsh woman's voice that he had heard on the road back from Yeovil said, quietly, 'So 'twas Meridiana you need after all, my heart's joy. Let your old bebee take a good look at you. Let we see what is to be done with all this gorgie meddling.'

Cold fingers touched him, probing and seeking out all his painful places.

'Ah, dordi dordi! But this is a proper butcher's business! Whatever was you thinking of to allow this? What sort of mother is you, Maris Carew?'

'Doctor said 'twould work wonders in him. 'Tis the latest operation to cure sickly children.' His mother's voice broke, 'If I'd only known –'

'You knows nothing,' said the harsh voice, 'spite of all your long head and sharp tongue.'

The deep man's voice broke in, 'Thass enough of that, Mother! Is we goin' to lose him? That's the question.'

Sev looked up into his father's face, and scarcely knew the contorted features. Tears poured down the man's cheeks, he felt the strong arms tighten round him. The woman's harsh voice spoke again.

'Lose him? Us'll never lose this one, Jye! He'm one o' my kind, he'm a fighter – and more gypsy than the ribs o' God!'

Sev recovered very slowly from the tonsils operation. The dark woman came every day, declining all offers of tea, refusing to sit down in his Granny's kitchen. She laid hands upon his head and neck, and a strange warmth passed into him from her bony fingers. Her medicine was made of honey, it slipped easily across his swollen tongue and sore throat. Within hours his head had cooled, he no longer saw four tables or two Granfers.

Unlike his grandparents and mother, the dark woman spoke seldom. Her words were like rough stones; Sev turned them over in his mind, wincing at the sharp edges of them.

'Knows you where I live, boy?'

'I knows it.'

She pushed back his flannel nightgown. 'You got legs like bits o' chewed string,' she told him. 'You 'ont never make a stone-carver like your father.'

'Don't want to be a carver!'

'What do 'ee want, then?'

'I'se goin' to be a shepherd, like my Granfer.' The woman laughed.

'Come to my house Sev, when you got strength enough to walk. Bring the whistle with you.' She looked sideways at him, grinning at his pink confusion. 'I've heard 'ee playing when you thinks nobody's listenin'. Proper liddle music-master idden you! You 'ont never make a sheepman. You got itchy feet and too much music in your head.'

He said, suddenly curious, 'Whass your name, then?' She did not answer for a long time. Her top lip trembled. 'So they diden tell 'ee about me?'

Sev shook his head.

'I be your father's mother. I goes by the name of Meridiana.'

It had never occurred to Sev that his father might have a mother; that so awesome and large a man could have been a child, a baby. He thought about it.

'So you be my Grandma. Have I got another Granfer?'

'He'm dead. He died from a fall of stone in the quarry. Long time ago.' She paused. 'He'm lying in the church-yard. There's a stone above his head, wi' his name writ on it. Your father carved it.'

At Christmas his mother and father came to see him. His father held him, turned him around in his huge hands. 'Why is he still so skinny, Maris?'

'I can't say. He gets good food here by my mother. He've been very sick, Jye. That'll all take time.'

His father spoke directly to him. 'Best if us forgets

about school for the time being, eh young 'un?'

In that moment Sev almost loved his father. He recalled the tears of the man, his question 'Is we goin' to lose him?' Sev reached out a hand to touch his father's face, and then remembered, just in time, that all his allegiance was sworn to Granfer.

*

The early snows of that November had been a false threat. The Christmas days were soft and green, the January weather positively spring-like. Mathilda and Keturah went back to school. Sev watched them go sedately down the village street, two sturdy girls, white-pinafored, black-stockinged, their hair braided neatly, self-righteousness written huge across their rose-brown features.

Sev's year at school had taught him awareness of his own intolerances. To read had come as naturally as breathing; to sing had given him exquisite pleasure. The practical skill of writing with chalk upon slate, he found impossible to master. Many times his ears had rung with the force of the smudgy slate cracked across his skull, and his knuckles bled from the sharpness of the teacher's cane. He disliked the classroom proximity of so many human bodies; was outraged by their mindless chatter, their coughs and sneezes. He simply could not abide the ugly sounds they made with their mouths when they chewed on acid-drops and apples.

The mysteries of lambing were still forbidden to him, although he pleaded daily to be allowed to go to Granfer. He accepted the pacifying gift of lambstails, but hid it away inside the box-bed in view of the approach of his sixth birthday. He was relieved when the bad smell obliged his grandmother to burn the surrogate lamb. Sev had, in the past year, experienced separation and pain. He had lost the ability to pretend.

Each fine day encouraged Sev to venture further from his granny's garden. With all the children safe in school, the deserted village streets felt peculiarly his own. He roamed, aimlessly; watched a song-thrush break a snail's shell upon a stone, and then devour the contents; took delight in early celandines, primroses under hedges. No one shouted 'ginger-nob'. No chanting voices repeated the sneering jingle 'Sev the fair, wi' carroty hair'. Daily, he grew stronger. Returning strength roused curiosity in him. He remembered the words of the dark woman.

'Come to my house Sev, when you got strength enough to walk. Bring the whistle with you.'

*

Meridiana had spied Sev's every exploration in that early springtime; had noted how single-minded was his absorption with certain matters, how total his unawareness of others. He appeared not to see her, although she made no great attempt to conceal her presence from him. His preoccupation with sounds was very marked. The crest of red hair turned, the head tilted sideways, at the song of a milk-maid, the notes of a bird's trill, the hymn tunes sung by the weary masons, as they returned from the quarry.

She was standing at an upper window, willing Sev to appear when he turned into the narrowness of Middle Street, walked without a glance, straight past his mother's window, and came in through Meri's garden gate.

His first observation was, 'Your house smells funny!'

His first question was, 'Where's your gloving-table?'

'My house,' she told him, 'smells funny to you, because it got no stink of leather in it.' She grinned. 'As for my glovin'-table – I never had such a thing.'

'What do 'ee do, then, all day long?'

She pointed to the heap of hazel rinds piled up on the hearth stone. Showed him the sharp knife and the strips of tin; the hawking basket in the corner. 'I makes clothes-pegs. Then I counts 'em out in ten-and-two, puts 'em in the kipsie, and hawks 'em door-to-door.'

She sat down in the carver chair, and motioned the child to take the low stool. The corduroy breeches hung limply on his thin legs, every bone showed clear in his narrow face. She remembered that Sunday morning when Jye had first brought him to her.

'How old be you, boy?'

'Comin' six in April.'

Meri thought of all the lost years; his first smiles, his first tooth; the faltering steps he had learned at Jemima's side. He was smiling at her now, a three-cornered smile of such peculiar sweetness, that she, who never wept, felt tears burn suddenly behind her eyes.

'Be you feelin' stronger?' she asked gruffly.

He nodded. 'Reckon I lost nearly all my blood in that hospital.'

'You remembers all that?'

''Course I do! You rode back wi' me and Granfer on the cart. You give me medicine for my bad throat.'

Sev stared at the cluttered room: the bed beneath the rear window, the colours of the Crown Derby china, the shelves of green glass bottles, the chests and cupboards packed close on every wall.

She saw a strange expression cross his features. He pinned her with that deep and penetrating gaze that was the hallmark of her people. He pointed to the tobacco packet and the clay pipe.

'Smokin' baccy is for men,' he told her.

Meri studied Sev. In that moment he looked exactly like his Chapel-happy mother. He stood up so abruptly that the stool tipped over. He picked it up, and set it carefully down upon the hearth stone.

She began to laugh. 'You speaks up well, for a young 'un. I like that in a chavvie!'

He said, 'Be you truly my grandmother?'

She nodded.

He stared at the room, at the clothes-pegs and the hawking basket, and finally at her.

''Tis a lie,' he shouted. 'You don't look like nobody's granny.'

He walked through the door, up the village street, and around the corner to the Honeybones' cottage.

Meri watched him go. She stood for a long time at the open window, and it took minutes before her heartbeat slowed, her breathing evened. She looked towards the churchyard where Luke lay. There had been no trace of Carew in the boy's face, no hint of Loveridge in him. For that moment she had almost doubted the truth of patteran; until he had outfaced her!

Three times he had spoken up, and not like a child but as a man, grown; and she hard put to find him an answer.

'You don't look like nobody's granny,' he had told her. Meri grinned; she looked down at her plaid skirts, bare feet, her silk embroidered pinna. So had she herself spoken out when a child, truthfully and without fear.

'He'm his mother's image, still,' she told Luke, 'but he got my spirit in him. He 'ont never suit the gorgio, Lord help him! But he'll outface that trouble too when the time comes.'

* * *

Annis mourned her mother, at first with anger at Eliza's abrupt desertion, and then with pain because she could not call her back. The winter months had seen many changes. The house in Greenbrook Terrace now had other tenants, its furniture shared out among Eliza's daughters.

Without the magnet of her mother, Annis had no place of pilgrimage; Mecca had vanished, all her sure things in the world were gone. She had inherited the circular table; she polished it daily, finding consolation in its mahogany splendour. She turned to Madelina but received no comfort. Annis, at the age of forty, was behaving like a lost child, and Mina was caught up in more important matters.

Eliza's Will was proven in late June. It was a simple document. 'All that I own is to be divided equally between my children.' When all debts and expenses had been settled, a sum of One Hundred and Thirty-Five pounds, Sixteen Shillings and Ninepence, was paid over to each of Philip and Eliza's surviving children.

For Simeon Greypaull, still serving with Prince Albert's Own in India, his share of the money was to be a nest-egg. For Candace, in her Hampstead apartment, an easement of financial worry. In Dawlish, Blanche waved the lawyer's Draft between thumb and forefinger.

'My inheritance,' she told Hugh, 'from what was once a big farm of many acres! But for Uncle Samuel, Mama would never have had this much to leave us!'

Madelina deposited her share in a Post Office account, and described it as a sure security against the poverty of old age. The piece of paper with its impressive rows of black marks, was for Annis the first comfort she had ever received from the printed word. Frank was obliged to explain many times the row of symbols that represented money. The brown-covered Post Office book was laid carefully away in an upstairs cupboard. But not for long.

Annis had always known what she would do, should she ever be so fortunate as to 'come into money'. Her expectations of wealth through the Castlemaine connection had not yet been fulfilled, but still she hoped. A row of newly-built houses had lately been completed in a little street that lay midway between East Reach and Holway. Annis sought out the landlord. A rare ability to pay one month's rent in advance ensured her a front-door key and rent book.

Annis took her family, on a Sunday morning, to survey their new home. 'Halfway up Nob Hill' was how a doubtful Frank described it.

'Well, 'tis further than we have ever been before! There'll be no more wading through the puddles at the back of North Street to get to our new front door.' She led him by the sleeve along a pavement of yellow brick.

They came to a mid-terraced house set behind a low wall. Frank pushed open the green-painted gate; he admired the quality of the fresh paintwork, the height and breadth of the bay windows. Annis opened the door to reveal a narrow hallway and a flight of steep stairs. She led him through the house, pointing out the spaciousness of the three bedrooms, the elegance of the bay-windowed parlour, the large middle room with its gleaming iron range; the little kitchen's brownstone sink and in-built wash copper. 'Every convenience, Frank!' Annis paused dramatically beside the kitchen door. 'Now this,' she told him, 'is the best bit of all, as far as you're concerned.' She turned the key and opened up to a small conservatory. 'You've always had a fancy to grow things.' She pointed further, to the small, walled garden. 'Well – now's your chance Frank. 'Tis a feature you don't find in many houses!'

'How much a week?' Frank asked quietly.

'Never mind how much. I can afford to pay more rent since I be come into money. Anyway,' she indicated the silent girls, 'they two gets bigger all the time. Us can't possibly go on living in that pokey old cottage.'

The weeks that followed were to be the most blissful that Annis would ever live. Her floors and stairs were covered with best quality linoleum; she bought a square of dark blue carpet for her front parlour, had dark green roller blinds fitted at the windows to keep out destructive sunlight. She sought and found elegant furniture, curtains and mirrors, ornaments, china and table linen.

On Sunday afternoons she walked with Eve to the St James's cemetery in Staplegrove. Annis knelt at the unmarked grave that held Louis and Jack, and now Eliza. She arranged flowers in a stone vase and begged approval for prodigality.

''Tidden really extravagance, Mama. Us needed so many things, and you always wanted my maidens to have nice clothes and boots, and a comfortable home.'

*

Madelina, who was sensible and practical, and to be relied upon in any crisis, had believed, in her secret heart, that Mama would live forever. She, of all Eliza's children was the one who remembered Larksleve and its legends; who had understood the joys and disappointments of Eliza's long life. The passing of her mother brought on an unusual restlessness in Mina. She also sought and found a larger house in another district, busied herself with curtains and carpets, as if the uprooting of her home and family could ease the pain of loss. The house in Holway stood on the edge of green fields. Once again Mina re-created the blue elegance of the Larksleve parlour and found comfort in so doing. She told her daughter, 'Now remember, when you come to the furnishing of your own home, blue is the colour always favoured by the Greypaulls.'

The engagement of Laura to Sergeant Patrick Quinn was to be a quiet matter since this was a family still deep in mourning. Laura wore Patrick's beautiful half-loop of diamonds; the sad year ended. When spring came, Madelina could no longer deny her daughter the happiness of wedding plans.

The marriage of Laura Lambert to Sergeant Patrick Quinn was to be remembered by those fortunate enough to be invited, as the 'wedding of the year', in Taunton. Patrick, a young man of good family, was tall and very handsome. Laura was beautiful; elegant and slender, she had inherited her father's dark blue eyes and quiet mannerisms. The red curls, kept short and hidden in the case of Eliza, had been allowed to grow long on Laura, so that they fell thick and gleaming to her waist. Her Aunt Annis had been invited to act as Matron of Honour; her cousin Abigail was to be chief bridesmaid. Dresses of Honiton lace with sashes of palest violet were to be worn by the young bridesmaids. Gowns of cream watered-silk trimmed with purple velvet was Laura's choice for her mature attendants. Her own gown of Honiton lace over satin would be worn with a head-dress of lace and a coronet of fresh Parma violets.

＊

Annis had at first felt proud that she and her daughters were to play a major role at Laura's wedding. But gradually her satisfaction was eroded by small irritations. Without the restraining presence of Eliza, Annis brooded on imagined slights. The close family involvement that was so essential to her nature, now encouraged feelings of envy to which she could not admit. An over-dependence on the love and approval of other people made her vulnerable, and at the same time roused her to anger. She disliked, so she said, the gown of cream watered silk trimmed with purple; as for the hat, expensive and made of ruched purple velvet, it was only, so she told Frank, her regard for Madelina's feelings, that prevented her from burying it deep inside the ash bin.

＊

Eve loved the wedding and everything to do with it; especially the soldiers in their bright red tunics, and shiny swords and helmets. They held her aloft, carried her upon their shoulders. The whitening paste, dabbed thickly by Mother on the new boots, had rubbed off onto those scarlet tunics, but they only laughed and brushed it carelessly away.

At the wedding breakfast, Eve ate too much for comfort. Abi explained how everything had been specially chosen in shades of white and lavender, and purple. Even the little cakes that were called sponge fancies had been iced in palest mauve, and topped with the sugary petals of crystalised violets. It seemed almost a shame to eat such pretty things, but Eve loved all kinds of cakes, especially those made by her Aunty Madelina.

Eve wished that Father had been there to see the lovely gowns and flowers, to eat the ham and chicken, and the wedding cake. He came in at the very last moment, just as Laura and her new husband were about to drive off to the railway station. All the people laughed and shouted, which frightened the horses and made them snort. Aunty Mina cried, and so did Cousin Laura.

Mother cried too, but not until she was at home in her own kitchen. She told Father how Aunty Mina had pushed her away to stand in the very back row of the wedding photo. Mother took off the purple hat and burned it to ashes in the fire grate. She told Abigail that she was finished for good and all with those haughty Lamberts.

Eve yawned as she unlaced the white boots. A crumb of violet icing had lodged in the laces; absentmindedly, she ate it.

It had, she thought, been a really lovely wedding!

*

A birthdate which falls on the first day of a New Year must inevitably carry with it a hint of resolutions and new beginnings. Jye seemed, on this day, to suffer a curious convulsion of the spirit; a compulsion to look back across his shoulder, an unwilling need to look forward. Even more disturbing, because he was power-less to prevent her, the spectre of Blanche Greypaull always came to share her birthday with him. He came awake slowly on that January morning, knowing this to be the day.

He remembered the North Porch of Westminster Abbey, and Blanche, dressed in wine-red velvet, a hat of soft grey feathers perched among her auburn curls.

'How old be you, Blanche?' he had asked her, then.

'Seventeen. Eighteen come next New Year.'

He had looked up from the place where he knelt among the worn stone.

'So be I', he had said. 'Eighteen come next New Year. We be both the same age, exactly.'

Words seldom passed between Maris and Jye and never in the early morning. He waited while she packed

135

his nammet in the old blue tin, and filled a stone jar with cold sweet tea. Maris, who was good with numbers, said, 'Forty-three years old today. You takes after your mother. Not a sign of grey in your hair and moustaches, you stoops a bit – but so do most stone-carvers.' She was standing at the kitchen table; the lamplight cast shadows across her fair hair and tired eyes. He felt that gaze upon his face, knew fear, and turned his head away. She moved, pulled at his sleeve and forced him back to face her.

'Look at me, Jye!' She formed her lips carefully, her whole attention focused on him. 'Living with you is like living by my ownself.' Tears formed in the corners of her eyes. 'I can't bear it. I can't bear it no longer!' Her words chased around the edges of his mind, but could not gain entrance. She waited, expecting some sign that he at least understood her. He snatched up the blue tin and the stone jar, walked swiftly from the house, pausing only when he came to the steepest incline of the Hill. He looked back along the empty road, saw the first pale streaks light up the eastern sky, and knew that he was not alone. Somewhere, Blanche also watched the winter dawn, caught in this spell of her own making, quite unable to break free.

Jye had always been a simple man; his mind obedient, his emotions disciplined, his whole life a system of tidiness and habit. In thirty years he had never missed a day's work, had been first mason at his banker every morning, and last in the column of men who came down from the Hill in the failing light. His garden was tended in every season, food provided for his growing children, fruits and vegetables in rotation; and he had learned other skills. Jye mended boots and shoes as skilfully as any cobbler; he was known to be a steady man, a good provider. That beneath his bedrock simplicity lay another, more significant stratum, was seldom guessed at by those who knew him, and suspected only vaguely by Jye himself.

136

'Deep' was how his mother described him; and Meridiana knew her son. But his only safety lay in denial of that 'otherness'. His life, built stone upon careful stone, had allowed no hint of the bright, the many-coloured; but there were fissures now in that tight construction, cracks through which his love for what was light and fancy welled up and would not be denied. His rosebushes stood in a long line, bisecting the vegetable garden, taking up precious space where potatoes should have grown. Jye had a need, aroused long ago by Blanche, to strive for the unattainable, to long for what was exquisite and yet totally impracticable. In summer, the roses almost satisfied that need. In winter, Jye remembered London, and all that had come to pass there.

He came up to the deepest quarry, stood for a moment and looked down on the base-bed of the yellow stone. He turned away, towards his place of work, entered the tin-roofed hut and stood before his 'banker'. He was hardly aware of the arrival of workmates, took no part in their early-morning grumbles; Jye examined his work of the previous day and found it to be good. This task of carving a rose-window for some distant Abbey required his total concentration; one slip of the chisel and all would be lost. Jye gathered his mind and trained his eye towards making the first cut of the day. He lifted the mallet, and then lowered it, without striking. His grip on the chisel grew slack so that he almost dropped it. A great weariness seeped into his mind and body. He began to tremble; but for the support of the oaken banker he would certainly have fallen. The spasm lasted for a full two minutes; when it had passed Jye found chisel and mallet still within his grasp; he laid them down carefully, and eyed them as if they were old friends who had betrayed him. The trembling had ceased, he could feel strength begin to flow back into his body; but his sense of unreality remained. He closed his eyes, and opened them, but the vision stayed with him. He could smell incense and flowers, and that perfume she had called 'Attar of Roses'. He was back in King Henry's Chapel, in the Abbey of Westminster; his banker was the Altar and he a supplicant before it. He had prayed in those days. 'Our Father, Who art in Heaven ...' Jye spoke the words aloud, but softly. Very slowly he came back to awareness of his true surroundings. He picked up chisel and mallet, squared his shoulders, breathed deeply, and willed himself once more to make the first cut of the day.

At the noonday break Jye usually sat alone beside his banker to eat bread and cheese, drink cold tea, and smoke a pipeful of tobacco. But on this New Year's Day nothing was as usual. For the first time in his forty-three years of life, he could not bear to be alone. When the quarrymen and masons laid down their tools and began to move towards the inn, Jye fell in behind them.

The Prince of Wales Inn stood foursquare among the deepest quarries. It was a necessary place of warmth and comfort for these men who toiled in frost and rain; its strong rough-cider a palliative in all seasons of the year. Jye was not, by nature, a public drinker. He stooped low to enter the long dark bar. A bright fire burned at each end of the room, in wide fireplaces carved from the golden Ham stone. Jye took his cider mulled; he sat down, tankard in hand, among the masons who had gathered around the left-hand fireplace. No one remarked on his unusual presence, although all had noticed his peculiar behaviour of the early morning. He was known among his workmates as a man 'best left alone'.

Jye drank one tankard of cider, and then another. He smoked two pipesful of thick-twist tobacco, and felt the dulled sensation that always eased the edge of pain. An elderly mason, forming his lips carefully to spell the words, said, 'Be you alright, my old acker?'

The concern in the older man's voice was lost upon deaf ears. Jye saw only the intrusive question.

'Right as rain,' he said, gruffly. 'I be right as rain!'

There is a certain age at which a child begins to discover his world; a time in which he first feels mystery and terror, delight and awe, and is convinced that these experiences are his, exclusively. Sev had lately felt that shift in his awareness which made him critical and noticing of adults. He had also learned that certain situations could be manoeuvred to his own advantage. Typhoid and scarlatina were rife throughout the village. All of his three sisters were absent from school, complaining of aching limbs, sore throats, and headaches.

'Scarlatina,' Sev told the teacher, 'wi'out the shadow of a doubt.'

The teacher moved swiftly backwards. 'Then go home at once, boy, and don't dare to come back here until you've all been passed as non-infectious.'

'Teacher told me to go home and bide there,' Sev told his mother. 'If you got sickly sisters they won't have you in school in case you spreads the trouble.' The argument sounded reasonable to Damaris. She placed her hand upon his forehead but he writhed away. 'I be alright! I had that operation, didden I? I don't never get bad no more!'

It was true. Pale and thin, with most of his bones accountable to human eye, Sev among them all, was the only child who walked fit and bright-eyed through every epidemic. He asked the usual question.

'Can I go to Granfer now?'

Maris nodded her agreement. With three ailing daughters, a tableful of gloving, and her heart still sore from the morning's episode with Jye, she was glad to see the boy go from her.

'Take a bag,' she told him, 'I need firewood and – '

But he was gone, running down the street towards his grandmother's cottage.

It was well after the noon hour when Sev reached the hill. Oh, but Granny had been glad to see him. 'You be jus' the boy I needs, my sonner! Your Granfer won't be comin' down this night, nor yet, for the next week. He got trouble betwixt the ewes. He've had to pen 'em close in, beside the hut. He dursn't leave 'em no more; not for a blessed minute.'

Sev felt happy when his Gran called him 'my sonner'. He was not truly her son, but, he told himself, he was 'nearly as good as'. It was a shame that his mother stood in between himself and his Gran and Granfer. Sev placed the heavy bags on the ground, and leaned against a boulder, to regain his breath. He had come up by the short cut, which was steeper than the main lane. From his resting place he could see the Prince of Wales. The quarrymen and masons were leaving the inn and making their way back towards the huts and quarries. They were a cheerful crowd, the younger men and boys jostled and pushed one another; the older men grinned at their antics, and all of them moved unsteadily across the tussocky grass. One man only walked apart from his own workmates. Sev recognised the tall dark figure of his father. At this distance the boy could see clearly the pathos of those stooped shoulders, that bent head. Once, Sev had asked his Granfer, 'Why is my father always by his ownself? Why do 'un always bide so quiet?' ''Tis the deafness', Granfer had said, 'that do cut a man off from human kind.' Sev had heard, but he had not understood. Now he saw, with shock, how a man might walk among a hundred others and still be solitary. Sudden pity for his father made him long to run forward, to cry out, 'Here I am – you've got me, Dad.'

Sev looked down at the hampering bags, filled with food and dry clothing. The distance between them was too great. His legs were too short; he could never catch his father. Already, the men were out of sight. He picked up the bags and began to walk towards the path that led down to Norton. In any case, thought Sev, his Granfer would be more than glad to see him.

*

Lambing had begun in mid-November. Granfer said

140

that strong winds always brought the lambs, and it was on a morning of gale so wild that Sev could scarcely keep his feet upon the hill-path, that he came to the shepherd's hut, and witnessed birth for the first time.

The hardy ewes were usually lambed out in the open, on grass. Sev was accustomed to the findings of twins, triplets even, already dry and fed, and following strongly behind their mothers. Provision had been made by Granfer for complications. A pen had been formed of straw, close-packed between double rows of hurdles. This pen, its roof lightly thatched, was sheltered on the one side by a thick hedge, and on the other by a haystack. The pen was used only for the most difficult of lambings. He knew that Granfer must be inside it; the dog Ruff lay across its entrance. Sev came, very slowly, to the sheepfold, eager and yet fearful to witness a complicated lambing. He knew all about the tarred cords which were used to secure the legs of lambs who could not, for some reason, get themselves born in the normal manner. To see those cords used in the way described by Granfer, to drag a reluctant lamb from its mother's body, was a drama Sev did not wish to witness. He peeped through a gap in the straw-packed hurdles and saw Granfer kneeling, the ewe lying on her side before him. The tarred cords were already attached to the unborn lamb's protruding hind feet. Granfer was crooning above the frightened ewe. Over and over, in a high soft lilt, he repeated the same chant.

'Quiet now, maid. 'Twill soon be over. Thy liddle one 'ull soon be with 'ee. Quiet now, my dearie. Quiet now.'

In a lower tone Granfer said, 'Come on in, boy. But move soft and steady! She'm a shearling and nervous, and her silly lamb have decided to come out backside-first.'

Sev came into the pen, head averted; he kept his gaze upon the ewe's white face, pink nose and gently curving horns.

Granfer murmured, 'I be proper glad you come, Sev.

This poor maid of ours is in a bad way.' He began to remove the tarred cords from the lamb's feet. 'Take off your jacket, boy. Roll up your jersey sleeves, and wash your hands in that bucket of Jeyes Fluid. 'Tis a gurt big lamb wi' all his legs pointing backwards. My hand is too broad to shove the front feet forward. Your liddle paw is the on'y thing left what can save her.' He looked up into Sev's frightened face.

'Come on, be quick now! Us'll lose 'em both, else!'

Sev removed his jacket, pushed his jersey sleeves back, and washed his hands in the milky liquid.

'Leave 'em wet,' Granfer ordered, 'an' come to kneel by me.'

The hindquarters of the sheep had been propped high on sacking. The ewe bleated once as Sev knelt down beside her.

'Now slip your hand in gentle,' Granfer whispered, 'and tell me when you've found his forefeet.'

Sev felt sick and cold. His hand slipped easily beyond the lamb's hind legs. Excitement made his voice shrill.

'I've found his front feet, Granfer!'

'Then go steady now. Take one hoof at a time an' ease it inwards.'

Sev did as he was told, and almost before his arm was withdrawn the lamb had started to emerge.

'Ah-h-h.' Granfer's sigh was long and heartfelt. 'A good big feller, and strong!' He turned to Sev. 'You done wonders and miracles my old sonner! A shepherd-born you be, an' no mistake.' He lifted the lamb and gave it to its mother. He gazed fondly at the shearling ewe. 'I thought you was a gonner, maid,' he told her. 'Never mind, 'twill be easier nex' time.'

*

Sev's sisters had, in fact, contracted scarlatina. Many children of the village died that winter. Without a need for words upon the subject, Sev was removed from the house of sickness, and back to the box-room in his

Granny's kitchen. He was watched closely for the development of fever symptoms, but none appeared. Jemima Honeybone still believed that the boy was delicate; when Sev begged to be allowed to stay out upon the hill with Granfer, she considered the spread of infection down in the village, and agreed that a few weeks on the hillside 'might be all for the best'.

It was said among farmers, that to see Shepherd Honeybone with his flock, was like seeing a devoted father with his children. To begin with, Sev had thought that one sheep looked very much like another. Now, with the help of Granfer, he could see the subtle differences, the characteristics which made each one special, and quite unlike its fellow.

The shearling ewe and her single offspring were of especial interest. Granfer showed Sev the lamb's fine points. His broad head well-covered with wool from brow to poll; a beautiful head, that would, when he was fully grown, bear long strong horns coming downwards and forwards in graceful curves close to his face; his full deep chest, and well-placed legs. Sev was glad that the lamb would not be 'goin' to market'; at weaning-time Sev was sent on an errand to the village. A tiny bell, brought by the Montacute carter from a shop in Yeovil, was paid for with a precious sixpence from Granfer's worn money-purse. Bells were expensive, and only awarded to Granfer's special favourites. The tinkling music now made by the ram lamb, was the sweetest Sev had ever heard. He would recognise it in a flock of hundreds.

Sev's particular task of each day was the cutting up of mangels into thin manageable slices. These were fed, with small quantities of pea-chaff and linseed cake to the weaned lambs. To be trusted with Granfer's sharpest knife was a proud yet fearsome business. The shadow of the dark woman, falling unexpectedly across him on that April morning, almost resulted in the amputation of his left-hand index finger. The cut was deep, revealing bone.

'Now look what you made me do!' he cried out. 'Granfer'll never let me use the knife no more!' He remembered the blood-stained straw of the farm cart, on that day when the dark woman had travelled with him from the hospital in Yeovil. He tried to pull the edges of his skin together; the cut hardly bled at all, but still he blamed her.

Meridiana took one look at the laceration and turned at once to the blossoming hawthorn hedge where a dozen cobwebs hung, the morning dew still wet upon them. She snapped off a sappy wand and bent it around to form an oval. The wand, passed across and behind each cobweb, gathered up a thicker web which she transferred to the damaged finger, which by this time had begun to bleed profusely.

'That'll stop the blood,' she said, 'and the next time you sees me – keep your wits about 'ee!' He watched her pick up the knife and begin to slice mangels. With her gaze fixed upon the knife she said briefly, 'Your sisters be already back at school.'

He knew what she meant. 'I be goin' back when Easter's over. Granfer had a need of me this winter.'

She laid down the knife. 'They do say that you can't read nor write.'

'Yes I can! I can read any page you like to give me.' His lower lip jutted. 'I can't abide writing. Anyhow, what for 'ud a shepherd-boy want wi' writing?'

'Your father cud read and write when he were seven. 'Course, he went to school every day – '

'I bain't like my father – I be Granfer's sonner!' The dark woman grinned.

She said, 'Honeybones is long-headed people. Scholars in the Bible College up to Bristol, both your uncles be! Seems like you idden neither Honeybone nor Carew.'

A slow flush rose beneath Sev's skin, he could feel his temper rising. 'You'm a liard,' he shouted. 'I be Honeybone all through, my Granfer said so.'

Sev looked down at his sore finger; the bleeding had

quite stopped. The colour drained from his face. He feared her, and yet the words would not be denied. 'They calls me diddecoi an' mumper, round the playground,' he whispered. 'My mother said I mus' never go to your house.'

*

Sev returned in May; to school, to his father's house, to the iron bedstead with its mattress of lumpy flocks, and the sisters, recovered from their scarlatina, who resented his presence more than ever. He had grown taller and stronger in the past weeks. Beneath the blankets each night, his bony heels paid back many hurts and insults on his sisters' shins and ankles.

The sickness had gone from the village, but many new graves had been dug in the churchyard. The Sanitary Inspector came out from Yeovil. He looked at the cottages in Middle Street and Wash Lane. He talked about overcrowding, and the need for vaccination. He advised the use of disinfectant, demanded better ventilation. New houses would be built, he said, to accommodate those families who had more than four children. Nobody believed him.

The evenings were light again, and long. Sev knew the whole hours of deep contentment; grass grew lush and green on the hillside. There was white clover in the meadows. The ram lamb, now independent of his mother, the little bell around his neck, skipped for joy at the sound of his own music. Sev learned new hymn tunes in the Baptist Sunday-School and played them secretly on the penny-whistle. The dark woman had approached him once only; she had asked if his cut finger was healed, and he had shown her the white scar.

Father spent every evening on his allotment garden, digging and planting, hoeing and weeding. Sometimes he knelt down among the roses; Sev saw him smile as if the flowers made him happy. Mother was sharp-tongued and ready to find fault. She used her gloving-stick, without fear or favour, across the knuckles of any child who disobeyed her, even Jemima!

Granfer, his sheep and lambs safely folded, came back to the village every evening. Supper was not allowed to be served in the Honeybone household unless Sev was present.

'Where's thik boy o' mine?' Granfer would say. 'Us can't never start our meal wi'out him.'

*

Eve lived in a state of permanent bewilderment, a crease of puzzlement across her forehead, a baffled expression in her eyes. She wished that her family was more like that of other children; she could not have explained, if asked, where the difference lay, except that all the blame was with her mother. Father was mostly to be found behind the pages of his daily paper. Eve had no place in which she might hide. In summer she would wheel her doll's pram up and down the yellow pavement. In winter there was no escape. That her mother loved her, she had no doubt. They went everywhere together, hand-in-hand; Eve was mother's 'liddle maid', her good child.

Abigail would sometimes shout at Eve and slap her for no reason, and then bring hot cocoa up to the school, in a mug, and pass it through the playground's iron railings. It was Abi who explained about their many relatives; but Eve was never sure whom she should love. Father was the only one she could rely on. Abi was to go to work like other girls. She 'minded' Eve, and cooked the meals, while mother worked in the shirt factory. She described the house in Dawlish, its fine furnishings and garden.

'You'll never be asked to stay with Aunty Blanche!' was Abi's favourite threat whenever Eve seemed likely to disobey.

Eve did not want to go to Dawlish unless Father could go with her. She considered her own house to be finer than that of most other children. It had seemed at first that the new house might make even Mother happy;

several weeks had passed without a single cup or plate being hurled and broken. They were visited solely by Mother's relatives. They came in twos or threes, but never all together at the same time. Nothing good was ever said about the absent ones, which was strange, when upon their subsequent arrival, the missing members were also greeted with smiles, and arms outstretched.

Mother's time of contentment had ended with Cousin Laura's wedding. The burned purple hat, sufficient of its velvet left intact for identification by Aunt Mina, had remained in the firegrate for several days. Eve and Abi had pretended not to know about the coolness that now existed between the two sisters.

It was on a Sunday in December, two days before Eve's seventh birthday, that the wedding photograph was handed over; Abigail paused on Holway Hill, untied the string and loosened the brown paper.

Eve said, 'You shudden never have done that! Aunty said to go straight home and show Mother the picture –'

'Oh my goodness!' Abi interrupted, 'this is bound to set the cat among the pigeons.' She bent down to show the photograph to Eve. 'Look there! You and me sitting right on the front row, and so is all the most important of the relations –'

'But where is Mother?'

'In the very back row. You can just see a bit of her face and that dreadful hat.'

Eve thought it over. 'But we already knowed about that. We knowed that Mother was stood in the back row of the picture.'

Abi held out the large square of cardboard and squinted at it. ''Tis all much different,' she said, 'when you sees your ownself image set down in black and white.'

*

The dinner was eaten in uneasy silence. They had waited for Mother's violent reaction, but she had propped the

147

photo on the mantelshelf without one angry word. Father, who often dozed for an hour on Sunday afternoons, said, 'Think I'll go for a walk, Anni.' He turned to Eve. 'You coming with me, Evie?'

Mother said, 'She bides here! I need her with me.'

Abigail said brightly, 'I'll do the washing-up for 'ee Mother, then I'll walk out to Staplegrove and see after Granny Greypaull's grave.'

Mother laid down her knife and fork, and looked straight at the photograph. 'They sisters of mine wudden never dared to treat me so bad if only my mother was still alive.' The high pitch of her mother's voice was more frightening to Eve than any smashing of cups and dishes. Mother looked at Abigail and Father.

'Go now,' she said, in the same strange voice. 'Go quick before the rain starts.'

The house seemed bigger and darker without Abi and Father. Mother said, 'Go upstairs. You'll find a hatpin on my dressing-table. Bring it to me.' The staircase was steep and very narrow. Eve held the little silver hatpin carefully before her, afraid that she might slip on the new, shiny lino. Mother sat before the fire, the wedding photo in her lap. She took the hatpin and said in her strict voice. 'You never tells nobody a word about what goes on inside these four walls, mind! Not even Abigail and Father. If I ever find out that you have told – I'll make you sorry for it.' Mother passed a hand across the picture. 'Our Blanche,' she said, 'don't bother no more with candlewax and pins. According to her, all you needs is a likeness of the ones you hate, and a good sharp needle.'

Eve stood at her mother's knee; she felt the dread creep across her mind and body. The hatpin hovered above the wedding-group. The room was so hushed that a coal, falling from the firegrate, made her start in terror. The hatpin began to move along the rows of faces. With great accuracy, Mother first put out the eyes of the bride and groom, and then every other wedding guest, save those of

148

herself, Abigail and Eve. She reached for Aunt Mina's brown paper and string, and rewrapped the photo, tying the string in a neat bow.

'Put on your shoes, and your hat and coat,' Mother said, 'us got a liddle parcel to deliver.'

The early twilight of December was already deepening as they walked up the steep hill to Holway. The gaslights looked like flowers on the long stems of the lamp-posts. Her short legs grew quickly tired, but Eve dared not complain. They walked at a fast pace, she holding onto Mother's hand and Mother holding onto the spoiled picture. Eve thought about Abigail and Father; she smiled into the darkness. Eve knew things that Mother hadn't even guessed at. Abi never went to the cemetery in Staplegrove; she'd be larking about at this very minute in Vivary Park, with the choir-boys from St Mary's church. Father never went for walks on Sunday afternoons. He called in on his father and mother in the shoemaker's shop in Silver Street. Eve had learned early how to keep secrets, and not all of them were Mother's.

The parcel would not go through Aunt Mina's letter-box. Eve ran back to the corner where Mother stood waiting behind a garden hedge. ''Tis too big,' she whispered, 'I can't post it.'

'Then push it underneath the front door.' Mother gave her a little shove. 'Go on, now! Be quick. You never know who's watching!'

*

Father came home with no appetite for supper. Eve worried about the cake crumbs, lodged in the creases of his best waistcoat, but Mother hadn't noticed. Her grandmother Nevill, thought Eve, made the nicest sponge cake in the whole world.

Abigail came in, cheeks flushed and hair loosened from its ribbons.

'You look very untidy,' was Mother's sole remark.

''Tis the wind,' said Abi.

Mother glanced sharply at her. 'There is no wind. 'Tis as quiet as a mill-pond.'

'Oh?' Abigail turned to Eve. 'Have you two been out then?'

''Course we haven't,' lied Mother. 'We've sat cosy by the fire all afternoon.'

Eve pushed away the horror of the wedding photo, the damaged eyes, and her own desperate attempts to force the brown paper package underneath Aunt Mina's door. She surveyed the supper table. Mother had made a fish pie. There was, Eve knew, cold apple tart left over in the pantry. Perhaps, if she asked nicely, Mother would allow her to have both. She studied the faces around the table, each one closed tight around its own little secret. Eve picked up her spoon and fork, and smiled. Not a single one of them was hungry.

*

The command that Hugh should go at once to their South African gold mines, had come from Aunt Porteous in mid-September; and Blanche, who had always feared to travel on water, declared at once her intention of accompanying him. To 'cruise' was considered 'smart' these days; all the best people did it; and a journey of such length would require a new wardrobe of summer dresses and elegant hats. Blanche, in fact, felt nothing but relief at this prospect of leaving England for a few months. Since the refurbishment of Summerlands had been completed, and Dawlish explored and found dull, her boredom had reached unprecedented levels.

Blanche was not, nor could she ever be, a country lady. Shopping expeditions to Exeter, visits to her sisters in Taunton, riding in the carriage with Hugh around the South Devon lanes, would never compensate her for the loss of London. At the age of forty-three she was still a remarkable beauty; she needed the glances of admiring men, the jealousy of plain women, as a flower needs sunshine.

Two days spent in London had been sufficient for the making of travel arrangements. Blanche had shopped in Regent Street and Bond Street, while Hugh visited the office of Thomas Cook and Son at number 13, Cockspur Street. There he had learned of the superior accommodation to be had on the Union Castle Line of Steamships. Entertainment was provided for passengers 'en voyage', together with the services of a qualified doctor and stewardess. The SS *Enterprise* carried bathrooms and electric light in all its staterooms. 'Recherché Cuisine' was a most desirable feature of the voyage. A Smoking Room was available, but only to gentlemen who travelled first class. Hugh booked a stateroom for two at a staggering price of thirty-one pounds and nine shillings. Blanche thought it wiser not to mention that she had visited Penhaligon's in Bond Street, and ordered a silver dressing-table set to be sent to Miss Laura Lambert in Holway, Taunton. They had sailed for South Africa on the very day of Laura's wedding.

*

When asked in the years to come about South Africa and its people, Blanche would confess that most of her time in that country had been spent beneath whirring fans in the bar and lounge of Cape Town's finest hotel. There had been certain compensations. With Hugh so often absent on expeditions to his gold mines, there was no lack of wealthy men who were ready to indulge in mild flirtation with a witty and beautiful woman, just arrived from London. But on Hugh's return, Blanche always listened with great attention to his anxious talk of Contango Rates and Debentures. Some of their money, he told her, was invested in the mines of De Beers and Lace Diamonds. De Beers had already fallen by two per cent before Hugh left England. Since his arrival in South Africa a sharp fall had occurred in all his other holdings. At a depth of 1,015 feet a banket reef had been struck in his principal mine which assayed only 2 dwt of gold to the ton.

'Is that bad?' Blanche asked.

'It's disastrous! It means that a stringer and not a real blanket reef has been struck.'

'How bad are your losses?

'Impossible to tell at the present time.'

'And what about dear Aunty? Did she put all her money in an empty goldmine?'

'Her investments are more widely spread.' Hugh looked embarrassed. 'As a matter of fact my holdings in that particular mine were bought on her advice.'

'Then it will be up to your aunt to make up the shortfall in our income! My father was ruined by the writing of his name on the wrong piece of paper. I never did think much of your Contango's and Debentures.' Blanche touched the safety chain on the brooch that spelled PERSIMMON in diamonds and gold; she twisted the square-cut emerald ring on her third finger. 'I keep my investments where I can see them. Don't worry,' she told him, 'there's a pawnshop in Exeter where I can get a good loan on my jewellery – should the need arise.'

Their balcony, furnished with cushioned wicker armchairs, and bright with flowers, was cool and pleasant at that time of evening. A silence fell between them; they sipped their drinks, careful not to look directly at one another. Suddenly Blanche said, 'I've been told that it's quite the fashion lately, in Paris and London, for a gentleman to take a black boy as a personal servant.' She waved a hand, and glanced downwards at Cape Town's crowded pavements. 'This city is simply packed with the sweetest little nigger-boys. You can buy one in the street-market, so I'm told, for no more than an English sixpence.' Blanche smiled. 'Now wouldn't that just liven things up around Dawlish Warren! There's a certain place where the black boys stand in line every morning, ready for inspection. I shall go there tomorrow, and if one takes my fancy, then I shall buy him for you.'

She had not expected to gain Hugh's attention, but he, grateful for any diversion, began to discuss the purchase of a servant with great enthusiasm.

'Not a little boy, I think. A youth would be better. Oh yes, Blanche! A black manservant in Dawlish would be piquant, to say the very least! We shall go together to this market, first thing tomorrow morning!'

*

Hugh Fitzgerald had learned, before he left Cape Town, that his seam of gold was no longer worth the mining. The news that his aunt's investments still flourished had at first annoyed, and then gratified him. For as Blanche pointed out, just as long as the gold continued to pour from Aunty's holdings, the impoverished Fitzgeralds would have little cause to worry.

On that leisurely cruise from Cape Town to Southampton, with his black servant in attendance, and Blanche admired and coveted by every man on board, Hugh enjoyed every pleasure offered by the SS *Enterprise*. The 'Recherché Cuisine' was all that Mr Thomas Cook and Son had promised; Hugh delighted in the electrical fittings of his luxurious stateroom; the Smoking Room where, dressed in velvet jacket and skullcap, a silk cravat knotted at his throat, he passed hours in pleasant conversation with men of his own class. The prospect of hard times to come was so unlikely that he and Blanche were able to joke about it.

It had long been Hugh's habit to read aloud to Blanche the more interesting columns of *The Times*. Newspapers, taken on board at their final port of call had contained one amusing snippet. From the first day of January, 1909, a pension of five shillings weekly had been paid by the State to any poor person who had reached the age of seventy. Any private income of more than ten shillings weekly would mean disqualification from this benefit called Old Age Pension.

'Well that counts us out at the moment, my darling!'

laughed Hugh. 'But who knows? By the time we reach our old age we may be extremely grateful for His Majesty's pension of five shillings.'

Hugh's first interview with his Aunt Porteous removed all humour from their situation. His news of the failure of his investments was overshadowed by the death of his brother Julian, of a fever, in the Windward Islands. A widow, left in straitened circumstances, would have to be provided for, not to mention the two nephews, being educated at present at Dartmouth Naval College.

For the first time in his life, Hugh found Aunt Porteous less than sympathetic; 'Go home,' she advised him, 'and review your expenditure, dear boy! I feel sure that economies can be made; your wine bills have always been excessive, and do you really need so large a carriage, in the country?' She paused. 'I am sorry, Hugh, but surely you can see that my commitment must be to your dead brother's family. Julian, it would seem, believed himself to be immortal. No provision was made – but there, it is all too late, now.'

Hugh returned to Dawlish, and Blanche, angry now and very frightened, travelled with him until the train reached Taunton.

'What I have to do,' she told him, 'will be best done alone.'

*

Mina saw the horse-cab halt before her gate, and the cabby climb down to unload the hat-boxes and trunk which invariably preceded her sister into the front hall. Mina tidied her hair and removed her apron; she opened the door to find Blanche looking nervous and unhappy.

Mina said, 'What's wrong? Where's Hugh?'

Blanche marched past her sister, through the hall and into the kitchen. 'Plenty's wrong, but I'll need a stiff drink before I can talk about it.' She gestured towards the cabby. 'Pay him for me will you. I have no change.'

Mina fussed around Blanche. 'Let me take your coat

and hat. You look ill. I'll just stir the fire and put the kettle – '

'I don't want tea, our Mina! I know that you keep in a bottle of Gilbey's for medicinal purposes.'

Mina fetched a glass and a small, unopened bottle of Gilbey's gin. Blanche drank quickly. She said, abruptly, 'Hugh's lost all his money. Every shiny gold sovereign. The fool bought an empty goldmine. He sunk every last penny in the digging of it.' She laid her left hand on the scrubbed wood of the kitchen table, and contemplated her bejewelled fingers. 'There's a pawnbroker in Exeter who'll advance me a good loan on my rings.' She lifted the glass and drained it. 'But it won't come to that of course.'

Mina said, 'Whatever will you do?'

'Live as we've always lived, at the same pace and in the same style. Our credit is first-class in Exeter and Dawlish. Tradesmen fight one another to gain our custom. People trust you, Mina, if you live in a large house, and keep servants and a carriage.'

'So they might – but for how long?'

Blanche lifted the gin bottle and poured herself another measure. 'For as long as it takes my fool of a husband to convince his dear aunty that this whole rotten business is all her fault.'

'And is it?'

'It was she who advised him to buy the bloody mine! I tell you, Mina, at this minute I should quite enjoy burying her in it! Oh, she'll pay up, don't you worry. She could never bear the disgrace of having her nephew sold-up by the Court Bailiff.' Blanche paused and assumed an expression of deep regret.

'Of course,' she said quietly, 'all this trouble will mean that I shall see much less of you and Annis.'

'That may not,' said Mina, 'be such a hardship for us as you seem to imagine.' She rose and went towards the kitchen dresser; from a drawer she removed a parcel wrapped loosely in brown paper.

'Take a look at that,' she told Blanche, 'and tell me whose handiwork you think that is.'

Blanche studied the photograph. 'Why, it's your Laura's wedding, the whole group. But full of little holes! Oh my God, Mina! Somebody has poked out all their eyes.'

'Take a closer look. Not all of the people in that picture have been ill-wished.'

Blanche said slowly, 'Our Annis is untouched, so is Eve and Abi.'

Mina's face was tight and angry. 'To use witchcraft,' she said, 'would never occur to Anni by herself. Bad temper is more her style. She breaks a few dishes and then feels better.' Mina faced Blanche across the kitchen table. She tapped a forefinger upon the photo.

'This Devil's work have got your thumbprint on it!'

'Don't be silly, Mina. I was in South Africa. I know nothing about it.' The words lacked conviction.

Mina said, 'I can't bring myself to speak to Anni. I've cut her dead in the street, and she my own sister. We've had our little ups and downs, but never anything like this.' She paused, made a visible effort to restrain tears. 'I won't cry,' she said, 'that'll only upset me. But there's only one person who could have planted that evil in our Anni's head – and that person is you, Blanche!'

'I might have said something on the subject. But just in fun, for a joke, don't you know?'

Mina nodded. 'Annis is a simple sort. She's suggestible and easy-frightened. She takes offence where none is intended. You were always a bad influence on her. Blanche. 'Tis all your fault that there's this rift between us.' Mina stood up. 'I think,' she said, 'that you had better go home to your husband. I'll fetch a cabby round here. You can be back in Dawlish before nightfall.' She looked meaningly at Blanche. 'Poor Hugh will need you with him now that he finds himself in all this trouble.'

Blanche smiled. 'Hugh is well looked after. There's no need for you to worry about him. We have an extra servant now, a black fellow we brought back from Cape Town.'

*

Nothing, thought Annis, had been quite the same since the passing of Eliza. The whole family had changed; Annis herself had done things she would have never dared to contemplate in her mother's lifetime. She had waited, with mixed feelings of anticipation and shame, for the owners of those photographed eyes to go blind or at least suffer eye afflictions. When, after a space of months, the bride and groom and all the guests retained their health and vision, Annis concluded with relief, that Blanche had, as usual, let her down.

The failures of Blanche were, in fact, proving an unexpected source of satisfaction and comfort. Abi's news, served up with the mutton and potatoes of the Sunday dinner, had quite altered Annis's view of her successful sisters. Eve, if asked to repeat conversations, would relate no more than the bare facts. Abigail, at the age of fifteen, possessed all of the Greypaull's gift for histrionics. Face flushed, voice lowered and then raised, her knife and fork stabbing at air, Abi more than repaid for permission to continue the after-church visits to the house of Madelina.

'Aunt Mina's ever so upset,' she reported. 'I never saw her so wretched. It seems that she's quarrelled with Aunty Blanche. Told her to go back to Dawlish.'

Annis smiled. 'Well I never! Did you hear that Frank?'

Frank spoke for the first time on the subject. 'Perhaps,' he said, 'perhaps you should go round and see your Mina? She've always been so good to you, Anni.'

'Me? Go to her, after the way I was slighted at the wedding? Never! 'Tis for Mina to come to me, Frank. I got some pride left I'll have you know.' She turned back to Abi. 'So tell me about Blanche, then. What have come to pass in Dawlish?'

Abigail, hands crossed upon her heart, a look of woe

upon her features said, 'Oh, 'tis such a tragedy, Mother! Poor Uncle Hugh have lost every single penny.'

'But he can't have.'

''Tis true enough. When they got to Africa they found out that the goldmine had no more sovereigns left in it.'

Abi grinned and said in her normal voice, 'Oh Ma – you'll never guess what they've brought home to Dawlish. They've brought a black man to clean the shoes and fill coal buckets in the winter.'

'No! Well I never did! Have you heard that, Frank! They lost all their money, and straightway took on another servant.'

'And his aunty up in London won't help him this time,' Abi's voice rose high with the drama of it all. 'Poor Uncle Hugh! Deserted by all in his hour of need!'

Annis pushed aside her untouched mutton and potatoes. She sighed her satisfaction.

'Oh my godfathers! What a sorry state they be all in. It do really grieve me to see it.'

*

Sev wakened early; he slid carefully from underneath the blankets, fearful that he might wake his sisters. His clothes lay in the kitchen, folded where he had left them across the brass-railed fireguard. He pulled on the corduroy breeches and skimpy sweater, and the coarse woollen socks knitted for him by Granny. He laced-up his iron-studded boots and went on tiptoe to the pump. A splash of cold water over his face, and wet fingers thrust through red curls, completed his morning routine.

His mother had asked him, once, why he left his bed to go roaming when the rest of the family still slept, but he had no answer for her. Sev himself did not understand this deep need to act independently, to have his own private time between darkness and full light. His mother rarely left her cottage; she knew nothing of those minutes described by Granfer as 'the charm of the morning', when Sev would slip between the iron rails that bordered

Montacute Park. He would stand quite still among deer in the tall grass, and wait for the note of the single bird that would set all the others singing.

Sometimes he would make for the sheeptracks that wound around Hedgecock, skirting the flock which lay folded in mist in the lower meadows, and coming to the beechwood which held the Wishing Stone. In springtime certain gypsies pitched beneath the beech trees. Sev had come to recognise their separate waggons, their lurcher dogs and goats, caged linnets and banty hens. He talked with a gypsy boy who said his name was Righteous. They argued about rabbits, and the best way to catch them.

The clock struck five as he passed the church; birds in Montacute Park had been singing for a good ten minutes. He turned towards the sheeptracks that led up to Hedgecock. He came to the beechwood, and there, in the grey light, watching through a gap in the hawthorn hedge, stood the dark woman. Sev hesitated, caught halfway between terror and curiosity. Without turning her head in his direction, she said in her gruff voice, 'Too late now for 'ee to run, boy! I knows that you be there, behind me. They old boots o' yourn do ring out louder than a team of horses.'

Sev went to stand beside her. A red and yellow blanket was pinned crossways upon her shoulders; on her head she wore a man's flat cap. A clay pipe smoked gently between her clenched teeth. He looked down at her feet, bare and brown in the wet grass. Sev appreciated, as he had never done, the shabby brilliance of her dress, the great hoops of gold which swung from her earlobes. He had always known that the dark woman was quite unlike his Gran and his mother. He looked through the hedge towards the painted waggons, and it came to his mind where the difference lay. With absolute conviction he told her, 'You belongs wi' they wandering people. Thass why you be always watchin' for 'em.'

She grinned. 'You watches, too. I sees you lookin' for

159

'em. One time I see'd you roker wi' that rapscallion Righteous. You mother wudden like that.'

'Righteous knows a lot about rabbits. He got a speshul dog what can catch hares in his bare teeth. He said I could have that dog to keep, if I g'ied a silver sixpence for 'un.'

The dark woman laughed. 'You likes catchin' rabbits?'

Sev nodded. 'The poachers come in the dark wi' their nets and sackbags, but Granfer don't never tell the Constable about 'em. Me and Granfer is allowed by Squire to take some rabbits.' Sev paused and glanced up into the listener's face, uncertain as to whether he should reveal so huge a secret. Her rapt expression led him on to make further revelations. 'We got a ferret name o' Rip. He'm better than any old mumper's dog.' Sev hesitated. 'I shudden, by rights, be tellin' about him.'

The dark woman sat down abruptly beneath the hawthorn bush. She tucked her skirts around her bare feet, and knocked cold ash from her pipe onto a flat stone. From her apron pocket she pulled a yellow paper-packet and a small knife. The packet held tobacco, thick and black; she cut a plug of the stuff, put it in her mouth and began to chew it. Sev sat down, absent-mindedly beside her, so surprised was he to see a woman chew tobacco. The dark woman chewed silently for several minutes, and then she spat tobacco juice towards the hedge, reaching a distance no man had ever achieved. Sev gasped his admiration.

'Cah! I never know'd a woman could spit like you can! Do it take much practice?'

She laughed. 'Tell I some more,' she said, 'about thy Granfer's ferret.'

Sev had never told a living soul about Rip and Granfer, but envy of the woman's spitting skills encouraged him to boast.

'Well,' he began, 'Rip lives inside of Granfer's shirt. He on'y comes out to answer calls of nature. By night he sleeps in a liddle wooden hutch what me an' Granfer made him. 'Tis on'y Granfer what's allowed to touch him.' He smiled. ''Tis best of all at supper-time. Granfer won't never start to eat unless he got me sitting opposite across the table. Well, 'tis then that Rip do get to feed,' Sev chuckled, 'you should jus' see how his liddle white head do come peeping up from the neck-front of Granfer's shirt! He got pink eyes that shine when he sees the meat on Granfer's plate. Rip's a very tidy eater. Granfer cuts the food up in tiny pieces, an' Rip takes 'em careful-like so as not to nip the fingers.' Sev sighed. 'We reckons he'm the best ferret in the whole world.'

The dark woman made a strange sound deep in her throat. She put a hand up to her eyes and rubbed them. She chewed hard on the tobacco, and spat again towards the hedgerow. She said at last, in her gruff voice, 'You had another grandfather. Long time ago. He would of been so proud o' you, boy! He've laid these many long years in Montacute churchyard.'

'I know,' Sev said, 'you told me about him. How he died in the quarry.'

'Did you go and read his gravestone like I said you shud?'

Sev grew restless. He stood up and moved away from her to lean against the safe trunk of a nearby beech-tree. 'No, I never did! I don't like the churchyard. Our 'Tilda reckons that there's ghosties hiding in there!'

'There's ghosties in most every place, boy.' Her face took on a strange look. 'I sees things what gorgies never see. My granny was a chovihanis. I be the seventh child of a seventh child.' Her voice had risen as she spoke.

Sev cried out, 'Don't talk like that! I don't like you when your face goes funny!'

At once her voice grew familiar and harsh, her features bland and smiling. 'I did'en mean to 'trash 'ee, my heart's joy.' She beckoned to him. 'Come yer, and I's'll tell a secret.'

Sev went, hesitantly, towards her.

'I got a present for 'ee. Bought from a big shop in

Yeovil. 'Tis better by half than thik old penny-whistle what you be always a-playing.'

'What is it, then?'

'They calls it a mouth-organ. You puts it in your mouth, and blows on it.'

'I do that with the whistle.'

'No, no. This is diff'rent. The mouth-organ got a lot more music inside of him. The shop-engro played me a tune before I parted wi' my silver.' She glanced sideways at the boy. ''Tis a dinky liddle thing. You can carry 'un easy in your breeches' pocket.'

'Have you got it on you?'

'Not so fast my young rai! I asked you to visit me reg'lar, and you never yet done it!'

Sev gazed at her, enraptured. 'I'll come tonight. Straight after school.' He turned and began to move back along the sheeptrack. 'I got to go now. Us gets caned if we'm late.' He paused. 'You won't give the – the mouth-organ to our Mathilda, will 'ee?'

The dark woman's face grew grim. 'Your sisters pass me by wi'out a word,' she muttered. 'Oh, they is surely the daughters o' their mother.'

*

Sev had thought Ham Hill to be in possession of two kinds of people. There were the quarrymen who hewed the stone, and carvers like Jye, his father, who shaped that stone for use in local houses and cathedrals. There were the shepherds like Sev and Granfer, who grazed their flocks across the Hill and in the lower fields that led down to Norton. There were the workers. The Hill for them was a place of toil; the source of their daily bread.

There were others who used the Hill as and when they fancied. For the vagrants it was a safe place to pitch their tents, light their fires, catch rabbits for the pot, and pick the wild strawberries. Their ponies were grazed across the short turf, they cut wood from hedge and covert for the making of their clothes-pegs, they caused trouble only when the young gypsy-bloods were drink-proud, or a fight broke out among their women. The children, spoiled and petted by their elders, ran free from dawn to dusk. Their skills were not those taught in the village classroom. Sev envied, but was still wary of them.

He had recognised lately that certain men roamed the Hill who were neither workers nor vagrants. Gentlemen of the leisured class, said Granfer, walked on Ham Hill just for the pleasure of it! They studied flowers and grasses, talked with common people like masons and shepherds, and then went away and wrote books. Sev's only contact with the upper classes had been to glimpse Squire Phelips and his family as they rode through the village in their high black carriage. The brothers Powys, on foot and dressed in baggy tweeds, stout shoes, and carrying walking-sticks, were a source of wonder and speculation to Sev. He questioned Granfer about them.

The Vicar of Montacute, said Granfer, although a Churchman, was friendly and well respected in the village. His sons had been educated at Sherbourne and Cambridge. They travelled to foreign places, but always came back to the Montacute Vicarage. Three of the vicar's sons were writers of books. The oldest, the one called John Cowper, was already a famous man.

'When your mother was a young maid,' Granfer reminisced, 'she liked to argue religion wi' Mister John.'

'My mother talked wi' the likes o' him?'

'Aye, boy. My Maris was a great reader of books when she had the time. Her was a long-headed girl – could of been a scholar so they told me in the school. But that sort o' thing don't do, see. Not in a female.'

Sev thought about his mother, seated day and night at her gloving-table. He recalled her pinched, unhappy face, her sharp voice and busy hands.

'Her don't never read books no more.'

'Well, she wudden, wud she? Not with all your four childer and your father to see after – and another chiel expected any minute,' Granfer sighed, 'things don't never turn out the way we expects 'em to. People change, Sev. Sometimes us can hardly recognise 'em.'

Sev studied the drabbet smock and black felt hat, the seamed face and bright blue eyes; the three-cornered smile that was meant to reassure him. He grasped Granfer's hand in a rare gesture of affection.

'You don't never change, Granfer. You be always the same, I always knows where I can find 'ee.'

Sev looked down towards the village and all at once his mind seemed to move several paces forward. 'Nobody cares about me, save you and Granny. Don't never go away, will 'ee Granfer?'

'You shudden say that, Sev. Your father and mother cares about you.' Granfer turned his head to where the sheep were grazing. 'Nothing stands still, boy. Look at you – eight year old already – an' the bestest shepherd-boy I ever see'd. As for my goin' away – why I never even gets so far as Yeovil.'

※

Hugh watched the morning come, saw the sky grow light and the sea, soft as a pigeon's wing, ripple gently in towards him. A bank of mist shrouded the horizon. The air was growing cold. He looked out towards the estuary; soon the long skeins of black Brent geese would be flying in from Russia. Full tides, and gales from the south-east would cause high seas to break across the roofs of trains; at such time the Exeter line would be closed down until the tide ebbed. He leaned against the sea-wall and looked upwards to where the white gables of Summerlands showed clearly above the red cliff. He loved this place in all its moods and seasons; but especially in winter.

The realisation that he was a ruined man had come slowly to Hugh Fitzgerald. A letter from his aunt, commanding that he should sell Summerlands, and that Blanche and he should return to their old apartment in her Russell Square mansion, had forced him finally to admit that he was, in fact, bankrupt, but Hugh also knew that he would never leave Dawlish.

He had visited his aunt at her house in Bath. 'Summerlands is my home now,' he had told her. 'I shall never give it up. I shall have to find work of some kind.' His aunt had smiled. 'You have never worked, dear boy, in all your life. No one would employ you.' She leaned forward and took his hand in hers. 'Come back to Russell Square, Hugh! I am not a young woman, I tire easily just lately. Your brother's death has caused me a great many problems – '

'– And your bad advice regarding my investments has brought me to the point of ruin, Aunt Letitia! Please understand this. I shall never, in any circumstances, return to your house in London. I would rather emulate my father, and throw myself out of an upstairs window.

For a moment it seemed that his aunt might faint; she sat down abruptly.

'Is it really so bad, Hugh? You still have your holdings in the Bristol lime-kilns, and the bonds I gave you on your last birthday –?'

'Not enough,' he interrupted, 'to keep a house the size of Summerlands, and support Blanche!'

'Ah – Blanche.' Hugh's aunt sighed. 'There, if I am not mistaken, lies the truth of this matter. Too late now for me to tell you that you should let her go. The poison is in your blood. Your mother destroyed your father. I have prayed that old history should never repeat itself in your case.' She paused. 'Money is all that keeps Blanche with you.'

'My money is gone,' he said quietly, 'and without Blanche my life is ended.'

'No Hugh! I can't bear to hear you speak so! There must be something we can do? Look here – I will make you an allowance – ten pounds weekly should be sufficient to –'

'Ten pounds? But I have a coachman, a gardener, three servants –'

'Dismiss them. Send the black man back to Cape Town. Employ your maids on a daily basis. Get rid of your carriage and buy a pony trap. Learn to differentiate between weeds and flowers. Lock up your cellar – you know that Blanche drinks brandy as if it were water!'

'But ten pounds, Aunt?'

'Don't provoke me, Hugh. A working labourer in this country draws a wage of about sixteen shillings. Thousands have no job at all, they exist on the charity of others. Ten pounds would keep a labourer and his family for three months. It is all that I am prepared to offer, and then only on certain conditions.'

'What conditions?'

'That you make the economies I have already mentioned. I shall also need help with your brother's children. As you know, they are both at Dartmouth Naval College. I shall expect you to invite them to Summerlands at the end of each term. There will be a small bonus to cover their expenses.'

'I shall have to speak to Blanche about this.'

'No Hugh. You are in no position to manoeuvre. Yes or no – I need your answer, and I need it now.' He had of course said yes. What else could he have done?

Hugh looked out towards the bank of sea mist, and shivered. He crossed the iron footbridge that spanned the train lines, and began to walk back, very slowly towards Summerlands and Blanche.

The memory of that capitulation was still bitter in his mind. He had returned to Dawlish, exchanged the carriage for a small gig, taken his black servant to the docks at Bristol and put him on a packet-steamer bound for Cape Town. The two maidservants no longer lived-in, but returned each evening to their homes in Dawlish. The gardener came, but for two days only in each week. Hugh had himself learned how to feed and groom the pony, and put on harness. He was forced into keeping proper accounts. Ten pounds, he now discovered, was indeed a lot of money; if properly handled.

❊

Blanche woke to the familiar slap and boom of waves as they broke upon the sea wall. She had always to remind herself on waking that the ocean was so close by. She still waited for that old prediction of Meridiana Carew to come true. 'No peace shall come to her,' the gypsy had said 'until she rests with her face towards the sea . . .' Blanche turned, uneasily, against the pillows. Peace of a sort had come to her in that first year in Dawlish; Hugh and she had been closer then, than at any time in their marriage. Together, they had furnished the house, planned the garden, explored the surrounding country-side, sometimes in the carriage, but more usually on foot. She had bought stout shoes suitable for walking, and a smart suit of fine tweed in a becoming shade of violet. A dash of glamour had been added to this unlikely outfit by a brilliant feather in her hat, a splash of expensive perfume, and the Persimmon diamonds, pinned as always, upon her lapel. They walked the lanes and hills around Dawlish Warren; picked blackberries so that Florrie the cook might make jams and jellies. Blanche had looked at her juice-stained fingers and been reminded, inevitably, of Larksleve and Loveday Hayes. Hugh had taken her to the estuary at Starcross, shown her curlews and redshanks, black geese and oyster-catchers. They had bid at local auctions for pictures and china, dined out in Exeter on special occasions. Hugh had been happy then; but it hadn't lasted. She had known it wouldn't. Blanche remembered those brief times of harmony on Larksleve between Philip and Eliza, always to be followed by quarrels and coldness. There was nothing new, Blanche thought, underneath the sun. The names and faces might be different, but the same old tragedy was acted out, the same sorrows handed on, from mother to daughter, from father to son. She shivered, and looked towards the empty firegrate. In other times the bedroom fire would have already burned brightly. But now, since the maids were employed on a daily basis, the lighting of the morning-room fire, and the cooking of breakfast were their first tasks on arrival from the village.

Blanche remembered Berkeley Square and herself at sixteen, sore-fingered and smudged from the cleaning-out of firegrates and the carrying of coals. There was nothing to prevent her, Hugh had said, from lighting her own bedroom fire, if she so wished. As for himself – he rather enjoyed the novelty of feeding the pony and pulling up weeds!

'I would rather,' she told him, 'turn blue and freeze in that icy bedroom than take one single step backwards!' It was true. But for the care of her clothes, which had always been of prime importance, Blanche could not bring herself to perform one simple menial task. She knew now, that far back in her mind, beyond conscious thought, she had always been waiting for this ultimate disaster.

She recalled her first sight of Hugh, on the steps of the Connaught Hotel. He had come towards her, hand outstretched, and Blanche had felt the heart contract within her. She half-turned and would have run from that place, but he had taken firm hold of her hand. She had looked up at the flaxen curls, the brilliant blue of his eyes and the high flush of colour that stained his cheekbones. At the touch of his fingers revulsion had seized her. He might well, she had thought, be the ghost of her Papa! Instinct had warned her in those first moments of their meeting, that this man brought with him the certainty of her own, inevitable end.

Every step she had taken since that day was to bring her towards this point at which she now stood. She had planned a life as different as that of Eliza as it was possible to be, and what had been the outcome?

Blanche left her bed, pulled on a warm robe, and went to stand beside the window. She saw Hugh, walking slowly, head bent and shoulders hunched, upon the foreshore. Even as she watched, the sun rose huge and golden from the sea, making a pathway towards him. Blanche trembled and pulled the robe close about her. It might well be Philip Greypaull who walked there, and Blanche herself, an echo of Eliza, watching her husband from an upper window. The thought once admitted, brought others with it. The parallels were too obvious for denial. Eliza had also married a man she did not want; a man who, nevertheless, brought land and possessions with him. Eliza had loved Samuel, the second son who would inherit nothing, but had denied that love. Philip, like Hugh, had trusted in the word of others. Bankruptcy had followed! Eliza, when in trouble had been abandoned by her family. Blanche remembered Madelina's words; 'Don't come here no more Blanche! I shall go out now and find a cabby. You can be back in Dawlish Warren before nightfall!'

Madelina would never know how much it had cost Blanche in pride, to come back to Taunton and admit Hugh's failure. To dazzle Annis had always been easy, but throughout their lives it had been Madelina, her respected older sister, whom Blanche had most needed to impress.

Hugh turned towards the house. Blanche saw him climb the iron footbridge, saw defeat in his drooping shoulders, and was reminded more than ever of her father, Philip. Another thought, unexplored, because she could not endure it, came back and this time would not be denied.

Eliza had loved Samuel, the second son who would inherit nothing.

Blanche had loved Jye Carew, who was also a poor man.

*

A shepherd, Granfer told Sev, must know his sheep as a loving father knows his children; but more than this, he must be so familiar with them that the slightest change in their behaviour will tell him if the animal is ailing or distressed. Ninety-nine sheep out of every hundred will be easily accounted; it is that hundredth absent creature which must at all times concern the shepherd.

Sev had learned where missing sheep were to be found. He sought them in the hawthorn hedges where their long fleeces caught up easily in briars. He knew all the stony outcrops and rocky hollows where a sickly ewe might creep. In the presence of Granfer, and because he knew himself to be trusted by the shepherd, the boy felt himself grow responsible and adult. In this year of 1910 Granfer had promised that Sev might help with the castrating and tailing of lambs. If all went well he could assist with dipping and shearing. In April Sev would be nine years old: almost a man.

They sat together in the winter hut and made summer plans. With lambing already well advanced, and snow lying deep across the fields, this was a night when they would not be returning to the village. A great frost had come down in the past few hours. It couldn't, said Granfer, be any colder in that Switzerland, where poor Mr Llewelyn had been sent to find a cure for his consumption.

The illness in the previous November, of Llewelyn Powys, youngest son of the Vicar of Montacute, had shocked the whole village by its severity and nature. Tuberculosis was accepted among village families; it was, they were told by the doctor, a natural outcome of poor diet and overcrowding. That it should strike down the most handsome and engaging of all the Vicar's eleven children was hard to credit.

'That young man had looked seedy for a long time,' said Granfer, whose greatest skill was the spotting of sickness in sheep. 'He were walking slower every day. I met up wi' 'un one time down along by Wulham's. He was coughing fit to split his lungs. "Why, Mister Llewelyn," I told 'un, "thass a graveyard cough if ever I heard one!" ' Granfer looked out across the snowy landscape. 'If 'tis snow an' frost what do cure consumption then he needed never have gone to they foreign mountains.'

Sev had come to the Hill in early afternoon, bringing with him a change of dry clothing for the shepherd. He had also brought cheese and bread, and a jar of rabbit stew: with potatoes roasted on the stove they would not go hungry.

'I shan't expect 'ee back this night,' Granny had said. ''Tis Sunday tomorrow, an' no school, save in the Chapel.' He had left her, knitting beside the fire, the ferret Rip asleep in his little wooden hutch in a corner of the kitchen. He found Granfer, exhausted from many nights without sleep, and soaked to the skin from digging lost sheep from the snowdrifts.

Dry clothes and hot food had made it impossible for the shepherd to stay awake. Sev filled lamps and trimmed wicks while Granfer dozed. He awakened, full of alarm, 'I could sleep for a week, but I dursent – not in this weather!' He rubbed a hand across his face, and Sev noticed for the first time the white tufts that had grown lately among the red beard. 'Is that mouth-organ in thy britches pocket, my sonner?'

Sev nodded.

'Then give we a tune, eh? 'Twill stop I from nodding-off.'

*

The mouth-organ had, at first sight, looked an unlikely instrument of music. Sev had gone to the dark woman's house, secretly, by night. He had taken the object, examined it briefly, and stowed it in his breeches' pocket. He'd gazed once around the firelit room, and instinct warned him that here was danger! The dark woman had tried to detain him with offers of tobacco and cider.

'I got to go home,' he'd lied, 'my father's waiting for me.'

'Play me a tune,' she'd begged, 'jus' so I can hear how that dinky liddle box do sound!'

Sev had run from her then. He could not see how music was ever to be called out from this piece of tin and wood, and he had no intention of allowing himself to be shamed before her. He had gone without a word of thanks out into the windy darkness. He had run from the village to stand beneath the tall white larch trees that lined the road to Ham Hill. Only then, when he was sure that no human ear could hear his failure, did Sev halt, regain his wind, and put the mouth-organ to his lips.

He'd breathed into it, just a whisper of air to begin with, and then strongly. He passed the instrument across his lips and the sound aroused in him an ecstasy of feeling, such as the penny-whistle never had. He arrived late in his grandfather's house, where the supper could not start without him.

''Twas all the dark woman's fault,' he excused himself. 'Her called me into her house, for to take a liddle present off her. Looksee! 'Tis called a mouth-organ, I bet nobody else in the world have got one.' The colour flooded to the very roots of his red hair. 'I can play 'un already.'

'Abide with Me' was Granfer's favourite hymn. Sev's slow and passionate rendition of the old tune brought tears to Granny's eyes, and robbed Granfer of words.

'Oh my dear Lord,' his grandmother whispered, 'you draws sounds from that liddle wooden box just like you'd had music lessons. There's nobody musical in our family.' She turned to David. 'Wherever do it come from Father?'

At her words Sev had grown cold and frightened. He knew exactly where the music in his soul had come from. His delight in the tinkling of sheep-bells, of men's voices singing, of his own attempts to make music, was, he felt sure, a direct inheritance from the dark woman, who said she was his father's mother.

Sev peered now through the gloom of the winter hut at

Granfer's drawn features and drooping eyelids. He looked out on the lambing pens, where five ewes were expected to deliver within the next few hours. It was snowing again. He pulled the mouth-organ from his breeches' pocket. Very softly, and with feeling, he began to play 'Abide with Me'.

The thaw came quickly, leaving the Hill a tender green, its paths slippery with mud. A sheet of white water covered Athelney and Sedgemoor. A gleam of silver in the lower meadows told where the river Parret over-flowed.

Ten lambs had been lost in the bitter weather; many of the ewes turned sickly. The ram lamb still walked proudly, his curved horns gleaming in the March sun.

Granfer's absence from home had this time been prolonged; his losses among the flock unusually high.

'I can't recall such a winter,' he told Sev, 'not in all my fifty-nine years. Reckon I be gettin' old, my sonner. 'Tis comin' time for you to take my place.'

They closed up the winter hut and took the short cut that led down to the village. Granfer halted once, the crook firm in his hand, the dog Ruff at his heels. He leaned for a moment upon the crook, and looked back across the great bulk of the Hill. In a tone Sev had never heard him use, Granfer said, 'The heart have gone out of me, boy. I shan't never see this place no more.'

*

Sev left his grandfather's house as dusk fell. 'Don't bide long,' Granny told him, 'your supper's nearly ready, and 'tis getting dimpsey.' He wandered aimlessly about the village, drawn out by some power he could not compre-hend. He halted at last beside the churchyard gate. From the Honeybones' cottage a wavering light came slowly towards him.

'No need to come lookin' for me, Granfer,' he cried out, 'I be comin' home this very minute.'

Sev tried to move but found that he could not; and the

173

light came on, glowing brighter all the time. It reached the churchyard wall, hung above it for a moment, and he could see that no man's hand had held that flaring brightness. All at once it disappeared across the wall and fell down into a far corner of the graveyard.

Sev had heard about corpse-candles from his sister Mathilda; how a light would appear just before a death, and trace a path from that person's house to the spot where he was, eventually, to lie. His mother had said that such tales were wicked, and that what people really saw were glow-worms. But whoever heard of glow-worms the size of a man's fist, or one that flared with such terrifying brightness?

Since their return from the winter hut Sev had slept in his old box-bed in his grandmother's kitchen; he dwelt once again in the House of the Lord. The light had come from the Honeybones' cottage; Sev had been a witness to it; he wondered how many before him had seen their own corpse-candles, and what form his death would take, if and when it happened? Perhaps he would get the consumption like Mister Llewelyn Powys? His sisters would be sorry then, for all the bad things they had done!

*

Sev was taken that night from his grandfather's house just as swiftly as he had been brought there, at the age of eight months. He was awakened by arms that lifted him up and out of the box-bed.

'Your Granfer's been took bad,' he could hear terror in his mother's voice, 'you can't bide yer no longer. You got to come home.'

For the rest of that night he lay awake at the bottom end of the iron bedstead. He slept towards morning, to awaken to his sisters' scorn.

'Well, well,' they taunted, 'jus' see what the wind blowed in! 'Tis Sev the fair wi' his carroty hair! What have you come back for? Don't your old Granfer want you no longer?'

174

David John Honeybone died, said the Martock doctor, from pneumonia, brought on by exposure to bad weather, and aggravated by chronic overwork and exhaustion. He was carried from his cottage to the place of burial prepared for him in a far corner of the churchyard. He had been a small man; his coffin was carried easily on the shoulders of his sons.

No one, not even his tormenting sisters, had dared to tell Sev what had come to pass. Jemima Honeybone, cast down with the burden of her own grief, said to Damaris, 'He'm a funny sort o' chiel. There's no tellin' how he'll take it. He'm what you might call many-minded. I be feared to tell 'un. You'm his mother. You must do it, Maris.'

Maris said, 'I can't bring myself to tell 'un. He idden used to me an' my ways. P'raps – p'raps 'tis best left alone? He'm a bright child. Let 'un see the coffin carried to the churchyard, and he'm bound to guess then what have happened to his Granfer.'

*

Sev had spent time in all his secret places until Granfer should be well again. Never before had he been refused entry to the shepherd's cottage. He had watched the doctor come and go, had seen his uncles arrive at the Montacute railway station. His mother's tears, his father's grim face, confirmed that something bad was happening to Granfer. It was April, the month when the charm of the morning was at its very sweetest. He heard the first cuckoo in Montacute Park, wallflowers bloomed on every Ham-stone wall. He went to Pitt Pond, where he and Granfer caught eels in summer; he climbed up to the beech wood on the way to Hedgecock, stood breathless on the Wishing Stone, and made the only wish that was in his heart.

He wandered aimlessly through the April evening, coming at last to the overgrown cart-track that led back down into the village. He heard the tolling of a single bell from St Catherine's Church, and knew that the sound preceded a funeral. He remembered his sighting of the corpse-candle, and began to run.

Sev crouched by the churchyard wall and counted the chief mourners. There was his granny, dressed all in black, his mother and father, and the oldest of Sev's three sisters. There were aunts and uncles from Tintinhull and Five Ash. Cousins from Odcombe, and as far away as South Petherton. But it was his mother's brothers, the two who lived in Yeovil, and the other ones, the clever Parsons who had come from Bristol, who carried the small coffin.

Sev's mind withheld the shock of truth for several minutes. It was not until the Baptist Minister said, at the end, as he always did, 'And now Brethren, we will sing the favourite hymn of our dear departed Brother,' that Sev finally conceded that the body in the coffin must be that of Granfer.

The whole village of Montacute had turned out to mourn David Honeybone; it was their heartfelt singing of 'Abide with Me' that covered the sound of a child's screams.

*

The way to the winter shelter seemed longer in the darkness. Sev took the path that led up to the beech-woods above Hedgecock, passed through the haunted place known as Forster's Gully, and felt no fear. The April night was cold; he crept into the cave, found Granfer's old brown blanket, and laid down on the straw and slept.

He awoke to full sunlight and the instant awareness of last night's horror. But for those brief screams, ripped from his throat and covered by the singing of the congregation, he had made no sound. He had not wept.

He threw off the blanket and walked towards the sunlight. The sheep and their lambs made a pattern of white against the green fields down by Norton Covert. He watched them, the way their faces always turned towards the sun, their woolly rumps into the prevailing wind. He could see the new shepherd standing in amongst them; the young strong man who had been brought out from Odcombe. The shepherd was not alone; the dark woman stood beside him. Sev moved back into the shadow. He could not believe in the reality of this brilliant morning, in these people who still walked the earth as if nothing of significance had happened. Even the sheep still grazed and fed their lambs, although a stranger overlooked them.

So that was how it happened? You could go right away from everybody, and no matter how good you had tried to be, nobody would miss you. They would dig a hole, drop you into it, cover you with earth – and then forget about you. Sev now knew what was meant when sick people were described as soon to be 'wearing a green overcoat'. He had watched the Sexton fill in Granfer's grave, had seen the green turves spread above him. Sev looked out from the winter shelter and could not believe in a world that no longer had Granfer in it. He felt the turning of his mind towards an evil thought, and there was nothing he could do to change it. If the shepherd was dead, then perhaps his sheep should also die; especially the ram lamb?

In those first nights and days in the winter hut Sev felt no real hunger. He drank from a nearby spring, and ate the wrinkled apples, stored by Granfer, in the previous autumn. On the fourth morning he saw smoke among the trees, and knew that the travelling people had come back, as they always did in April, to the lanes around Norton Covert. The smell of frying bacon caused his stomach muscles to contract in an agonising spasm. He crept closer to their atchin-tan than he had ever been. The boy called Righteous appeared suddenly beside him. The dark-skinned boy looked closely at Sev.

'Shepherd Honeybone's dead,' he said, flatly.

'No he idden! You'm liard!'

'Us heard tell about it on the Petherton drom. Some uncles was comin' from Odcombe way. Shepherd's dead, they told us. Watch out for the new feller!' Sev said, "Tis I what they uncles o' yourn had better watch out for! That new feller don't know nothing. He got to do 'xactly what I tell 'un to.'

The lie lacked conviction. Righteous said, 'You be hungry idden you?'

'I wudden eat your food. They reckons you eats toads and hedgehogs.'

'You better go home, Sev. The gavmush stopped us on the road to ask if we had see'd you.'

'What do Constable want wi' me? I done nothing wrong.'

'Your mother's lookin' for 'ee.'

'I got no mother.'

Sev walked back slowly to the winter shelter, avoiding the paths where men might pass. Shepherd Honeybone's dead, the boy had said. Go home to your mother. The words would not leave his mind. A desolation more terrible than he had so far known, took hold of him now. He began to run towards the cave. He flung himself down upon the straw and began for the first time to weep for Granfer. The tears, once loosened, could not be controlled. Throughout that day he sobbed and slept, and sobbed again. It was evening when the dark woman found him. 'I know'd you was here,' she said, 'but I never told 'em. There's times when a man needs to be by his ownself.'

'I dursen't go back now. Father'll strap me.'

'Not him! I had words wi' my Jye about all this. I put the fear o' God in him. I told him you'd likely done away wi' yourself.' The golden hoops in her ears swayed with the sharp nod of her head. 'You's'll come back along o' me. That witless mother o' yourn 'ull be glad to see thee.'

He followed her from the winter shelter, and did not look back. His thoughts were muddled. He kept his gaze on the muddied hemline of her plaid skirts, heard the slap of her bare feet on the slippery sheep track, and knew that in all his life he would never again tread these paths that he had once walked with Granfer.

*

At a quarter to midnight on Friday May 6th 1910, King Edward VII died peacefully in his sixty-ninth year. His body was taken to lie in state in Westminster Hall, where many thousands of his faithful subjects filed past the catafalque to pay their last respects. At the funeral, it was his fox-terrier Caesar who, at his late master's wish, was led by a footman immediately behind the gun-carriage which bore the coffin: the dog taking precedence over the Emperor of Germany and eight other reigning monarchs.

Candace McGregor stood among the crowd on that fine May day and watched the passing of the cortège; Candace had approved of Edward Albert. A sporting King – in every sense of the word; a heller, a chancer, a merry feller! Even in death he had bested his detractors. No one in that vast crowd appreciated more than Candace the joke of a dead man's dog which was allowed to walk ahead of Emperors and Kings.

The funeral procession moved slowly towards Paddington Station. Candace walked with it along the crowded pavements, keeping pace with the solemn music and the terrier dog. Her feeling of loss was deeply personal. Her very best bets had been placed on good old Bertie's winners. On the day of his death she had won five shilliings on his filly 'Witch of the Air' which had come in first to take the Spring Two-Year-Old Plate at Kempton park. For years she had glimpsed the King on racecourses and in saddling enclosures. His presence among the racing crowds had given an air of excitement and romance to a scene that for Candace had always been the most enchanting in the world. It was, so the newspapers said, the End of an Era. The faithful subjects of King Edward VII had been privileged to witness the passing of the greatest Edwardian of them all.

The procession turned into the station precincts. The Royal Train was to take the King to his last resting place at Windsor. The people around Candace seemed inclined to linger, as if they could not bear the solemn pageantry to end. She watched the coffin and the dog called Caesar until both passed from her view.

It was late in the evening when Candace returned to the tall and narrow apartment house which overlooked Hampstead Heath. She gazed up at the first-floor windows and saw that her curtains were open and the gas light burning. It was Billy who insisted on pulling the brass chain which sent gas hissing into the little white mantel; Candace, when alone, preferred the candles and oil lamps of her childhood. A smell of cigar smoke on the stairs confirmed his presence, and she wondered, as she always did, what trouble had brought him home to her, this time.

He was sitting on the sofa, her picture-albums stacked high beside him. Candace sighed; even as a small child Billy had seemed to find comfort in the family portraits. He laid down the album which held his cousin Laura's wedding photo. He stubbed out his cigar in the pot which held his mother's finest aspidistra; he came towards her, held her firmly by the shoulders, and shook her.

'Where the 'ell 'ave you been, Ma? I've sat here all bleedin' night a-waiting for yer.' The tension in his face alarmed her, and then he smiled. 'You knows how I worries abaht yer. There's only you and me, Ma! What ever would I do wiv'aht yer?' The tears in his eyes seemed genuine, although with Billy she was never sure. Long ago she had accepted that her son was an actor, on-stage and off; his whole life was a performance. Every gesture and emotion, every move he made, was a direct reflection of whatever role he happened presently to be playing. The fact that his role altered frequently and without warning confused Candace. But as she so often said, the one certain thing about her Billy was his love for his mother, and his determination that he would one day see his name 'up in lights'. She smiled back at him, and pushed him gently away.

'Cup o' tea – or could you fancy something stronger?'

Billy brightened. 'Come into some more money 'ave yer?'

'I had a win – on the King's horse. "Witch of the Air" come in first at Kempton. I had a nice bit on her – '

'But that was weeks ago, Ma!'

'I had a feeling you'd be back, soon. I got a few drinks in – just in case you needed cheering up.' Candace took two glasses from a cupboard, and set a full bottle of whisky on the table. 'That's where I've been all day.' She pointed at the bottle. 'I've been down to Paddington to say cheerio to the feller who paid for this lot!'

Billy grinned. 'Always had a soft spot for old Bertie, eh Ma? Well he's gone nah, more's the pity! They say that young George is a regular, stiff-neck what don't go much on racing.' Billy scowled. 'The peelers is hard enough already on the bookies and their runners – '

Candace poured whisky and handed it to him. 'What is it this time? Coppers on your trail again? You should pick your pubs more careful, Billy, and always wear a cap! That yellow hair of yours is a dead giveaway. They only caught you passing bets just the once, but they've remembered you for it!'

Billy shook his head. 'Nah, it ain't the Law, Ma.'

'What is it then? Some girl – ?'

He laughed. 'You know me better than that. I'm too fly for any girl to catch me.' He sat down on the sofa, retrieved his cigar from the flower pot, and re-lit it. Candace went to the armchair beside the fireplace. She looked up at the mantleshelf and saw that the faded photo of the dead McGregor was slightly out of place. Billy had been studying his father's likeness; always a bad sign.

He followed her line of vision and said softly, 'If I'd

only 'ad a Guv'nor it might 'ave all been different. I can 'ardly remember 'im no more, Ma.'

'What is it, Billy? Is it Reeves – or Karno what have upset you?'

*

Fair, waving hair, blue eyes, and a frail physique had made it possible for Billy to play juvenile parts long after he had reached mature years. Only he and Candace were aware of his true age, but lately his style of living had made him look older even than his twenty-six years. He leaned back against the cushions of the blue brocade sofa, a whisky glass in one hand, a cigar in the other, and Candace could see nothing of the dark McGregor in him. Billy was and always had been, a facsimile of her father, Philip. The space of years had brought tolerance to Candace, and observation of her son had given her insight into the characters of both men. They could not be termed liars, neither should they be judged insincere, since such a verdict could not be applied to characters for whom reality had no literal meaning. Once again she asked him, 'You in some sort of trouble wi' Fred Karno?'

'Not exactly trouble.' Some new quality in Billy's face and voice warned Candace that this was no act.

'It's a number of things, Ma. First of all, I'm twenty-six years old. I've been on the 'alls since I was eight or nine. I thought I was doing alright, and now, all of a sudden there's younger blokes in the Company, taking leading parts – '

'But that's not fair, Billy!'

'Yes it is, Ma. I've watched 'em, they're better than I shall ever be.' He paused, drained his whisky glasss, and began to turn the empty tumbler between his fingers. 'There's a per'tickler one – a moody little swine name of Chaplin. Hardly ever speaks to any of us. Never has a bet or a drink. Rumour is that he banks his wages every Friday! A comedian wiv a bank-balance – I arsks yer, Ma – did you ever hear the like?' Billy gazed straight at

Candace, and she felt fear at the sick look in his eyes. 'He's good, Ma. Karno thinks the world of 'im. He just arsks for a leading part and Karno gives it to 'im.' Billy looked away towards the faded photo on the mantel-shelf, and then at the albums stacked at his elbow. He said quietly, 'I know I can act. It's a feeling – I can't describe it, but I've always had it. But it takes more than just knowing – and I'm getting older. A few more years wiv the Karno company –' He tapped the albums, 'I've been studying their faces, wondering which ones I favour. Or perhaps I take after poor McGregor. He was a failure, too. He copped-aht and died when he was only thirty – perhaps I shall go the same way?'

'Don't talk so foolish! You be nothin' like your father. You comes down in a straight line from my father Philip, to my brother Simeon. They was both powerful singers and stage-struck!' Her sharp voice softened. 'You looks exactly like 'em, Billy. Make no mistake, you be a Greypaull. Everybody in the family have said so.'

'But they never got nowhere, did they?'

'That wasn't their fault. They both had their chances but circumstances went against them.'

Billy had grown up with the tales of his grandfather Philip. He had loved the stories of this hell-raising farmer, who had defied his church-warden father, and sung songs at the old Victorian Free-and-Easys, that were held in the roughest pubs in Taunton. He had also heard about the marriage, arranged and sweetened by a dowry of gold sovereigns. There had been Uncle Simeon, who had actually auditioned on a proper stage for the impresario George Edwardes, and who, because of his illiteracy, had also turned down his chance of fame and fortune.

Billy said, 'You reckon that a bloke should chance 'is arm, do yer Ma? Even if it means going miles away, for years and years?'

Candace sighed. 'You've been trying to tell me something ever since I walked in the door. Might as well

183

get it said, Billy.'

He was silent for a moment, and even as he sought for words it occurred to Billy that he was still quite masterly when it came to the dramatic pause.

'There's talk of Karno sending a company to New York. I've already asked him about it. He won't pay my passage, but he'll give me a contract to tour America if I buy my own ticket to sail.'

'Who else is going on this tour?'

'Oh there's quite a crowd. Some of 'em is taking their wives and children wiv 'em. Charlie Chaplin's going of course, and another up-and-coming bright hope called Stan Jefferson.' Billy paused, and the break in his voice was not assumed.

'I'm finished here, Ma. I knew it when Karno refused to pay my passage. He said I was welcome to tag along with the rest – if that's what I wanted. I do want it, Ma! They're making moving pictures in America – all I want is a chance – '

Candace said, 'America's a long way. You'll be on your own, for the first time. Until now I've been able to help you.'

'P'raps that's my trouble, Ma. I've thought a lot just lately abaht Grandfather and Simeon. They never 'ad the guts to step off the straight-and-narrow. A man got to chance 'is arm, just once in his life.'

'When does the ship sail?'

'Oh, not for weeks yet.'

'You'll be wanting money?'

'Not much – just enough to buy a ticket.'

Candace rose and began to walk slowly towards the kitchen. 'I'm more tired than I thought. I'll put the kettle on and make some supper.' Her attempt to smile did not quite succeed. 'Fancy,' she said, 'I've seen my King go to his last rest, and heard that my only son is to go to the New World; and all in the space of a single day.'

*

At the end of September a cattle-boat, the SS *Cairnrona*, set sail from Southampton, bound for Quebec. On board was a twenty-one year old actor named Charlie Chaplin, and an even younger Stan Jefferson, later to be billed Stan Laurel. They docked at Quebec, and travelled by train calling at Toronto on their way to New York.

Billy McGregor, with two pounds, ten shillings, in his trouser-pocket, and a watch he could pawn if ever forced, would remember always his first sighting of the New World, and the words of Charles Spencer Chaplin, 'America, I am coming to conquer you!'

*

There were ways, Abigail had found, of persuading Eve to reveal her secrets. A few careful questions, together with a gift of sweets or chocolate, and Eve would chatter as she chewed.

They were walking the Staplegrove Road towards St James' Cemetery; Eve carried flowers for Eliza's grave. Abi drew from her pocket a sticky three-cornered bag filled with sugar-fondants.

'I saved these for you,' she said, offhandedly, 'I know they're your favourites.'

Eve bit into the soft pink oval. She glanced sideways and upwards. 'You wants to know what happened between Mother and Aunt Mina.'

'Don't tell if you don't want to.'

'Mother said she'd kill me.'

'She won't kill you. You're her liddle maiden.' Abi's voice changed. 'I won't split on you, Eve. Promise!'

Eve bit into her second fondant. She said slowly, 'Mother took a hatpin and poked out the eyes it Laura's wedding photo. Then she made me push in underneath Aunt Mina's door.'

Abi halted. 'You mean she – ?'

'Oh, not her own eyes, nor yours or mine. But everybody else's, every single one! I thought they'd all go blind. I watched 'em for ages and ages, but they never didden.'

'But that's witchcraft, Evie. That's wicked witchcraft.'

'Mother said how Aunty Blanche had told her how to do it.'

They walked in silence for some minutes. As they entered the cemetery gates Abi said, 'So what happened when Aunty Mina saw the photo?'

'I don't know. The next time we met her up in North Street she took one look at Mother and then cut her dead.'

Abi went to the tap and filled a jar with water. The sisters knelt, one on either side of Eliza's grave; Eve arranged chrysanthemums in the thick glass jam-jar.

'Things have gone from bad to worse,' whispered Abi, 'since Granny Greypaull died, I don't like all their quarrelling and upset. I can't bear it when they argue; I never could, even when I was quite tiny.'

Eve said, 'You've been sleep-walking again. Father heard you go in the middle of the night. He followed you into East Reach. You was out in the town in no more than your nightgown. He found you staring in at a butcher's window.'

'I know,' said Abi. 'They always tell me about it the next morning.' She stood up, abruptly. 'Sometimes – sometimes I feel so wild that I could smash things. But if I did that – then I'd be like Mother.'

'You don't look very well, our Abi. You really ought to eat your dinner, instead of pushing most of it onto my plate. You look thin enough to be consumptive. Father says – ' Eve paused.

'What do Father say, then?'

'He reckons that mother should have let you go out to work in the factory instead of keeping you cooped up indoors to mind me and do the housework. "Abi needs to mix with youngsters of her own age." That's what Father said.'

'And what said Mother?'

'Oh – you know – the usual stuff about you being a

lady and too delicate for hard work.' Eve placed the final chrysanthemum in the jam-jar. She stood up and adjusted the wrinkles in her black woollen stockings. 'I wish she wouldn't make us wear these. It's not even winter yet, and anyway, 'tis you that's the sickly one.'

They stood side-by-side at Eliza's grave in its quiet spot beside the stone wall, then they turned and walked away beneath the Cedar-of-Lebanon and yew trees.

Abi said, 'What else do they say about me when I'm not there?'

Once past the cemetery gates, Eve felt free to eat another fondant. Through a mouthful of sugar-icing she said, 'Mother reckons you got money coming to you.'

'I know. She've been saying that for as long as I can remember, but I'm not supposed to know about it.'

'Is it true, then?'

'It might well be.' Abi paused. 'Something happened when I was little. Mother thinks I can't remember, but I can. There was this old lady, this very rich old lady. She used to come in a carriage and put money in my two hands. I thought she was my grandma, but she couldn't have been. Nobody can have three grandmothers.'

'She could have been,' Eve reasoned, 'perhaps you was an adopted child. Perhaps you truly belonged to that old lady. Why else would she have give you money?'

Abi halted. She grabbed Eve's wrist and shook her. 'No,' she cried, 'I was never an adopted child! I belong to Father, same as you do! He's so good to me. He's the only one what understands the way I feel, he always did –'

Eve freed her wrist and rubbed it. 'Well there's something special about you. Mother went back herself to work in the shirt factory so that you should stay at home.'

'Mother likes the factory. She goes into the Half Moon pub on a pay day and drinks cider with the rest of them. Father'd be mad if he found out.'

Eve said, 'I know something else what you don't.'

'Tell me!'

'A letter came yesterday from Dawlish. Father read it out to Mother. You was gone early to bed, all worn-out with walking in your sleep. Aunty Blanche and Uncle Hugh wants us both to go down there, for a holiday. I thought that Mother would say no, like usual. But guess what – she said we could go, you first, and me later on, if only to spite Aunt Madelina!'

*

Abi's journey to Dawlish was made on a fine day in mid-September. Mother came with her to the railway station, warned her about talking to strangers, and had words with the guard about the rowdy sailors, bound for Plymouth, who filled the third-class compartments. The train began to move; Abi waved until the tall figure of her mother grew insignificant and tiny. She touched the broad leather strap that secured the window, but had no intention of obeying the final instruction that she was to close it. She sat down, leaned back against the plush upholstery, thankful to be alone in the small, enclosed world of the train, and away from the admonishing voice and commanding index finger. She closed her eyes, and the warm sun and the train's rhythm calmed her anxious fears; she opened them to find that smuts from the engine had flown in and settled, as Mother had said they would, on the cream serge of her new dress and jacket. Mother's fondness for the ladylike qualities of cream serge was well-known in the family. Why could she not have bought the smart and practical navy-blue for which Abigail had pleaded? She began to brush at the smuts, which only smudged and spread them wider. Abi's eyes filled with tears. Nothing ever went right for her! What would the Fitzgeralds think? Aunty Blanche was so beautiful and well-dressed, Uncle Hugh immaculate, in his frock-coat and topper, a silver-topped cane in his white undamaged fingers. An image of their faces, shocked at the sight of her dishevelment, rose up to torment Abi, and all at once the nervous frustration which had caused her recent illness made her clutch at the cream serge skirt and bunch it together in her sweating fingers. Her heels began to drum, the sound keeping time with the wheels' clatter; her screams lost in the long blast of the steam-engine's whistle.

Her rage lasted only a short time, leaving her exhausted; and then calmness settled on her. Abi began to experience a state of self-awareness that she could never have known while still in Taunton. It was as if she hovered in a high corner of the railway compartment, and looked down on herself, coal-smudged and tear-stained, but seated primly, now, hands in lap, feet placed tidily together. Her straight brown hair had been put-up that morning, for the first time. Abi watched the girl that was herself shake her head quite deliberately until hairpins and combs flew in every direction; and with that action came a memory so clear that she could almost hear her Aunt Mina's voice, warning Mother that Abigail would be bound to disgrace the Fitzgeralds. She was back again, sitting on the worn doorstep of the cottage behind North Street; she could see the fuchsia bushes, and the skirts of white broderie anglais bunched in temper in her grubby hands. Compassion filled her for the seven-year-old Abi. She seemed to hear Eliza's voice. 'Now come you here to your Granny, my lovely, and tell me all about it.'

No one had ever guessed how badly Abigail missed her Granny Greypaull. The bond between them had, for some reason not known to Abi, been very special; and quite unlike that of Eliza with any other grandchild.

The train slowed; though the open window Abi saw the Fitzgeralds waiting for her on the station platform. She gathered up combs and pins, and pushed them hastily into her hair; made one final disastrous sweep of her hand across the cream skirt, and stepped down into outstretched arms. Once aboard the little train that went to Dawlish, Aunty Blanche smiled and shook her head at the ruined dress.

'Nobody but my sister Anni would have dressed you all in cream to travel on a steam-train.'

'She said I was to close the window,' Abi confessed, 'but I disobeyed her. Things always go wrong for me when I don't do as Mother tells me.'

Her aunt reached across to touch the half-pinned hair that straggled over Abi's collar.

'Pinned-up for the very first time, eh?'

Abi nodded. 'It's a dreadful mess – '

'Don't you worry about it! Tomorrow we'll have a hairdressing lesson. You've got lovely hair, it just needs careful pinning. What do you think of her, Hugh? Hasn't she grown as pretty as a picture? Oh, she'll pay for dressing! I see her in well-cut navy-blue, a costume I think, skirt ankle-length, and a blouse of pleated white shantung, with a gold-pin at the throat. Shoes of matching navy, with little bows, to set off those tiny feet and slender ankles. She'll have to be measured of course. She's so tiny and slim that nothing off-the-peg is liable to fit her.' She turned to Abigail. 'It's your birthday next week. We'll take you to Exeter, won't we, Hugh? We'll have you looking like a Princess!'

Uncle Hugh smiled and nodded, but said nothing. He was, thought Abi, in spite of all his money and position, quite a lot like Father and Uncle David Lambert, who also tended to be silent when in the company of their wives.

It was almost dark when they reached Dawlish. The horse-cab drove slowly out along the coast road towards the Warren. The rising moon showed Abigail the sea; they came in sight of the fine white house called Summerlands that stood upon the cliff-edge. They drove in through the open gateway, and Abi saw with surprise the two maids standing in the lighted doorway. A smell of roasting meat came from the kitchen. There was no sign of the reduced circumstances spoken of by Mother. She walked through the hallway, glancing into lamplit rooms as she passed open doorways. The furnishings and carpets seemed even grander than she had remembered; the whole house still smelled of flowers and beeswax. For a man who had recently lost all the gold in his mine, her Uncle Hugh, thought Abi, lived in some considerable style!

*

Dawlish was quiet in late September. A few trippers came on bicycles each Sunday, carrying picnic boxes and bathing costumes. They sat on the sandy beach and ate egg sandwiches and apples. They sang music-hall songs, the chorus lines of which were quite audible to Abi from her high point at the edge of the kitchen garden. Aunty Blanche heard her singing the words, 'You can do a lot of things at the seaside that you can't do in Town.'

She laughed, and then said seriously, 'Would you like to live at the seaside, Abi?' Abigail sensed the invitation that lay within the question.

'I – I don't know. Mother and Father might not – '

Aunty Blanche interrupted. 'You came here this time at your mother's expressed wish,' she said sharply.

'I know, Aunty. It's very kind of you to have me, what with all your troubles. I've got this nervous illness you see. I get headaches, and I sleep-walk. I can't eat, and the doctor says I'm too thin already.'

'It's no wonder you get headaches, cooped up in the house all day, by yourself. Why, when I was sixteen I was out in the world, on my own, looking for my fortune in the City of London!'

Abi said diffidently. 'But you were beautiful. No artist in his right mind would want to paint my picture.'

'Don't denigrate yourself, child. There's nothing in this world you can't achieve if only you want it badly enough. Always remember this. You've got breeding on your side. You come from a long line of distinguished people. All you need is the right setting, a few smart clothes, and the proper introductions, and you could also make an advantageous marriage. Don't ever be tempted to settle for some factory-hand or ledger-clerk. Look in your mirror, Abigail, and always be proud of what you see there.'

*

The cheval-mirror of Mr Page of Exeter, Bespoke Tailor to the Gentry, showed Abigail exactly what her aunt had meant. The navy-blue costume with its well-cut jacket and ankle-length skirt satisfied Abi's own innate good taste and developing instinct for what was fashionable and stylish. The navy shoes, also made-to-measure, felt light and easy on her feet; she loved their Petersham bows and the neat raised heels which made her appear taller. Aunty Blanche had shown how Abi's straight brown hair could be dressed high with combs to give her added height. A gold-pin brooch, bought that morning by Uncle Hugh at Exeter's largest jewellers, added the final touch of elegance to the shantung blouse.

They lunched at the Grand Hotel, and for the first time since her arrival, Abi felt at ease, and as if she belonged with the Fitzgeralds. For some days now, she had observed her aunt's every move and gesture, her manner of speech, the charm and graciousness which captivated everyone who met Blanche. Almost unconsciously Abi's voice had modulated to a more musical one; her head inclined at a flattering angle when listening to conversation. She was conscious, for the first time, of the possible impression she might make on others. 'Don't denigrate yourself,' her aunt had said. 'You've got breeding on your side – you come from a long line of distinguished people.' The improvement had not gone unnoticed. Aunty Blanche leaned across the luncheon table to pat Abi's hand.

'I am very proud of you, my dear, and so is your uncle. You look so chic and self-possessed. Several heads have turned to take notice of you. I do believe that people think you are our daughter!'

'I owe you both so much,' Abi murmured, 'I don't know how I can ever – ?'

Uncle Hugh held up his hand. 'No need for thanks, my child. It is our pleasure.'

A look passed between the Fitzgeralds, and all at once Uncle Hugh excused himself and left the table.

'I'll order coffee for you, dear!' Aunty Blanche called after him. To Abi she said, 'A business matter he had forgotten – he'll be back almost directly.' She reached for her handbag and withdrew a small package. 'You spoke of gratitude, Abi – well, there is one small service you could render for me. You remember the jeweller's shop where your brooch was purchased? Now, I have a small transaction to make with Mr Trimbold, the owner, but it is business that I don't care to do in person. There is this package to be handed over. In return you will be given a large brown envelope. Just say that you are Mrs Fitzgerald's niece. He is expecting you to call so there will be no problem. I shall wait for you here. The jeweller's shop is just across the road; it won't take but a few minutes.'

The parcel weighed almost nothing in Abigail's hand. She identified herself, Mr Trimbold was fetched, and the exchange was made. She returned to the luncheon table to find Uncle Hugh and Aunty Blanche drinking coffee. The bulky brown envelope was stowed swiftly away inside a crocodile-skin handbag. As her Aunt snapped shut the clasp which made the bag secure, Abi noticed that her aunt's left hand no longer bore the square-cut emerald ring.

*

It was late October when Eve came to Dawlish. She was placed by Annis in the guard's van of the Exeter train, a label tied around her neck which stated her name and age, and destination. Eve was also dressed in cream serge, with bows of stiff pink satin in her curling hair. She would, Annis knew, sit quietly throughout the journey, on a little wooden fold-down seat, among bicycles and luggage, and wicker-baskets full of homing pigeons. When she left the train at Exeter to be claimed by the Fitzgeralds, her cream serge dress and coat would be quite unmarked; the pink ribbon bows still stiff and neat in her hair.

*

Abi watched her little sister step down from the dirty guard's van, labelled like a parcel, but quite immaculate and unconcerned. Eve submitted to the hugs and kisses of her relatives, and said that the journey had been 'alright, thank you', and owned up to a ravenous hunger. Her first sign of awe at her surroundings was when she saw the high tea she was to share with Abi. 'All that food,' she whispered, 'just for you and me?'

'You get a whole egg all to yourself,' Abigail informed her, 'as much as you can eat of everything.'

Eve studied Abi's narrow waistline. 'You don't look any fatter.'

'There are other things in life besides food. Hurry up, now. Finish your cake. I want to show you the house and gardens.'

Abi took Eve by the hand and led her through the many rooms of Summerlands. She was not a talkative child, but Abi knew when Eve was most impressed with her surroundings by the sudden pressures of the little girls' fingers, and the widening of her green eyes. The mysteries of the bathroom were explained; the absence of a hip-bath remarked on, the purpose of the silver chain with its flowered handle made quite clear. It was not until the door of the drawing-room was opened by Abi, that Eve was finally moved to speak.

'Oh, my goodness,' she whispered, 'just look at that carpet! Jet-black, with great bunches of pink roses all over – can I walk on it?'

''Course you can! But only in slippers. Aunty Blanche is most particular about that carpet. It's the exact same kind as she once saw in a Lord's house up in London. Millie has to scatter damp tea-leaves on it once a week, to pick up the dust, you see!'

'And the sofas and chairs,' said Eve, 'why, they looks too good to sit on; and all that pretty glass, and the china figures! Oh, I never see'd anything like it did you, Abi? 'Tis like the King's palace – '

'You mustn't say "'tis",' Abigail corrected, 'and you must say "I never saw", not "I never see'd". You must talk like the gentry when you live amongst them.'

'I never thought they was gentry? Aunty Blanche is Mother's sister.'

'She married gentry. Don't you know anything at all?'

'I know this much. My name is Eve and not Blanche. She keeps getting it wrong, but I didden like to tell her, not straight away.'

Abigail looked stern. 'And you mustn't tell her! Your proper name *is* Blanche. 'Tis on your Certificate of Birth – I see'd it when you started school.'

Eve giggled. 'You said "'tis" and "see'd" when you never ought to.'

Abi flushed. 'Well I can't remember every time, can I? Anyway, Eve is only Father's pet name for you. In Dawlish you must answer to Blanche. I'm surprised that Mother didn't explain it to you.'

'She might of done. I don't always listen when Mother's ranting on.'

'Now don't you get cheeky, Eve Nevill! Aunty Blanche is a very gracious lady. You should think yourself honoured to be named for her.'

Eve grinned. 'You uses big words, lately. They'll laugh at you when you comes home.'

'I might not come home.'

'But you'll have to. Mother'll see to that.'

Abigail said, 'We're to share a bedroom, in case you get nervous by yourself. You can see all the way to Teignmouth from our window.'

'I never get nervous. Can we see the sea?'

195

'You can see the ocean from most windows in this house. It must be lovely to live here always.'

Eve's dark green eyes narrowed slightly. 'I'd better,' she said, 'go and hang my clothes up in the wardrobe. They'll be all full of creases if they bide much longer in that carpet-bag.'

'Don't be such a silly child! There's no need to do your own unpacking.' In a tone that parodied exactly that of her Aunty Blanche, Abigail said, 'Haven't you noticed? We have servants in this house!'

Eve surveyed the bedroom with a coolness that enraged Abi; she said nothing about the deep-rose carpet or the rose-sprigged curtains. At the sight of her few clothes, hanging in the walnut wardrobe, the carpet-bag set neatly beneath them, she remarked, 'I don't like strangers touching my belongings.' Determined to draw some response from the annoying child, Abi walked to the other walnut wardrobe and flung wide its door.

'Look there! See the clothes that Aunty Blanche has bought me!' She lifted down the navy-blue costume, and blouse of pleated white shantung. 'I was measured specially for all these. Aunty says I look very sheek in them. Sheek is French for smart, don't you know?'

'Well, why don't you say smart?' Eve asked, absently. All her attention was for the navy-blue shoes; she touched the ribbon-bows and the high, slender heels.

'Can you walk in these, our Abi?'

''Course I can. They were made to measure for my feet. I've got very tiny feet, you know Eve, with extra high arches. I bet you didn't know that.'

Eve stroked the shoes; 'Can I try them on?' she whispered.

'No you can't! Your feet are already broader and bigger than mine. None of my things will ever fit you, so you needn't get ideas about them.'

Abi went to the dressing-table and picked up the jewel-box.

'I'll allow you to wear my golden brooch until the

morning,' she relented. 'You can pin it on your night-gown. If you're very good and promise never to tell a living soul, I might tell you a few secrets.'

Eve had always been a safe recipient of Abi's secrets; nothing confided here in Dawlish would be repeated to Mother when they were back in Taunton. Abi pinned the brooch and its safety-chain on the thick white cambric of her sister's nightgown. She picked up a strip of folded brown paper, and began to wind a strand of Eve's long hair around it.

'I don't know why I have to do this,' she said, irritably. 'Your hair curls by itself.'

'Mother said you must.' It was a statement for which Abi could never find an answer. She wound hair and tied ribbon until her little sister's head began to resemble a long-fringed lampshade.

'So tell me about *them*,' Eve said softly. 'What else do they do, besides giving you whole eggs, and buying you new clothes?'

'They don't do much of anything,' Abigail said slowly. 'Come to think about it, they don't seem to like each other all that special!'

'How do you mean?'

'They put on a good face in front of the servants. They call each other "dear" and "darling" but you can tell they don't really mean it.' Abi paused, a strip of brown paper in one hand, a strand of Eve's hair in the other.

'I'd rather,' she said, 'have the sort of rows we get at home, with Father acting stubborn, and Mother throwing shrimps and butter at him. You know where you are, with them. There's something funny goes on in this house, Eve. You just take notice at the breakfast table. They never do a hand's turn of any proper work, and yet they both look near-dead first thing in the morning. They only eat a bit of dry toast, and drink pots of coffee.'

'What a shame,' Eve said, 'with that pantry full of food! I see'd a whole side of bacon hanging from a hook – '

'You saw,' corrected Abi, absently. 'But that's not all.' She lowered her tone to a dramatic whisper. 'They act very strange when we go out all together!'

'How strange?'

'They like it when people think that I'm their daughter.' A wondering note came into Abi's voice. 'I'll bet that's why they bought me posh clothes, and a gold brooch.'

Eve said, 'P'raps you really is their daughter? Mother's always saying that the gentry's too clever to be hindered with pesky babies. P'raps they was too posh when they lived up in London with the King, to be bothered with a sickly child like you!' Eve turned her strange green gaze upon Abigail. 'There's something different about you. I'll bet anything that you and me is not real sisters; like I said before, you is probably an adopted child!'

*

Aunty Blanche was very careful of them; Eve and Abigail might walk in the gardens, but not too close to the cliff-edge. They were permitted on fine days to stand on the little footbridge that spanned the railway lines, and wave at the 'Devon Belle' as the steam train roared and puffed beneath them. The beach was considered too cold and damp for them to stroll on; the autumn tides too swift and high for safety.

Abigail observed the ways of moneyed and leisured people. 'We must,' she told Eve, 'remember every single thing that happens here. You know what Mother is; she'll want to know every little detail.' The day began with the arrival of Florrie and Millie from Dawlish village. Grates were cleaned, fires lit, a quantity of empty bottles thrown into the ash-bin. The breakfast gong sounded punctually at nine. Eve poured cream and spooned sugar onto her plate of porridge, she counted the silver dishes filled with kedgeree, bacon and kidneys and smoked haddock; the racks of toast, the crystal bowls that held three different sorts of preserve. She thought about Father, coming home at about this time from French's Tanyard, to eat bread and the egg laid by the brown hen. She saw the faces of her aunt and uncle grow pale at the sight and smell of so much food, so early in the day. Uncle Hugh read aloud the letters that were brought by the maid to the breakfast table.

'Aunty can't neither read nor write,' Abigail told Eve. 'You'd think she'd be ashamed – but not a bit of it! It saves me an awful lot of worry and trouble, that's what she says. 'Tis – it is my belief that she can't even sign her own name!'

The Dawlish tradesmen called daily at the house. The fishmonger and butcher were given their orders and soon dismissed. The baker, who was said to feel the heat in summer, and the cold in winter, was not allowed to leave the morning-room until he had joined Aunty Blanche in a mid-morning sherry and water-biscuit. Florrie disapproved of such familiarity. 'The Master,' she told Eve, 'is a proper gentleman,' she sighed and shook her head, 'but oh, the madam – !'

An old man came in every Friday to mow the lawns and sweep up fallen leaves. His bonfires produced a thick pall of smoke that was, said Abi, most likely mistaken by passing ships as a distress signal sent up by the Fitzgeralds. It was mild on that October evening; the bonfire sent out yellow smoke, a light breeze was blowing in a southerly direction.

They were seated at dinner when a liveried footman, insisting that his message must be delivered in person, was shown into the room. The young man touched a finger to his forehead. 'Sorry to intrude, sir.' He held out a slip of folded paper. 'From my master, sir.'

Hugh laid down his knife and fork. He read aloud, 'Mr W.H. Wills of Charlton House, will be obliged if Mr Fitzgerald will take immediate steps to abate the severe nuisance caused by his infernal bonfire. Mr W.H. Wills and his distinguished dinner-guests have been forced to dine behind closed windows due to the smoke and smuts blown into Charlton House by Mr Fitzgerald's bonfire.'

Eve and Abi exchanged glances and then turned to look at Aunty Blanche. She had snatched the note and handed it back to the nervous footman.

'Your master is W.H. Wills, the tobacco millionaire?'

The young man nodded. 'Then deliver this message to him from Mrs Blanche Fitzgerald. Tell him that since he has made a considerable fortune out of smoke he should not object if a whiff or two floats in at his dining-room windows. In fact, he should quite enjoy it.'

The footman went away. Uncle Hugh said, 'Oh Blanche! You really should not have sent back such a message. Our bonfires do create a nuisance! I'll see to it, straight away!'

Eve said, before she fell asleep, 'What will happen, Abi? Will Aunty Blanche get into trouble for being so rude to a millionaire?

Abi laughed. 'No, of course she won't! What's the use of being rich yourself, if you can't be rude to other rich people?'

'But what about consequences?' Eve sighed. 'You know how frightened Mother is of consequences. She's always saying so to Father.'

'Aunty Blanche has spirit,' Abi said, 'she looks into her mirror and she's proud of what she sees there! You mustn't ever denigrate yourself, Eve. There's nothing in this world you can't achieve, if you want it badly enough!.

'They do a lot of boozing.'

Abi said, 'Well they have to pass the time with something, don't they? Anyway, it's not called boozing if you're gentry. It's an aperitif or a pick-me-up, or a hair-of-the-dog.'

'They get drunk, Abi. They get drunk at night and shout at one another.'

'I know, I've heard them.'

'Shall you tell Mother about it when we get home?'

'I'm not sure yet. I might – and then – I might not.'

*

The lace-edged hankies fluttered from the compartment window like two white birds escaping; Blanche stood on the platform of St David's station and watched the train grow small. They were gone, her surrogate children; back to Annis, to the terraced house in East Reach, to a life and future which she had, herself, found impossible to bear.

Annis had reared them well. They trod quietly through the house in slippers, treated with reverence Hugh's many treasures. They knew their table manners, were polite at all times to all people. What had pierced the heart of Blanche was the sound of their childish laughter wafting through the house and garden. Abigail, at sixteen, was still a child when in the company of her little sister. Blanche had watched them from an upper window, picking beans for Millie; sitting on the white seat which faced seawards, pointing to ships as they crossed the harbour bar.

Abigail, impressionable and highly-strung, was still capable of change. But the little one, who had said, almost straightaway, that her name was Eve, had left Blanche defeated and confused. There was no getting past the obliqueness of those jade eyes, the firm set of that small mouth.

Blanche had experienced, on the eve of their departure, a hopelessness such as she had never known. Until now, there had always been a dream of some kind, a plan, a possibility that she might remake the world a little closer to her heart's desire.

'Supposing,' she had said to Abi, 'supposing your uncle and I should purchase a position for you at Chapman's big store in High Street, Taunton? We could buy you an apprenticeship in the millinery department – it's a very ladylike occupation. You would meet a genteel class of ladies in such a situation.'

But Abi had refused. 'Thank you,' she had said, 'but no. You see – Father wouldn't like that. I just know he wouldn't.'

*

The grief of a child is seldom acknowledged by a mourning family. To begin with, Sev had tried to hold on to the thought of Granfer; to recall their good times together, the birth of the ram lamb, the gift of woolly tails that had been his first plaything. But remembering was painful, and Sev's capacity for grief was vast and unchildlike. The enormity of his loss was so far beyond the boy's comprehension that evasion of hurt now became his sole defence.

The first anniversary of David Honeybone's passing occurred in April. Sev stood at the graveside, between Maris and Jemima; he observed how the green-turfed mound had sunk low so that the primroses and violets laid upon it were almost level with the surrounding earth. In that moment of realisation, Sev's image of Granfer slipped away, taking with it the very substance and core of love.

The cool wet days of April, 1911 were followed at once by an extraordinary summer. Sev would still talk, when a very old man, about those boyhood days of great heat and long drought when the river Yeo ran so low between banks that it was possible to wade from one side to the other through water that was only chest-deep. The countryside turned brown beneath long days of sunshine, and Damaris Carew, her body heavy with her sixth child, saw her only son become lethargic, his expressive features grow sullen, the lower lip mutinous. To her mother she said, 'Our Sev haven't never been the same since he lost his Granfer.'

*

The sheep were to be washed before shearing. Sev lay beneath a parched hedge in Drayton's meadow and watched the flock come down to the only pool for miles around that still held a necessary depth of water. In other days he would have been there, busy and excited, standing waist-deep in the muddy water, Granfer beside him. The tinkling of copper sheepbells came clearly across the heat haze, and Sev clapped both hands across his ears to shut out the sound. He could still hear the voice of the new shepherd, swearing and cajoling. The clipping would begin soon, the white fleece curling away from the shears, the shorn ewes, released from their burden of wool, skipping awkwardly away between the hurdles. Sev closed his eyes and concentrated upon emptiness; it was possible, he had discovered, to reach a state where not a single thought would stir his mind. He lay for a long time, hands across his ears, until the sheep and their bells had been returned to the high pastures. He opened his eyes and looked at the newly-washed flock as they wandered aimlessly in the noon heat. He stood up, and began to walk without direction, taking care to avoid the cracks that had lately appeared in the dry earth. He should have carried his father's dinner up to the quarry. He knew that on both counts he could expect a beating; cuffed about the ears by the schoolmaster, and across the knuckles by his mother's gloving-stick. He was never asked to explain his truancy; he could not recall the last time his father had spoken to him. His granny had grown silent and withdrawn since the death of Granfer. It was only Righteous Lock, and the dark woman, who ever talked directly to him. Sev's preoccupation with graveyards and burials, with corpse-candles and hauntings, was a private matter about which he could not speak. It became his mission to observe the invalids of the village, those who were said to be sick and about to die. He believed in his child's mind that such people carried special knowledge; if he watched them closely he might discover how Granfer had managed to slip so secretly away.

*

Llewelyn Powys had come back to England in the spring of the year, looking so thin and changed that Montacute people were sure he would 'never last out the summer'.

His bed had been placed on the terrace-walk of the Vicarage garden; his days were passed in reading and writing. All his family came to visit. Sev watched their arrival at the railway station; he followed John Cowper Powys as the famous author strode the short distance from the train to his brother's bedside. People said that the Vicar's youngest son had come home to die. Sev spied from a tree that overhung the Vicarage garden, he saw the bowed shoulders and heard the deep cough of the severely consumptive. When Llewelyn Powys, instead of dying, began to attempt short walks in the surrounding country, Sev's disappointment was bitter. He began to trail the young man over fields and through lanes, and every day the walks grew longer, the cough less frequent.

Gentlemen's sons, Sev now discovered, wore white shirts in summer, and cream flannel trousers which were always clean. The Powys brothers often carried books from which they read whole pages to each other as they walked. They talked all the time, in accents and using words that Sev found difficult to follow. His fascination with them made him reckless. The day came when Sev's presence could no longer be ignored. He heard John Cowper say, 'That boy is following us. I've noticed him on several occasions.' They were walking in the clover-field that lay beside Mill Copse. Sev wanted to run, but the sight of these two giants as they turned back to face him, held him rooted and without words.

It was Llewelyn Powys who spoke first. 'Is there something we can do for you, boy?' Seen full-face, the golden-haired man looked like the Bible pictures of God's angels. His eyes were kind, his voice gentle. The great head bent towards Sev.

'What is it? Did you want to ask me something?' Sev's throat was dry; at last he said, 'They says – in the village – that you'm as good as dead, already.'

The words came out awkwardly, but with great force. Llewelyn Powys's smile was of an unexpected sweetness.

'What else do they say of me – in the village?'

'My – the dark woman – she reckons as you 'ont never make old bones.'

Sev thought that the giants would be angry with him, that threats would be made to inform his father. The golden-haired man turned towards his brother. 'This child's preoccupation with death would seem to be even greater than my own. I find that interesting, John. Very interesting!' He turned back to Sev. 'Is that why you watch me? Because I am dying?'

Sev scraped a bare foot across the parched grass; he studied the dry dust between his toes, the bramble scratches on his ankles.

'I don't know – ' he muttered.

'I think you do!' The voice of John Powys was deep and vibrant, and like music. Sev gazed up into the craggy face and strange, compelling eyes. 'I think you know exactly why you follow us, but you do not intend to explain yourself – and why should you? If it gives you pleasure to gaze upon us, then do so, by all means!' He paused. 'You may tell your father and your mother that you have, this day, exchanged words in the Mill Copse field with that great and gifted author – John Cowper Powys!' The man moved one step towards Sev and held out the books he carried.

'You may follow six paces behind us,' he said gravely, 'but on one condition only. That you carry our books, and close all field gates behind us.'

*

Llewelyn Powys did not die that summer. He walked each day in that extraordinary heat, and his bowed shoulders straightened, his cough almost disappeared. The barley fields turned golden, apples ripened in Mr Coles's orchards, and still Llewelyn Powys lived.

School closed down in August. Maris Carew was delivered safely of her sixth child. Sev carried dinner to his father every forenoon, careful to avoid those hill-paths he had once trod with Granfer. The tall, white-shirted Powys brothers were not difficult to find among the scorched pastures and harvest fields. Sev opened and closed gates for them, carried their books, but did not walk six paces behind. Every day he drew closer to the cream-flannelled legs, the intriguing conversations, his bare feet making no sound in the white dust of the lanes. The giants called at every tavern in the surrounding district; between halts they talked about books, how and when they should be written, and by whom. Sev listened carefully to the long words and peculiar accents; these men were more than just long-headed. Something moved far back in the boy's mind; he experienced the first stirring of awakened interest since the death of Granfer. He sat on the broad step of the Jolly Ploughman Inn and looked for the first time at the book he carried, the weight and size of it, its soft green binding, the gilt-lettering on its spine. He spelled out the name, John Cowper Powys.

So it was true; Sev hefted the book in his hand, and the pages fell open. He began to read, skipping over the long words, of which there were many. A shadow fell across the page, and he looked up into the face of John Powys.

'So you can read, can you?'

''Course I can!'

'So what do you make of my book, eh?'

'Cudden understand the half o' it. But I bet it's clever!'

'Wiser men than you have reached the same conclusion. Did you hear that Lew? He can't understand the half of it, but he bets it's clever.'

Sev felt the blood creep beneath his skin, felt his anger rise at the giants' laughter. He slammed the book shut, stood up, and then threw it down onto the tavern step. His lower lip jutted, his eyebrows came together, the look directed at John Powys was deep and disturbing.

'You can rot in hell,' he told the astonished author, 'afore I ever carries a book for you again.'

*

The November gales brought waves crashing clear across the train lines; the wind howled about the house, tearing at the high white chimneys, until it seemed that Summerlands might be uprooted and hurled into the ocean. Blanche could no longer wait for the fishmonger's arrival; her first drink of the day was the measure of brandy now slipped secretly into her breakfast coffee. It was Hugh's refusal, on that wild morning, to tap a cask of brandy just delivered, that so enraged Blanche, and was to end in black tragedy for both. He drove off to attend a local auction in silver and fine china. Florrie was sent to Dawlish village to do some unnecessary shopping. It was Millie, the younger of the maidservants, who accompanied her mistress down the cellar steps. Blanche surveyed the brandy barrel.

'Fetch me a hammer and a chisel!'

'Oh madam – do you think we ought to?'

'Do as I say, girl!'

'But madam – if we make a big hole in the barrel, Master's bound to notice. Why don't we bore a tiny hole and push a straw through. Do it that way and nobody'll be any the wiser. You can nip down any old time and take a drink. He'll think he was sold a half-empty cask.'

Blanche grew thoughtful.

'You could be right. Fetch a skewer from the kitchen – a very thin one; and bring two straws while you're up there. Such cleverness as yours deserves a reward.'

When Hugh returned three hours later, maid and mistress lay together, dead-drunk across the cellar floor.

*

Blanche awoke in late afternoon to find a tray of coffee on her bedside table. Florrie looked angry and reproachful. 'I'm off now, madam, I shall have to take Millie to her home, she's in no fit state to walk the cliff-path by herself. I've had to do her work, this day, as well as my own.' The maidservant paused in the open doorway. In a voice that lacked all respect she said, 'Master want to see you in his study – as soon as you can walk there.'

Blanche leaned back upon her pillows, sipped scalding coffee, and began to evaluate her physical condition. She felt slightly nauseated but that would soon pass. Brandy suited her. Very gradually the bedroom and its contents ceased to sway, her head cleared sufficiently for thought. So he wished to see her, did he! She was summoned to his study like a dishonest servant, obliged to stand before him and explain her crime. This state of affairs could not go on. The servant had not even tried to conceal her contempt.

Blanche rose from her bed, and made her way unsteadily towards the dressing-table. She sat down on the little gilt stool and studied the three faces in the triple-mirror. I was beautiful once, she thought. So beautiful that gifted artists wished to paint me. Simeon Solomon compared me to some woman in the Bible. She began to speak. 'Who is she that looketh forth as the morning, fair as the moon, clear as the sun, and terrible as an army with banners?' Blanche leaned closer to her mirrored image.

'Well who is she then? What happened to her? I'll tell you, shall I? She's an unlucky woman. She always finds the little foxes. The foxes that spoil the vine.' She picked up the silver-backed comb and began to drag it through her unpinned hair; she reached for the rouge-pot and placed a dab of colour underneath each cheekbone. A favourite peignoir of lilac-coloured satin lay across a chair. She pulled it on, and began to walk, very slowly, along the crimson-carpeted corridor that led to Hugh's study. She entered without knocking.

He was standing beside the open window that led onto the balcony, a half-full whisky tumbler in his hand – or was it half-empty? Blanche giggled. How foolish he looked, in his blue silk smoking-jacket, the tasselled cap upon his head.

'Caught you,' she cried, 'caught you in the very act!'

'I needed something to steady my nerves after your

disgusting exhibition of this morning.' He did not look at her, but continued to gaze downwards at the darkening garden. 'You know that this sort of thing cannot go on, Blanche.' She began to laugh. 'Don't talk to me as if I were a scullery-maid! Why! You drink twice as much as I do! You always did! Remember how I took the blame – allowed your aunt to put me in an Inebriates' Home? Why, you sanctimonious bastard, you're a bigger tippler than your crazy father! Threw himself out of an upstairs window, didn't he, when he was full of whisky?' Hugh turned to look at her, and for the first time there was no love in his eyes. 'My aunt was right after all,' he said quietly, 'you and I should not have married.'

'Do you think I don't know that?' Blanche screamed. 'I've regretted it every day – oh I could have done so much better for myself if I had waited. I should have had children. That was your fault too. You're a failure, Hugh Fitzgerald! A bloody rotten failure!' She moved towards the side-table which held glasses and bottles. She pointed at the heavy crystal whisky-decanter. 'That's where your courage comes from,' she taunted. 'I'm more man than you could ever be! Who spat in the eye of Mr W.H. Wills, eh? Who sent him a message that told him to swallow our bonfire smoke, and be glad about it? Who had to pawn her jewellery in Exeter, because her husband bought an empty goldmine?'

Hugh's face took on a strange expression. At last he said, 'I shall write a letter to your sister Annis. I shall explain your drinking problem to her. She must be told the truth about you. Happy as I am for Abigail and little Claire to visit Dawlish, all such holidays must now cease. Your sister Blanche, I shall say, has become a hopeless drunkard and is no longer a fit person to be put in charge of innocent children.'

Blanche sought support, and her hand found the pie-crust edgeing of the side table. 'Abigail and little who?' she whispered.

Hugh smiled. 'You thought her name was Blanche,

didn't you my dear? Well it isn't! Frank showed me her Certificate of Birth. He and Annis observed *my* wishes in the matter. Her name is Claire!'

Blanche looked at Hugh but saw Philip, her father; and she felt all that old horror and loathing rise up inside her. Her hand sought and found the slender neck of the whisky-decanter; she lifted it to shoulder height and hurled it. Her aim was deliberate and true; the heavy cut-glass object caught him full in the neck, just below his right ear. What she had not expected was the force of the blow, which unbalanced Hugh and sent him backwards. She watched in total disbelief as he fell back through the window, across the low balcony, and out of her sight. She took three steps forwards towards the desk, and leaned upon it, willing herself not to faint. Time passed and she, incapable of sound or movement, studied the green leather of the armchairs, the pale Indian carpet, the paintings around the walls which Hugh had once told her were very valuable, and known as the 'The Cries of London'.

Blanche became aware of a voice calling from the garden; an old man's voice with the burr of Devon in it. 'Oh master! Whatever have happened to 'ee? I was about to go home when I see'd you fall. I came up as quick as ever I could. Can you stand, now? Hold on to my shoulder. Never mind thik old decanter! Us'll pick that up later on. Good job that tiv' been raining so much lately, master! Leastways you falled on soft ground!'

*

Hugh seemed unhurt. The fall had left him shocked and winded, slightly bruised perhaps, but sober. He walked unaided to the bathroom. Blanche heard the gas geyser hiss and the bath water running. Ten minutes later and the study door opened and closed; she heard the key turn in the lock. If he slept at all that night, it was on the chesterfield or in an armchair. He came down to breakfast quite intact, but for the darkening bruise underneath his right ear.

Blanche said, 'It was an accident.'

He raised an eyebrow. 'Was it?'

She looked at him across the table, and knew that this time there was no way back. In the days that followed, Hugh's hand moved frequently up to his neck; the bruise faded quickly, but he continued to stroke the spot beneath his right ear as if deliberately to remind her of the hurt she had inflicted on him.

The swelling appeared in the week before Christmas. Blanche pretended not to notice. She gave orders to the Dawlish poulterer that a turkey and a brace of pheasants was to be sent to each of her three sisters. Boxes of chocolates, and hand-embroidered blouses were posted to Abigail and Eve. A fir-tree was brought into the hall and trimmed with red candles.

The swelling had increased by New Year. Hugh found it difficult to move his head in any direction. He was, quite obviously, in great pain. On New Year's Day Dr Lovely was called out from Dawlish. He examined the lump and at once asked for towels and scalding water. When Hugh emerged later, from the bathroom, his neck was bandaged.

'What is it?' Blanche asked.

'He's not sure. He thinks it might be some kind of abscess. He's removed skin and tissue from my neck. It's to be sent to a laboratory in Bristol. The result will be back within a week. He's to call again next Tuesday morning.'

Blanche said, 'Today is my forty-seventh birthday.'

Hugh said, 'My father died of a fall from an upstairs window.'

It was to be a week of silences and tensions. Hugh walked daily on the foreshore, the wind whipping at his long cloak, his neck and head enveloped in scarves. Blanche remained sober, as if by so doing she could influence the verdict. They were sitting together in the morning-room when Dr Lovely drove in through the opened gates. At the sound of carriage wheels Hugh glanced towards the window.

'That man,' he said, quietly, 'is carrying my death warrant.'

*

Hugh Fitzgerald faced death as if all of his life had been no more than a rehearsal for the final act.

'I want the truth,' he told Dr Lovely. 'There are plans to be made, affairs that must be set in order. I know that I am a dying man, all I need to know from you is how long I might have to do all that must be done.'

The doctor looked to Blanche. She nodded her assent.

'The verdict is cancer, Mr Fitzgerald. Inoperable and rapid. You may have a year – no more. I can make it easy for you. A nurse can be engaged who is experienced in such cases. With care, your life might be prolonged beyond my first prognosis.'

'No,' Hugh said, 'let's not make it a drawn-out business.'

He turned to Blanche. 'My father had it easier, eh Blanche! His death was also accomplished by a woman, but he died in a matter of minutes.'

*

Good news and bad always come together. The white envelopes, drifting like snow through Madelina's letter-box, brought her joy and sorrow, and a new experience of wild frustration. Talking to David was less satisfying somehow than an hour or two across the teacups with her sister Annis, and there was such a lot to be confided! Mina reached for the tin that contained her best fruit cake. She cut a large slice and wrapped it in greaseproof paper. Classes would be out at four; if she hurried she might just meet Eve on her way home from Trinity School.

Eve, who rarely hurried, was the last child through the school door.

Mina said, 'You haven't been to see me for a long time.'

'I went down to Dawlish with Abi. Since we got back I've had a lot of ear-ache.'

'So how's your mother?'

Mina took Eve's hand and placed the parcel in it. 'I brought you a piece of my cake. I know how you love it.'

Eve smiled. 'You put raisins and sultanas in your cakes; Mother only ever puts currants in hers, and then not many.'

Mina said, off-handedly, 'Oh yes – well speaking of your mother – I've got a bit of good news she might like to hear. My Laura gave birth to a baby boy, down in Exeter. The news came in a letter just this morning. Now don't forget to tell her, Eve, the minute she gets home from work!' Mina paused. 'I got other things to say to her too, sad things.'

'Father goes out on Sunday afternoons,' Eve said helpfully, 'he walks up to Silver Street to watch the traffic. There was twelve motor-cars came past last week, in the space of two hours. Father says that Taunton is getting more like London every day.'

*

Annis said, 'That's our Mina's cake you're eating!'

'She met me from school. She sent a message for you. Cousin Laura got a baby boy, and there's something else she wants to tell you, what is very sad.'

'Is she coming round to see me?'

'I said Sunday was best – '

Annis reached for her coat and hat. 'What time is it, Evie?'

'Five to seven.'

'Your father's working late. His supper's in the oven. Dave Lambert goes to Bible class on a Wednesday evening. Abigail has gone to bed with one of her sick headaches. I'm just going round to see your aunty – I shan't be long – '

Annis stood before Mina's front door; she lifted a hand to the knocker and felt her heartbeat quicken. Did Mina really wish for a reconciliation? What if Eve had been mistaken? At the sound of the drawn bolts she clasped her hands together.

Mina was smiling. 'Well, how nice to see you, Anni! I thought you might be round. I made a fish-pie and an apple-dumpling, in case you hadn't had your supper.' Mina bustled about, turning up the gaslight, placing chairs before the fire.

'Here – let me take your coat. Warm your hands, you must be frozen!'

Annis sat down in Mina's tidy kitchen. Her heartbeat slowed, colour came back to her face. She half-turned towards her sister.

'There's something I got to say – I done a very wrong thing with that photo. I regretted it afterwards. Many's the night I've laid awake – '

''Tis all forgiven and forgotten, maid! We'll say no more about it. I expect there was faults on both sides.' Mina poured boiling water onto the tea leaves, 'Anyway, I got news that you must know about.' She put the lid back on the teapot, and then gestured towards the two envelopes that lay on the scrubbed-top table. 'Come this very day from Exeter and Dawlish, one holding good news, the other bad!'

Annis said, 'Your Laura got her baby, then? I thought as how you'd be down there with her?'

Mina smiled. 'Seems like he was in a hurry. He arrived three weeks early. I shall go down to Exeter of course, and see her through the lying-in.'

'So what did David say?'

Tears filled Madelina's eyes. 'Oh Anni, I never saw my Dave so happy. He always wanted a son you know; well now he've got a grandson. The baby is to be called David Patrick, so Laura says. Dave's already making plans to teach him woodwork and take him fishing.'

Annis sipped her tea. 'What news from Dawlish then?

My maids was down there some time ago and no trouble much to speak of.'

Mina put a finger to her lips. 'Reading between the lines,' she said slowly, 'something very bad have happened to poor Fitzgerald, and all the fault of our Blanche, if I'm any judge!' She sat down, her chair close to Annis, the closely-written pages in her hand.

'Don't trouble to read it all,' Annis' voice was nervous. 'Just tell me what have come to pass.'

Mina sighed and put a hand up to her white hair. 'I never knew a family so plagued with accidents, our Anni! 'Tis like there's some curse put on the Greypaulls, and the ones they marry. From what I can make out, there's a balcony runs around the upper storey of the house in Dawlish. You get onto it by stepping across the low sill of the window.'

'That's right! That's exactly how my Abigail described it.'

'Well it seems that poor Hugh fell out of his study window, over the balcony and onto the lawn beneath. He got no more than a few bruises at the time, the ground being soft from rain. But six weeks later and his neck swells up; a lump comes underneath his ear.' Mina paused dramatically. 'The Dawlish doctor have given him less than a year to live Anni. Hugh Fitzgerald have got cancer!'

Annis covered her face with both hands. For the moment she was silent.

'Cancer?' she whispered. 'But how could he get cancer in his neck from a fall onto soft ground?'

Mina nodded. 'And how could he fall *over* a window sill, *and* the balcony rails. Even if he was drunk, that would have taken some doing!'

'You don't think,' Annis whispered, 'you don't think she might have pushed him?'

'Who knows what our Blanche might do when in a temper.'

Mina said, 'Did you get a turkey and a brace of

pheasants from her at Christmas?'

'Oh yes – well they can afford it, Mina! According to Eve there was more food on a single breakfast time in Dawlish than you and me can afford to buy in a month of Sundays. 'Twas all done for show if you ask me, so that my girls 'ud come home and tell me about it. Our Blanche always was a show-off!'

Mina refilled Annis's teacup. 'I was given to understand,' she said slowly, 'that Blanche and Hugh was bankrupted, and yet by the sound of it, they live grander than ever.'

Annis nodded. 'You should see the clothes and shoes they bought for Abigail; all hand-made, and to measure. But Abi come out with a strange tale the other night. It seems that our Blanche sent her into a jeweller's shop in Exeter. She was to hand over a liddle package and get a big brown envelope in return. Abi noticed later on that Blanche's engagement ring was missing!'

Mina gasped. 'You don't mean to tell me – ?'

'There's something else. You know how Blanche always flaunts that big gold brooch with the diamonds in it?'

'Never off her chest!' confirmed Madelina.

'Not a sign of it! Not all the time my maids was down in Dawlish!'

Mina looked wise. 'You know what she did, don't you? She used your Abi to do business in a pawnshop. A signature would have been needed for such a big sum of money – and the Golden Goose can't write her own name.'

'Oh my godfathers!' Annis paled. 'Just think of my maid, in the city streets, with Blanche's jewels in her hand, and all that money. Why she could have been killed for it, Mina!'

Mina leaned forward to pat Annis's knee. 'Best not to get mixed-up with the Fitzgeralds, Anni; goodness knows what's going on this minute, down in Dawlish.'

*

The February day was mild and still. Hugh had walked to the estuary at Starcross; he had experienced a longing to see the Brent geese for the last time. He watched them for some minutes as they fed from the eel-grass on the mud flats. When the long black skeins came flying in again from Russia, he would be –? He caught at the thought, did not allow it to go further. Time was a factor that filled his mind. Next month, next week, tomorrow? Hugh had accepted Dr Lovely's verdict with a bitter resignation. He had always known that Blanche would, one day, annihilate him. He had heard her quote the Song of Solomon; the words that had been used once by an artist to describe her beauty. 'Fair as the moon – clear as the sun – and terrible as an army with banners.'

Mist creeping in from the sea, plunged the bright day into semi-darkness. Hugh began to walk back towards Dawlish; he took the coast road for safety, and then smiled at this superfluous habit of ingrained caution. Walking, as always, cleared his mind. In spite of the pain in his neck and shoulders, his awareness of increasing weakness, he was still able to make plans and take decisions. Hugh thought about his life. Since birth he had been passed, like a parcel, from the hands of one scheming woman to another. Abandoned by his mother, reared by his Aunt Letitia, jilted by Claire, and destroyed by Blanche. He resolved that the time remaining to him should be his own, and lived in an isolation as comprehensive as his condition would allow. He smiled. His purchase of a lone house, set upon a cliff-top, could not have been improved upon for such a purpose. Every hour, and each remaining day must be made significant, and totally for him. He counted the months from February to November. He would not set ambition too high. Just to see the return of the Brent geese would satisfy him.

*

Blanche had not at first believed in Hugh's illness. It was

only the constant rubbing of his bruised neck, she told him, that had brought up the swelling. Even when told by Dr Lovely that the lump would prove fatal within the year she had thought his prognosis an overstatement. As the doctor's gig drove away down the Exeter road she told Hugh, 'Don't believe that old quack! He's just trying to earn the fat fee you'll have to pay him.'

'I already knew the result, Blanche, before the doctor entered the house. That man is carrying my death-warrant, those were my very words.' The accusation hung unspoken in the air between them. Blanche, who was never ill, and who abhorred all deformity and sickness, said swiftly, 'It's only a little lump. It'll go away if only you'd stop dwelling upon it!'

To link cause with effect was at this point quite beyond her; to feel guilty over any of her actions was not in the nature of Blanche. 'We'll take a ride in the train. It's been simply ages since we were in London. A few dinners at the Café Royal, a visit or two to the theatre, and you'll soon feel like your old self.'

She could not read the look he gave her; his subsequent actions were also beyond her comprehension. He no longer consulted her on any matter. It was while she and Millie were in Exeter on a shopping expedition, that Florrie and the gardener moved a single bed from a guest room, to stand in a corner of Hugh's study. The newsagent's boy no longer called night and morning. All newspapers and periodicals had been cancelled. When questioned Hugh said simply, 'What goes on in the world beyond this house is no longer my concern.' He had written, he told Blanche, to relatives and friends, advising them of his condition, and instructing that they were not to call except on his expressed wish.

'But why?' she pleaded. 'Why cut me off from everybody? If you really are ill, and I don't for one minute think you are, then I shall have need of people round me. I can't care for you. I know less than nothing about sickness.'

'Nurses,' he said, 'nurses will do all that's necessary. Dr Lovely said so.'

'Not in my house, they won't! I've heard stories about private nurses. They march in and take over the whole household. But it won't come to that. All this fuss about a little lump! Men are such cowards about their ailments!'

Spring came, and with the lengthening of the days came awareness of her isolation. Blanche began to watch Hugh, to mark his loss of weight, the increased swelling beneath his right ear. She felt certitude slip just sufficiently to allow doubt in, and doubt infiltrated all her mind until every hour was touched by greyness. Her first twist of fear came with the thought, if he dies – what will become of me?

The summer was unreal; they lived as if suspended in a vast glass bubble. Blanche planned trips to London. She examined her wardrobe, shortened hems according to the fashion, trimmed hats, and posted parcels of discarded clothing to her sister Annis. The trips to London were never taken. Hugh continued to walk daily on the foreshore, and then in late September his study began to take on the appearance of a sick-room, the chesterfield and desk removed, a nurse installed in the adjoining guest room.

The nurse was young and pretty; she sat at Hugh's bedside in the night-hours when pain made sleep impossible for him, and read aloud his favourite books. Blanche questioned the girl about Hugh's condition.

'I want the truth now! Is he really ill, or is that a charade put on to make me feel uncomfortable in some way?'

The girl looked suspiciously at Blanche, 'This is not a subject for joking, madam.'

'I am not joking, young woman!'

'Then you know nothing about illness, madam. Cancer of the neck is not a disease that can be faked. Your husband is gravely ill – but surely you can see that?'

Blanche said quietly, 'What causes such a condition?'

The nurse, who had heard the gossip in the kitchen, said with equal softness, 'It's impossible to say exactly, madam. In your husband's case it would seem that he suffered a blow – a heavy blow – to the neck – just prior to the appearance of the tumour.'

'Is he going to die?'

'That's not for me to say. You must ask the doctor.'

'I'm asking you! Is my husband about to die?'

The nurse looked uncomfortable. 'Well – let me put it this way, madam. I shall expect to be back home in Plymouth to celebrate Christmas with my parents.'

Blanche turned away; she walked towards a dining-room window that looked out onto the ocean. With her gaze upon the water she said, 'He keeps the cellar keys underneath his pillow. As soon as he is sleeping I want you to get them for me.'

'I'm afraid I can't do that, madam. I am a nurse. My whole concern must be for the welfare of my patient.'

Blanched laughed. 'Well sleeping with keys underneath his pillow isn't likely to cure him, is it?'

'I refer to Mr Fitzgerald's peace of mind. He warned me that you would make such a request. I promised that I would not give you the keys on any condition.'

Blanche turned and surveyed the nurse; she spoke sharply, 'This job is well paid, and easy. You have comfortable living-quarters, maidservants who will do your every bidding, an undemanding patient. You would do well to consider these things when I ask you to oblige me in such an unimportant matter.'

'The matter is not unimportant. If it were, then you would not have asked me.'

Blanche moved towards the door. 'I'll get them myself. If he is as sick as you say he is, there is very little he can do to stop me.'

'No, madam!'

The nurse, angry now, stood between Blanche and the door.

'No, madam! You've had your daily allowance of brandy. Florrie follows Dr Lovely's orders in the matter – '

'So what else do you know about me?' Colour flared suddenly in the girl's face.

'I know that a good man lies dying because of your drunken temper. He allows you sufficient brandy to keep you quiet, so that you won't insult the tradespeople of the village, and antagonize the servants!'

'What else do they say about me?'

The nurse, all discretion gone, said, 'You want to hear the gossip do you, madam? Well, opinions about your husband's "accident" are divided. There's one camp that thinks he tripped over the window-sill, and another that swears to it that you must have pushed him!'

'And what do you think?'

'I think you're a fool.' The young nurse, all her anger gone, spoke gently to Blanche. 'I've seen those paintings of you, when you were young. You were beautiful then; you're still a very handsome woman. The drink is spoiling your good looks, but you know that, don't you?' She sighed. 'Ah well, my tongue has lost me a comfortable billet. Don't worry, madam. I'll be gone from here tomorrow morning. Dr Lovely will send up a replacement, I should have left soon in any case. I can't stomach what is going on here.'

*

Many nurses came to Summerlands that autumn, and were dismissed by Blanche; some of them within hours of their arrival. Hugh, too weak now to leave his bed, and totally dependent on their special skills, asked finally that pen and paper be brought to him.

'I intend,' he told Blanche, 'to ask your sister Madelina to come here.'

'She won't even consider it.'

Hugh said, 'I believe she will come. Your sister is a kind and compassionate woman. A good nurse was lost to the world in Madelina.'

To be needed in a house of sickness had always brought out the very best qualities in Mina. By the end of the week she had arrived in Dawlish, prepared to stay for as long as she was needed. She and Blanche dined together on the night of her arrival.

'Dave said at once that I must come to you,' she told Blanche. 'Our Anni will do his washing for him. His sister will cook his dinners. Laura will be coming up from Exeter to spend Christmas in Taunton. Hugh might be well enough by then for me to go home and see my grandson?'

Blanche shook her head. 'He's never going to get well, Mina.' She leaned confidentially across the dinner table. 'Truth to tell, I'm very glad that you have come. There are things on my mind that I can only talk about to family.' Blanche paused. 'You're the first visitor we've had, apart from Dr Lovely and those nurses.'

'But what about his aunty? Surely she – ?'

'He won't let me send for her, Mina. Time is getting short. I'm afraid if he leaves it much longer it'll all be too late.'

Mina said, 'Oh that's awful, Blanche! You can't possibly let him die without saying his last farewells to his aunty. Why, she's been more than a mother to him!'

'I'm not worried about his last farewells! It's the money she allows him that concerns me. That old bitch hates me, Mina! When Hugh's gone she'll cut me off without a penny, and enjoy the doing of it. Without that ten pounds a week I can't possibly live here!'

Mina cried, 'Ten pounds? That's almost three times as much as my David earns, for sixty hours of work in every week.'

'You'll have to persuade him for me, Mina. Point out to him that I shall be left destitute without his aunty's allowance. Tell him he must send for her, right away. You've seen the state he's in. Anything could happen!'

'Still thinking only of yourself, Blanche. You never

change, do you?'

'I've fended for myself since I was sixteen. I was put out on the street by my first employer, and that's a dangerous place to be in London. You've had it easy, sister! Cosy and safe – that's your life. But I wanted more than the rest of you.' Blanche waved a hand at the Sheraton sideboard loaded down with silver, the matching dining table and its fine apportionments. 'You don't think I would let all this slip away, after all it has cost me to achieve it?'

Mina said, 'What has it cost you?'

Blanche pushed her plate away; she picked up her brandy glass and studied its contents. 'They all say that he's going to die, so it won't matter if I tell you now. I never wanted to marry Hugh Fitzgerald. There was somebody else.'

'Well that's no secret, Blanche. Even down in Taunton we heard rumours of your so-called friends in London.'

'Jye was no friend. I met him first when I was sixteen. He was a mason at the Abbey. Our birthdays fell on the same day of the same year. He was totally deaf, couldn't hear a word I said.' She smiled, 'He was a lot like you in his ways, Mina. Buttoned-up tight against the wicked world. Reading his Bible and praying in the Abbey.' Her voice changed, 'Ah, but you should have seen him, Mina. I've met all kinds of men in my life, but never one to equal Jye. I worked magic on him, you know. I hammered six iron nails across a threshold and made him step across them. For as long as I draw breath, Jye Carew's soul is mine, and there is nothing he can do about it.'

'How much brandy have you drunk, Blanche?'

Blanche laughed. 'Let me inform you of the situation at present prevailing in this house. My dear husband keeps the cellar keys underneath his pillows. The servants have been told how much brandy to allow me. Just enough to keep me civil to shopkeepers and skivvies! So what do you think of your fine brother-in-law now,

Madelina?'

'I think he should have done all this a long time ago. Depriving you now is like locking the stable door when the horse has bolted. The damage has been done. I saw the fishmonger's boy slip a bottle to you, soon after my arrival. You've been drunk since tea-time. You hide it very well, Blanche. Nice steady walk, from one room to another. Hardly a stumble on the staircase. Words only slurred just the tiniest bit. But I've known you since the hour of your birth. You were never one of us. There was always something different about you.'

Blanche looked bemused at this battery of accusations; she seized on the one that held most relevance for her.

'What did you mean when you said that the damage had been done? Have you been gossiping with my servants?'

'I didn't need to. The cabby who brought me out here, from the station, couldn't wait to tell me what he knew.'

'And what did he know, Mina?' Blanche's voice was dangerously quiet.

Mina put a hand up to her white hair, tucked a stray strand into its plaited coils. 'He spoke such broad Devon, I couldn't catch it all.' She sounded nervous. 'Anyway – you know how tales spread around a village – what starts off as a bit of an accident gets exaggerated until they're saying it's a murd –' She clapped her hands across her mouth.

Blanche smiled towards Mina's wine glass. 'You shouldn't touch brandy, dear sister, when you're not accustomed to it. Not if you want to keep secrets from me. Come on now. I insist on knowing what the cabby said.'

Madelina looked down at her plain dark dress. 'He must have thought I was a nurse or a new housekeeper. He warned me to be careful. He said I was the twentieth one he had driven out to the Warren, and none of them stayed more than a week! He said that the master of

Summerlands was dying. That his wife had attacked him with a crystal decanter and pushed him off a balcony into the garden. That the cancer in his neck was due to a blow.' Mina's tone fell away into a whisper. 'Was that how it happened, Blanche?'

'I don't know, and that's the truth. We had both been drinking. He said terrible things. I had never thought him capable of deliberate cruelty. He told me that little Blanche had been registered as Claire – and after all that I have done for our Annis! He said he would write to Frank, and tell him that I'm a hopeless drunkard. That I am not a fit person to be in charge of children. I remember picking up the decanter. I saw it strike his neck, just underneath his right ear. But then he fell backwards across the window-sill and over the balcony. The timbers must have been rotted or something.'

'Did you mean all that to happen?'

'Perhaps I did, and perhaps I didn't. It was like that time when I cursed Father as he lay dying. I just wanted an end to it all.'

Mina looked away deliberately; 'I don't understand what you're saying. I don't want to understand it. There's something terrible about you.'

'Somebody else told me that, a long time ago. "Terrible as an army with banners", that's what he said.'

All at once, Blanche sat upright in her chair. Her tone changed. She spoke coldly to Madelina, as if to a servant. 'So don't forget what I told you. Tell Hugh that without his aunt's money I shall end up in the Poorhouse. Talk to him, Mina. He'll listen to you.'

*

The whole house seemed different with Madelina in it. Her first act had been to have Hugh's bed moved from its gloomy corner and positioned beneath the long windows that overlooked the Bay. She had changed the bedlinen, demanded extra pillows; banished beef-tea and calves-foot jelly from his meal tray and ordered that he was to be allowed any food or drink that he so fancied. She trimmed his unkempt hair and ragged moustaches; assisted him to shave, brought his pomade and colognes from the bathroom cupboard. From the hour of Mina's arrival, Hugh felt comforted and secure. No one dared to question the authority of this tiny, dark-clad woman; not even Blanche.

Hugh smiled at her across his breakfast tray. 'Thank you for being here, Mina. It was kind of David to let you come.'

'My husband is a good man; he said straightaway, when he read your letter, that I must go to wherever I was needed most. These so-called professional nurses are all very well, Hugh, but they can never take the place of family.' He looked towards the door. 'Blanche –?'

'Not up yet.'

'No – no, of course not. She rises later and later every morning. This is a difficult time for her. We must do all we can to make things easy for her.' He laid back upon his pillows, and Mina removed the laden bed-tray.

'Aren't you going to scold me for not eating more?'

'You shan't eat a morsel more than you got a fancy to – now tell me, what was your favourite dish when you were little?'

'I always loved apple-dumplings.'

'Could you eat one for your lunch, instead of that broth I just saw bubbling on the stove?'

Hugh grinned. 'I can't remember when I last ate apple-dumpling. Will you share one with me?'

'We'll eat together,' promised Mina, 'I'm quite partial to a dumpling. But not with custard!'

'Oh I do agree. Custard ruins the flavour. A touch of cloves perhaps?'

Mina picked up the tray. 'I'll speak to Florrie about it.'

Hugh said, 'I have to talk to you, Mina. Privately, and as soon as possible.'

'I know.'

'Blanche walks the Lady's Mile every afternoon. We'll

talk while she is absent.'

The apple-dumplings, unadulterated by custard, were served on dishes of dark-blue Chelsea. Madelina, tray on lap, sat beside a window; she could see the splintered wood of the balcony across which Hugh had fallen. She turned back to study the man in the bed, his drawn features, the hair that was almost as white as her own. Propped by many pillows, the bed-tray before him, Hugh picked up fork and spoon with obvious reluctance.

'I'm sorry, Mina. I really thought that I could eat it – '

She said swiftly, 'Now there's an odd thing!' She looked closely at the dumpling on her plate. 'There's no seam to show where the pastry has been joined together around the apple. Now I wonder how Florrie manages to do that?'

Hugh glanced at his plate, and all at once his interest was caught. He began to move the dumpling this way and that. 'By Jove you're right! Not a sign of how the apple got inside it.' He stabbed his fork into the crisp brown pastry and the smell of spiced apple filled the room. He began to eat, very slowly, but with obvious enjoyment. When the food was finished he asked if he might have coffee.

'The nurses said it was bad for me. They never allowed me a single cup.'

Mina said, 'A pot of coffee is on its way, with plenty of cream and brown sugar.'

Hugh smiled. 'And then we must talk, Mina.'

He fell asleep quite suddenly, the coffee cup still in his hand. Mina removed it, and then sat down in the armchair beside the window. So busy had she been since her arrival, that she had noticed only vaguely the beauty of the house and its surroundings. She thought about Blanche, walking the cliff-top path that was called the Lady's Mile. Her sister's need to escape the house must be severe, if she was prepared to go on foot. Since Mina's arrival Blanche had hardly visited the sick-room. Mina tried not to look at the damaged wood of the balcony, but gazed out instead across the dark-grey ocean. She leaned back against the jade leather of the armchair, and allowed the thought that she had resisted since the hour of her arrival. Madelina, prosaic and unimaginative, knew for certain that something evil walked this house; even the servants had remarked upon it.

'There's been a bad feel about the place,' Florrie had confided, 'ever since they two dear girls went back to Taunton. I'd sooner not work here any longer, Mrs Lambert, but times is hard in the village.'

Mina looked at the man in the bed, and remembered Hugh as he had been at their first meeting; tall and fair-haired, elegant and slim, and so proud to have won Blanche. How, she wondered, did he feel now about his present situation?

Hugh opened his eyes. 'Don't look so concerned, my dear. I've known my position for a long time. There's a curious inevitability about all that has happened to me. My father also died in his mid-forties. My mother was responsible, indirectly, for his death.' He turned his head towards the Bay, although the movement clearly caused him pain. 'The Brent geese must be in from Russia. I've been watching for them, but no sighting so far. They roost at sea, you know. When at rest they crowd very close together. They make a fascinating study; they resemble a vast black island far out in the Bay.' He smiled, faintly. 'Wise birds, Mina. They avoid all contact with the human species. I had the same urge to cut myself off from human kind when I first learned the doctor's verdict. I feel better since you came – more at peace with myself, able to face up to my responsibilities in the matter of Blanche. Provision will have to be made for her.' He raised an eyebrow. 'I expect she has already broached the matter with you?'

'She did mention something.'

'Don't be embarrassed, Mina. We both know Blanche. She can't help her nature. I wrote to my aunt, telling her about my illness. A reply came in this morning's post.

She'll be arriving from Bristol in time for tea on Sunday.'

*

The rumble of carriage wheels sounded in the driveway; the front door opened and Mina's raised voice welcomed Hugh's aunt into the house. Blanche hid in the bedroom she no longer shared with Hugh, the room she had furnished in every shade of green from palest eau-de-nil to deepest turquoise.

'I won't see her,' she had told Mina.

'But what shall I say?'

'Say anything you like – just see to it that she and I don't come face to face.'

'But what will she think?'

'She'll think that I'm drunk, but that is of no importance. I want to be told when she is about to see Hugh; now don't forget that, Mina, and don't close the study door completely.'

It was early afternoon when Mina came to Blanche.

'Hugh had a bad night,' she whispered, 'but he feels strong enough now to see his aunt.'

Blanche opened her door just sufficiently to allow a sight of Mrs Porteous as she climbed the stairs and went into Hugh's study. The woman had aged; but still it seemed likely that she would outlive Hugh. Blanche trod carefully along the crimson carpet. The door of the study was not quite closed. She leaned against the lintel, and the sound of voices came clearly to her. Mrs Porteous was weeping.

'But why did you not send for me earlier, Hugh?'

'There was no point, Aunt. There is nothing to be done, and I had no wish to distress you sooner than was necessary.'

'And what of Blanche? I've seen nothing of her since my arrival.'

'Blanche is herself unwell; she is distressed by the illness of other people.'

'How very convenient for her! The sister is a wonderful woman. One would never suspect that the two are related.'

Hugh said. 'I owe a very great deal to Madelina. She has given me comfort and peace of mind in my last days.'

'Oh Hugh, surely there is something to be done –?'

'No Aunt. We must face the truth together, you and I. I am not unhappy. My mind is still clear, and I have Mina to tend to me. There is only one matter that gives me cause to worry.' He paused, 'After my death – what ever will become of Blanche?'

'But surely that is for Blanche to decide? As I recall she was never lacking in initiative in the old days!'

'She is older now, and we have no friends in Dawlish. All her family is in Taunton, and as you know she is quite unable to deal with any kind of business matters.'

'Can't even write her own name,' Mrs Porteous said drily. 'Oh I can see why you are concerned about her.'

'There is something else – ' Hugh's voice grew weak, so that Blanche could scarcely hear him. 'The money you allow me – the ten pounds, weekly. Could that not continue after my death? Blanche will be destitute without it.'

'But there is this house, Hugh, and all the valuable items you have collected.'

'We have massive debts. An illness such as mine tends to be expensive. The debt-collectors will descend like vultures after I am gone.'

'But I have other relatives to consider! Your brother's sons are still at Dartmouth Naval College, and Julian's widow is totally without means. No, Hugh. I cannot possibly continue to support Blanche. It is quite out of the question!'

The small sounds of the house came to Blanche as she crouched beside the study door. She could hear the faint rattle of dishes from the kitchen, the tick of the hall clock; and over all the slow, insistent boom of the waves as they broke against the sea-wall. The extended silence was alarming. She felt sick and faint, and then Hugh's voice came again, stronger and louder, and with a strange note in it.

'I had not anticipated your refusal, Aunt. I had thought that a dying man's last request would have been impossible to ignore. I see now that I had misjudged you. I had thought you a kind and compassionate woman.' Blanche heard the breath rasp in his throat, and she clenched her hands together, willing him to speak again.

'One thing only remains to be said between us. My time is very short now, but of this I am certain.' He paused, and then said in a firm voice, 'You and I, Aunt Letitia, will never meet in heaven!'

'Oh no! You must never say that!' Blanche heard the sounds of renewed weeping. 'If it means so much to you,' the voice hesitated, 'if it means so much to you, then yes! I will continue to support Blanche – '

' – For the rest of her life?'

'For the rest of her life, Hugh.'

*

The Brent geese appeared in Dawlish Bay late that afternoon. They flew in, making ragged lines against the grey sky; Hugh heard their distinctive croaking growl, saw them settle close together, to form a vast black island upon the water. He smiled at Madelina.

'No reason now for me to linger. Blanche is secure and my Brents have come back. I am content.'

He died as the early-morning tide turned towards the ebb, cradled in Madelina's arms.

*

Abigail had waited for something significant to happen, some sign that would mark her out and confirm that she was, indeed, a special person. The mis-spelled and blotted sheet of paper trembled in her hand. The message was more than she had hoped for. It said simply,

Dear Annis,

Send Abi to me with all haiste. My need of her is urjent.

Your sister. Blanche.

Abi fingered the first-class ticket that had come with the letter. By this time tomorrow she would be in Dawlish.

*

Abi tugged on the rope that rang the front doorbell, but nobody came. She stood for a long time, the wind from the sea catching at her skirt, and whipping it smartly about her ankles. Her fingers turned blue around the rope; at last she dropped it and moved away towards the seaward windows, only to find that all the curtains were drawn tight across them. The letter crackled in her pocket. 'Come with all haste,' it had said, 'my need is urgent.' She moved quickly around the house, knocking on doors and tapping on windows. It was the kitchen door that gave way to her frantic turning of its handle. She stepped inside and glanced cautiously about her; the room was dim but even in the half-light she could see the piled-up dishes and dirty saucepans. She called out in a small voice not expecting any answer, 'Florrie – Florrie where are you?'

Abi moved into the hallway, her carpet-bag in one hand, her handbag in the other. The house no longer smelled of beeswax and flowers. She peered into the dining-room, the drawing-room, the little morning-room that was furnished in many shades of yellow. Dust lay thick on every polished surface; a sour stale odour filled the house. A little twist of fear turned deep inside of Abi; she felt panic rise into her throat but could not scream. She set down her bags very carefully upon the crimson carpet; both fists clenched, her back ramrod-straight, she began to climb the stairs.

Aunty Blanche lay on her bed of turquoise-ruffled satin, her face so white and still that Abi thought she might be dead.

'Aunty Blanche?' she whispered.

The pale lips moved. 'Is that you, child?' The voice was husky. 'They've all left me, Abi. They say that I killed him. They won't stay here any longer. I'm so ill and tired, and nobody cares.'

Abi lifted the limp hand and rubbed it gently. 'I care about you. I won't leave you.' She moved to a window and opened the curtains just wide enough to show up the many empty brandy-bottles, the spilled perfume and face-powder on the dressing-table, the plates of congealed food, many with a blue mould growing on them. She turned back to the bed and looked down on the slack mouth and swollen eyelids, the matted hair that hung about the puffy face; and just for that moment the life went out of Abi. She gripped her hands together, and tried to make her voice sound strong. 'Perhaps – perhaps we should send for Aunt Madelina?'

'No! I won't have her anywhere near me! It's only you I want, Abi.'

'Alright. But I have to go downstairs now, Aunty. You need some strong hot coffee and some food inside you. Just let go of my hand, there's a dear. I'll be but a few minutes.'

Abi opened the curtains in the blue and white kitchen, let in winter sunshine, and could hardly believe in the state of the place. She found matches, lit the gas beneath the kettle, found two clean cups and a coffee pot and placed them on a tray. While the water boiled she ground beans, concentrating on the task so as not to cry. She looked up to see Florrie's face pressed against the kitchen window. The maid came in, closing the door carefully behind her.

'So you came then?'

'You wrote a letter didn't you, telling me to make haste? Oh Florrie, how could you have left her in such a condition? She's a sick woman, she might have died – and where's Millie and the gardener, and why have no

233

deliveries been made? All I can find is coffee beans and biscuits.'

'The gardener and Millie stopped coming a long time ago. Then I told the missus that I was leaving. She got me to write that letter for her.' The girl's plump features crumpled suddenly, 'I cudden bide yer no longer. She've turned strange miss. She was always a queer one – but now! Oh my dear Lord! As for deliveries, no bills have been paid since Mrs Lambert left. 'Twas alright in Mr Fitzgerald's time – '

'My aunt is a very rich woman. She will pay her bills, it's just that she's – '

' – Too drunk to attend to any business?' Florrie pointed to a pile of envelopes on the kitchen dresser. 'Not a single letter have been opened since Mrs Lambert went.' She gazed beseechingly at Abi. 'I'm sorry, really I am! Tidden fair to put such a burden on one of your age. How old be you, miss?'

'Eighteen.'

'And you so thin and tiny! I never thought you'd come here by yourself. Like I said to my mother, they'll surely send Mrs Lambert down yer to sort out this lot.'

'Your letter said nothing about my aunt's illness, or that you no longer worked here.'

Florrie coloured. 'I don't make much of a fist when it comes to letter writing, as for your aunty being ill – there's something you'd better know right from the outset. She's not sick but drunk, and not like my father on a Friday night, that's something I be used to. Your aunty never sobers-up no more, and she's violent sometimes. You'd better send for your mother or Mrs Lambert. You'll never manage this lot by yourself!'

'Stay with me, Florrie. I'll see that you get paid – '

'I got another job, Miss. Anyway, my father wudden allow it. This house have got a bad name, lately. There's been talk in the village.'

'What kind of talk?'

'They says your uncle never fell of his own accord. The

gardener see'd what happened. You watch out for yourself!' At the sight of Abi's stricken face Florrie paused. 'Tell 'ee what I'll do though. I'll go round all the tradesmen, tell 'em that you be come here, and that all bills 'ull be paid in full.' Florrie moved towards the door. 'If you want my advice, your best bet is to get the first train back to Taunton.'

She pointed a finger towards the ceiling. 'That's a mad woman what you got to deal with. You should never have come here on your own!'

*

Abi fed her aunt with strong black coffee and Osborne biscuits, then she lit the gas geyser in the bathroom. The house felt damp and very cold. She raked ashes from the bedroom fireplace, searched for kindling wood and coal and found both in an outbuilding. When the water was hot and the fire burning brightly, she guided her aunt towards the flowered bathtub, helped her to remove the soiled nightgown and peignoir, bathed her emaciated body and washed her matted hair.

Abi set to rights the squalid bedroom. She found clean sheets and pillowcases in a linen cupboard, mopped up spillages and breakages, picked up scattered garments and replaced them in drawers and wardrobes. She paused at last to look down on her sleeping aunt. Already the face had a more normal colour, the skin seemed less puffy. With her long red hair spread out across the turquoise pillows, Aunty Blanche was still the most beautiful woman she had ever seen. Abi slept that night curled up on a sofa beside the bedroom fire.

Her first task in the morning was to tend her aunt. In her weakened condition Aunty Blanche was quiet and docile.

'We can't live on coffee and Osborne biscuits.' Abi smiled. 'I shall make up your fire and see you settled nicely, then I shall walk the Lady's Mile into Dawlish village. I must talk to the tradesmen, there's no food left in the house.'

Suspicion flared in the violet eyes. 'You won't come back. You'll catch the first train home to Taunton.' The husky voice broke down in weeping. 'I'm very ill. I've been ill since Hugh – '

'I know, Aunty! I know how ill you are, and I think it's shameful how that Millie and Florrie went away and left you. You were good to me when I was little. Do you remember that birthday when you took me to dinner at the Castle, and the waiter fetched cushions so that I could reach the table?'

The sobbing ceased. 'Do you really remember all that, Abi? You were such a pretty thing in your starched skirts and blue ribbons. I wanted to keep you then. Oh you'll never know how much I wanted to – ' Blanche wept again, and Abi put an arm about her shoulders.

'Don't cry! I'm here with you now, and I shall never leave you. But you must let me go to Dawlish.' Abi's tone was hesitant, 'No bills have been paid since Uncle Hugh died. What's happened, Aunty? Don't you have any money?'

Blanche nodded gently, as if the question gave her huge satisfaction. 'Oh I have money, child. I made certain of that. Madam Porteous was prevailed upon to continue the allowance she had always paid to Hugh. The money is lying in the bank.' Blanche giggled. 'Only trouble is, I can't write my name on that bit of paper called a cheque. It's all there, child, just waiting for me, and I can't sign my name on the lawyer's papers.'

Abi said, 'There's a stack of letters piled up in the kitchen, some of them with Exeter postmarks. We shall need help with all that, Aunty. But first of all let me fetch some food, or I'm liable to faint away from hunger.'

'You'll come back? I'll die now if you leave me.'

'I promised didn't I?'

Blanche said softly, 'You're a dear child Abigail, and you won't be the loser, I can tell you now. Meanwhile – I need a drink. I need a drink very badly. Just to bring my strength back. Just to see me through the lawyer's business. After that, I won't touch another drop. You and I will have a lovely life together.' Blanche opened her eyes and smiled at Abi's worried face. 'Go round to the Mount Pleasant Inn. Ask for a quart of Martell's Four Star. Say that Mrs Fitzgerald has been indisposed, but that all outstanding bills will be paid by the week's end.'

News of her arrival had been spread by Florrie long before Abigail reached Dawlish village. The fishmonger and butcher agreed, reluctantly, to resume deliveries that very day. The baker filled her basket with hot bread and spiced buns. She collected eggs and butter from the dairy; milk and cream, she was promised, would be sent to Summerlands forthwith.

In the days that followed, Abi cleaned the house from cellar steps to attic bedrooms. She lit fires in all the damp rooms, washed and ironed, and arranged the kitchen to her satisfaction. Cash in hand was still her most pressing problem. In a house full of rare and valuable objects there was not a single farthing to be found. Worry about money kept her wakeful in the night, in spite of her physical exhaustion. Her aunt's consumption of Martell's Four Star seemed to increase daily.

It was on that morning when the landlord of the Mount Pleasant Inn refused her further credit, that Abi made her stand. She stood at Aunty Blanche's bedside and eyed the half-inch of brandy that remained in the dimpled bottle. 'No more brandy,' she said briefly. 'The innkeeper wouldn't serve me. You said that you needed a drink just to get your strength back. All outstanding bills paid within the week, that's what you promised!' She began to cry tears of quiet despair. 'I don't know what to do anymore.' She stepped away from the bed. 'I promised not to leave you – perhaps I should send for Mother or Aunt Mina – '

Blanche reached out a hand towards the brandy bottle.

'It's your last,' warned Abi, 'there'll be no more until

we get some money.' She turned back towards her aunt, 'Isn't there something I can pawn?'

Blanche came back, reluctantly, from a far place. 'Don't cry,' she murmured. 'It'll be alright. I made provision long ago for this sort of trouble. Anything that will pawn well, your highness. That's what I told him.' The lids that came down across the violet eyes looked like crumpled tissue paper. The voice slurred. 'Down in the cellar – a loose brick behind the wine-racks – empty wine racks. Pull out the brick and you'll find a jewel case. Bring it to me!'

*

Exeter station was full of drunken sailors; Abi stepped from the train, her thin arms clutched tightly around the crocodile handbag. She shivered. The navy blue costume gave no protection against the winds of March. The jeweller recognised her. 'From Mrs Fitzgerald?' he asked, as he opened the package.

Abi said, 'It's something very special this time. I'm only thankful to have reached here safely.'

The man was shocked. He gazed at the brooch on its bed of crimson velvet. He whistled softly. 'You walked through the streets carrying this?'

'I came down on the train from Dawlish,' Abi told him.

'How much is she expecting for it?'

Abi sought and achieved the air of cool command that she had once observed in Hugh Fitzgerald. In the tone and accents of her Aunty Blanche she said sharply, 'The best loan possible, of course! The piece is unique, surely you can see that?'

He turned the brooch slowly in the morning sunshine. 'Persimmon,' he muttered, 'wasn't that the horse that won the Derby. Belonged to his Royal Highness, didn't it? They said he gave presents to his lady friends.' The man's eyebrows climbed almost to his hairline. 'South African diamonds of the very first water. I've never seen finer in all my life.'

Abi tapped the glass-topped counter with a gloved hand. 'I have to catch the next train back to Dawlish. I must get there before dark falls. I shall,' she said meaningfully, 'be carrying a considerable sum of money.'

The bills were paid, a stock of food laid by, a full cask of brandy stood once again in the Summerlands cellar. Aunty Blanche came downstairs. She walked, supported by Abi, through the neglected garden, in the April sunshine. The gardener was re-engaged; newspapers were ordered from the Dawlish newsagent. Abi spent her evenings reading snippets that might distract her unhappy aunt. Gents' smart suits were on offer in Gray's Inn Road, London, at a bargain price of ten shillings and sixpence. A Mister Godfrey Elliot-Smith of Ludgate Circus was offering a treatment which guaranteed strong nerves and absolute self-confidence. Send three penny stamps, he advised, and I will cure your nervous blushing in only twelve days. A piano, read Abi, could be delivered for an initial payment of ten shillings and sixpence. For five shillings monthly you could become the proud owner of a Coventry High Grade Bicycle. The whole world, said Aunty Blanche, seemed to be living on extended credit, and she really couldn't imagine how it would all end!

Blanche learned from Abi how to write her name in a shaky script. Wincarnis, said Abi, was a better pick me up than brandy; all the newspapers advertised it. Blanche signed the documents necessary for her collection of Aunt Porteous's allowance. Iron Jelloids, said Abi, cost only one shilling for a fortnight's supply, and were guaranteed to restore vitality and give a cheery outlook. An advertisement in *The Weekly Despatch* was offering Pawnbroker's Bargains in a Sale of Unredeemed Pledges. 'How much would it cost,' Abi asked, 'to recover the Persimmon brooch?'

*

Sev walked into the schoolroom on that April morning, he smelled the sharp odours of ink and close-packed bodies; heard the raised voices of his classmates, their sniffling and coughing. It was said that the school bell and railings had been brought here from Ilchester gaol soon after the closure of that dreadful place. He stood, indecisive, until the prison bell began to toll, then he turned and ran out towards a path that would take him upwards into a quiet place.

St Michael's Mount was its proper name, but to Montacute people it had always been known as Miles Hill. Sev thought it an eerie place, its steep woodlands given over to colonies of rooks, and haunted, so people said, by fairies and hobgoblins. Since it gave no grazing for sheep, had no quarries which held stone, there had, until now, been no good reason why he should climb it. But on that morning of grey cloud and wild wind, the Folly that crowned Miles Hill beckoned to him like a finger.

The need to roam had grown more powerful in him lately; his intolerances for certain smells and noises heightened to the point of frenzy. But these were his own peculiarities and easily set to rights. Not so simple were the matters which involved other people. Last night's trouble with his mother still rumbled on in his mind to spoil the morning. He had stood before her in the light of a single candle, and even as she scolded, the thought had come to him that although he was days short of his thirteenth birthday, his height was already equal to her height. The round-ended gloving stick had been pointed at him.

'You're not to go near her, never again! Now you mind my words, David!' His mother always called him David whenever there was trouble over the dark woman.

'Did you think I wudden smell tobacco smoke on you? 'Tisbad enough for me to watch your father burning good money!'

''Twas only a drag or two what I took from her clay

pipe.'

'Clay pipes is the Devil's playthings! Why, there's men I could name who'll see their wives and children go barefoot and hungry, just so long as they can puff tobacco.' The gloving-stick had changed direction; it pointed to the middle drawer of the big oak dresser.

'He've locked it against me.' His mother's face was bitter. 'There's silver in that drawer, give to your father by his mother. Money that's to be spent on tobacco and cider.' She pointed to the loaded gloving-table. 'Here I sit from sunshine to dimpsey, working for the money to keep the six of you children fed, and clothed decent. There's times just lately when I've been hard put to it by Tuesday to find tuppence-ha'penny for a loaf of bread.' Sev looked at his mother's face and learned his first lesson in resentment. He recalled his father's stooped shoulders and tired features; the man also laboured long and hard, according to the dark woman. A slow anger had lit in the boy, against the world and all the people in it, and there was always the sore place in his heart that could never quite heal over. He paused on the steep side of Miles Hill, he sat down in a sheltered place between furze and blackthorn bushes. He watched clouds blow apart, felt the sunshine warm in the sudden stillness. Beyond the golden village, patchwork fields and church spires fell away towards the soft horizon. Sev wondered if that blueness could be the sea. He sat for a long time, listening to the wind, and the rooks crying in the tall trees, and quite unaware of the approach of Llewelyn Powys. The tall tweed-clad figure of the Vicar's son appeared suddenly upon the path. The man sat down among ferns, his spine propped against a fir tree. Sev glanced briefly at the great head covered with tight golden curls. He saw the kind eyes and compassionate features, and knew that no one, since Granfer, had looked at him in that concerned way.

'You are crying, boy.'

Sev turned his face away to where Quantock crouched

low against a wild sky. He fixed his gaze upon the hills, willing his voice to remain steady.

'I idden crying. 'Tis this wind what do smart my eyes.'

'Are you still angry with me?'

'No sir.'

Llewelyn Powys smiled, and that smile Sev thought was like a light coming on in a dark place. 'Well, I didn't die after all. As you can see I've grown strong enough to climb Miles Hill in a half gale.'

Sev said, 'Where's the other one? Him what never stops talking.'

'My brother John? He's in America. He gives lectures – talks to people about books and writing. He'll be home within the week. Our mother is very ill; in fact she's dying.'

'An' what do you do all day long?' Sev felt suddenly curious about this man who had cheated death.

Llewelyn Powys considered. At last he said, 'I write stories in an apple-scented loft above my father's stables. I've had one published recently. Are you a reader, boy?'

'There's nothin' much to read in our house, save the *Sunday at Home*, and the books what come from Chapel. I like the penny dreadfuls but they be hard to come by.'

'Do they punish you for playing truant?'

Sev grinned. 'That don't faze I half as much as sitting in the schoolroom. 'Tis worth a beating now and again to get away from teacher. I won't be there much longer, anyhow. Next week I got my thirteenth birthday.'

'And what does that signify?'

'I leaves school o' course! I shall be a man then.'

'What will you do? Has your father apprenticed you to the masons' craft?'

Sev's lips thinned into a hard line. 'They idden bothered about I. 'Tis on'y the maidens they be concerned for.'

'You have sisters?'

'Five of 'em. All smart as paint, and good as gold. I be

242

what they calls the black sheep. They didden never want me in the first place. I was took to live wi' Granfer when I was o'ny months old.'

'Your Granfer being Shepherd Honeybone who died a few years ago?'

Sev looked surprised. 'You know'd my Granfer?'

'Indeed I did. We talked many times upon Ham Hill.' Llewelyn paused. 'You miss him, don't you? I recall, you were always with him as a small child.'

'Fancy you taking notice o' that!' Sev's top lip trembled, and just for a moment he could not speak. When the words came back to him they were bruised and quiet.

'They never told I he was dead! I see'd the corpse-candle leave his house, and go flittering along until it come to a churchyard. I saw it go down behind the wall onto the very spot where he lies buried.' He turned an anguished face towards Llewelyn Powys. 'I cudden believe that he was gone. I kep' on lookin' for 'un. Nobody told me nothin'. They wudden let me talk about it. All for the best, they said. He's wi' Jesus in Heaven.' Sev's top lip steadied; he said in an angry tone, 'What do Jesus want wi' Granfer? He promised me once that he 'ud never go away. Why, I never even goes as far as Yeovil, thass what Granfer said.' Sev worried at a loose thread on his shabby sweater. 'I thought that corpse-candle was meant for me. There's times when I cud wish it had been. I've thought and thought about it. Granfer know'd he was all I had in the world, yet he goes away an' leaves me.'

Llewelyn said gently, 'Is that why you followed John and me throughout that extraordinary summer? They told you I was dying, and you wanted to see for yourself where the dead go! I wish I could tell you, boy, but I cannot.' He smiled. 'I've contemplated mountains in Switzerland and asked myself that very question. Stay away from mountains. That silence is designed to shrivel a man's soul!'

Damaris went to the school; she stood in the classroom where she herself had excelled in every subject taught. She asked, tentatively, about Sev. The schoolmaster had nothing good to say about him. Insolent and lazy, he told her. Rude and outspoken. Shiftless and a dreamer. Has spent most of his days – when he deigns to honour us with his presence – in looking out of windows, and distracting those who wish to work.

Jye was no help. 'That do take a certain kind o'boy to train up for mason and carver. He'm too flighty, too many-minded. Can you,' he asked her, 'see that boy tied for seventy hours a week to a mason's banker?'

Maris thought about it, but hard as she tried she could not call up this satisfying picture. She remembered Sev riding on her father's shoulder; the small boy running to and fro between the sheep; spending bitter nights without complaint upon the Hill, when ewes were lambing.

'He might look like me,' she said reluctantly, 'but he got the restless roamin' ways of your old mother. He might make a shepherd, given time and a good master?'

'Drayton's farm,' she told Sev. 'He wants a boy to train up as a shepherd.'

'Not sheep,' Sev's face was pale. 'Never sheep! I can't abide the creatures!'

'Well, you'll have to go as general help then. There's nothing else for you.'

Farmwork was for the dullard, for those who were strong in the arm and thick in the head. To be marked down in this way was both shocking and unexpected. Sev started work on a Monday morning, uneasy in the stiffness of new corduroy breeches, his feet encased in hobnailed boots of cheap black leather. The monotony of each task was an intolerable burden; sent after milking, to pick stones and flints from a distant field, Sev lay down beneath a hedge and slept. He was always tired. Still small for his age, his bony frame lacked the muscle necessary for carrying milk pails, the lifting of heavy tackle. At the end of that first week his wage of two shillings and sixpence was paid directly into his mother's hand.

'And he's not worth that much!' the farmer told her. 'A more dislikeable liddle tyke 'ud be hard to find. His sour looks is enough to turn the milk off!'

Sev's misery had, until now, been of the variable kind. In other summers, small escapes had still been open to him. He had lain beneath the honeysuckle hedges that led out to Odcombe, and read forbidden copies of the novels known as penny dreadfuls. He had talked on Miles Hill with Llewelyn Powys, exchanged words that had fired his imagination and stretched his mind. 'Stay away from mountains,' the tall man had said. 'That silence is designed to shrivel a man's soul.' 'Are you a reader?' he had asked; for weeks those words had lain dormant, but now among the tedium of stooking sheaves, the drudgery of cleaning cow-sheds, Sev knew that to be a reader, like Llewelyn Powys, was the one thing in the world he craved to be.

The penny dreadfuls, so called because of the gaudiness of their jackets and their low price, contained nothing more harmful than stories of adventure, and heroism of the more improbable kind. These tales, told in simple language, satisfied some deep need in him to know more of the world and the people in it.

He now slept on a truckle bed in the corner of the living-room, on a cot of narrow canvas that was unfolded nightly. When the house was quiet, Sev read by rushlight, straining his vision over smudged print on yellow paper, to fall asleep and dream of India and Egypt, of soldierly valour and gentlemanly conduct. Leaving a poor home and uncaring parents, was, it seemed, a necessary spur to every hero of the penny dreadfuls. London was the place where transformation occurred. Puny boys turned overnight into handsome, six-foot mashers, who committed some small crime out of desperate need, and were promptly obliged to flee the country and join the Foreign Legion.

Sev asked his father about London. He had found Jye on that summer's evening in his usual spot among the rose bushes that bisected the long vegetable garden. They gazed warily at one another, like strangers who meet for the first time in a place of danger. Sev noticed nothing of the scents and colours, all his attention was for the big man with the stooped shoulders and dark, unhappy face. He moved his lips carefully so that his father might understand.

'London,' he said, 'you was once in London, wasn't you?'

'Aye.'

Sev watched his father's hands move among the blooms; the month was July, the roses at the peak of their perfection.

'What's it like – London?'

The answer, spoken slowly in the deep voice, was not at all what he expected.

'A bad place, full of wicked people. A place for the likes o' we to bide away from.'

Something terrible must have happened to his father up in London. Sev probed further.

'You was living there for a long time.'

'I worked on St Paul's Cathedral and Westminster Abbey.'

'There must have been a lot of life goin' on there?'

His father looked meaningly at him. 'I was there to do important work. I never was a flighty feller.' The hard tone softened. The lips beneath the black moustaches twisted briefly into a near smile. 'Don't 'ee like that farm job?'

'Not much.'

'I'll ask roundabout, see if I can find something better for 'ee. You be on'y thirteen. 'Tis too soon for thee to be thinking about a place like London.'

They had never spoken together at such length or in so personal a manner, the rare trace of gentleness in his father's voice almost unmanned Sev. He felt tears burn behind his eyelids. He fell back on his resentments, pulled them, like a cloak, around the exposed places of his heart. Without the conviction that he was, and had always been, the unwanted member of his family, he was nothing.

*

Bank Holiday that year fell on Monday, the third of August. Jye Carew walked to Martock in the evening sunshine; he sought out and spoke to the foreman carpenter who worked for Hebditch.

'I got a boy what needs employment. Is there a chance that you might take 'un on?'

The man looked doubtful. 'In the normal way I'd have said no. But with all this trouble what they say is coming – well, I cud be left short-handed if all my young joiners gets conscripted.'

Jye said, 'What trouble's that, then?'

'Good God man! Don't you never read the papers?' He pushed a newspaper at Jye. The headlines read 'Europe Drifting to Disaster'. 'Last Efforts for Peace'. 'German Yacht Withdraws from Cowes'.

Jye said, 'Whass it all about then?' He laid down the paper. 'I be hard of hearing,' he explained, 'I don't catch the gossip what goes about, and my wage don't run to the buying of news-sheets.'

''Tidden no gossip, man! We be on the brink of war. Some bloody old Archduke got hisself shot in a place called Sarajevo, and the upshot is that our poor soldiers have got to go and fight the Kaiser!'

Jye said, bemused, 'So you'll gie my Sev a job, then?'

'Send un over in the morning. Us'll see what he can do.'

Sev had started walking soon after first light. His mother had packed a hunk of bread, a piece of cheese, and a raw onion in his satchel. The food was to last him for the whole day. The road to Martock was covered with the fine pale dust of summer. Sev took off his boots and hung them by their leather laces around his neck. He liked the feel of the dust between his toes, felt a lift at his heart to see the white road stretching out before him. The day was the fourth of August, 1914. The weather for some days past had been fine and hot.

Hebditch and Son, Joiners and Carpenters of Martock, made sheds and chicken houses for the local farmers. Sev thought he might like to be a joiner, it must be less hard and more interesting than farm work. His father had said that there might be a war. His mother had said that this was the day of Mrs Mary Powys's funeral. John Cowper had come, looking older and thinner. It must be hard work, this business of being a great and famous man. Sev did not like work. There were scarlet poppies growing by the roadside; he picked a handful of them and stuck them in his cap-band. He chased a rabbit until it disappeared into a ditch. He paused to hear a linnet singing. He thought about work; the way it never seemed to end. Already he was hungry. He sat down by the wayside and ate half of the bread and cheese. When Sev arrived at Hebditch and Son, men had been hard at work for half an hour.

The foreman-joiner looked at the scarlet poppies wreathed in Sev's cap.

'The country's at war with Germany,' he said, 'and you come in half an hour late on your first morning!' He reached for a broom. 'Take this! Sweep up all the shavings, keep all the floors clean. That'll be your job for the next six months!'

*

The sunshine days of that early August made war seem unlikely. To the trippers who sat on Dawlish beach, the newspaper headlines were a subject for discussion while their children built sandcastles and paddled in the warm blue water. For Abigail Greypaull, standing high above them, picking beans in Summerlands' kitchen garden, the talk of war made a convenient diversion; a ploy to distract her aunt in the long summer evenings from an overwhelming need to drink.

In those first months of their time together, Aunty Blanche had made promises to Abi. She had foresworn brandy, vowing never to touch another drop if only Abigail would stay with her. The puffiness had left her face, her red hair had regained its lustre. There had been good times, days when they had travelled to Exeter on the Devon Belle, shopped for clothes, taken lunch at the Grand Hotel. Heads had turned to admire the handsome woman and her young companion. Abi had been happy then; she hardly ever thought of Taunton.

She picked the last bean and placed it in the vegetable basket. She went back to the blue and white kitchen and began to assemble bowls and saucepans, moving confidently from cupboard to table as if the house belonged to her. Abi sliced beans and peeled potatoes. She thought about Florrie, who had said that evil walked the house. Summerlands in summer held no hint of danger. Abi had filled the light and lovely rooms with roses, opened windows to let in the sounds of the sea. One room only had been closed against her. The door of the study had remained locked since her arrival, Abi set a saucepan on the gas stove with an unnecessary clatter. Aunty Blanche was not mad but unhappy; and miserable women always turned to drink, even those who couldn't afford it. Since the balcony rails had been repaired, no sign remained of poor Uncle Hugh's mishap. Abi tried not to think about him, except at those times when she and Aunty Blanche took flowers to his grave. She broke eggs into a bowl and began to beat them. It was, she felt sure, those visits to the cemetery that had caused the brandy habit to creep back. Just lately there had been the bouts of black depression; the nights when her aunt, wakeful and restless would pace the house, blaming herself for the manner of Hugh's death. She reproached herself for all the hard words she had ever spoken to him, the way she had failed to appreciate his goodness to her.

'Even in his last hours,' she told Abi, 'all his concern was for my comfort.'

Victory over Mrs Porteous seemed to be her aunt's only satisfaction. 'Ten pounds a week for the rest of my life, that's what she vowed to Hugh, and let me say this, Abigail! I intend to live forever!'

*

The roses had all fallen. Abi picked chrysanthemums and placed them in tall vases, until their bitter-sweet scent filled the house. The rooms smelled once more of flowers and beeswax polish. She closed all the windows against the cold air of October, but could not shut out the moaning sounds made by the wind. The war had come. Already there were shortages of food in Dawlish. Several banks were said to have closed their doors, so that paper money might be substituted for gold coin. Lord Kitchener was demanding the voluntary enlistment of one hundred thousand men. Sermons had been preached in local churches about the Angels of Mons; the ghostly bowmen who were said to have come to the aid of the defeated British Army. Rumour said that ten thousand Russian troops had landed at Southampton. But nothing could conceal the truth that the British were in full retreat. Placards and posters appeared in every town and village; the pointing finger of Lord Kitchener told every fit young man 'Your King and Country Need You!'

Aunty Blanche needed Abi. No mention had been made of engaging another servant. 'So much nicer, dear,' Aunty Blanche had said, 'just the two of us together.' But it was Abigail who cooked the meals and washed the dishes, who polished windows, cleaned firegrates and silver, dusted and scrubbed. The black carpet with its sprays of pink, embossed roses was her greatest torment; her aunt was particular about it, the use of dustpan and brush seemed only to aggravate the problem. She asked her aunt what she should do.

'Damp tea-leaves,' was the answer, 'spread thickly every morning and brushed-up when dry. That was the method I used when I was a servant girl in London.'

Those final words had lodged in Abi's mind and would not go away. She had not, until then, considered what was her position in this household. Was she the beloved niece, the stay and comfort of her bereaved aunt? Or was she a servant, to be petted and patronised at her aunt's whim? On those trips to Exeter, when they had dined at the Grand Hotel, Abi had needed to keep silk gloves on her hands in order to conceal their chaps and blisters. There were days when she could do nothing right, nights when she lay wakeful, remembering Uncle Hugh and all that had come to pass in this house.

Martell's Four Star, she felt sure, was brought regularly to Summerlands beneath the apron of the fishmonger's boy. Despite all her promises to Abi, bottles were secreted by Blanche in improbable places. Sometimes she would lie, outright, pointing to the empty bottle and denying that she had touched a drop.

'I dropped the whole bottle,' Blanche would cry. 'Every single drop has soaked into the carpet. If you don't believe me, then get down on your knees and sniff.' Oh, her aunt was clever! Just enough brandy had been spilled to create an odour, but Abigail was not deceived.

Abi wondered for just how much longer she could endure this strange enclosed existence. It was with feelings of relief and terror that she read the letter penned by Eve.

Dear Abi,

Please come home as quick as you can. Father is very ill with double pneumonia and pleurisy. The crisis is expected to come at the weekend. Mother wants you here, and so do I.

Your loving sister, Eve

Blanche was rarely surprised by her own emotions; she was, she believed, quite a simple person, one who had always known what it was she required in life, and whose wants, with two major exceptions, had been satisfied beyond her dreams. That she should feel sorrow for Hugh, remorse about the manner of his dying, was so unexpected that she could hardly recognise as Blanche, this grieving widow that was herself.

Brandy had become her master; she no longer needed food or warmth or the company of others. Even Abigail, her beloved daughter, had failed her in the end. She had pleaded that Abi should call her 'mother', but the chit had refused.

'Oh yes,' Blanche had cried, 'your mother is in Taunton, but when you go home to her, ask her where your father is?' She had not meant to say it; it had been the brandy talking. But Abigail had only looked perplexed and walked away. It was with mixed feelings that she heard Abi read to her the letter sent by Eve.

'So you'll be going back to Taunton?'

'I'm sorry Aunty, but I've got no choice. Eve says that Father's dying.'

It was early in the morning, in that tricky time between her first drink and her second. 'All the men die young in this family,' Blanche spoke with difficulty. 'No stamina – no guts. They just give up the ghost and die.' The words made her think of Hugh, and tears filled her eyes. 'I never meant that he should die. It was an accident, Abi.'

'Of course it was. Lots of people die of cancer. Nobody thinks that it was your fault.'

'I wanted it to end,' Blanched sobbed, 'I wanted a stop to all the arguing and trouble. But I never wanted him to – '

Abi placed an arm about her shoulders. 'Don't cry,' she said, 'I'll bring you some coffee, and a poached egg on buttery toast, done just the way you like it.'

'Don't want toast and egg.' The petulant voice began

to wheedle. 'Just fetch me the new bottle, there's a dear girl! You'll find it in my hatbox underneath my sable bonnet.'

Abi said, 'I'll go into Dawlish just as soon as it's full light. I'll find Millie and ask her to come up and stay with you for a few days. You'll be alright with Millie, won't you?'

'I'll be alright when you hand me that bottle! Now bring it you little bitch. I shan't ask for it again!'

Abi opened the heavy wardrobe door; she removed the lid of the green and white striped hatbox and felt beneath the sable bonnet. Her fingers found the bottle, but there was something else! She pulled out a metal object not much longer than her hand.

'I never knew,' she said, 'that you kept a pistol, Aunty?'

Hugh had slept, when in South Africa, with the pistol underneath his pillow. He had shown it to her once, but would never allow her to touch it. 'I keep it for our protection. Of course, it isn't loaded. One would only need to point it, and wear a threatening expression.' He had put it in her hatbox on their return to Dawlish.

'Somewhere away from our curious servants,' he had joked, 'we're not likely to need it here, in any case.'

Blanche held out both hands. In one, Abi placed the brandy bottle; in the other she laid the pistol.

'I'll just pack a small bag, Aunty. I don't suppose that I'll be gone for long. I'll call and see Millie on my way down to the station. She won't mind coming in for a day or two, especially if you pay her well.'

Abi left the house without a backward glance. All her thoughts were with poor Father back in Taunton. She called on Millie, who agreed reluctantly to go to Summerlands at once, and stay there until Abi should return. The morning was cold; a white frost rimed the fields of Devonshire. There were Christmas trees in cottage windows. She wondered, vaguely, if Christmas had passed or was it yet to come? Abi wore her navy blue costume, and the dainty shoes with their bows of petersham. A long cloak of scarlet wool, with a fleck of navy woven in it, was her aunt's most recent gift. Abi wore it with style, as she did the scarlet cloche hat with its navy feather. The train was filled with soldiers; aware of their admiring glances, Abi lifted her chin and gazed coolly at them in the best manner of her Aunty Blanche.

'Now that's what I calls a classy bird,' she heard a sergeant say.

'Not your sort, Jacko!' laughed a corporal. 'You couldn't afford to keep the likes of her in shoe-leather.' Abi smiled, and pressed her chapped hands together, thankful for their concealment inside her fur-backed gauntlets. It felt strange to be out in the world, among normal people, and away from the hushed splendour of thick pile carpets and delicate china; from the white house and its locked room; and the daily search for concealed brandy bottles.

The soldiers were celebrating. Abi thought they might have won a battle, until she recognised their song. 'Auld Lang Syne' was a tune sung only at New Year. Abi turned to the woman who sat beside her. 'What month are we in?' The woman looked surprised. 'Why, it's New Year's Eve, my dear. Tomorrow will be the first day of 1915 – and God only knows what dreadful things that year will bring us.'

Abi knew then with a sense of shock, that Christmas had come and gone, quite without her knowledge.

*

Eve had put clean sheets on the big double bed that she would have to share with Abi. She had sneaked two of Mother's best lace-edged pillowcases in an effort to live up to the standard of elegance to which Abi must have grown accustomed after one year lived in Dawlish. She smoothed the clean white honeycomb-bedspread, gave a final polish to the bedstead's brass rails and knobs. She shook the bowl of pot-pouri that stood on the dressing table, until a fragrance of roses filled the room. It wasn't Summerlands by many a long mile! But it would have to do!

Through the open doorway of her parents' bedroom, Eve could hear the sounds of Frank's laboured breathing, and the quiet voice of Aunt Madelina, soothing and reassuring him that all would, in the end, be well. Eve bunched her fingers, pressed knuckles against her mouth to stiffle sobs. If anything should happen to Father, however would she bear it?

The sound of a knock had her rushing down the narrow staircase. She flung wide the front door to find Abi standing on the doorstep in her scarlet and navy, the feather on the cloche-hat nodding gently in the wind. Abi came into the dark little hallway. She surveyed Eve with shocked eyes. 'You're taller than me,' she said crossly, 'And you're only fourteen. I never expected that to happen.' She held Eve's arm and turned her around. She studied Eve's legs in their black woollen stockings. 'You've got long legs,' Abi sounded envious, 'and you're not fat any more.' Grudgingly, Abi said, 'When you put your hair up you'll be almost pretty.' She walked into the living-room moving elegantly on her high-heeled shoes. She flung her cloak down on one chair, her hat upon another; Eve watched, admiring every move until Abi stripped off her gloves.

'Oh your poor hands! Oh Abi, whatever have you been doing down in Dawlish?'

Abi sat down close to the fire. 'Never mind my hands. Tell me about Father!'

Eve said, 'He went to watch a rugby match – his nephew Joe was playing half-back for Somerset. Mother told him not to go in the pouring rain, what with his overcoat being so thin, and there being no shelter much to speak of. But he would go! He came back soaked to the skin. The very next day he started with a cold. It got onto his chest, and in no time he had a fever. Now the doctor says that 'tis double pneumonia and pleurisy on both lungs. The doctor wanted to use leeches on him, but mother put her foot down! They expect the crisis tomorrow night – that's when it'll go one way or the other. Oh Abi! You don't think he's going to die, do you?'

'Of course he won't! Aunt Mina's up there with him – I recognised her hat and coat hung up in the hall. Father won't dare to die if Madelina says he musn't.' Abi kicked off her high-heeled shoes and spread her toes before the fire's warmth.

'Put the kettle on, maid. I'm tired enough to sleep for a whole week. It'll be nice to be waited on for a day or two. I've had a hard time down in Dawlish.'

Eve filled the kettle and set it on the hob. 'But I thought she had servants. I imagined you being all posh, drinking tea in that drawingroom, and eating your dinner off pretty dishes, with wine and stuff.'

Abi leaned back in her chair. Eve studied her sister, alarmed at the pallor and thinness of her. 'Did she make you do house-work then? I thought you went down to Dawlish as a lady's companion? That's what mother's been telling everybody.'

Abi said, 'Don't repeat a word of what I'm going to tell you. Mother'll have enough on her plate with Father's illness; and you know what she's like about her own family. Well, when I got there, the maids had left. The house was like a pigsty. You'd never have recognised Summerlands, Eve. It broke my heart to see it. I cleaned the place through, from attic to cellar.' Abi paused. 'Things seemed to go along quite well, after that. I persuaded Aunty not to drink so much, and she was sober for most of the day. It was when the headstone was put up on Uncle Hugh's grave that the trouble really started. She kept going to the cemetery, and ordering me to read the words that his Aunt Porteous had said should be engraved on it. The text said "He giveth His beloved sleep," and it was this that seemed to upset her most.'

'I was his beloved,' she kept crying, 'and I was the one

who gave him sleep!'

Eve said, 'Do you think she's gone mad, our Abi?'

'Mad or drunk.' Abi's voice was sleepy. 'Makes small difference in the long run. I was glad when your letter came – not because of Father, of course, but just to get away for a bit. I'd forgotten what the normal world was like. Some soldiers whistled at me on Exeter station –' The tired voice slipped into silence. As Eve brought the teacup towards her sister she saw that Abigail already slept.

*

To survive the crisis of pneumonia and pleurisy was rare among the very poor. Even for those of the respectable working class, like Frank and Annis Nevill, recovery from such an illness would depend on a sufficiency of good food and warm blankets. Most of all, and more difficult to come by, it required nursing of the skilled and devoted kind.

Madelina came just as soon as she was told about Frank's sickness. She had pushed the tearful Annis gently from the bedroom, instructed her on the preparation of beef tea and calves' foot jelly, and showed her how poultices for the chest should be made.

The crisis began on that New Year's Eve, soon after the arrival of Abigail. Mina sponged Frank's feverish body, laid cold compresses across his burning forehead, wetted his parched lips, and changed, repeatedly, his sweat-soaked sheets. It was Mina who refused to leave him through his hours of delirium and bouts of ague; she who slept, fully-clothed, on a hard chair at his bedside, when weariness finally overcame her.

By the afternoon of New Year's Day, Frank's fever had broken. Pale and exhausted, but his temperature normal, and in his right mind, he lay back on piled-up pillows and glimpsed his reflection in the dressing table mirror. He grinned weakly. 'Who's the old fellah in the bed?' he asked Madelina.

She smiled. 'It suits you very well, Frank; makes you look quite distinguished.'

In the two weeks of Frank Nevill's illness, his dark brown hair had turned a snowy white.

*

Without Abi to chivvy her into getting dressed and coming downstairs, Blanche remained in bed. She had waited after Abigail's departure for Millie to arrive. The girl came, but with obvious reluctance, persuaded only by Abi's promise of good pay.

'What day is it?' Blanche asked.

'Why, 'tis New Year's Eve, madam.' Millie sounded nervous. 'I shan't be stopping overnight, madam. Us got a bit of a party planned in the village. There's some soldiers on leave from the front – but I'll see you safe and comfortable before I leave.'

'I don't need you here overnight,' Blanche said sharply. 'I was never a nervous woman, and in any case I have this for protection.' She waved the ancient pistol vaguely in the direction of Millie, and laughed when the girl began to scream.

'It's not loaded, you ninny! But don't spread that information round the village. Now bring me my handbag, there's a good girl.' She placed five sovereigns in Millie's hand.

'A sovereign for yourself, and with what remains you shall purchase brandy for me. Go to the Mount Pleasant Inn and tell them Martell's Four Star for Mrs Fitzgerald.'

She waved the girl away from the bedside. 'You shall bring me a light lunch on a tray. I intend to enjoy myself in my daughter's absence.'

Millie brought the brandy, and hid it in unlikely places, as instructed by Blanche. One bottle and a clean glass stood on the bedside table. She looked doubtfully at her mistress.

'Oh madam, I don't think it's wise for you to – '

'Go away!' Blanche screamed. 'You're as bad as that

snivelling daughter of mine! I deserve a little pleasure. It's my birthday tomorrow.' She smiled suddenly, and just for that moment her face held all its old charm and enchantment.

'Go to your home, my dear,' she said softly, 'enjoy your celebration with the gallant soldiers. I'll see you in the morning, but not too early.' She glanced towards the bottle. 'I have every intention of sleeping late.'

Millie said, 'You'll come downstairs and lock the doors behind me? I've drawed all the curtains and lit the gaslights.' She watched as Blanche rose unsteadily from her bed.

'Are you sure you'll be alright, ma'am? I could stop a bit longer.'

'For mercy's sake go, girl! You'll drive me to drink with all your twittering and moaning.' Blanche laughed heartily at her own joke. 'My daughter is just the same, you know, she worries about me too.' Blanche pulled on her lilac peignoir and stood by the bedside, swaying only slightly. 'Look,' she cried, 'steady as the rocks that this old house is built on.'

Blanche pushed home both locks across the front door, making as much noise as she was able. Millie waited, she knew, upon the doorstep, to hear the reassuring clicks. The sound of the girl's steps grew faint across the driveway. Blanche heard the gate close. She began to move, very slowly, through the silent house, visiting each room, and seeing Hugh in every one. The house was clean and well cared for. How fortunate she was to have such a daughter. Abi knew how particular she was, especially about the black, rose-patterned carpet. When Abigail returned from Taunton they would take a holiday together. Paris would be nice in April. Blanche moved back into the hall, she looked upwards, and the stairs seemed to have multiplied, they looked much steeper; she doubted her ability to climb them. She stood, both hands around the newel-post to prevent herself from falling. She remembered the half-empty bottle beside her bed, and all the other bottles hidden safely in places where Abigail would never think to look. The need for a drink suddenly became urgent. She began to stumble upwards, the hem of the lilac peignoir catching dangerously in the high heels of her velvet slippers. She came to the locked door of Hugh's study, paused momentarily beside it, her ear pressed against the panel. She knew that he was in there; but the key was underneath her pillow. He could not escape. She entered her own bedroom and closed the door, very carefully behind her. Millie had tended to the fire before leaving, and its glow now lit the room. Blanche gazed with pleasure at the ruched satin of the turquoise bedcover, the pillows and cushions of eau de nil lace. She reached for the bottle and began to drink from it, tipping it high so that its golden colour reflected firelight. She moved to the dressing-table that was loaded down with matched silver mirrors and brushes, the perfume bottles and jewel boxes once bought for her by Hugh, from Penhaligon's of Bond Street. Bowls of white hyacinths stood on little tables and on window-sills. The warmth of the fire drew out their scent; Blanche breathed in the perfumed air and smiled. She touched polished walnut and emerald velvet, pale green silks and darker green brocades.

Every single item was of the very best quality; all of it expensive. Hugh was dead, but nothing had been lost and much was gained. She had Abigail and Summerlands; she had ten pounds a week for as long as she might live. She had learned to write her own name. Money came from the bank at a few strokes of her pen.

Blanche sat down in an armchair; she watched the shadows of the fire's flames go chasing across the pale green of the carpet. Once again she tipped the brandy bottle and drank deeply from it. The clock in the hall began to strike, and without needing to count the strokes she knew that it was midnight, and that this was the first day of 1915, and her fiftieth birthday. Half a century of life behind her, and still she did not feel old. *I intend to* live forever, she had told Abi, and was ever a woman more comfortably placed so to do?

Blanche waited, and the image of Jye Carew rose before her, as it always did on the last stroke of this particular midnight; and this time she saw him more clearly than ever. His dark face was beaded with moisture, the yellow fog of London swirled thickly about him.

'I'll say it slow and clear,' he told her, 'so that you can understand me. I don't want you! Not now – not never.' She reached for the brandy bottle and again drank deeply from it, but the vision of Jye would not go away.

'My mother said that death will come to the man you choose. That you and me would never come together.' He placed a hand on the parapet of Westminster Bridge, and looked down towards the water. Blanche hooked her arms into his and swung him back to face her.

'There's more! I know there is. You had better tell me, Jye. I shan't leave you alone until you do!'

He spoke the words in a voice made terrible by its tonelessness. 'No peace shall come to her,' quoted Jye, 'until she lies silent beneath the stone; until she rests with her face towards the sea, the sound of the ocean beating in her dead ears.'

'Sweet Jesus help me!' Blanche heard her own prayer with a sense of shock; she reached for the brandy bottle, and finding it empty she hurled it across the room. She lay back in her chair, closed her eyes, and willed the image of Jye Carew to depart from her; but he remained, superimposed upon the darkness of her closed lids. Blanche became aware of tiny sounds. The slight shift of burning coals in the firegrate, the drumming of her fingertips upon the chair's arm; and above all, the roar of the winter ocean beating loudly and endlessly upon her eardrums. She reached a hand towards the bedside table. Blindly, she sought for and discovered the cold metal pistol. The image of Jye grew threatening and huge. 'No peace,' he repeated, 'until she rests with her face towards the sea, the sound of the ocean beating in her dead ears.'

Blanche steadied the pistol against her heart; she pointed it at Jye's head. Her finger crept around the trigger; quite forgetting that Hugh had said the gun held no bullets, and took aim and fired.

She had always linked blood and pain together; she looked down at the small scarlet stain spreading outwards and downwards across the lilac peignoir, and was surprised that she felt nothing. The image of Jye began to fade. Her head dropped forward and her eyes closed. The last sound she heard was the pounding of the winter ocean against the sea wall of Dawlish Warren.

*

Jye wakened, suddenly, a sense of great fear gripping at his heart, making it painful for him to draw breath. Damaris, who slept lightly, became aware of the laboured sounds of his breathing. She sat up, lit the bedside candle, and held the candlestick above him. She studied his ashen face.

'Oh, whatever is it? Have you took a chill or something?'

His dark head moved upon the pillow. He placed both hands across his chest, and moaned.

'I'll make you a hot drink.' Damaris set down the candle. 'It could be a – ' Jye clutched her forearm. 'Don't leave me,' he whispered, 'not for a single minute! Say the Lord's Prayer! Say it for me!'

Damaris began to pray, both her hands held tight within Jye's grasp. When her prayer was ended she asked again, 'Oh, Jye, whatever is it?'

''Tis the Devil leaving me,' he murmured. ''Tis the Evil departing from me.' His features contracted as a spasm of pain more terrible than any he had yet felt, convulsed his body. Damaris placed her thin arm around his large frame.

'I've got you safe,' she cried, 'hold on to me, Jye!' She

felt him relax within her grasp. She heard him say in a clear voice. 'No peace for either of us until she rests with her face towards the sea, the sound of the ocean beating in her dead ears.' They lay quietly together for some minutes. Normal colour crept back into Jye's face. Maris placed her hand across his heart. 'I've heard tales around the village about possession of humans by evil spirits, but I never could believe it.' She spoke wonderingly, but with conviction. 'All these years, since the very first evening when you came to Father's cottage, I had this feeling that there was something – something absent in you. 'Twas like you was here with me in your body, but missing in your spirit.' Her tears fell upon his face to mingle with his tears. She moved her lips carefully so that he might understand.

'I don't know what happened to you up in London. I don't never want to know, Jye. Only tell me that 'tis over now!'

''Tis over, maid. The demon have left me.'

He lifted a hand to touch her thin face, the broad streak of white that ran back through her fair hair.

'What have I done?' he asked her. 'What harm have I put upon thee?'

'You've been a good and faithful husband, a hard grafter in quarry and garden. A quiet man what makes no trouble. A good provider for your children.'

'Not enough, maid. You deserved more than that from me.'

'We still got time, Jye, to put right all wrongs between us. 'Tis New Year's Day, and your fiftieth birthday, and the beginning of a New Year.'

*

Abi came back to Summerlands to find all doors and windows bolted against her. She circled the house on that winter's morning, shivering inside the scarlet cloak, calling her aunt's name, seeking some way that she might gain entrance. She came at last to the wide wooden flaps that covered the outside steps which led down to the cellar. She found the flaps unbolted and began to descend, moving carefully in the dim light. Annoyance turned to anger as she read the note left by Millie on the kitchen table.

Dear Miss Abigail
　　have left yore anty comfortabul. Shall be back in the morning but you mite get there befor I do.
　　　　　　　　　　　　　　　　　Yores. Millie.

Abi walked into the hall, she removed her cape and hat and placed them on a chair. The house was always quiet, but today the silence had a curious quality; she placed one foot on the first tread of the staircase.

'Aunty Blanche,' she called out, 'it's me Abi! I've had a dreadful journey down from Taunton. I'll make some tea, and bring you a cup, I'm really put-out by that Millie. She promised faithfully to stay here.'

Aunty Blanche made no answer, but Abi had not expected any. Eleven o'clock in the morning had never been a good time for an exchange of words between them. She lit the gas and filled the kettle, set a tray with cups and saucers, put the teapot to warm, and found the biscuit barrel. While the kettle boiled, Abi moved from room to room pulling back the curtains. All was just as she had left it. The house felt very cold; she would need to light fires in every room. She stood for a moment on the troublesome black carpet, and studied the sprays of pink, embossed roses. She wondered how much brandy had been brought into the house in her absence, and how many new hiding places her aunt would have discovered for it.

Why had she come back here?

Lying beside Eve, in the big double bed, Abi had confided her secret fears; her resentment that Aunty Blanche, while calling her 'daughter', should continue to use her as an unpaid skivvy.

'I don't know how much longer I can stand it, Evie.'

'Nobody makes you bide down in Dawlish. You could come home any time you wanted. There's plenty of gloving to be had now that there's a war on. Mother and me have got more work than we can handle!'

'It's that house, Eve. The way she lives. I've got used to silver cutlery and crystal glasses. You've been there. You've seen it. There's carpets on every floor, fires in every room; a proper bathroom and hot water, and an indoors privy!'

'But 'tis still you what lights her fires and cleans her carpets. Still you what tries to stop her drinking, and gets shouted at for it.' Eve's voice had been curious. 'Is it worth all that much, our Abi, just to have fine feathers?'

Abi had blushed in the darkness, surprised at the wisdom shown by Eve.

'You've been away for a whole year,' she went on 'and that have changed you. You have a different look about you. It's not just your clothes and hair, it's the way you walk and talk. Excepting for your sore hands, anybody 'ud think that you were a lady.'

Abi said, 'Well – I have to be like *her*. It's what she wants, and anyway, I can't seem to help it when I'm with her. She frightens me sometimes – and yet I've always got this feeling that I belong in her sort of life, and not here in Taunton.'

'I wish you'd come back, our Abi. We could go around together.' Eve's tone had been wistful. 'I've been left school for a whole year now, I sit home all day sewing gloves with Mother. She won't let me out of her sight for a single minute. 'Twould be different if you were here.'

The pink embossed roses blurred suddenly, and Abi brushed away tears. Steam from the kitchen floated through the hall, she remembered the kettle. Abi made the tea and poured a cup for Aunty Blanche. She placed one foot upon the first tread of the staircase, and the cup in her hand shook so violently that tea spilled into the saucer. It's the cold, she told herself, this awful chill of a house without fires. She came to her aunt's bedroom door, opened it, and entered. The room was dark.

Abi set down the cup and pulled the velvet curtains. She turned back towards the bed and saw that it was empty. She walked towards the armchair, and without needing to touch her, Abigail knew that Aunty Blanche was dead.

*

Abi's life had been filled with small catastrophies. There had been the spoiled dress on her seventh birthday; the fact of her straight hair in the face of Eve's curls; the delicate health that had kept her so close to Mother, and Mother's family. Her reaction to trouble had always been emotional and instant. Her temper tantrums had become a by-word, her sleep-walking a family legend.

True terror, she now discovered, had a strange effect upon her. She felt no desire to scream or run, or faint away. She stepped back towards the fireplace and gazed about her. The room was as beautiful and orderly as it had always been, the bedclothes only slightly disarranged, even the empty brandy bottle lying on the carpet was nothing out of the ordinary.

She looked last of all upon her aunt's face. The features were calm and youthful, the lips faintly smiling; her expression almost triumphant, as if she had finally discovered some valuable secret. She looks, Abi thought, like a woman who is happy for the first time in her life. Except that there was no life left in her.

*

People came. Millie was the first, flustered and apologetic about her late arrival.

'Mrs Fitzgerald is dead,' Abi told her calmly, 'shot by her own hand. Go back to Dawlish as quickly as you can. Inform the Constable and Dr Lovely, and then come back to me.'

Abi threw away the cold tea and made a fresh pot. She

drank it at the kitchen table, but still the coldness that had settled on her would not go away. Millie returned, bringing Dr Lovely and the village policeman. She and Millie told their stories; Aunty Blanche was examined and pronounced dead. A clear case, said the Constable, of a foolish woman tinkering with an old and unreliable firearm. The pistol, he said, had exploded as Aunty Blanche had pulled the trigger. Death said Dr Lovely, had been instantaneous. There was hardly any blood.

*

They buried her on a January morning, beneath the granite cross, and beside her husband; her face turned towards the shore, in this place where the sounds of the ocean were to beat for all time in her dead ears. Madelina and Abigail stood together, two small, black-clad figures, beside the open grave. Mina remembered the wilful and beautiful child who had lived on Larksleve; the exquisite young girl who had sat to England's finest artists. Abi remembered the Castle Hotel and her own seventh birthday; Blanche in the blue satin gown that revealed her shoulders, the lovely red hair dressed in tiny curls across her forehead. How beautiful she had been, and how kind to Abi! It was Uncle Hugh's death that had unhinged her mind.

Abi turned to Mina. 'She was never the same after Uncle Hugh died!'

Madelina sighed. 'Blamed herself,' she said sadly, 'loved him more than she knew, and discovered it when all was too late.' They began to walk away down the steep hill which contained the little cemetery of Dawlish.

'A sad life,' said Mina, 'for all her furs and jewels, and her fine house on a cliff top.' She paused and looked back towards the granite cross. 'He giveth his Beloved sleep,' she said quietly, 'well let's hope so, Abi. It's the best that we can wish her, now.'

*

Abigail came home to Taunton, dressed all in black, her face sad, her shoulders drooping. Eve found her less formidable than the Abi of the scarlet cloak and high-heeled shoes; she lay propped up on pillows in the brass-railed bed, and Eve brought her trays which held nourishing milk puddings, and the beef tea and calves' foot jelly that had been scorned by Father. Abi's need to talk of Dawlish, and the tragedy that had come to pass, was compulsive and frightening. Eve chatted about other, more cheerful subjects.

'Father's getting better. He's not well enough yet to come downstairs, but he's asking for prawns and brown bread and butter, and according to Mother, that's a good sign.'

Just to say aloud the magic words gave a lift to Eve's heart. Supposing Father hadn't gotten better – the thought was so awful that she turned her mind back towards her recent anger. Mother, for all her fine words and high temper, had been a broken reed. Eve had for the first time, really studied Mother, and found her wanting. Without the devoted care of Aunt Madelina, Father surely would have died.

Abi recovered, very slowly, from her experience in Dawlish. To begin with she had recounted daily those moments when she had discovered the body of her dead aunt. But now, as the horror faded from her mind, the talk around the gloving-table turned to other matters. The war had caused shortages in Taunton. Rumour said that butter and sugar were to be had in Bridgwater. Eve offered to borrow a bicycle and cycle with a girl friend to that town on Sunday, and to her surprise, Mother at once agreed. Having Abigail at home made life easier in many ways for Eve; with her older daughter to fuss over, Mother hardly noticed her own little absences, her white lies.

*

Annis rose early on that Easter Sunday. She whitened the

doorstep, cleaned the windows, polished with beeswax the red, inlaid lino, and shook out the pegged rug that laid before the hearth. She had managed, in spite of rationing and shortages, to fill the pantry shelves with good food. A piece of pork had been bought at great cost. A cake had been made by Madelina with the butter and sugar brought by Eve from Bridgwater. Potatoes had been sent round, no questions asked, by a cousin of Frank who worked in the Castle Hotel. After several months of bedbound illness, Frank was that day to be allowed downstairs.

Annis scored the rind of the pork joint with a sharp knife, and rubbed salt into it; she chopped onions and sage, peeled potatoes and put cabbage to soak. She began to mix pastry for an apple pie, and as always, the familiar tasks helped to calm her mind. This was a day she would always remember. With Frank recovered, and Abigail returned from Dawlish, their little circle was complete. She recalled the Casualty Lists in the Post Office window, those black marks on white paper which meant nothing to her, but spelled heartbreak and loss to so many wives and mothers. Annis did not understand about the war, had made no attempt to understand it. Such matters, she considered were man's business. She trimmed the apple pie and made a pastry rose with the remnants. The rose was for Eve, it had always been her special treat since childhood. Not of course that she was even close to growing up; she still wore the long black woollen stockings and abbreviated skirts of her school-days. Annis smiled at the thought of Eve's docility, her willingness to be still her mother's little maiden.

Frank came downstairs very slowly, supported by Eve and encouraged by Abi. Annis felt a twist of anguish at the sight of his thin frame and white hair. In those hours of his 'crisis', she had known at last how much she loved him, and how great was her debt to her sister, Mina. She had sewed extra cushions for his carver chair; to see him seated now beside the fire, his briar pipe drawing well, a smile of contentment on his face, was more than Annis had ever hoped for. They had eaten the pork and apple pie. Eve had read aloud from the Sunday newspaper; the war news for Frank, and the fashion notes and serial story for her mother. A knock at the door roused them all from the light doze into which they had fallen.

'I'll go', said Abi, 'I'm the only one who's wearing shoes.'

Abi opened the front door, and was gratified to know that the smart navy court shoes were on her feet. She was also wearing, in Father's honour, her best navy skirt and blouse of pleated white shantung. At sight of the good-looking soldier standing on the doorstep, her hand went up to touch the golden brooch pinned at her throat. The man smiled.

'I'm looking for a family called Greypaull. I was given your address by a man I met in the saloon.'

He looked enquiringly at her, but Abi made no answer. His voice was deep and very quiet, his words peculiar, his accent foreign to her.

'Greypaull,' he insisted, 'the man in the saloon said –?'

'My mother's name was Greypaull. Before she married.'

'Do you think that I might speak with her?'

Annis came into the narrow hallway, her slippers pulled hastily onto her feet, her face flushed from the fire's glow. She saw the soldier.

'Well, ask the young man in, Abigail. Don't never keep one of our gallant boys in khaki standing on the doorstep.'

Abi stood aside so that he might enter. As he passed her she read the flash stitched across the upper sleeve of his tunic. The one word CANADA explained his accent and the strange words, but what was he doing in Taunton, and what had he to do with Mother? She closed the front door; on her way through the hall she patted her hair and pinched her pale cheeks. Mother was apologising. 'You'll have to excuse us, young man. We used to sit in the front parlour on a Sunday, but with coal being so short we can only afford to have but the one fire.' Mother paused. 'Did I hear you mention the name of Greypaull?'

'Why, yes, ma'am. I never expected to find myself in Taunton, but now that I'm here it seemed like a good chance to seek out my father's family.'

Frank spoke for the first time.

'And who was your father?'

'James John Daniel Greypaull, born on Larksleve Farm in the Parish of Buckland St Mary. Late of Greenbrook Terrace, and killed by a fall from a horse while taking part in a steeplechase, in a place called Ashmeadows.'

Annis sat down, abruptly. 'Oh my dear Lord,' she whispered, 'you must be the baby, took away to Canada all they years ago.'

'Nicholas Greypaull, ma'am! Sergeant of the Canadian Cavalry. Wounded at Ypres. Frostbitten feet and a chest wound, I've spent six months in a place called Netley, a special hospital for soldiers.'

Frank smiled and nodded. 'I know it well, boy.'

Annis was crying. She went to the young soldier and took his face in both her hands. 'Jack,' she said, 'I can't hardly believe it. You're the living image of my dead brother.' She turned to Eve. 'Put your coat on, maid! Run quick and fetch your Aunty Mina. Don't say a word to her about all this!'

Mina came, breathless and irritated at being roused from her Sunday doze.

'Whatever is it, our Anni? Have Frank been took with a relapse –?'

She halted at the sight of the soldier, drinking tea beside the fire.

'Whoever's this then?'

Annis said, 'Take a good look at him, Mina. Don't he remind you of somebody?'

Mina studied the dark curling hair above the thin face.

She looked at the pale skin and light green eyes, the ploughlines of worry that ran from nose to chin. Mina bit her knuckle, as she had done when a child on Larksleve, and screwed up her eyelids so as not to cry.

'Jackie,' she murmured. 'Oh, our Anni, did you ever see such a likeness?'

She read the flash on the soldier's sleeve and smiled her comprehension. 'I've often wondered lately, when I've seen the Canadian soldiers in the streets. I worked out dates and ages, but I never believed that it would come to pass.' She hesitated. 'What about your mother?'

'She died, ma'am. Long time ago.'

'So how did you know about us?'

'Papers,' he said briefly. 'I found them in an old tin box, after her funeral.'

Mina said, 'I loved your father best of all. My hair turned snow white when he died. He was such a brave little chap, so sweet natured and always laughing. But he was daring too, especially with horses. He always rode bareback, but I expect you know that?'

'No ma'am. My mother hardly ever talked about him. I think it pained her in some way that I was so much like him.'

'Then you don't know exactly who we are?'

He laughed, 'Well I kinda guessed that you and the tall lady are my father's sisters, which must make the gentleman my uncle, and the two young ladies my first cousins.'

'That's right! I'm your Aunty Mina. This is your Aunt Annis, and these are her two daughters, Abigail and Eve. Poor Uncle Frank there, is just getting over pneumonia, and you had another aunt called Blanche, but she shot herself accidentally on New Year's Day. Then there's your Aunt Candace of course, now she lives in London – '.

Abi sat on a hard chair, away from the fire and in the shadows, grateful that all attention was caught by Aunt Mina's catalogue of family members, and that no one noticed the bright colour that came and went in Abi's face. She gazed at Nicholas Greypaull and thought how much she liked him. The drawl in his speech was what Aunty Blanche would have termed fascinating. She loved the way he held his head a little to one side and listened gravely to her mother's questions. He spoke slowly, each answer considered and thoughtful; oh, but he was charming!

'So what will happen to you now, Nick?' Father was smiling.

'They say I'm unfit for active service. I'm staying in a camp just outside of Taunton. I expect I'll be put on cookhouse duties,' he grinned towards the shadows where Abigail was hiding.

'So I guess you good people will be seeing plenty of me, for a while at least.'

*

Annis worried about small things; she built a barricade of tiny problems and then cowered beneath it, believing herself so to be protected. She discussed at great length the misfortunes that beset other members of her family, finding in such conversations a distraction from the threats that shuffled daily closer to Abigail and Eve.

The bombing of London was a drama about which Annis could take practical action.

'I've had Eve write a letter to our Candace,' she told Mina.

'I've told her to come to Taunton. I'm willing to clear my front parlour so that she can bring her bits and pieces. I can't bear to think of her up there, at the mercy of they wicked Zeppelins!'

The letter, written in Eve's strong, backward-sloping script, had been answered promptly and the offer of sanctuary accepted. Candace would, she said, be with them inside a fortnight.

'We shall have such a lot to tell her.' There was a sharp delight in Annis's voice. 'She knows that Blanche passed away, of course, but not the whole shameful story. Poor Blanche!'

But even as she spoke, the shadow of Nick Greypaull grew huge in Annis's mind, and Mina, as she so often did, seemed to sense her sister's secret panic.

'You'll have quite a houseful, what with Candace in your front room, Abi home to stay, and young Nicholas knocking on your door every five minutes.'

'He won't be in these parts for much longer. His frostbite is much better. He can wear boots now.'

''Tis the wound to his chest that's still giving him trouble.' Mina spoke with authority.

'There's been mention of a medical discharge for him, so he told my David. He talks about settling down in Taunton.'

Mina looked directly at Annis. 'First cousins!' she said softly.

It was almost a relief to have fear put into speech. Annis sighed. 'I don't know what you mean.'

'Yes you do, maid. Don't tell me 'tis you and Frank he comes to visit. I could see from the very start how it was between him and Abigail. They got eyes only for each other. In any case 'twould be a fine match, but facts got to be faced, our Anni!'

The memory of their brother Louis, tall and handsome, but retarded and incontinent, lay heavily between them.

'First cousins,' Mina repeated, 'there's no getting round it. You and Jack were brother and sister. Our mother and father were first cousins. I don't need to say more, do I?'

*

Eve listened and watched, and voiced no opinion on any subject. Sometimes she worried about her own lack of lustre. She sat beside mother at the gloving-table and sewed the thick hedgers' gloves, making neat black chain stitches, every one of equal length. She glanced up to find

Father gazing at her; the look they exchanged was one of perfect understanding. Abi spoke into the silence.

'Back to work on Monday, is it Father?'

'Yes, maid, and I'll be glad to go.' He tapped the empty bowl of the briar pipe clenched between his teeth. 'First thing I'll buy when all our debts is paid is a half-ounce of Diggers' Best Shag,' he smiled at Annis, 'and a fuchsia for your mother from the Saturday market.'

'Don't you worry about flowers for me, Frank. Us have managed very nicely so far, and now that Abi's back we've got an extra hand at the gloving-table. Just don't try to do too much in your first week. You know what our Mina said. There's not many men of your age what come through pneumonia and pleurisy. You got no call to worry about money. We've managed to pay the rent, and the grocer's bill is only two weeks behind. There's coal in the coalhouse and food in the pantry.'

Eve tried not to look up at the fancy china teapot where the pawn tickets were hidden. If Father had noticed the absence of certain items, he had known better than to say so. He smiled in Abigail's direction, and Abi smiled back.

Mother said, 'Our Candace'll be here soon. She's bringing her bed and the rest of her things on a pantechnicon. We shall have to put all our front room furniture in the spare bedroom. I thought she could make a bed-sitter for herself. Be more private for her, don't you think Frank?'

Mother rarely waited for Father's answer. 'She'll find Taunton very quiet, of course, after London, but like Mina said, Candace won't be lonely. She'll have all her family round her, and about time too!'

Eve said quietly, 'But you don't know her, Mother.'

'Don't know her? Whatever are you saying, maid? She's my sister, of course I know her, we grow'd up together.' Mother's voice was complacent. 'That's the best of families like ours. People stay the same.'

*

Abigail had not stayed the same. How strange that Mother seemed not to have noticed how changed was her elder daughter. Eve ached with envy for Abi's tiny elegant figure, her slim feet, the hand-tailored suits and blouses which bore labels of Exeter and London. Abi had style! She knew about rouge and face powder, talked knowledgeably about shampoos and perfumes, Abi could roll her hair into a French-pleat or a chignon, add a little scarf or a silk rose that could change a simple outfit into something very special. Eve had waited for Abi's speech to slip back into the broad vowels and soft drawl of the Somerset-Devon border, but still she retained what Eve thought of as her 'Aunty Blanche accent'.

Abigail wrote notes to Nicholas Greypaull, and received answers from him. There was no need to hide the letters, since Mother would not recognise her own name if she saw it written. The handwriting, like Abi herself, was impulsive; it sprawled extravagantly across the page in great loops and whirls, and flourishes which declared her undying love. Eve, who was good at English and composition, always checked the spelling of the big words, before slipping the note, secretly, into Nick's jacket pocket. His replies, written in a fine copperplate hand, promised love and devotion, an inscribed gold-watch for Abi's twenty-first birthday, and a wedding ring by Christmas.

Candace arrived on a day in August. She brought with her a brass-railed bedstead, a dressing-table and an aspidistra. Several tin trunks held her bedlinen and clothing, her many photograph albums, and at least two hundred copies of a racing newspaper called the *Pink Un*. Eve helped with the arranging and unpacking; a canary in a brass cage was carried into the house by Candace herself. Mother's parlour of soft blues now had a raffish look; the canary's cage swung from the gas lamp bracket, and copies of the *Pink Un* made an unsteady pillar that reached almost from floor to ceiling.

Eve liked Aunt Candace; she had expected her to be an older, even more depressive version of Mother and Aunt Mina, but Candace was a bustling, jolly little woman, dressed from head to toe in black, a small lace cap covering her grey hair. Eve unfolded sheets and helped with the making up of the brass bedstead. She eyed the towering column of newsheets. She said politely, 'You read a lot I see, Aunt Candace.'

Her aunt laughed. 'Them's racing papers! I follow Form, I've made a lifelong study of it. I could tell you the pedigree and performance of every race horse just as far back as records go.' She winked, broadly. 'Anybody ever risk a bet in this house, eh?'

'Well – Father has a flutter on Derby Day, if he can afford it.'

'That's no good! He'll never make a profit that way.' Candace smoothed the bedspread, and studied Eve. 'You've made a fine big girl. You've got your father's good looks, there's not a bit of Greypaull in you. Where do you work?'

'I stay at home with Mother. We do the gloving. I go up to French's Tannery every morning to take the finished work, and fetch a new batch.'

'Do you like it?'

'No I don't! I hate it!'

Eve clapped a hand across her mouth to stop the wicked words, but it was too late.

Aunt Candace said quietly, 'That's alright, my dear. You have told the truth and shamed the Devil. You should never be here in this house all day long, cooped up with a bunch of gossiping old women.' She sighed. 'Funny, how some people never learn. Your grandmother kept your own mother close up beside her, and just look what befell our poor Annis!' She paused, and looked searchingly at Eve. 'You got something else in mind, eh maid?'

Eve nodded. 'I fetch Mother's wages every Friday morning. There's a card in Mr Stenlake's office window.

They want a girl to learn the job of examiner. I'd be working in the making-up room with six machinists – '

Candace said, 'You get on well with Frank?'

'Oh yes. Father's always lovely to me.'

'Then tell him about it. Get him on your side.'

'But Mother's always so – '

'Never mind our Anni! She always was all wind and water! I'll remind her about her own young days, that'll shut her up!'

Candace pointed to the six framed prints that leaned against the wall. One was of Queen Victoria, the others were of famous horses and their riders. 'Get me half a dozen nails,' she told Eve, 'and a hammer. We'll hang up my pictures, and then I'll have a word with Frank.'

*

Abigail was in love, and in some contrary way that she did not understand, the opposition of her mother was making her passion for Nick Greypaull even more delightful and exciting. Not that mother had said anything definite against him. Well, how could she? As a wounded soldier come from the Dominion of Canada to fight for the British, and her own nephew, she could hardly forbid him the house. Ah, but how she would like to! Abi knew her mother; she recognised from the increased cooling of manner, the tight face, that Annis was controlling with difficulty her ungovernable temper. Plates might well be hurled at heads, when the time was ripe.

*

Meri knew that Sev had no real affection for her, but she had reached that point in her life where she no longer hankered for what was out of reach. His visits to her cottage followed no regular pattern; he came as and when his needs demanded. His taste for tobacco had become a craving that she alone could afford to indulge and satisfy. His liking for the 'rough' juice of the apple made sure that her cider keg was never empty. Even so, her hold upon him was tenuous and not of the spirit, but she would not have had it other. The uncertainty of their relationship, the brittle and abrasive tone of the words exchanged between them, made every meeting an event to be pondered upon and remembered in the long night hours when she could not sleep. Sev had reached that painful time in his life when a boy is no longer a child, and yet not quite a man. His voice had deepened by several octaves; blood on his chin revealed his first attempts at shaving. He came after dark on that autumn evening, entering without knocking as she had bid him do. He sat down without a word of greeting, in Luke's old carver chair, before the fire. It pleased her to see him sit so; she handed him a new clay pipe, and a fresh plug of tobacco.

'Cider?' she asked him.

'Not yet. I needs a smoke first.' She noticed his heightened colour, and rapid breathing.

'Maidens been chasing thee again?'

He drew smoke deep into his lungs, and trickled it slowly through his nostrils. He grinned.

'One of these nights I'll let the silly creatures catch I! Then they'll wish I haden!'

'You got a keen way with the girls, Sev. 'Tis they blue eyes o' yourn what brings 'em.' Her voice was sly. 'You be partial to dark-haired maids I notice.'

The colour came up beneath his fair skin. 'You been spying on I again; you been watching me from behind the hedges!'

''Course I have,' she chuckled. ''Tis my finest entertainment. You'd be surprised what I know.' She laid a forefinger alongside her nose. 'There's not much goes on in this village what escapes Meridiana. There's goings on up to Montacute House that 'ud shame the devil. That Lord Curzon ought to draw his window curtain. He got that red-headed woman living up there. Her what behaves as if she owned the place already.'

'You mean the one that writes books, that Elinor somebody?'

'Glyn,' Meri said, 'that's her!' She took a long draught from her cider tankard. 'If you wants my opinion, there's a damn sight too many books what gets writ by the gentry in this village.'

'Books,' Sev said carefully, 'is the hoarded treasure of the great minds of our nation.'

Meri screeched. 'Hoarded treasure, my backside!' She patted the money belt around her waist. 'Thass where treasure lies, my heart's joy. Anyways, you pinched they big words from that Llewelyn Powys, didden you?'

'So what if I did! You can learn a lot from book readin'.'

'Found that out a bit late, didden you boy? You was hardly ever in the classroom, as I remembers.'

Sev dismissed the Montacute school with a wave of his fingers. He leaned forward, elbows on knees, his body tense with the importance of his thought. Meri studied him with pain and pride. His bright hair had darkened to a burnished auburn, it lay in thick deep waves that reached from brow to jacket collar. His voice was deep, with a tone like music, even as Luke's had been. His gaze was blue and fierce, terrifying to those unfortunate enough to cross him. His head was high-crowned, his ears well shaped, and capable of catching the smallest sound. It came to her then, that in her heart she feared him, she who had never knuckled under to any man or woman, now stood back in awe from this chal who carried the fair looks and keen brain of his mother Maris, and the waywardness of heart and spirit of her own Rom people.

'Did you know,' he was asking, 'did you know that we got four great writers all living roundabouts?'

'No,' she murmured, 'no I didden know that.'

'There's Mr Thomas Hardy over to Dorchester; then there's that Elinor Whatsit up to the big house. Then we got Mr Llewelyn, and John Cowper Powys!' He glanced briefly at her, and there was caution in his look. 'I might – I might write a book one day. My head is always full o' stories.' He held out his left hand. 'Want to read my fortune? Want to tell I what is writ there?'

The words brought Luke back to her, in a way that no visit to the churchyard had ever done. Luke laughing at her, holding out his hand with that selfsame gesture of defiance and disbelief, and she refusing to be drawn. 'No,' she had said, 'I can't never tell for family.' She took Sev's hand and turned it palm downwards across her own. 'A small hand for a man, but neat and long-fingered. You got the hand of a music maker. My father and brother were so blessed!' She gazed keenly at him. 'You 'ont never make no ploughboy, no shed maker's apprentice.'

'I knows all that,' he said irritably. 'Read the lines, like you do for other people!'

She shook her head. 'No, boy. I don't care to tell for family.'

'You must,' he cried, 'I got to know what is coming to me.' He frowned and his black look caused a tremor in her stomach.

'Alright. But you might not like what I got to say.'

'Nuthin' could be worse than this dead village and the people in it.' He thrust both hands towards her now. 'Tell me!' he demanded. 'Tell me what you sees, or I shan't come round yer anymore.'

Meri took his right hand and turned it palm upwards. She began to trace the lines with her mind's finger, and all her reluctance to read for anyone of close blood was overcome by a curious excitement at what she saw there.

'Long life,' she told him, 'ah, you's'll live to be a very old man. No sickness. A near drowning. But nothing what'll finish you off, my heart's joy!' Her voice changed. 'Guard your fingers like they was pure gold. Take care o' your hands, for that is where your soul is.'

'Why for?' he interrupted. 'Do that mean I shall one day write a book?'

She frowned. 'No, somethin' else. I can't rightly see it yet, but 'twill change your whole life.'

She relaxed and grinned. She tapped his outstretched palm with her own index finger. 'You'm a warm feller wi' the maidens. Leastways – you soon will be.'

Embarrassed, he tried to pull his hand away, but she held firm, and all at once that rare feeling came to her that had nothing to do with the lines of the hand. She looked up into his face.

'You'll go to a far land,' she crooned, 'and bide away from us for many a long year. You'll find your only true love and be parted, straightways from her. But after a long time, and when you leasts expect it, you 'ull find her again.' Meri closed her eyes; she felt the boy's fingers tremble within her own. She spoke again in a high chant, ''Tis that maid o' yourn what'll bring back my coral pendant – '

'Stop it!' Sev shouted. 'I only wanted to hear about the far land and the music! I don't like you when your face goes funny.'

Meri opened her eyes and saw his pallor. She released his hands, and he at once wrapped both arms tight across his chest in a gesture of protection.

'Never shud have asked you,' he mumbled.

'No,' she said, 'it don't never do for me to tell to family.'

*

Jye came in the hour before noon, while the Sunday worshippers were still in Church and Chapel. Meri sensed a new shyness in him; it was as if a small lamp had been lit in his dark mind, and he not yet accustomed to the wonder of it. Her son was not a man who could be questioned, and yet the signs of change were in his face. Life had returned to his dulled eyes. It seemed almost that Jye might be in love.

He sat down in the carver chair, and as always Jye's likeness to his dead father was both a pleasure and a pain.

'You'm lookin' smart, boy.'

He touched the white silk muffler at his throat, and smiled.

''Twas a gift from Maris.'

'Her must be in the money,' Meri said sourly. She glanced keenly at him.

'So 'tis presents these days, is it? Things must be lookin' up betwixt the two of you.'

Jye's hand came up, involuntarily, to touch the place in his chest where the heart dwelt. The joy in his face, fleeting and swiftly hidden, was sufficient to tell his mother where the answer lay.

'The whore is dead, Jye.'

'Dunno what you means.'

'I think you does know. The evil have gone out of you. I've see'd it often enough to read the signs. Remember what I said? No peace until the sound of the ocean beats in her dead ears. Her'll be buried somewhere close to the seashore. That woman is dead, my son, and you a free spirit!'

He looked at her, and then away. 'I had a tearing in my chest, like something fighting for to leave me.' He paused, and she could sense his indecision. He reached a hand towards her as if he were a blind man. He said quietly, 'I feels different, Mother.'

Jye had never before, in his whole life, reached a hand towards her. He had hardly ever called her 'Mother'. Meri hardly dared to draw breath, so tender was the moment.

'I seem to see everything with new eyes. There's my girls, growing up to be young maidens. There's Maris, what have had to bear with all my coldness towards her.'

'And the boy?' Meri interrupted. 'What about Sev?'

Jye bowed his head; Meri felt the increased pressure of his hand within her own.

'Reckon 'tis too late for me and him. He'm idle and good for nothing; up to all the devilry and mischief he

283

can find. He'm a roamer and a lightweight. I found 'un a good place wi' Hebditch of Martock, but they finds him readin' rubbish among the woodstacks, and playing tunes on that dratted mouth-organ.'

Meri grinned. 'Don't you worry about Sev. He'll go further and do better than any o' your maidens.'

Jye said, 'I was right not to apprentice him to the masons' craft. He'd of shamed me afore my whole Lodge.'

'The boy is many-minded,' Meri said sharply. 'He got music in his hands, like my brother Ephraim and my father. He'm razor keen in his brains. He do read they clever old books what Mr Llewelyn Powys give him.'

'Book learning is for rich men, likewise music. Better the boy be a good ploughman, or a decent cowman!'

Meri shook her head. Jye released his fingers from her grasp.

'Sev's coming up for sixteen years in April,' she said drily, 'You'se have noticed many years too late, Jye, what manner of child your only son is.'

*

There were times when Sev was shaken by such powerful feelings that he could only conceal his emotions by a front of coldness and indifference. Resentment towards his mother had become difficult to sustain; but still he did not know that what he felt for her was love. He had fought since a small child against this tender feeling, the aching need to protect her from all hurt and burden. From his superior height he could now look down upon the crowning braids of her neat head. He looked into the mirror and recognised with shock how much of her nature had gone into the making of him. There were days when he longed to put an arm around her shoulder, to lay his head in her lap and weep for all the lost years; and yet, in some strange way Sev still knew himself to be Granfer's sonner. He closed his mind to the thought of Granny, living with her son in Yeovil. Towards Jye, his father, he felt nothing but resentment; he envied the man's great height and powerful body, the steady strength of him. He had noticed, could not fail to notice, the new warmth that had grown lately between his mother and father. Sev saw it as a betrayal. He could, he thought, bear the fact of his parents' indifference towards him, just so long as they were equally distant one with the other.

It was his sister Mathilda, who had always known best where to drive home the knife and then twist it, who informed Sev that Maris, their mother, was 'expectin' a happy event'.

*

Making hen houses and sheds for Hebditch's of Martock had turned out to be a matter of sweeping up shavings and straightening bent nails. Sev crouched among the woodpiles and read a strange tale by Llewelyn Powys called 'The Stunner'. He played his mouth-organ when out of earshot of the foreman. He had learned new tunes, whistled by soldiers on leave from the Front. Songs called 'Tipperary', and 'Pack Up Your Troubles'. He stood in the Borough in the evenings and listened to the soldiers' talk. He envied their uniforms, their talk of foreign cities, the wounds of which they boasted.

He climbed to the very top of Miles Hill, and gazed out towards the blueness he had always believed to be the sea.

'How old must I be,' Sev asked a limping soldier, 'before they'll allow me to enlist?'

'Eighteen,' he was told, 'but they don't ask for proof any more. If you're standing upright, and walking on your two feet, they'll take you easy, no questions asked.

He walked the five miles into Yeovil, and found the recruiting station. 'Do your mother know you're out all by yourself?' the recruiting sergeant asked him. 'Come back in a couple of years, and then we'll see.'

Sev stood on the road to Sherbourne; he looked up to the green slopes of Windham, and the steep rise of Babylon Hill. He felt his heart lift at a memory, and knew that the memory was not his own; and even as he watched, the white dust of early summer rose up in a great plume on the hill's crest.

The waggons were beautiful. He caught his breath at the colours of them, the intricate carvings, the many styles and shapes that made every vardo different from another. He felt the old tension knot his stomach muscles. Sev stood by the roadside and watched the gypsy tribe come rolling down into Yeovil, and in that moment he seemed to reach out beyond time and space, to a far land and an alien people. A shout from a flat cart brought him back into himself.

'Hey Sev! What you doin' here, mush?'

It was Righteous Locke, grown tall, his voice deep, a shadow of black stubble on his chin. The gypsy leapt down from the flat cart, thrusting the reins into the hands of a boy only half his age.

'You'm a long way from home. What you doin' here in Yeovil?'

'Come to join the Army,' Sev muttered, 'but they wudden take I.'

Righteous laughed. 'Dinilo!' he shouted, 'you gurt fat-headed ninny! Whatever you want to go an' do that for? Wants to get your head blowed off do 'ee?' he spat. 'Let they rotten gorgies fight their own wars. They 'ont get I to carry no rifles for 'em!'

'Be you old enough to enlist?'

'Old enough by more'n six months. But the gavmush can't prove that, not one way nor t'other. Us don't carry bits of paper, cudden read 'em if we did.'

Sev was impressed by this nonchalant attitude towards law and authority. His mood changed at once from deep depression to recklessness.

'Take I with you!' he pleaded. 'Let I come, Righteous! I be sick an' tired of old Hebditch's bloody chicken houses.'

Righteous hesitated. 'Dunno 'bout that. Us have just come out o' Dorset. Mean devils they be!' He jerked a thumb towards the flat carts filled with crying children. 'No bread for two days,' he spat again, 'and us won't pitch this night in time for the women to go calling.'

Sev said, 'I know a loft where apples is stored. I know too a bakery when I can pinch a loaf or two. Only let I come with you – I don't never mean to go home anymore.'

All at once Righteous grinned, revealing black and broken front teeth. 'Come on then!' he shouted, and began to run towards the disappearing flat-cart. Sev ran with him; together they flung themselves across the tailboard and onto a heap of faded canvas sheets.

'Best if you gits underneath they covers,' Righteous advised, 'My sweet father 'ud brain me with the crane-iron if he know'd I brought you wi' us.'

Sev crawled underneath the canvas; he slept at once, waking only when the cartwheels ceased to turn. He lay for a long time, aware of voices and movement, the jingle of harness, the smell of woodsmoke. A hand found his shoulder and shook him fully awake.

'You'll have to git outa there,' Righteous told him, 'us needs they covers for the bender-tent.'

Sev crawled out into a night of soft winds and brilliant starlight. He jumped down from the cart and looked about him. He recognised fields and trees; the crouching shape of Ham Hill. A scarf of cloud lifted from the full moon and he saw clearly in the hillside the entrance to Granfer's winter-hut. He turned on Righteous.

'You never told I that you was bound for Norton Covert!'

'You never asked.'

'But I got to get far away,' Sev moaned.

Righteous said, 'Us'll bide yer until the gavmush sends us packing, and that cud be a tidy three weeks. They'se a decent sort here roundabouts.

Sev began to walk, and weariness and hunger, and a small fear at his unexpected isolation took his feet towards the Montacute road. At a bend in the lane he halted briefly to look back on the waggons and flatcarts, the tethered dogs and horses; at the smoke rising straight in the warm night air. He moved on, stopping many times; he slept for an hour beside a newly-made strawstack. He came into Montacute in that magical time between darkness and dawn. From Montacute Park he heard the first note of the first bird. The charm of the morning brought Granfer to his mind, and he wept like a small child.

Sev came back to the cottage he had meant to leave for all time. He lifted the latch and went in to find a lamp already lit, and his mother in her usual window-corner, head bent above the gloving-table. She laid down her stitching and surveyed his condition.

'You've been sleepin' in a straw stack?'

'Aye.'

'What else have 'ee been up to?'

'I went to Yeovil. I tried to enlist, but they wudden take I.'

She said, 'I waited up all night for you to come back.' Her voice changed. 'Whyfor do 'ee fret me so bad, my sonner?'

'I idden your sonner! I belongs to Granfer!' The words were out before he could control them. He saw the anguish in her face, and in some shameful way he was glad to see it. His mother's head bent low, her hands became busy with gloving-stick and shears.

'So thass how 'tis with you still,' she said quietly. There were tears in her voice but he refused to hear them. 'You wants to be gone from us?'

'I went wi' the gypsies but they was on'y Norton-bound.'

His mother sighed. 'There's a position goin' beggin up at the House.'

Sev was wary. 'What sort of position?'

'Odd-job boy to Lord Curzon. But not here in the village. You'd have to go away to a place called Carleton House Terrace. 'Tis in London so they tell me, in the same street where the King lives.'

'How soon can I go?'

'There's two housemaids travelling up on Monday. You're to go with them.'

''Tis already settled then?'

'Only if you wants it.'

Sev grinned. 'I wants it. Oh yes, I wants it.'

Jye spoke to his son on the eve of Sev's departure. 'So you be off to London in the morning?'

Sev nodded.

Jye looked hard at him and then away. He said awkwardly, 'You mind yourself now. 'Tis a wicked city full of evil people. There'll be Montacute folk working in that big house. You bide close to your own sort, then you'll be alright.' He paused. 'I was near enough your age when I first went to London,' his voice became gruff. 'I found it hard to live among strangers. I was homesick all the time.'

Sev moved closer to his father. He stood before him and looked up into that dark face. He moved his lips carefully so that his meaning should be clear.

'I want to go. I want to be among strangers. I got no home here what I shall ever feel sick for.'

*

The two housemaids who boarded the west country train on that Sunday morning were young and pretty. Once a year, they told Sev, they were allowed to come home to see their parents. They flattered him with admiring glances. They spoke as if he could not hear them.

'We cud just do with something like him in the kitchen. Whoever would have thought that skinny Sev 'ud have growed up to be so 'andsome?'

Mary giggled, 'Pity he idden old enough to be footman. He'd of looked fetching in a pair of knee-breeches.'

"Course he'll have to get that wavy hair cut,' Jane said sadly.

'God's butler 'ull have a fit when he sees they red curls on his collar.'

Sev said, 'Who's God's butler?'

'Never you mind. You'll find out quick enough.'

'Anyway,' Sev mumbled, 'tidden red no more. 'Tiv gone a darker colour since I growed up.'

Mary moved from her window seat. She sat close beside him. 'I minds,' she said softly, 'when your hair was carrot red. You must remember me, Sev? I sat beside you in school. I helped you with your sums. I saved you from many a hiding from Mr Baldon.'

'I mind you,' Sev said sourly. 'You near drove I crazy with your sniffing and coughing. You always had a cold. You wiped your nose on your sleeve, and ate apples wi' your mouth wide open.'

'Did I?' Mary yawned to show that she was unconcerned. 'Well I knows better these days.'

Jane said. 'You better forget they fussy ways from this day on, Sev Carew, and you needn't look at me so fierce wi' they eyes o' yourn.'

'Don't say that,' Mary cried, 'I get goose bumps all over when his eyes go funny.' She wriggled closer to him. 'I quite fancies you, Sev Carew. I like it when you goes all strong and moody. It makes you look like Valentino.'

'Who's Valentino?'

Jane said in a hushed tone, 'Oh my dear Lord! He've never even heard of Valentino.'

Mary nodded wisely. 'He'll have to be took in hand.' They began to take stock of Sev. 'A haircut'll be the first thing. Then there's his teeth. I noticed a front tooth what have turned black. Then there's his clothes. We can't do much in that direction until he gets some money.'

Sev said, 'How long have you two been in London?'

The housemaids considered. Mary said, 'Us went straight from school. Must be comin' three years.'

'What's it like,' he asked, 'London?'

They giggled. 'Depends what you mean,' Jane said. ''Tis noisier than Montacute. There's soldiers everywhere. The East End got bombed a few months ago. There's been a lot of bombing lately. The people go down to the Underground for shelter when the Gothas come over.'

'What's the Underground?'

''Tis a railway what runs underneath the streets – oh I can't explain it!' Mary patted his sleeve. 'Us'll show you round when we gets our half day.' She turned back to Jane. 'We cud take 'un to the Picture Palace first of all, and then down to Piccadilly –'

'And then there's the Waxworks,' Jane interrupted, 'and Hyde Park Corner.' She smiled at Sev. 'Don't you worry,' she told him, 'me and Mary'll see to it that you be never lonely.'

*

Sev had dreamed of a brilliant city, of wide streets lit by a million gas-lights, of great buildings, loud traffic, and pavements thronged with elegant people. He had known how London was bound to look; he had read about it in the penny-dreadfuls. The city he came into on that autumn evening was as quiet and dark as the village from which he had just come. The traffic was thin, few people lingered on the streets. The recent bombing of East London had brought the war to the heart of the capital city.

He paused on the area steps of Number 1, Carleton House Terrace, and looked up at the dark sky. It was taller than Montacute church, more impressive than anything he had seen in Yeovil. He turned to Mary. 'Which bit of it do we live in?'

'We works at the very bottom,' she said drily, 'and we sleeps up in the attics. The rooms in between is all for the gentry. You better take your boots off to go up the back stairs. You're lucky; you won't have to share a room with anybody. Staff's on the sort side. The butler'll see you first thing in the morning.' Mary showed him to a sort of cupboard that held a narrow bed and a hook behind the door. A small table held a tin bowl and jug, and a stump of candle. Mary lit the candle. She turned to face him.

'Don't look so worried,' she said, 'me and Jane 'ull show 'ee what's what.'

Sev watched the door close behind her; he heard her footsteps grow faint along the bare boards of the corridor. When he was sure that she would not return, he set down his boots, and removed his jacket and trousers, and hung them on the hook. He climbed into the narrow bed. He felt weak and close to tears. In some vague and muddled way he had thought that to leave a source of pain must inevitably put an end to suffering. He did not want to think about Montacute and the people who lived in it. He closed his eyes and turned his face into the lumpy pillow, and at once his mind was filled with the image of the dark woman.

He had visited her that morning, just an hour before the train's departure. She had given him tobacco and a mug of cider.

'So you'm leavin' us?'

'London,' he had said, 'odd job boy to Lord Curzon.'

'And what do that mean?'

'Dunno.' His voice had been cheerful. 'Don't care all that much. I'll be gone from this place, that's all that matters to me.'

She had studied him with her sloe-eyes. 'I's'll miss thee,' she said quietly.

'No you won't,' he had laughed.

'I'll miss thee, my heart's joy,' she had repeated, 'don't forget about the music will 'ee?'

He had patted his jacket pocket. 'Mouth-organ goes everywhere I go. He'm the best friend that I got.' As he turned to go, he said back across his shoulder, 'Miss me if you wants to. You'm the only one what will!'

The opulent mansions known as Carleton House Terrace had been built by John Nash in 1827. Overlooking the Mall and in the vicinity of St James and Pall Mall, it was the most prestigious terrace of houses in all England. Number 1 was the London home of George Nathaniel, Earl Curzon of Kedleston; Ex-Viceroy of India, and present Leader of the House of Lords. A man who was, by his own assessment, 'a most superior person'.

Lord Curzon's favourite occupation, after politics and the friendship of beautiful women, was the purchase and restoration of historic houses. The Elizabethan house of Montacute had been recently restored and refurnished by him, with the help of his close friend, the famous novelist Mrs Elinor Glyn.

The recruitment of servants for his many great houses was no easy matter for his Lordship. He was known to be an exacting and difficult master. The numbers required to run and maintain a city mansion were so great that Sev Carew was never to know all of them by name. The company that worked below-stairs was an ever-shifting population.

When it came to the running of his household, Lord Curzon did not believe in delegation. The Leader of the House of Lords made a personal assessment of each new servant he engaged. His domestic staff were obliged to parade before him every morning. The long line to be inspected on that September day began with the butler, and came down through the ranks of chef and cook, parlour and housemaids, footmen and grooms, scullery-maids and, last of all, that lowest form of human life, the boots and odd-job boy.

Sev shifted impatiently from one foot to the other. He could hear the flat and autocratic tones of the man referred to by his servants as 'God's Butler'. Uniforms were being examined, fingernails inspected. As the voice came nearer Sev stood quite still, his gaze cast down towards the black and white tiled floor.

'So. What have we here? Your name, boy!'

'Sev – I mean, David John Carew.'

'You will address me as My Lord!'

'Yes – M'Lord.'

'H'mn. It's difficult to know quite where to begin. An immediate haircut, better get it cropped – half an inch all over. The neck looks like a potato-field just ready for planting. Use a scrubbing brush, and soap and water! Hold out your hands. Get those nails cut!' The keen gaze travelled downwards towards Sev's feet. 'You are here to clean boots and shoes among many other duties. Start with your own footwear, boy. Do you understand me?'

Sev continued to look downwards.

'I said, do you understand me?'

Sev mumbled a reply, not daring to open his mouth in case the great man should spy his black tooth and insist on its immediate removal.

'You are the one just up from Montacute. Your father is a mason, your mother is a glover.' Sev heard the contempt in the clipped tones; he looked up for the first time; his eyebrows drew together and he stared long and hard at the Ex-Viceroy. He saw a change that might almost have been fear touch the features of his new employer. As the man moved away, Sev heard him say to the butler, 'Watch that new boy! There's something insolent about him. See that he is kept busy, and for the sake of Heaven, attend to his deplorable appearance!'

The working day for lower servants began at five every morning. If there were no house-guests or important functions, Sev might go to his bed at nine in the evening. For this first month of his employment he was under instruction, and so did not merit any free time.

So much to remember, so many ways of breaking rules and offending people! On Drayton's farm and in Hebditch's woodshed Sev had worked alone. They had called him lazy and good-for-nothing. Here in London, away from all that was painful and familiar, something stirred and stretched in his mind. As he toiled, he also watched and listened, and with this new awareness there came a certain caution. His face, he suspected, was like a mirror that revealed his feelings; there was also some power in his eyes which had a strange effect on people. His speech was sharp, his words incautious. In that first month Sev learned to crouch low inside himself; he saw how to deflect unnecessary attention, how to hood his eyes, and still his tongue. It was not, he now discovered, so much the work that he resented, as the order to perform it. But in Lord Curzon's household Sev learned a new word that put right all wrongs.

Perks, so Mary told him, were a part of the job. Without perks they would all go barmy! After the first week of haircut and new clothes, and the forced application of carbolic soap and hot water, to his person, Sev began to see where compensations might be found. Food was plentiful and good. Produce from Lord Curzon's country estates was brought daily to London. Upper servants, he discovered, ate better than their employers, and the leavings from the butler's table were served to the lower orders. Sev tasted game and chicken for the first time. He sampled peaches-in-brandy, salmon-in-aspic, and out-of-season strawberries.

The disciplines imposed by Lord Curzon upon his household had little power beyond the green baize door. Life in the basement of Carleton House Terrace was haphazard and bizarre; the fate of a boot-boy depended on the whims and eccentricities of liveried and upper servants. Each senior member of staff had his or her own way of supplementing the quarterly wage paid by his Lordship. A thriving barber's business was carried on by a footman, who, in a cubby-hole just off the laundry-room, shaved the faces and cut the hair of his own colleagues, and that of servants from adjoining mansions. After clipping Sev's hair to an all-over length of one inch, the man licked a stub of pencil and turned to a clean page in his notebook. He entered Sev's name and position in the household.

'That's a tanner you owes me. Have to charge you tuppence extra this time, on account of your head being so well-thatched.'

Sev said, 'I got no money.'

'You will have. You got a sharp look about yer. 'Ave a word with Charlie. He'll put you in the way of something. Pay me when you gets fixed up.'

Charlie was the tallest footman. He doubled both as racing tipster and bookmaker. Within the month Sev had become his runner, employed to carry bets and winnings from the staff of the other great houses in the terrace, and from servants in the exclusive Clubs of Pall Mall and St James's. 'You got to have an angle,' Sev was told. 'Wiv' aht an angle you gits nowhere. Sixteen hours a day on yore bleedin' feet, and all for a measly five bob a week all found!'

Chauffeurs came and went more rapidly than footmen. The present driver of his Lordship's motor vehicle had worked when a young man as a dentist's assistant. Mr Jones, Sev was told, was available for the drawing of loose or aching teeth, in the very early hours of most Sunday mornings. The fee of ninepence per tooth pulled, would include the half-glass of Lord Curzon's whisky, administered before every operation.

Work did not seem so arduous when perks were to be had. Sev was shown the proper way to clean boots and shoes. A drop of flat champagne added to the final rub was said to improve the shine. It also quenched a boot-boy's thirst. He was measured and fitted for a suit of dark green, but the narrow trousers and monkey jacket were to be worn only when working above stairs. He earned sixpences and florins when carrying luggage for his Lordship's house guests. A Member of Parliament, when very drunk, once pressed a sovereign into his hand in mistake for a shilling. On his first free day since coming to London, Sev Carew had a total of twelve shillings and sevenpence half-penny in his trouser pocket.

*

His first tentative venture away from Carleton House Terrace was made on a day in late October. Until now Sev had been obliged to move swiftly through the Terrace and its precincts, as he collected bets and paid out winnings. On this still afternoon of blue skies and hazy sunshine, he walked slowly among falling leaves in Carleton Gardens. He observed, for the first time, the amazing grandeur of his surroundings. His father, when in London, must also have looked upon these mansions of the wealthy, but all he had ever spoken of to his family was the glory of Westminster Abbey and St Paul's Cathedral.

Sev came back towards the Duke of York's statue, and stood at the top of the flight of white steps that led down into the Mall. He had viewed the Mall from the window of his attic bedroom, but always by moonshine, or in the half-light of early morning. He walked down the steps and turned his face towards the Palace and knew that this was a moment he would never forget. The Mall was wide and straight, set on either side with a double row of plane trees; he remembered the driveway to Montacute House, and how impressive he had once thought it. He stood indecisive, and a little frightened, he jingled the coins in his pocket and wondered in which direction the shops lay. The craving for tobacco had intensified in the tensions of Lord Curzon's service, and he had used up all of the dark woman's thick-twist, filling the clay pipe and smoking it surreptitiously behind the kitchen boiler. He looked once more towards Buckingham Palace and began to walk quickly in the opposite direction. He came through Admiralty Arch and out into Trafalgar Square.

The tobacconist shop sold thick-twist and loose-shag tobacco. It also sold cigarettes. Sev examined the coloured packets; there were Turkish and Egyptian, American and French. He saw the deep yellow packet with Gold Flake written on it. The butler smoked Gold Flake. Sev had envied the sophistication of the man, the way he held the white cylinder between index and second finger, and trickled smoke negligently through his nostrils.

'Four packets of Gold Flake, and two boxes of matches.' Sev tossed a handful of assorted coins across the counter.

The man slammed down the cigarettes and matches and began to count Sev's money. His manner was truculent, his gaze suspicious.

'Not in uniform then?'

Sev looked surprised. 'I tried to enlist but they wudden take I. Said I had to be eighteen.'

'Lucky for you! I lost two sons at Passchendaele. I got no time for artful dodgers.'

'I be o'ny sixteen,' Sev insisted; his eyebrows drew together. 'You calling me a liar? You want proof or something?'

The man met his gaze and looked quickly away. He grinned, nervously.

'I believes yer, son. No offence meant. What brings yer up ter London then?'

Sev opened the Gold Flake packet and withdrew a cigarette. He placed it between his lips, struck a match and applied flame. He drew smoke deep into his lungs, and trickled it slowly from his nostrils. He held the cylinder loosely between index and second finger; offhandedly he said, 'I be come as footman to Lord Curzon. I works over there, in Carleton House Terrace.'

'How long you been there?'

'Couple o' months.'

The tobacconist looked awe-struck. 'Forget what I said about uniform, son. You'd be better off in France, digging trenches, than working for that swine.'

Sev came out of the dark little shop; he stood in the autumn sunshine and savoured the pleasure of his first cigarette. He began to walk back towards the Mall and Buckingham Palace. He thought about the tobacconist's words, and recalled the cold gaze and flat tones of the Leader of the House of Lords.

'Best keep out of his way,' Mary had advised. 'That way you'll sleep sounder and last longer!'

*

Keeping out of the way of George Nathaniel Curzon was to prove more difficult than Sev had thought. His Lordship was an admirer of Napoleon; he believed that success in life was dependent on the giving of great attention to small detail. While his food and best wines were enjoyed by the toilers in the basement, George Nathaniel sought for dust on the carved handrail of the staircase by wiping it on his descent each morning, with a white handkerchief of pure silk. It was said that he went out secretly after dark, and by candle light counted every last knob of coal in the coal-cellar. Sev did not believe this; his Lordship certainly kept count of the cans of hot water brought up by Sev to fill the hip bath in his bedroom.

'He's got a bathroom,' the second footman had confided, 'but he won't never use it. Likes to make work for us, he does. Has to have his bath afore a roaring fire, and behind a screen.'

Sev had been instructed in the proper stoking of the boiler that provided the hot water. He was put in charge of the six brass cans to be filled each night with near scalding water and carried upstairs, wrapped about in towels to preserve the heat.

'He likes a real hot bath,' the footman warned Sev, 'so for Gawd's sake keep that boiler stoked. Another tip for you. He got something the matter with his spine. They reckons it's the pain from it what makes him so bad-tempered. According to the valet he wears a steel corset padded out with leather, but we ain't supposed to know about it. So don't hang about in his rooms, and don't ever get caught there when he's dressing or undressing.'

Another of Sev's tasks was to wait upon the upper servants, who took the main course of their dinner in the servants' hall but then retired to the butler's room to eat their dessert and drink their master's port wine. There was little that escaped the notice of these men and women upon whom Lord Curzon's physical well-being depended. The gossip Sev heard in the butler's room was better than anything he had ever read in the penny-dreadfuls.

'He've got a new corset!' Sev reported back to Jane and Mary. 'And it's giving him gyp according to the valet.'

'I heard', confided Jane, 'that her Ladyship still won't come back to London. He's always writing letters to her. She's at Hackwood until Christmas. She can't abide Kedleston, you know. As for Montacute she won't never go there because it was furnished and decorated by that Elinor Glyn.' Jane giggled. 'You shud hear the rows they have, Sev. She's ever so jealous of him.'

Sev said, 'How many houses have 'un got, then?'

Mary counted on her fingers. 'Six or seven at the least. Last I heard he'd just bought up some old Castle.'

Sev whistled. 'He'm no fool,' said Mary, 'I'll say that much for 'un. He gets wed to American heiresses whose fathers have got pots of money.'

'How many times have 'un done that?'

'Oh, only the twice, so far. You've seen the painting in the drawing-room? Well that was the first Lady Curzon. I never see'd her in life, but she was very beautiful. Her name was Mary. They say he went crazy with grief when she died.'

'What about number two,' Sev asked, 'what do she look like?'

'Oh, she's a stunner for looks, and what's more, according to her maid, she's even richer than the first one.' Mary grinned. 'The diff'rence is that this one got his measure! She won't be no doormat for him. Her name is Grace, but he calls her Gracie, and sweet girlie. Us can't hardly keep a straight face sometimes. She goes to Hackwood whenever he's been acting up. That's to punish him, you see.' Mary sniffed. 'Can't see what the women find so fetching about him. Poor old devil, trussed up in that corset. He's losing his hair too, and he gets the toothache.' She looked at Sev. 'Time we got something done about that black tooth of yourn. 'Tis the one thing what's spoiling your appearance!'

It had been easy at first to put family and Montacute firmly from his mind. Whole days would go by without a thought of anything but the curious and challenging aspect of his new life in London; and then, all at once, there was talk of Christmas. The servants' hall was hung with mistletoe and holly, and paper chains made by Mary and Jane. The weather turned colder; from his attic window Sev could see the plane trees in the Mall, their last leaves fallen, their branches frost-rimmed. In those early morning hours of mid-December, when he shivered and blinked his way into a new day, he would feel a sadness settle on him that had nothing to do with the harsh words of Lord Curzon, or the unpredictable behaviour of his fellow servants.

He cleaned boots and shoes, carried coals, stoked the boiler. He noted absently the disappearance of two footmen and a housemaid, and heard without really listening the dramatic tale of their dismissal by his Lordship. The constant and unavoidable company of his fellow servants became suddenly abhorrent to him; he began to notice their more annoying personal habits. The butler sucked mints, holding the sweet far back in his cheek, and swallowing with unnecessary loudness. Mary sniffed; Jane had a habit of cracking her knuckles. The chauffeur made a crunching noise with his teeth when eating acid drops and humbugs. The accents of the Cockney servants, intriguing at first, now grated on his eardrums. All Sev's childish intolerances for offensive sounds were compounded now by his inability to escape them. His need to be alone and quiet became urgent; on his next free day he avoided the company of Mary and Jane and went into St James's Park. He sat on a bench beside the lake and watched the antics of the wildfowl.

It was lambing time in Montacute. He looked down at the sooty grass of London and remembered the cropped turf of Ham Hill; Granfer's winter shelter, and the smells of paraffin and tar, and warm oils. He closed his mind against the memory of Granfer, but another came to take its place. His mother, seated in her corner close beside the window, her red-gold hair a nimbus in the lamplight, her head bent low towards the stitching of the leather. The threat of tears burned suddenly behind his eyelids. He stood up, abruptly, and walked towards the water's edge, alarming the wildfowl so that they scattered and took wing across the lake. He could not bear the thought of the child that would be born soon; the brother or sister who would not be sent away and then claimed back when it was too late. He looked down into the water and saw his image, wavering and distorted on the rippled surface. He would never return to Montacute; never put himself in the way of suffering the pain of witnessing yet another cherished child in his mother's arms. He shivered, and the threatened tears ran cold upon his face, and into his shirt collar; without wiping them away Sev began to walk back, very slowly, towards Carleton House Terrace.

*

Abi picked up the lump of black wax and drew a length of hempen thread back and forth across it. She selected a newly sharpened needle, threaded it, then placed two halves of a glove carefully together. She began to sew, winding the stiff hemp around the gloving needle to make a chain stitch. The room was cold, the coals not yet caught into a blaze. The gaslight flickered in its fragile mantel, making her head ache. Her eyelids felt stiff from last night's weeping.

Eve stood before the mantelshelf-mirror, her reflected eyes were sympathetic. Through a mouthful of hairpins she murmured, 'Are you alright? I heard you crying in the night.'

Abi stabbed at the leather, and nodded significantly towards the kitchen. 'Tell you all about it, later on.'

Eve reached for her coat. Her face was compassionate, her voice fearful. 'You could try to be a bit more diplomatic with her. There's no point in upsetting her before you have to. Even with my head underneath the blankets I could hear you shouting.'

'Diplomatic?' Abi turned in her chair. 'You want me to pacify her? You want me to fuss around her, like you and father? It's alright for you. You've got a job to go to. I'm boxed-up with her, here. Day-in, day-out!'

Abi's raised tone brought a warning echo from the kitchen.

'You'd better hurry up, Eve. It don't do to come late on a Monday morning.'

'I'm just going, Mother.' Eve lingered beside the gloving-table.

'Can I take a message to him?'

Abi shook her head. She said bitterly, 'Just you be a good girl and do all that mother tells you. You're a fine pair, you and Father. The both of you are frightened silly of her.'

Abi heard the front door close quietly behind Eve. She waited for some acid comment from the kitchen, but none came. So today the weapon would be silence, with Mother's lips compressed into a pained line. Well, two could play at that game, and when it came to muteness, she could outlast Mother. The small sounds of the house settled round her. The careful pyramid of coals collapsed into a sudden blaze. From the front room she could hear a discussion on racing-form carried on by Aunt Candace with her caged canary. At nine o'clock sharp Aunt Mina would arrive to inspect the battlefield, and bind up the wounded.

Abi hitched her chair closer to the gloving-table. She laid down the glove and picked up the stick of black wax, and thought how much the elongated lump looked like her mother. She held it firmly in her left hand, the gloving-needle poised above it. She felt ashamed, and then the frenzy of resentment seemed to galvanise her fingers. She bent low across the table; there was a malevolence about the wax that was also a challenge. Abi bit at her lower lip, and glanced at the half-open kitchen door, then she stabbed the lump of black wax quite deliberately with the newly sharpened needle.

Eve closed the front door very gently behind her. Any hint of a slam might well be construed by mother as a sign of sympathy for Abi.

'Keep out of it, maid,' Father had advised. ''Tis the sort of family complication what'll get decided by your mother and her sisters.' There was an indecision in his voice and face that disturbed Eve. 'I always feel,' he went on, 'that Abigail is more your mother's business.'

'And what about me? Whose business am I? Who will you side with when my turn comes with Mother?' The words had shouted in Eve's mind, but she would never bring herself to say them.

'I can't see,' she had said, 'what all the fuss is about. Most mothers are keen to get their daughters married.'

'Nick and Abi are first cousins, and there's a history of mental trouble in the Greypaull family.'

'But there's no taint on your side, Father.'

Eve remembered the way he had snatched up the briar pipe, and the leather pouch that held his tobacco. She had looked at him then, really studied him as she might have done had he been a stranger. Something stirred in her mind; all at once she felt unsteady, as if the earth had moved beneath her feet.

'My side don't count in the case of Abi,' Father was saying. He looked at her with the tired and patient eyes that made her want to cry. 'There's things you don't know, old matters that come back to haunt a man when he least expects it. Let the subject drop, Evie, there's a good girl! Just remember, whatever happens, your sister is your mother's business.'

Eve walked through the light snow of the January

morning, glad to be out of the house and away from its tensions. She came into Tancred Street and felt an easement in the tightness of her facial muscles. The shouting of last night, the sound of Abi's muffled weeping in the bed beside her, had brought back fears, and posed questions she could not evade. Her heart ached for Abigail and Nicholas but there was nothing she could do to change things; and her sister was quite right, of course. Eve and Father, both, were terrified of Mother.

The difference between herself and Abi had become more marked in the past year; when measured against the formidable Greypaull women Eve knew that she was considered at best to be mediocre. She lacked her sister's fire and daring spirit, showed no sign of the musical talent possessed by her cousin Laura. Comparisons had long ago been made which placed Eve in the category of unremarkable but inoffensive. She had been a contented baby, a placid child, a willing and conscientious pupil at Trinity School. When voices were raised and tempers high, it was Eve who exchanged the long look of understanding with Frank, her father. Eve who still wished that her family was more like that of other people.

But the move to French's, encouraged by Aunt Candace, and grudgingly approved by Aunt Mina, had taken her much further than Tancred Street and the tanning factory. It had plucked her from the repressive and female world of Mother, and set her down safely in the uncomplicated and masculine atmosphere in which Father spent his days. The job of examiner, Mr Stenlake had said, was a responsible one. The good name of French's, it now seemed, rested solely in Eve's hands. Her task was to check the outworkers' stitching, to ensure that each hedger's glove was fit to bear the heavy strains that would be put upon it. Any signs of weakness in the chain stitch, any careless fastening-off of threads must be made good by Eve. When working at home with her mother and sister, she had been the least important person at the gloving-table. Now she was in the unique position of overseeing the work done by Abi and Mother. The fact that their gloving was always faultless, and passed without need of correction, hardly seemed to matter. Sixteen years of comparison with the Greypaull women had blunted Eve's perception of herself, and leaked confidence away. She would come only slowly to a knowledge of her own worth, but already when people asked about her job, Eve was heard to say, 'Oh me? Well, I don't work at home any more, I hold the position of examiner at French's.'

*

Annis shredded suet, measured flour and baking-powder, and stirred the mixture to a stiff paste with a cupful of cold water. She floured the cloth and tied the pudding securely into it; after several hours of steaming, and served with onions and liver, and a jug of Candace's special gravy, it would last for two meals, at the very least.

The suet and liver was an under-the-counter favour from the butcher's son. To begin with Annis had worried about the ease with which Eve could obtain the little extras that supplemented their legal rations. Eve tended lately to be noticed by young men, but in a subdued way about which a mother could do nothing. Annis fretted about the tannery workers; she had questioned Frank upon the subject.

'Who does she meet? Does she walk home with anybody? Our Mina saw her talking to a boy last week. They were standing under French's archway.'

Frank had grinned. 'The only men left in the tannery these days are either too old, or too sick to be caught by conscription. The most of them are boys of Eve's own age.' He had laid his newspaper aside to give weight to his words. 'She's in no danger, Anni. She's a shy maid.'

'You believe that, do you? Well, it's to be expected. She

was ever your favourite. I'll tell you something about Evie. She've got hidden depths. She's only shy-of-manner, what is something altogether different.'

Annis stood, indecisive in the icy kitchen, and thought about her daughters. The instinct to 'manage' their families, so strong in all the Greypaull women, was fiercer in Annis than in any of her cleverer sisters. She felt compelled to anticipate every possible danger, to forestall every threatened blight and scandal. Certain subjects were unmentionable, even between herself and Frank, and self-deception had become habitual. The facts of Abi's birth were overlaid by so many years of subterfuge and small lies, that Annis could hardly remember that Frank was not Abigail's true father; except at those times when she and Abi quarrelled. It was then that Castlemain's daughter showed the Castlemain breeding and fiery spirit. Last night's upset had frightened Annis. She had seen the small proud head rock back in anger, the fine bones of the face etched sharply beneath the pale skin. Abi's cool grey eyes had burned suddenly with such hatred that her mother had flinched and looked away.

*

Eve blew out the candle and snuggled down into the softness of the feather bed. She could sense the rigidity of Abi's body lying close beside her. Her feet sought the searing heat of the stone-jar filled with boiling water. It was easier to talk in darkness. A faint whiff of hot wax lingered on the air, the smell forever to be linked in her mind with the sharing of secrets. She said quietly, 'So what happened last night between you and Mother?'

'She said she would never allow me to marry Nick, that she'd rather see me dead first. That it was all for my own good and that one day I would thank her for it. She said that Granny and Grandfather were cousins, and to remember all I'd ever heard of her brother Louis. If cousins should marry twice, she said, within three generations, then their children would be imbeciles, monsters even. I might have a child with two heads or no legs.'

Eve's voice was husky with fear. 'But that's terrible! I'll bet she's made it all up, just to bend you to her will.'

'I don't think so. I remember Granny Greypaull telling me about Louis; and it's a fact that grandfather and she were cousins.'

Eve said swiftly, 'But you're of age. She can't stop you marrying Nick.'

'Can't she? You don't really know her, do you?' Abi's voice broke on a sob. 'He's asked me to go back to Canada with him.'

'Now Mother wouldn't like that.'

'She says I'm not strong enough to marry anybody. As for living in Alberta, well she reckons that would kill me.'

Eve said, 'But that's silly, Abi. Aunty Blanche worked you like a skivvy and you never died. It was you that found her body, and what a shock that was to your nerves! In Canada you'd have a husband beside you.' Eve sounded hesitant but curious. 'You do care about him don't you?'

'Of course I care for him! I'm crazy about him. I'm just afraid that he'll get tired of waiting for me. He says that the war will be over by the autumn. Oh Evie, whatever shall I do?'

Eve lay silent for some moments. The passion in her sister's voice when she spoke of Nick Greypaull had been unexpected. She said at last, 'I never guessed you felt that strongly about him. You never gave a sign in front of the family. It's all been going on such ages, and I know he gives you presents, but I thought that it was more from friendship, and you being kind to a wounded soldier.'

Abi's laugh had a note of hysteria in it. 'Oh, you're such a child. You can't imagine how I feel. Of course I've made it look like friendship! We've had to be so careful. Mother would have banned him from the house if she'd guessed that we were serious about one another.'

Eve giggled. 'Aunt Mina tried to warn her. I bet Mother's wishing now that she had listened to her.' Eve paused. She said, admiringly, 'That was clever of you, Abi, to hoodwink Mother.'

'Deceitful is what she calls it! Mother called me a bare-faced liar, last night. It's not true. I've never told her a deliberate untruth.' Abi went on in a different tone. 'Now you – you tell her lies, Eve. I've heard you do it.'

'Well I have to, sometimes. I'm doing her a favour, really. She'd only get upset if she knew where I'd really been, and who I'd met.'

Abi said, 'But you always seem so frightened of her.'

'So I am. When she starts to rant on, and lose her temper, why, I almost wet my knickers!' Eve laughed softly in the darkness. 'I learned a trick or two from watching Father. I found out when I was quite small, that there's ways and means of diddling Mother.'

'Like what?'

'Like him telling us that he'd been watching the motor traffic pass by up in North Street, when all the time he'd been having Sunday tea with his mother and father. He spends more than he ought to on cider and tobacco, but he buys Mother a fuchsia and it stops her moaning and complaining.'

'That might work for Father, but if Mother catches you lying, then she's bound to kill you!'

'I know. I have nightmares about it. But she makes me a liar, Abi! It's all her fault!'

The silence that fell between them lasted for so long that Eve was drifting into sleep. She roused to hear her sister say, 'I can't seem to find the right words to tell Nick that we can never marry.'

'But you can't give in, now. Don't let her break your heart and ruin your life. If you really loved Nick, why you'd chance anything for his sake!'

Abi's tone fell to a whisper. 'You don't understand. It needs so much will-power to stand out against her. You're only sixteen. You play little games and think yourself clever. But just you wait and see, Eve Nevill! Wait until there's some man in your life that you can't live without. That's when Mother will take hold of you! That's when she'll make damned sure that you can never have him.'

*

It had, thought Candace, been good of Annis to take her in when the bombing of London had made life in the capital unsafe. But lately, the tensions of the house, although not her direct concern, were powerful enough to unsettle the mind and make concentration difficult. Her study of the *Pink Un* was interrupted frequently by the sharp exchanges between Abi and Annis; her sleep made uneasy by the sound of weeping in the night.

There was no one, save Frank, with whom she might discuss her passion. She would wait for the noonday factory whistle which preceded his arrival for the midday dinner. She would hover around his chair while he ate, waving the latest issue of the *Pink Un* before him.

'Frank!' she would cry, 'tell me what you think about Dancing Bear for the three o'clock at Goodwood.'

She had overheard Eve say, 'I don't know how Father stands her! He can't even eat his meals in peace, since she came here.'

Abi had said, 'Do you think she means to stay forever? Mother was complaining that all her best furniture was turning mouldy, stored away in that damp back-bedroom.'

Candace took out Billy's latest letter; she counted the dollar bills that made the envelope bulky, and wondered how many pounds they would yield in the Taunton Bank. There was a little house to rent out at Rowbarton. She would ask Mina to go with her to view it. She took the smudged and ill-spelled letter through to the middle room of the house, where Annis and Abi sat silently beside the gloving-table.

'Word came from Billy on the morning post. Seems

like he's doing very well in this Hollywood place. He sent me fifty dollars!'

Annis said, 'Oh Can! How much is that in proper money?'

'I don't know yet. I have to take what the Bank is willing to give me.' Candace tapped the envelope. 'It'll be enough for me to rent that house I was telling you about.'

Annis said, uncomfortably, 'You don't have to go, Can.'

'Yes I do, maid. It's been good of you and Frank to have me all this time, but with money coming regular from Billy, and with my winnings – well I can afford my own place.' She pulled out the letter from her apron pocket. 'I'll make us all a cup of tea. Our Mina 'ull be here any minute now, then I'll read to you what Billy says.'

The letters that came from her cousin Billy, might well, thought Abigail, have been written from the moon, so incomprehensible were they. Abi sipped the scalding tea and listened to the flat tones of Aunt Candace as she read the familiar opening phrases.

Dear Ma,

Hope this finds you as it leaves me at the present. In the Pink! I trust you had a good Christmas. Don't worry about me. Life never been so good. Hollywood is a fine place. Went bathing at Malibu on Christmas Day, in the Pacific Ocean. Chaplin is bilding a new film studio at the corner of La Brea and Sunset Boulevard. Yours truly hoping to move over from Mutual when said studio is finished. Charlie is by now the most famus film star in the world. Cant stand the little beggar, but got to go where the work is. Bet you never thowt I would make a proper actor. In my last film I played a bank robber. Get cawt just as I am emptying the safe. Dont worry about me Ma. Life here is fine and dandy. Parties every night, booze flows like

water. You must go to see my pictures when they come
to England. How are you doing on the gee-gees? Still
making a bob or two I bet, and worrying the bookies.
Take care of yourself. Dont do anything I wouldnt.

Love from your son Billy.

Annis said, 'He must be doing well for himself if he can
afford to send you all that money.'

Mina said, 'That sounds like a fast life, our Candace!
Be far better if he'd stayed in England.'

'If he'd stayed in England,' Candace said sharply,
'he'd have got caught by conscription, and knowing my
Billy, he'd have been the first one in the trench to cop a
German bullet.' She folded the letter and put it in her
apron pocket. 'At least,' she said quietly, 'I know where
he is and what he's doing. He's only young once. It's
only natural that he should want to have a good time.'

*

Moonlight, so people said, had a lot to do with air raids.
Sev stood at a high window and saw the moon appear
through clouds above the Mall and St James's Park. Even
as he watched, the window sashes rattled and the great
houses in Carleton Terrace seemed to shift on their
foundations. A great glow lit up the night sky, he could
hear the drone of airplanes and the clanging of a fire bell.
Many of Lord Curzon's servants had declared themselves so frightened of the bombing and gunfire that they
had given notice and returned to their villages. Sev felt no
fear, merely annoyance, as the departure of so many
nervous footmen and maids laid a heavier burden of
work on those who remained. He allowed the folds of
crimson velvet to fall back across the window, and
turned to the table where his Lordship had just dined
alone. The meal, a concoction of messes created by the
French chef, had scarcely been touched. Sev piled plates
and tureens, cutlery and glassware onto a large tray, and
carried them carefully down the long flights of back

stairs and into the kitchen. His Lordship had forbidden all use of the dumb-waiter after he had dined. The sound of the pulleys, and the rattle of descending dishes would, he said, reach the study and disturb his concentration. Three journeys were required to clear the dining table. Sev met the valet on his way into the study with a newly-opened bottle of champagne and a single glass. He glimpsed his Lordship, seated at his desk, stiff-backed in his leather corset, the boxes of State piled high around him. He heard the testy voice raised in complaint about the picked-over dinner. Sev grinned. There was to be roast beef and Yorkshire pudding in the servants' hall that evening, with apple charlotte to follow, and a nice bit of Stilton.

*

Intercession Sunday had been held on January 6th. Sev had gone to Westminster Abbey, at his Lordship's command, with the rest of the servants, but as Mary had said, God must have turned a deaf ear. The war went on; battalions of wounded passed through London on their way to hospitals and convalescent homes. Every day brought rumours; the latest was that poison gas bombs were about to be dropped on London.

'P'raps us ought to go home?' Jane said.

'You do what you wants to,' Sev told her. 'God's Butler'll have to kick I down the front steps, before I leave London!'

Sev felt the same sharp excitement run along his veins, whether he was darting among crowds in Piccadilly, or strolling quietly beneath the plane trees down the Mall. The city was a great pulse that beat inside him; he could never see enough of it. He had grown taller; good food and money in his pocket had given him an assured air that was almost jaunty. His cropped hair had grown out to a more respectable length. On his seventeenth birthday, while on an errand for the butler, Sev had sneaked away to a gentlemen's outfitters in the Strand. For ten shillings and sixpence he had bought a suit of smart blue serge, a brown bowler hat, and a walking stick that was topped with a knob of imitation silver. A new housemaid had been engaged, a saucy-looking girl who at once made it clear that she would quite welcome a kiss and a cuddle in the china pantry, should he feel so inclined. He had not yet availed himself of the offer. She was, he felt, a here-today, gone-tomorrow sort of creature. Already he had sampled the jealousy of Jane and Mary, who were equally available to him, but permanent.

'Fancies yourself lately, don't you, Sev Carew?' Mary had sniffed.

'Jus' because you got a blue suit and a bowler, you thinks yourself a bigger swell than his Lordship!' She surveyed him, hands on hips, her eyes half-closed. 'You'd be just passable on a wet night,' she said spitefully, 'if wasn't for all they rotten front teeth o' yourn.'

'I only got the one bad tooth,' he mumbled through closed lips.

'Oh no you haven't then. The rot have spread through all four of your top front gnashers. Like Jane was saying t'other day, us can't fancy kissing you no more. That Flossie is more than welcome to you!'

It was Sev's task to polish bedroom silver every Tuesday morning. He usually handled with disinterest the silver-backed brushes and combs, the silver-topped perfume bottles and heavily embossed hand-mirrors. But finding himself alone in the butler's pantry, Sev turned over the mirror that belonged on Lady Curzon's dressing-table. He gazed at his reflection, then lifted his top lip. Mary was right. The blackness had spread. Another few months of neglect might see him toothless. A visit would have to be paid to Mr Jones, the chauffeur, in the early hours of next Sunday morning. Sev closed his mouth, but continued to study the face in the mirror. Not a bad-looking chap, he told himself, just as long as he remembered not to smile. With the black teeth removed, and new dentures fitted, there was not a girl in the house who would be able to resist him. He laid down the mirror, and even as he did so, Sev felt that change of mood which he had come to dread. As always, the slow ebb of confidence was followed by a swift plummet into misery. He picked up the mirror and held it at arm's length. The face that looked back at him was that of Granfer and his mother. He began to touch with his mind's finger each separate feature. He gave way to the bitter-sweet recognition of his inheritance of high, domed forehead, straight nose, and deep, wide-set eyes. The dark red hair sprang away from a deep peak, in the exact same way as did his mother's; he had her fresh colouring of skin – her long and sensitive mouth. He remembered the lips that curved upwards, but all too rarely lately, with irrepressible humour. A picture of her, as he had last seen her, rose up before him. The new child would have been born at Christmas. His mother must have survived the birth. If she had died, he thought, somebody would have remembered to let him know. She had witten to him just once, but he had never replied.

Sev felt the depression settle on him. He laid aside the mirror. He whispered to himself, 'The black dog is on my shoulder,' and wondered from whence the strange words had come.

*

The denture lay like an expensive jewel, on a bed of cottonwool in a little box in Mr Jones's living quarters. Sev studied the four pearly teeth and their attachment of gold wires.

He looked anxious. 'You're sure they'll be a good fit? That could be awkward at certain times if they was to go adrift.'

Mr Jones grinned. 'Twenty times I've measured you already, boyo! But we'll never know for sure if they fit until you let me draw your own teeth.'

Sev had never visited a dentist. He remembered the tonsils operation, and how much blood there had been.

'Will I bleed much, Mr Jones?'

'I don't expect so. In any case, I shall put your new denture in straight-away. You'll hardly know that anything has happened.'

Mr Jones was the sort of practitioner who required to be paid before the operation was begun. 'Four teeth at ninepence a time, that comes to three shillings. Then there's the denture. Got to charge you five bob for that, I'm afraid, on account of the price of gold.' Sev handed over eight silver shillings, and received a full tumbler of whisky in return.

'Drink it all down,' he was told.

'But I'll be dead drunk. I've got work to do –'

'It'll be alright. His Lordship's gone down to Montacute for the weekend, and I've had a word with the butler. He says you can go back to bed for an hour or two while the booze wears off.'

Sev choked and gasped, and managed to drink half the whisky.

'I'll save the rest for afterwards.'

'Very wise,' said Mr Jones, 'I expect you'll need it.'

It was cold on that September morning. Sev sat on a straight-backed chair borrowed from the kitchen, and held on to the seat, as bidden by Mr Jones. The walls of the garage advanced and receded. He giggled helplessly as the chauffeur came towards him, wearing one of the cook's white aprons, and holding a pair of nutcrackers in his hand.

'Now open wide, boyo. This won't hurt a bit.'

*

Two weeks were to pass before the anguish and swelling had subsided; another month before he could eat meat, or spend minutes with Flossie in the china pantry; but the denture fitted, the new teeth indistinguishable from his own. Sev practised his smile in Lady Curzon's silver hand-mirror. The attentions of the housemaids reinforced his own conviction that he was now the most handsome male member of Lord Curzon's household. He grew confident and careless. When sent on errands for the butler or housekeeper, an hour of exploration on his own account was now included in the outing. Lady Curzon had returned to London. Sev had helped to carry in her luggage. Her arrival caused great excitement beyond the green-baize door.

'Oh, idden she just lovely!' cried Mary.

'I'd forgot just how elegant she was,' said Jane.

Sev knew better than to gaze directly at the faces of his employers; his sightings of her Ladyship were always from a distance, or through partly-opened doors. His new Monday morning task, since her return, was to take a linen-covered wicker basket to Mr Taylor of Bond Street, into which was packed the lotions and creams, the rouge and powder ordered by the lady's maid. This trip, which should at most have taken twenty minutes, had gradually lengthened to a lapse of two hours. He strolled, bareheaded in the autumn sunshine, the dark green of his uniform-suit a perfect contrast to his red and waving hair. Women looked at him twice; he pretended not to notice. Sev had lately found an interest that absorbed him more than casual flirtation. India was the one word on his mind in that October of 1918.

George Nathaniel Curzon, Ex-Viceroy, and present Leader of the House of Lords, had filled his town house with mementoes of his former glory. The walls of Number 1, Carleton House Terrace were hung with his hunting trophies; tiger-skins stretched before fireplaces, strange ornaments and statues gathered dust on every polished surface. A marble replica of the Taj Mahal, a delicate thing all tiny domes and minarettes, caused complaints from every housemaid whose task it was to keep the object dust-free. Statues to many famous men had been erected in the vicinity of Carleton House Terrace and Waterloo Place. Sev began to study their inscriptions; distinguished service in India was mentioned on almost every stone plinth. In late October he discovered a book about India on the stall of a second-hand dealer. For the price of two pennies, Sev learned through prose and pictures, that the British had held India for many years, and that seven years in that fascinating country was the usual span of service for a regular soldier.

The valet, because of his privileged position had frequently pretended to a knowledge of State Affairs which he did not have. The war, he told the servants' hall, would be over by the middle of November. On a morning of low cloud and damp winds Sev heard the sounds of gunfire and church bells. He looked down onto the Mall, and saw that crowds were gathering; people had a look of purpose about them, there was a sense of important things about to happen.

Lord Curzon had, in that month, dismissed two footmen and a housemaid. Sev thought about the extra tasks that awaited him in the kitchen. Already it was mid-morning, and the boiler not yet raked-out and stoked. He began to move away from the window, when a roar from the crowd drew him back. 'The King', they were chanting. 'We want the King.' Sev knew then that the valet was right. The date was November 11th. The war was over. Sev moved; down the stairs, past little groups of excited servants, past heaps of unwashed dishes, unpolished boots and table-silver; past the unstoked boiler. He came out into the Terrace to find a city gone mad. He stood for a moment by the Duke of York's monument and looked down on the surge of men and women who had left homes and jobs, offices and hotel kitchens, to be out in the streets on this extraordinary day.

A sudden quickening in the crowds around the palace rippled back along the Mall. A cry went up, 'The King and Queen! They're on the balcony!' People started to run towards Buckingham Palace. Sev glanced back at the tall white mansion where duty lay, but already his feet were on the flight of white steps that led down to the Mall.

It was dark when he returned to Carleton House Terrace. He crept down the area steps and into the kitchen, to find Mary and Jane waiting for him. They gazed disapprovingly at the marks of lip-rouge on his face and collar.

'Been having a good time, have you?' Jane said sourly. She inclined her head towards the huge black boiler.

'You'm in trouble my fine boy! All day us have been wi'out hot water, thanks to you. Now the word have just been passed round that His Lordship is to dine this night with the King and Queen. He'll be wanting his bath in less than an hour.'

The boiler was difficult to light when wood and coals weren't dry. Sev struggled, without success, to coax flames from damp sticks. He dragged a kitchen chair into the yard, and ignoring the cook's wrath, he smashed it into short lengths, and fed the pieces to the sulky stove. The result was six cans of lukewarm water.

The euphoria of the day's events had not yet left him. He whistled 'Pack Up Your Troubles' as he hefted the towel-draped brass cans up to His Lordship's bedroom. The hip-bath stood ready before a blazing fire. Laid out across the bed and chairs were the knee-breeches and jacket, the fine white linen, and the leather corset. Sev put down the last of the cans, and left the room. He had reached the top of the back stairs when a great roar echoed through the house.

'Carew! Come back, at once!'

Above the dressing-gown of blue silk, his Lordship's face was white, the skin drawn tight across the bones. Sev approached very slowly; for a moment he believed that Lord Curzon was about to strike him.

'Do you know with whom I am to dine this night?'

'The King and Queen, your Lordship.'

'The bath-water is cold. You knew this to be the case when you brought it to me.'

Lord Curzon turned to the valet. 'Go to the butler. Tell him this ruffian is to be returned to Montacute forthwith.

Tell him that he is to pay any wages owing to him and rid me forever of his presence.'

*

Sev had never ridden in a motor-vehicle. At any other time he would have found the experience exhilarating. He sat up beside the driver, a Montacute man who was older than his father. Sev wore his blue suit and brown bowler hat. A wicker suitcase tied around with string had been loaned to him by Mary. The case had clanked and rattled as the driver stowed it among casks of wine and Fortnum and Mason hampers.

'What have you got in here, then?' the man had joked. 'You haven't pinched the Crown Jewels, have 'ee?'

Sev shook his head. He ignored all attempts to draw him into conversation. They drove slowly through city streets where people still celebrated the end of war. Flags flew from every building, and Sev watched them flutter through a haze of tears. Last night he had been angry; rage at the unfairness of his dismissal had prevented him from sleeping. This morning he felt cold and sick. He glanced sideways at the driver's seamed and rosy face.

'Do 'ee know why I got sacked, Mr Dearborn?'

'Way I heard it,' the old man grinned, 'you tried to make his Nibs take a cold bath.'

Sev's hands bunched into fists. If he had only been sacked for some huge and daring misdeed he could have better borne the shame of it all. But Montacute people would find humour in his delivery of cold bath water to the Leader of the House of Lords; especially since he was to dine that night with the King and Queen. Sev jerked his head back towards the wicker suitcase.

'I done something much worse than that,' he hinted, 'I shall prob'ly be sent to gaol when they finds out about it.' He peered through the van's misty windows. 'You needn't take I all the way home to Montacute. I'll get out when us comes to the next big town.'

'Oh, no you won't, my bucko! His Lordship's order

was that I should deliver you home to your mother, and that's what I intend to do.'

Sev slumped in his seat. He began to think about Montacute, about ridicule and humiliation.

'Bad time for you to lose your place,' the driver told him. 'People do say that there'll be terrible unemployment when all they soldiers come home, wanting their old jobs back.' He paused. 'Your Ma won't be none too pleased, either. Not now her got another mouth to feed, poor 'ooman!'

Sev turned to the driver and stared at him from beneath drawn eyebrows. He saw the man's hands grip the steering wheel until the knuckles shone. 'Hey, hey! There's no call for you to give I one o' your black looks. I was on'y trying to warn 'ee what you got to expect.'

Sev lifted the familiar latch, walked into the house, set down the wicker suitcase and stood awkwardly beside it. His mother showed no surprise at his abrupt arrival. She was sitting in her usual place at the gloving-table, close to the window; there were streaks of grey in the gold of her bent head. Her foot moved, without pause, on the ledge of the old rocking-cradle. He felt the tears well-up inside him. He longed to go to her, put his head in her lap, and be comforted. He took one step towards her, but a cry from the cradle wrenched her attention from him. The warmth of his tears cooled to a cold indifference. He said, 'I got the push from his Lordship. I let his bathwater get cold so he sent me home.'

His mother studied him from crest of shining red hair, to toe of smart brown boots. 'You looks well, David,' she said gently. 'No wonder all they maids was after you, up in London.'

'I got sacked,' he repeated. 'Old Curzon gave me the shove, don't you hear what I say?'

'I hears you. 'Tis a wonder to me that you lasted so long; from all what us hears about the man, he'm a devil to work for.'

Indifference changed to gratitude, and gratitude to

love. Sev bent to the wicker suitcase. He loosened the
string and threw back the lid. He lifted out the knives
and forks, the heavy silver spoons that had Lord
Curzon's monogram stamped upon them.

'Look at that, Ma!' he said proudly. 'I brought you a
present back from London!'

His mother's face changed. Indulgence and sympathy
turned to fear and horror. 'You stole these things.' It was
a statement, not a question.

'No I never! They got hundreds of 'em. Drawers and
cupboards full what they never use. I thought about you,
and your bent tin forks, and the knives what don't cut. I
thought you'd be pleased.'

She looked long and thoughtfully at him. She said at
last, 'If you had meant to steal, I reckon you'd have
taken something of real value. But the consequences is
the same whether 'tis diamonds and gold or knives and
forks. When they find out what you've done you'll be
sent to prison. You cud get the birch or the cat o'
ninetails.'

Sev picked up a silver spoon and stared dumbly at it.
He remembered the anger he had felt on being called a
ruffian by Lord Curzon. He had taken the brass water
cans back to the kitchen after his dismissal; on his way
past the butler's pantry he had spied the unpolished
silver. On an impulse he had grabbed up all the cutlery
that he could possibly carry in two hands, and taken it
swiftly to his room. He had heard about the cat
o'ninetails, the whip of nine ropes, each one with a knot
tied at its end.

'What'll us do, Ma?' he muttered, assuming her
complicity and willingness to help him.

'The van goes back up to London on a Friday. If I take
these – these things, to Mr Dearborn, p'raps he'll be able
to slip 'em back where they belong, and nobody the
wiser.' Sev's mother had not smiled once since he had
walked in the door; now she leaned forward suddenly
and patted his hand.

'You took up cold water for his Lordship's bath?'

He nodded. His mother's long and mobile lips began to curve up into a smile. He felt his own mouth twitch. He said, ''Twas an important dinner that night with the King and Queen. His Lordship was proper put-out I can tell 'ee, Mother!'

The amusement bubbled in her throat, her head went back in a paroxysm of helpless laughter. 'Oh I bet he was,' she gasped, 'did – did 'un acshully get into the water?'

'From what I could see,' Sev admitted, 'he had at least one wet foot.' He grinned, 'Come to think about it, that must have been a bit of a shock when he was expecting to step into hot water.'

Sev began to laugh. The sounds of their combined mirth woke the baby in the cradle. Sev peered down at the small red face, all laughter spent. 'What's she called?' he asked awkwardly. His mother bent to the rocking cradle. 'Her haven't got no proper name yet. Us just calls her Baby. I was waiting for the time when you came home, so that you cud name her.'

*

The only work available to a dismissed boot-boy was that of farmhand. The November days were spent in idle wandering; he walked to the crossroads at Five Ash, where it was said that the body of a long-dead gypsy was buried. He climbed Miles Hill and looked out to the long blue line of the horizon that might even be the sea. He would never do farm work; could not, however great the pressures, stand before a farmer and plead to be taken on. He gazed out across the muted greens and browns of Somerset, the golden villages, the tidy homesteads. The itch of discontent intensified, until it was a torment. He had seen London. He had felt the pulse of that great city beat in harmony with his own pulse. A loathing for every field and copse, every hedgerow and covert, seized his mind. He remembered standing on this selfsame spot with Llewelyn Powys; they had talked about mountains. Stay away from mountains, Mr Powys had said. That silence is designed to shrivel a man's soul. Sev wanted to feel his soul shrivel; he ached for the experience of strange lands and risky places. The months spent in Lord Curzon's service had fired his mind with images of India. He recalled the dark woman.

'You'll go to a far land,' she had crooned, 'and bide away from us for many-a-long year. Guard your fingers,' she had said, 'Take care o' your hands, for that is where your soul is.' Sev looked down at his hands, considered their neat shape, the smallness of them. He had a sudden memory of his father's hands, wide and clean, from contact with the limestone, the nails short, the skin roughened. The hands of a practical man, a worker, one who tended roses, and carved lettering on tombstones. Sev could feel the elation draining from him; he pushed the inadequate hands into the trouser pockets of his London suit. The ebb of confidence was followed, as always, by the plummet into misery. The black dog of depression, that had followed him from London, leapt now onto his shoulder. His need for a smoke turned into a craving, and all his severance pay from Curzon's had been handed over to his mother. He turned abruptly on the muddy summit of Miles Hill, and began to plunge downwards towards the village.

Meridiana heard the swift light footfalls halt before her cottage, and knew at once who it must be. She felt a blankness, a negation of all feeling for him. Safer so! She did not turn upon his entry; face averted, she said grudgingly, ''Tiv took 'ee long enough to make your way to my house.' But even at a distance of six paces she could sense the glory of him. Slowly, she moved her head until her eyes rested foursquare on him. She gazed into his face and felt the soul melt inside her. She remembered the pale and puny baby, placed in her arms by Jye, all those years ago. His small body had warmed her heart then; now her whole spirit was set alight by the brilliance of him.

'Come you over to the fire,' she murmured. 'Sit you down in your grandfather's chair.' She noted the way his eyes swivelled upwards towards the mantelshelf, the nervous plucking movements of his fingers.

'You needs a smoke?'

'Dying for one!'

She reached for a clay pipe and a packet of thick twist. 'Smoke or chew?' she enquired.

He grinned. 'Smoke! I never did get into the chewing habit.'

No further speech passed between them until the pipe was lit and drawing. She studied him, but slowly, savouring the sharp delight of his presence at her fireside. The brown boots and smart blue suit, mud-stained and already shabby, spoke to her of London. The cleaning of silver, the carrying of coals, had not damaged his hands. She came last of all to his face; to the bright hair that sprang away from the high forehead in a widow's peak; the thin skin that had the glow of health beneath it. He was taller than Damaris his mother, but would never now reach the great height of his father Jye. He had filled out, the hollow look had left him; his shoulders had broadened. But still he was not quite a man. The eager looks of a young boy still overlay his assumed pose of sophistication. Her love for him rose up like a great shout inside her. He was hers, although he did not yet know it; blood and sinew, nerve and spirit, he was her creation. He would do all those things in his life that she would have done had she only been a man.

' – and so,' he was saying, 'I shan't be staying yer much longer. I cudden abide to do farmwork, not after London.'

'So what will 'ee do, my heart's joy?'

'Find a ship. Sail to India. See the Taj Mahal and the River Ganges.'

'From where did 'ee learn about such things?'

'Curzon ruled India once upon a time. You shud of

seen that house of his'n! I read his books when nobody was looking.' Sev raised his head; he transfixed her for the first time with the full power of his gaze. 'You've been about quite a bit when you was a young girl; up and down the country, so you used to tell me. Where,' he asked, 'where's the nearest port what the big ships sail from?'

Meri fought the urgency of his words, but he was too strong for her.

He leaned forward, his eyes came all the way open.

'Tell me!' he demanded. 'I know that you knows all about such things!'

Meri spoke, and each word felt like a small death. 'Bristol,' she whispered, 'Bristol 'ull be your closest port. Thass where the big ships sail from.' She paused. 'You's'll need money. I got money. Be you certain sure that this is what you want to do?'

'Never more sure of anything.'

She stood up, and a great weakness gripped her body. For a moment she clung to the mantelshelf, and then her head cleared.

'Very well,' she said, in a strong voice. 'I'll give 'ee twenty gold sovereigns. But this must bide for all time a secret betwixt thee and me.'

*

The lights had gone up again in Taunton, people had linked hands and danced around the Praed. But as Madelina said, whatever would they talk about now that the war was over? On that memorable night of November 11th Abi had put on the navy-blue costume and the blouse of pleated white shantung. She stepped into the high-heeled court shoes and felt the confidence bestowed by extra inches. She pinned the gold brooch at her throat, stood before the dressing-table mirror and gazed at her reflected image. The expensive costume, bought by Aunty Blanche in Exeter, showed hardly a sign of wear. She pulled on the little cloche hat and swung the scarlet cape around her shoulders. Through the mirror she observed her mother, the thin figure elongated by a trick of light.

'You're going out then?'

'Well, I'm not exactly dressed for bed, am I?'

'That'll be rowdy in the town, tonight.'

'It's not every day a war ends.'

'The streets'll be full of drunks.'

'I feel like getting drunk myself.'

'You're going out to meet him. You might as well tell the truth, I shall find it all out later on.'

Abi whirled around upon the high heels. 'Yes I am! I'm going out to meet him! I'm going to tell him it's all over. That you won't let us marry!'

'Don't bring my name into your affairs. All your life you've been warned what happens when close cousins marry. You should never have got mixed up with Nick Greypaull in the first place.'

'I won't be mixed-up with him after this night. He's going back to Canada. That should be far enough away to satisfy even you!'

Abi turned back to the mirror. Her voice changed. She said in a light tone, 'I was talking to an old workmate of yours the other day. A woman who remembers you from Cook's factory.' She paused, but no comment came from the doorway. 'She was saying how smart you were as a young girl. A very striking looking maiden was what she said.' Abi sensed her mother's stillness and took courage from it.

'When Annis Greypaull walked in Vivary Park on a Sunday morning, why she was noticed by officers, not by common soldiers!'

Abi smiled into the mirror. 'If you were that good-looking I'm surprised you waited all those years for Father. What year was it that he came home from Burma?'

'I don't remember,' said the watcher, 'I never was very good on dates and figures.'

'It's not easy,' said Abigail, 'to know your own mind when all your waking hours are spent in the company of your mother. The war is over, and you're the winner this time. But I'm quite good at dates and figures, Mother; and you of all people must know how spiteful women love to talk.'

*

Mother, Eve noticed, was being especially nice to Abigail now that their cousin had gone away. Whenever Mother spoke of Nick, it was almost as if he had died bravely in the trenches, defending England.

'Ah,' she would sigh, 'he came to fight for us even though he didn't have to! He was a stout liddle fellah, just like his father. Of course, he won't have long to live. That wound in his chest never healed proper, did it Frank? A delicate-looking chap was Nick.' She looked meaningly at Abi. 'They say the winters in Canada are dreadful. You'd need to have been born there to withstand that cold. From what Nicholas said, 'tis a rough sort of life on his stepfather's farm. Good enough for Canadians I dare say! But no sort of place for a well brought-up girl from England.'

Abi grieved for Nick as if he had in fact died in the trenches. It had, Eve thought, been a curious affair of snatched meetings and passed notes. Once aware of his aunt's opposition to their marriage, Nick had no longer visited the house. He and Abi had been seen standing close together under lamp-posts on street corners, and walking hand-in-hand in the lanes beyond Holway. He had not come to say goodbye. Eve shed tears for the sadness of it all. Abigail remained dry-eyed, and dangerously bright.

A party, Mother said, was what this family needed; one that would serve several purposes and cheer them all up! Eve was surprised at the jollity of Mother. Aunt Candace had moved recently to the house at Rowbarton. The mould-streaked furniture was retrieved from the damp back-bedroom, wiped clean and polished, and restored to its proper place. The party was to mark the end of the war, Eve's seventeenth birthday, the departure of Aunt Candace, the return of Laura Quinn to Taunton; and Christmas.

Eve and Abigail made paper-chains and hung them; Father bought a Christmas tree from the Saturday market on the Praed. Aunt Candace made a fruit cake that had brandy in it. Aunt Mina promised jellies, and as many iced-fancies as the rations would allow. Eve charmed a pork loin from the butcher's son. Mother borrowed a piano from the next door neighbour; every family in the Terrace had received an invitation, a particular welcome extended to those with sons just home from France. That Christmas night was to live forever in Eve's memory; she was never to forget the sound of beer barrrels rolled up the slight incline of the Terrace by ex-soldiers who sang 'Tipperary' and 'Nellie Dean'. Never to forget the bright beauty of her cousin Laura, the tall and handsome Patrick Quinn, and their obvious love and joy in one another.

Laura played all the old tunes, like 'Lily of Laguna', and 'Goodbye Dolly Grey'. Patrick stood beside her and turned the pages of her music, and remembered, Eve felt sure, the magic of their first meeting. People sang and wept, and when the cider and beer ran out, new barrels were fetched from the Half-Moon Inn. Abi laughed and laughed, two patches of hectic red burning on her pale cheeks. Eve moved from one group to another, listening to conversations. She heard Uncle David Lambert confiding to Father.

'Wonderful to have a grandson, Frank! He's seven years old, you know, and they say he favours me in looks. We go fishing together. We like to do the same things; he's very keen on woodwork; he already handles my tools with skill! He's my second chance, Frank. The son I wanted but never had.'

Father glanced to where Abi clinked glasses with a

bandaged boy from the Dardanelles.

'A fine thing, Dave, to get a second chance in life. He's a grand liddle chap. You're a lucky man!'

It was after the party, when Father and Abi had gone to bed, and Eve picked up paper hats, and collected empty glasses, that mother appeared with the little box.

'Leave all that mess, maid. We'll straighten-up tomorrow morning. Come here to the fire. I've got a birthday present for you.'

Eve opened the box to find a silver pendant; a crescent of leaves, set with soft pink stones in the form of petals. She lifted it and fastened it about her neck. She looked into the mantelshelf mirror; she said uncertainly, 'Does it suit me? I don't have your fair colouring, Mother, and it was yours, wasn't it? I recall it from years back. Are you sure you want to part with it?'

'I made a promise to your Granny Greypaull that you should have it. It's supposed to be a charm against evil. There's an old story in the family that when my mother was a girl she did some trading with a gypsy. She bartered a blue china bowl in exchange for a similar pendant.' Annis sighed. 'Coral is said to be lucky for some people.'

'And was it for Granny?'

''Twas the losing of the necklace that seemed to bring the bad luck.'

Eve thought about Abi, the false gaiety of her, the unhappy eyes. She gazed at her mother's anxious face. 'Then I'll wear it,' she said. 'You never know, it might make all the difference.'

*

Leaving Montacute should have been easier for him this time, there were so many reasons why he could not stay. Sev stoked his anger with memories of Granfer and Granny. My parents never wanted me, he told himself. This never was my home right from the beginning. His sister Mathilda had gone away into domestic service, but

330

still the house was full of young ones; little girls who watched him, and giggled from behind their fingers. There was the truckle bed in the corner of the kitchen which marked Sev's uncertain position in the household. His father had spoken to him once since his return from Curzon's.

'That'll take a bit o' time,' he had said in his slow tones, 'for 'ee to settle down again, after London. Best if you can find work as quick as you can, I'll have a word about the village.'

The concern in his father's voice was to do with the fact that an extra plate upon the dinner table would place yet another burden on the crowded household. 'Stealing,' his father had said in his flat voice, 'was a very bad thing for 'ee to do. One slip could lead to another. A boy can begin by taking a halfpenny, and end up on the gallows.' He waited until the household slept, and then filled the pocket of the blue suit with his few possessions. He took with him the mouth-organ and the penny-whistle, a penknife, the blades of which were stiff with rust; and a coloured picture of the Taj Mahal that he had torn from a book in Lord Curzon's library. On the tenth day of the new year 1919, Sev walked the five miles into Yeovil. He bought an overcoat of Melton cloth, a white silk muffler, and a pair of smart shoes. At the Yeovil railway station he asked for a one-way ticket to Bristol.

The dockside pub was full of helpful sailors. Sev asked about ships to India, and was told that he had come to the wrong port. Southampton, they said, was the place he should make for. Meanwhile, what about a game of cards, and a tot of rum to keep out the cold? The dark woman's gold brought him instant friendship. He drank rum, felt sick, fell asleep, woke to find himself out in the street, propped against a wharfside lamp-post. They had left him the penny-whistle, the mouth-organ and the rusty penknife. The overcoat had gone, along with the smart shoes, and the money.

He had trod barefoot as a child, in summer. Now, he

stood up and began to walk along the wharf, his numbed feet slipping on the greasy stones. A fine rain began to fall, soaking the blue suit. Sev had seen gypsies and tramps go unshod through snow and over frozen grounds. He looked down on his bare feet. In winter his mother had always managed to buy him boots, of some sort. A sense of hopelessness gripped him. He found an open-sided shed stacked with timber and huddled in its shelter. The sun crept up to the height of its January zenith. Sev thought about drowning; how it would feel to have that black and oily water close above his head. People said that when you drowned your whole life came back to haunt you in those final seconds. He remembered the ball of woolly lambstails that had been his first toy. He recalled the ferret Rip that had lived inside Granfer's flannel shirt; lambing-time upon the Hill, the ram lamb that he had himself delivered.

'Stealing,' his father had said, 'is a very bad thing. One slip can lead to another. A boy can begin by taking a halfpenny, and end up on the gallows!'

Sev had never played the mouth-organ since that winter's day in St James's Park. Now his fingers sought its reassurance; he breathed life into the squat shape and the notes of 'Abide with Me' fell softly on the cold air. He thought of the dark woman and felt ashamed. He perceived, but dimly, in that moment, the nature of her love for him. He had taken all her money, got drunk, and allowed the sailors to steal it from him. You could almost say that it was Sev himself who had been the thief. Sev who was, according to his father, already heading fast towards the gallows.

The wood and tin had at first struck cold upon his lips; warmed by his steamy breath the mouth-organ now felt like a live thing, leading him on from one thought to another. There was the picture of the Taj Mahal folded in his pocket. He looked out towards the estuary, and saw great ships moving slowly across the sun's path. There was Montacute, restrictive and hidebound. There was love which made him weak when he needed to be strong; his mother's blue eyes, and the shy three-cornered smile that was reserved for him.

'No wonder,' she had said on his return from London, 'no wonder all they housemaids took a fancy to 'ee. You've growed to be such a handsome feller.'

Tears filled his eyes; the breath that formed the music lodged deep in his throat. He pushed the mouth-organ into his jacket pocket. He could never go back! He stared hard into the winter sunlight; when he looked away the awful thought was etched in fire against the sky.

Soliders served in India. He had seen photographs in Lord Curzon's study, whole battalions and regiments. The nearest recruiting barracks was in the county town of Taunton. He stood up and began to walk.

*

The horse-drawn cart had J. Minns, Bridgwater, painted on its side. Bridgwater, Sev thought, must be somewhere in the vicinity of Taunton. He raised a hand as the cart drew level. 'I needs a lift to Taunton.' The elderly driver looked doubtfully at him. 'I on'y goes so far as Bridgwater. Taunton is a fair step on from there.'

Sev swung himself up to sit beside the old man. 'That'll do for me,' he said wryly, 'I've see'd all I ever want to see of Bristol.'

They travelled in silence for several minutes. He began to shiver. The man looked sideways at Sev, assessing the state of the blue suit, his unshaven face and his bare feet.

'There's a heap o' clean sacks in the back of the cart. Find the biggest one and put it round your shoulders. There's a pile o' rags in there somewhere. Tie 'em round your feet. 'Tis the best I can do for 'ee.' The man shook his head. 'You been in some kind o' roughhouse, young 'un?'

Sev came back to sit beside him. 'I was looking for a ship to India, but I fell in wi' some sailors. They got me drunk on rum, when I woke up, they'd pinched my coat

333

and shoes, and all my money.' He adjusted the sack round his shoulders, and studied his rag-bound feet. 'I'm making for Taunton and the barracks.'

'Best thing you could do,' the man said. 'There's no jobs to be had, up or down the country. There's a bit o' bread and cheese in my bag there.' He sighed. 'I had a boy – looked a lot like you. He never came back from the Dardanelles.'

Sev said swiftly. 'I tried to enlist, but I was too young.'

'You'll be safe enough in the peace time Army; if they'll have you. How old be you now?'

'Eighteen come April.'

The man grinned. 'Close enough I reckon. There's trouble, so I've heard from they Feenians in Ireland. They say that the Army is taking all the young chaps they can get.'

Sev ate the bread and cheese, and a little warmth came back into his body.

The cart, pulled by a pair of strong horses, moved along at a good speed. Sev slept, and woke to hear the old man saying, 'We be coming into Bridgwater. 'Tis nearly dark. I got a barn you can shelter in overnight. Better if you start out fresh for Taunton.'

They came to a crossroads, and the cart slowed. Sev said, 'You can set me down here. I got to be in Taunton by morning.'

The carter looked first at the frost-rimmed road and then at the thinness of the blue suit. 'You knows your own mind best, boy. But like I said, 'tis a tidy step to the barracks. You better keep my sack, else you'll freeze to death this night.'

Sev jumped down from the cart. 'Thanks,' he said, 'I'll remember you!'

The signpost said Taunton, 11 miles. Sev calculated distance; to Yeovil from Montacute and back again was roughly ten miles. He flexed his toes inside the swaddling rags, pulled the sack about his shoulders, and took the road that led to Taunton.

The euphoria that carried him from Montacute to Bristol had seeped away in the timber shed on the wharfside. But the fumes of rum had still soothed his deepest hurts, allowing him to see the Army as a haven and the life of a soldier his only salvation. Now, as he tramped the uphill and downdale road, a little nervous, and alone in the frosty darkness, the true nature of Sev's position came slowly to him. The final seductive rum-fumes were dispelled. Supposing, he thought, supposing the Army won't have me? He remembered the verminous tramps who had passed through the village of Montacute in his childhood; young men dressed in rags, their bearded faces hollow, a flush of fever in their cheeks. They had slept under hedges and begged for bread. Well, the war had seen an end to all that! The message, 'Your Country Needs You', had included vagabonds and gypsies. But the war was over, and Sev not yet the magic age of eighteen years.

The rags on his feet began to wear thin on the flinty road; the sack across his shoulders was inadequate against the bitter cold. Hunger-pangs began to slice through him; except for the carter's bit of bread and cheese, he had eaten nothing since leaving Yeovil. Sometimes he staggered and almost fell; the need to lie down and sleep filled his mind. The darkness was lightening towards the east; he could make out a tall hedge, an open gateway, a ridged field that was used for the storing of potatoes. He turned off from the road and began to walk between the earthen ridges. He paused and swayed, no longer certain of the location of the blackthorn thicket. The weakness seemed to start at his ankles and move swiftly upwards; he felt pain as his knees hit the frozen ground. He made one, ineffectual move towards the sheltering hedgerow, but it was too late.

Awareness returned, and brought with it the agony of numbed limbs that contracted with cramps each time that he attempted movement. Even his eye-muscles seemed to be frozen; he peered out through slitted lids at the hummocks of red earth that stretched away on all sides. The sleeves of his blue suit were stiff and glittering with hoar frost; the hand that gripped his wrist was wrinkled and small.

'So you idden dead after all, then? My dear Lord, but you give I a nasty turn, young man, as I come past the gateway, I made sure you was a gonner! Be you damaged in some way?'

He sat up and the pain of returning circulation made him cry aloud. The woman was older than his mother.

'No damage,' he reassured her, 'jus' frozen stiff wi' the cold.'

'Rub your arms and legs,' she told him; she gestured towards a smoking chimney. 'You cud of come in an' had a warm afore my fire, but my husband is to-home this day, and he don't hold wi' strangers.'

Sev said, 'What day is it, then?'

'Why 'tis Monday, young man.'

'What place is this?'

'South Petherton.'

He tried to rise, but could not. He said, 'I got to get to Taunton.'

She looked concerned. 'You idden fit to go nowhere, not in that state.' She peered closely at him. 'Tell 'ee what I'll do! I'll fetch a hot drink and a bit o' bread an' jam.'

He rubbed at his arms and legs, made one more attempt to stand, but could not. He was sure she would not return, but all at once a steaming cup was thrust into one hand, and a thick wedge of bread, spread thickly with marmalade, was put into the other. The tea was hot and sweet, the bread fresh. He ate and drank and felt his strength return. He handed her the cup and tried to smile.

'Reckon I'll be alright now,' he told her; he stood up, swayed a little, and began to put one foot before the other. The old woman gazed up into his face. 'Be you makin' for the barracks?'

Sev nodded.

'I thought you might be. Well, thass a pity! 'Tis a shame when a nice-looking feller like you is brought to that low state!'

He managed this time to give her a wide grin. 'I'll remember thee!' he said. 'Oh yes. I'll remember thee!'

There had been no need for Sev to seek direction, the sounds of marching music led him into Taunton. The scarlet tunics brought him up through High Street; he turned the corner into Mount Street, his rag-bound feet keeping strict time behind the big drum. The good feeling leaked away as he watched them out of sight. He looked down at his shabby state and felt certain of rejection. He stood before the barrack entrance, read the word JELLALABAD inscribed across the high arch, and knew without doubt that this was the hour in his life that would make or break him. He spoke to a corporal who pointed to a door marked GUARDROOM, and said that he'd 'tell the Sergeant'.

Sev stood close to the coke-fired stove, and the steam from his frozen garments rose about him in great clouds. He touched a hand to his stubbled face, and curled his swaddled toes together. Two sergeants came in; they walked slowly round him, waving away steam.

'Jesus Christ,' said one, 'whatever next?'

''Tis a bloody walking scarecrow!' said the other; he grinned.

'Well, what have brought you here, my 'andsome?'

Sev remembered Lord Curzon; he cast his gaze downwards, made his voice respectful. 'I've come to join up, sir.'

'What's your name?'

'David John Carew.'

'Occupation?'

'I – I was a waiter in a big hotel in London.'

'Anything else?'

'I was a carpenter's apprentice.'

The older sergeant nodded. 'I might just place you as a mess-orderly or chippy. How old are you?'

'Eighteen sir.'

'Right! Medicals will be held at ten sharp. Meanwhile, you will go to Ablutions and clean your filthy self.' He pointed to the door. 'There's a Corporal out there. He'll show you where to go.'

As Sev turned away the Sergeant called him back. 'Tell the Corporal he's to find you a pair of boots before you can see the doctor.'

Sev did his best with the cold water, a piece of yellow soap and a threadbare towel. His hair had grown long since leaving London; he pushed wet fingers through it. The boots were at least three sizes too big, but he was grateful for them. It was, he thought, in the interests of the recruiting sergeant that he should look his best before the doctor. These sergeants, Sev had heard, were paid a fee for every man enlisted by them.

The Medical Officer was a dour man who at first examined him without comment. His questions were few. No illnesses, Sev confirmed. No operations. No disease in any member of his family. His hearing was acute; and no, he had never needed to wear glasses.

'You are better-nourished than most of your kind. How did you achieve that?'

Sev remembered his half-lie to the recruiting-sergeant. 'I worked in a hotel kitchen, sir. There was perks, if you know what I mean?'

The doctor smiled. 'You're a strong specimen for your age. Better than most that come before me. We'll just test your eyesight, to be sure.'

The white board had black letters printed on it. Sev was told to place his hand over one eye, and then read the letters. He covered his right eye and saw only a grey blur. He lowered his hand and gazed anxiously towards the doctor, but the man, still busy with forms, had not noticed his dilemma. Swiftly, Sev covered his left eye, and the letters showed up black and clear. He read them aloud, willing each line to remain in his memory. The doctor was watching him now. Sev began to cough in order to gain time, his gaze still fixed upon the board. He covered his right eye, and repeated the letters parrot-fashion, then came back to stand before the doctor's table. The long white form was signed without further questions.

'A good physique,' the doctor told him. 'You're A1 in every department.'

Once again Sev presented himself before the recruiting Sergeant. To pass the Medical it seemed was not enough. Sev's possible usefulness to His Majesty's Army had still to be assessed.

'A waiter in a London hotel, eh?' There was doubt in the Sergeant's voice.

'Yes sir!'

The man stood up. 'I'll be in the Officers' Mess,' he told the watching Corporal, 'if anybody wants me.'

*

White-coated orderlies were spreading cloths across tables; a trolley filled with cutlery and glasses stood beside the nearest table. The recruiting Sergeant looked down at Sev.

'Set a dinner-placing,' he commanded. Sev had not known before the eyesight test that he was capable of total recall, that objects and letters, seen once, however briefly, could be brought to his mind by a simple act of will. He closed his eyes and at once Lord Curzon's mahogany dining table stretched out before him; he could see every piece of monogrammed silver, every crystal glass and goblet. He stepped forward, and without hesitation he set a perfect dinner-placing. The Sergeant grinned.

'You'll do,' he said.

The forms were filled in, and a Pay Book issued; Sev's name was listed as David John Carew; his trade as waiter; his marital status single. His date of enlistment was January 12th 1919, and his Term of Service was to be for five years and two. The Unit and Corps to which he now belonged was the 2nd Battalion, Somerset Light Infantry. In company with four other young men who had that morning found acceptance in His Majesty's Service, Sev went to the Quartermaster's Stores and was issued with two uniforms and a topcoat, and more shirts, boots and socks than he had ever in his life possessed. The meal of Irish stew lay uneasily upon his stomach, so long had it been since he had eaten the bread and marmalade given to him by the Petherton woman. His bed was an iron cot that held a straw-filled mattress, two calico sheets and two rough grey blankets. From the barrack-room windows he could just see the trees in Vivary Park. His last thought before sleeping was of his mother. Twelve weeks of training, the Sergeant had told him, and then you'll be in the next draft bound for Ireland. Perhaps he would write her a letter from Belfast; and perhaps he would not.

*

Abi's mind had, from childhood, garnered secrets and hidden them instinctively away until time was ripe. She had absorbed without question those significant looks, the conversations overheard but not understood, the sly sideways glances, the insinuations. There had been times when she was tempted to reach out and grasp the speaker's meaning; to challenge the insult implied. But to do so would have been disloyal, both to Mother and Father, and loyalty was inbred in Abi; a direct inheritance from her grandmother Eliza. There was no particular moment when she had thought, Frank Nevill is not my father. It had taken the shock of her loss of Nick Greypaull to release the knowledge that had always lain just beneath the skin. Now, she felt certainty seep like a poison along her veins, knowing that in some respects it would make her weak; that because of it in some subtle way she would always be the loser. The thought, that was less than a thought, walked beside her, seeking confirmation of its own pain. The proof that she was not Frank Nevill's daughter had come on the day when he had abandoned her; on the day when she had heard him say to Eve, 'My side don't count in the case of Abi. There's things you don't know, old matters that come back to haunt a man when he least expects it . . . just remember, whatever happens, your sister is your mother's business.'

*

People believed that the end of the war would see a swift return to old ways and values. But demobilisation of the Army proceeded only slowly; restive troops, anxious to go home, were rioting in camps at Dover and Folkestone. 'A land fit for heroes to live in' was the slogan but the bitter-faced young men who came back to walk the streets of Taunton were so changed that old soldiers like Frank Nevill were bewildered at their inability to 'come to terms'. In March 1919, the number of men unemployed stood at over one million. Demobilised soldiers, who found women employed in their old jobs, had a particular grievance. One young man, who had returned from France to find a girl working at his leather-cutters bench, was especially bitter. Together with three friends he waited in North Street for the delivery van that served the Devon and Somerset Stores. While one man pinioned the driver, the other filled army kitbags with delicacies intended for the tables of the wealthy. Within seconds the whole business was over; within minutes the young men had vanished among the streets around Pig Market, and were distributing their loot among family and friends.

The ringleader was caught, and brought before the magistrate. 'Well of course he was recognised,' said Annis, 'everybody in the town knows Joey Santini! They were our neighbours when we lived in the cottage behind North Street. When Mr Santini died they moved away to Bishop's Hull.'

'I remember them,' said Abi. 'Mr Santini roasted

chestnuts and played the barrel-organ in the winter. He had a little monkey that wore a yellow jacket. In the summer-time he sold ice-cream. Joey Santini must be about my age. I sat next to him in school for one whole year. He had big dark eyes and the blackest curls you ever saw.'

'He's in plenty of trouble now,' Annis said, 'but what else can you expect? I don't know what the world is coming to. Young people had more respect for their elders when I was a girl.' She gazed fiercely at Abigail's shorn head. 'Look at you, miss! All your lovely hair chopped off just to follow some silly fashion!'

'I once heard,' Abi said, 'that you had a red-hot needle pushed through your earlobes, because you wanted to wear earrings.'

Even as she spoke her spirits lifted at this evidence of her own daring. The flash of fear in her mother's eyes encouraged her further.

'The world is changing, Mother. Or hadn't you noticed? Long hair is a thing of the past, we have the bob and the shingle these days. Skirts are getting shorter too.' She pointed to Annis's ankle-length black dress. 'Like I said to Eve, it's time we got busy with the scissors. Well, you wouldn't want us to look frumpish, would you?'

They were sitting together at the gloving-table on that Friday morning. It was that time between the departure of Frank and Eve for the Tannery and the arrival of Madelina for tea and gossip. Annis laid down the half-sewn hedger's glove. Her voice was dangerously quiet.

'You get to sound just like your Aunty Blanche. It's not just the way you speak anymore, it's the things you say.' She raised her index finger and shook it, close to Abi's face. 'I will not,' she said, 'have you going behind my back and persuading your young sister to do things she would never have thought of, left to herself! Our Blanche interfered in my life, with what dreadful consequences I can't ever tell you!'

Abi lifted her head, and for the first time in her life she

faced her mother quite without fear.

'You don't need to tell me. I already know. *I* was the result of what you choose to call your sister's "interference", wasn't I Mother?'

The silence in the room was absolute; they gazed at one another unaware at first of the presence of Madelina.

'The door was on the latch, so I came straight in.' Mina stared from one white face to the other. 'Is something wrong – ?'

Annis said, uncertainly, 'Put the kettle on, Abigail. Make some tea for your aunty.' She turned to Madelina. 'I've got to go round to see Mr Stenlake. There's been some mix-up with our wages. Come upstairs with me while I fetch my hat and coat. I want a word with you.'

*

It was Mina who explained to Abigail across the teacups on that Friday morning. 'You mustn't blame her; your mother had always been a bit silly – easily persuaded, if you take my meaning.'

'I don't take your meaning. I've never known her to be less than unreasonable and bad-tempered. If she had her way why, Eve and I would never leave this house.'

Mina sighed. 'Can't you see? She's frightened for you. She was only a young girl at the time – '

'No she wasn't,' Abi interrupted. 'I've worked it all out. She was twenty-seven years old! Old enough to know better!'

'Don't sit in judgement on her now. There were plenty who did that at the time. Poor Anni. She's had a hard life!'

'No she hasn't. She's had more good than she deserved. Father – ' Abi stumbled across the word – 'Father must have married her soon after I was born.' Her voice broke down in tears. 'I don't ever remember being without him. He was so good to me when I was little. Always so quiet and patient. Never lost his temper

343

with me. Oh, Aunty, whatever would have become of me without Father?'

Mina said, 'Your mother knows the debt she owes Frank Nevill. Make no mistake Abi, that's a good and loving marriage. 'Tis with you and Eve that she finds it hard; we all want the best for our daughters.' Mina paused. 'You've never yet asked about your natural father.'

'I don't think I care to know.' Abi coloured and glanced away. 'From hints that are dropped to me by women who worked with Mother at that time he must have been a common soldier from Jellalabad Barracks.'

'Not a common soldier, Abigail. He was an officer from a high-born family. Landed gentry they were; titles among them, plenty of money. When you were little they sent presents for you. His mother – '

'I remember now! The old lady dressed in velvet, who came to North Street in a carriage! She put sovereigns in my hands and told me to take them to mother.'

Mina nodded. 'Your mother has always believed that an inheritance would come to you from that family. He never denied that you were his child.'

'An officer and a gentleman? Well, well! So that explains a lot, eh Aunt Mina?' Abi's tone was bitter.

Mina hesitated; she said in a careful voice, 'There's just one more thing, my dear. Your mother asks one favour of you. Eve is never to know anything about this. Promise me that you will never tell her.' 'I won't promise anything – but you needn't worry. I shan't want to tell her! There are plenty of gossiping old biddies walking around Taunton, who will, sooner or later, do that very thing!'

*

The need to confide in Eve was at times overwhelming, and yet Abi could not bring herself to say the words. To know that Eve was her half-sister set a distance between them; a sense of separateness grew up in her and Abi felt strengthened by her compensations. Now, it was possible to admit to old jealousy and childish resentment; she remembered the times she had pinched and bruised the baby Eve, the delight she had taken in her tears. Now, all her envy of Eve ebbed away. Without that close tie of blood they could be friends; together they would conspire against Mother. Abi looked at Frank Nevill's daughter, and saw her clearly for the first time. There was not, nor had there ever, been one single point of similarity between them. Abi studied Mother, who had taken love from two men, and born a child to each. Mother who, in her middle-age, was sanctimonious and strict, but still vulnerable in certain quarters. At last Abi understood why too much closeness between herself and Eve had always been discouraged. Singly, they were no match for Mother. Together, they could not be bested.

The house in the Terrace allowed its inhabitants few secrets. Eve knew that there was a mystery in the family; she was aware of the nature of that mystery, she could even, if forced to do so, have picked out the precise time and situation in which Abi herself became aware finally of the truth. Eve knew the secret about Abigail, and yet she did not know it. Frank's habit of coming to terms with difficult situations had, in Eve, progressed to an outright inability to admit unpleasant facts; and still she wished that her family was more like those of other people.

The enmities and intrigues of the Greypaull family had, since her early childhood, seemed perilous to Eve. She had long ago taken the one step backwards that allowed her to observe them with minimal involvement. Her inborn mistrust of deep feeling had lately been confirmed by the agony of Abi at Nick Greypaull's departure. She found strangely embarrassing the vitriolic and double-edged exchanges that now took place between Mother and Abigail. What she could not deny or escape was Abi's new brilliance of mood, the determined sharpness of her, which even Mother could not blunt.

'And where do you two think you're going?' Mother had asked.

'Window shopping,' Abi said. 'We need new Easter outfits.'

They strolled arm in arm through the soft spring evening, pausing beside the plate glass windows of Hatchers and Chapmans, discussing the merits of this coat and that dress. Going out with Abi was a new experience for Eve. She found it stimulating to linger like this in the warm dusk, with the street lights coming on, and the scent of flowers wafting out from Vivary Park.

Young men stood about in small groups; they lounged within shop doorways and under lamp-posts. They wore shiny suits and cloth caps, and loosely tied white mufflers instead of collar and tie. As Eve and Abi sauntered by, the more daring among them whistled, and made low remarks. Eve's arm twitched nervously in Abi's grasp.

'Take no notice,' Abi murmured, 'we've got other fish to fry.'

A costume in powder blue linen was displayed in Hatchers's window. They could, Abi said, make quite a stir in Taunton by dressing, and going out together, in identical outfits. 'After all,' Abi said, 'mother got herself noticed in her day, so why shouldn't we?'

'It'll come expensive,' warned Eve. 'We shall need new hats and gloves, and shoes to match.'

'So we'll do extra gloving in the evenings! Or perhaps you'd rather spend your evenings reading the newspaper to Mother, or helping Aunt Candace pick out winners for the big race?'

Abi's tone was sharp. Eve glanced sideways at the dainty profile, made even more attractive by the bobbed hair, and as always she was confused by her sister's superior air and quick tongue.

'I – I don't really know what you want me to do. Mother's not too keen on us going around together.'

'But what do *you* want?' Abi insisted. 'Would you rather go on as you are – meeting fellows after work, under French's archway, and telling Mother that Mr Stenlake wanted you to stay late? In any case,' Abi said, 'Father knows that you're lying.' Her voice became persuasive. 'Now, if we were going out together, we could walk arm in arm as far as North Street, and then go each our separate ways! Just so long as we go home together – well, what ever can she say?' Abi paused. 'Don't make the same mistake as I did. Don't let her rule your life. Things are going to be different for you. My mind is made up. I'll come up to Hatchers first thing on Monday morning. Five shillings paid down, on two powder-blue costumes, and we'll knock every fella's eye out on Easter Sunday.'

Eve had known only the daytime face of Taunton. But now, in the company of her sister, she began to discover an unsuspected charm in the familiar streets. Taunton after dark was filled with the excitement of unplanned encounters; she realised fully, and for the first time, that hers was a military town. Recruits, their callowness made obvious by nicks in freshly shaven chins, and stubbly haircuts showing from beneath caps, walked in pairs along the main street, hobbling uneasily in their brand new boots. The officers, it seemed, also hunted in couples. Young lieutenants, their swagger sticks tapping smartly against boot tops, could be seen emerging two by two from Jellalabad Barracks at the evening hour when the bars were opened. The Castle Hotel, Abi said would be their destination, or perhaps the County. Corporals and Sergeants were to be found in the Four Alls or The Winchester Arms. Recruits, having little money, were obliged to drink the watered-down beer in the Barrack's wet canteen.

Eve thought that her sister's term 'unplanned encounters' must be a euphemism learned long ago from Aunty Blanche. Such behaviour, she pointed out, would in plain words, be called a pick-up, especially by Mother.

'Well how else,' demanded Abi, 'are we to ever meet a better class of chap? You're hardly likely to find an officer-type curing sheepskins at French's. As for me – I'm shut away all day. No!' Abi said. 'If it happens at all it'll have to be accidentally.' Exactly what it was that Abi hoped for from a casual meeting, Eve dared not enquire. In the company of her sister, Eve could go to those places where alone she would not have dared to venture. Together they sat in the best seats of the Lyceum Theatre, with two smiling lieutenants in close attendance. They drank port and lemon with them in the Lounge Bar of the County Hotel, and dined, on one memorable occasion, at the Castle.

'We'll be perfectly safe,' Abi said, 'just so long as we don't get separated!'

The powder-blue costumes saw them through from Easter into autumn. Worn with pure silk stockings and high-heeled shoes made of crocodile skin, Eve and Abi were known in that summer of 1919 as the 'two little girls in blue'. The frequent drafts for Ireland made sure that no particular pair of licentious lieutenants remained long enough in Taunton to become a problem to them. At the end of September they began to window shop for warmer outfits. Hem lines crept higher; silk stockings became a necessity. Annis predicted pneumonia. Cream coats, suggested Eve, worn with smart shoes of green suede would make a striking note when they walked out together. 'There would be,' Abi said, 'tea dances at the County Hotel in the winter season, not to mention the cinema and the theatre.'

But it was on a wet October night, in weather too cold for the powder-blue and before the purchase of the cream coats, that Abigail was to fall, quite accidentally, into the outstretched arms of Guiseppe Marco Carlo Santini.

*

The war had ended on a note of disillusion. The land fit

for heroes, was, it seemed, yet another unlikely slogan invented by the politicians. People wanted to forget the horrors of the trenches; all the deprivations of the past four years. Young people especially were demanding some distraction from the grim reports of soaring unemployment, rising prices and threatening strikes. A new sense of freedom had been felt in that springtime and summer of 1919, and as always, there were those entrepreneurs of enjoyment in London's West End, who were more than willing to fulfil a need. Restaurants and dance halls, night clubs and theatres were opening up to do roaring business and, as Abigail said, what ever London does today, the people of Taunton are swift to copy!

Old words had taken on new meanings. To be up to date had nothing to do with punctuality, but meant the wearing of silk stockings, shorter skirts, and an ability to dance the fox-trot. People talked about jazz, and ragtime and syncopation. To be modern in Taunton required from Abigail and Eve a modest wardrobe of at least two fashionable outfits; an aptitude for dancing; and sufficient nerve to deceive their watchful parents by inviting unplanned encounters, and applying for membership of the Tipperary Club.

The licensing laws, introduced in wartime, still restricted the daily times of public drinking to six and a half hours. In Taunton's only night-club, gin was drunk, it was said, at all hours; but discreetly from flowered-china teacups. Bath Place, according to Aunt Madelina, had been a dangerous thoroughfare in the time of Grandfather Philip Greypaull. There had dwelt the sedan chair carriers, the pickpockets and ladies of ill-repute.

Her first visit to the Tipperary Club held for Eve all the risky fascination she now came to expect when in the after-dark company of Abigail. Membership of the club was granted only on the personal recommendation of an existing member. Eve wondered how the bright green cards had come into her sister's possession. The night was dark and stormy, great gusts of wind blew them like leaves into the narrowness of Bath Place. There was a door set deep among the thick old walls, a black iron knocker, which Abi had said was shaped like a shamrock. They were to knock four times, and ask for Joey.

The door opened slowly and they were admitted into total darkness. As they moved further into the hallway, a dim light began to glow high up on the wall. A table and chair stood within a recess, beside them a man, his features unclear in the poor light, his hand outstretched to receive their tickets. It was at that moment, in the act of handing over the cardboard squares, that Abigail chose to slip on the damp tiled floor. Her scream brought a man with a powerful torch; as he came through the swing door Eve heard laughter and music. The light revealed Abi, now clasped firmly in the arms of a tall and handsome man. A man from whose embrace, Eve observed, her sister showed no inclination to disengage herself.

'Oh Joey,' she cried breathlessly, 'how lucky that you were there to catch me!'

*

Joey Santini was a jack of all trades. It was only in the art of attracting and seducing young women that he was so obviously the master. The Italian parentage that made him restless and volatile had also bequeathed to him the kind of good looks made fashionable by Valentino and Ramon Navarro. He was tall and broad-shouldered, narrow-waisted and slim of hip. Black curling hair, bronze skin, dark eyes, and a smile that revealed white and even teeth, were assets that could not be matched by the sturdy, but home-grown variety of Somerset's young men.

As he shepherded them through the swing door and led them to a little table, Eve took note of his astounding charm. Only an Italian could have worn the shabby dinner jacket and unmatched trousers, the bright green satin cummerbund and bow tie, with so much style and panache. Even the faint smell of mothballs that hung inevitably about a pawnshop purchase, did nothing to detract from Joey's fascination. Abigail, she observed, still clung helplessly upon his arm, her tiny slimness made even more appealing beside his great height.

Eve sipped at weak tea laced with gin and gazed bemusedly through cigarette smoke at the dancing couples. She raised her voice in order to be heard above the syncopation of a five-piece band. She grinned at Abi. 'You little devil! You already knew him, didn't you? And not just from your schooldays, like you said to Mother.'

Abi smiled a smile of pure contentment. She said, off-handedly, 'Oh, I've come across him a few times just lately. Well – he's been in so much trouble since the Army let him go. I just had to sympathise with him, didn't I?'

The band stopped playing. Eve whispered in the sudden quiet, 'What's he doing in this place? Is he the bouncer?'

Abi shrugged. 'Nothing would surprise me about him. He reckons he's a founder-member – whatever that means! He's mixed up in all kinds of things. He says that good luck just seems to gravitate towards him.'

Eve giggled. 'Like that stack of groceries from the Devon and Somerset Stores van?'

'That was just a bit of fun. He did it for a dare.'

'You seem to know a lot about it.'

Abi laughed. 'Remember that Dundee cake I brought home? I'll give you one guess as to where it came from?'

'Oh Abigail!' Eve gazed admiringly across the table. 'Why, Mother would have choked to death if she had known what she was eating.'

✳

The winter months of 1920 were to prove even more exciting than those of spring and summer. Dark nights, Eve now discovered, made it easier to lie to Mother.

Identical cream coats, worn with green suede shoes and little hats of emerald velvet, had, according to Joey Santini, made Abigail and Eve a walking advertisement for the Tipperary Club. The door in Bath Place opened up to admit them at least three times in every week. They learned to fox-trot and tango. Abi smoked Egyptian cigarettes in a long jade holder, and drank a cocktail called 'White Lady'. 'They were being,' Abigail assured her sister, 'quite madly modern! And wouldn't Mother and Aunt Mina die of shock if they could see us now!'

*

There must, it seemed, always be a ludicrous element in Sev's great adventures. In his search for a ship to India he had gone to the wrong port. On the troopship to Ireland he had started to be sea-sick long before the mooring ropes had been cast off. His period of duty in Belfast had been marked by several minor mishaps. Nothing of sufficient seriousness to appear on a charge sheet, but he had been warned to 'watch it, soldier!'

His claim that he had been a waiter in a big hotel in London had been disproved in the first few minutes of an important top brass function. Sev, white-jacketed and nervous had leaned over the shoulder of a seated Major General; the plate had slipped in his gloved hand, and a stream of Brown Windsor soup had run steadily down the General's shirtfront. He had learned several new oaths in the ensuing uproar, and been demoted at once from the prestigious job of 'silver service' to the clearing of tables and washing up.

The Battalion came back to Taunton on a mild October morning. They marched from the station to the music of 'Old Comrades', and Sev recognised the tune as the one he had once followed; nearly two years had passed since that January morning when he had crept hungry and barefoot through Jellalabad's gates. He had learned a great deal in that time. His natural inclination was towards indiscipline. Rules existed only to be broken. It had taken the greatest effort of will he had ever known to put a curb on his sarcastic tongue; to hold down his destructive temper. But a new kind of pride had grown up in him in Ireland. He had withstood the shocks, performed the pointless duties; paraded in full marching order under a sadistic Provost Sergeant while serving his time as a defaulter. The time in Ireland had been bad. As he marched into Mount Street and wheeled through the tall arch of red brick, Sev saw the Barracks as his place of salvation. He began for the first time to see himself as an 'old soldier'. A few open-mouthed recruits watched from a window as the Battalion halted. Sev's shoulders twitched inside the scarlet jacket; his lips twisted wryly to a three-cornered grin. He thought, surprised, 'I've come home! This is the place where I belong. This is my stepping stone into the world.'

Within hours of their arrival, Sev's Company was told of their inclusion in the next draft due to sail for Bombay. 'Three weeks,' the Sergeant said, 'during which time seven days' leave will be granted to any man who wishes to go home to say his farewells to family and friends. Remember,' he warned them, 'you'll be gone for five years at the very least.'

Sev sat on his bed and watched the departures of his comrades. Of the twelve iron cots in his room, two only were still occupied by that Saturday evening. He looked to where Taffy Richards counted money out onto his blanket.

'Not even enough left to get drunk on,' the Welsh boy grumbled. 'What about you, Chippy?'

'I lost my cleaning brushes just before we left Belfast,' Sev said. 'It took every last penny to replace 'em.' Personal remarks and enquiries about family made a man unpopular, Sev had learned, among his fellow-soldiers. On this occasion he could not hold back the question.

'You not going home then, Taff?'

'Got no bloody home to go to. Brought up in an

orphanage, I was. What about you then?'

'Same sort o' thing,' Sev said, abruptly.

Taffy grinned. 'Sergeant-Major'll have to keep his promise I reckon and be mother to us both. Never mind eh? We got three easy weeks in Taunton. Find ourselves a nice girl each, that's our answer boyo! One what'll write to us when we get to Agra.' Taffy sighed. 'Have you noticed how you and me is the only poor sods in this room what never gets a letter? That's going to be ten times worse when we're on a foreign posting.'

Sev had thought about writing to his mother. In Belfast he had gone so far as to buy a few sheets of notepaper and a pencil from the Quartermaster. He had sat on his bed for one whole evening unable to form the opening words, 'Dear Mother'. Almost two years had passed since he had relieved his parents of his presence. They should, he reasoned, be grateful to him. Never again would his father need to tout for jobs around the village. The shame of the stolen silver must by now have been lived-down among his mother's Chapel members. It was not, he told himself, as though he had ever truly been their son. The memory of Granfer dropped into his mind, and tears filled his eyes. He looked up to find Taffy Richards staring at him. To cover his embarrassment, Sev pulled the mouth-organ from his pocket. He began to play a tune he had heard, whistled by the porters on Holyhead station.

'That's called Alice Blue Gown,' said Taffy. He began to sing in a light tenor voice. ' "In her sweet little Alice blue gown – when she first wandered down into town . . ." Them's all the words I know,' he admitted. He crossed the room to stand at the end of Sev's bed; he nodded towards the mouth-organ. 'Who learned you how to play that thing?'

'Nobody. Just picked 'un up and did it. Same as wi' singing.'

Taffy said, 'I had this idea once, to go on the Halls but it never came to nothing.' He looked thoughtful.

'Now you and me – we'd make a bloody good act between us!'

They gazed hopelessly at one another, at the bareness of the room, at the blackness of the uncurtained windows. Sev stood up.

'Reckon we'd better go out for an hour or two. Start looking for these girls you say 'ull write letters to us.'

*

Walking-out uniform consisted of dark blue trousers with a scarlet side stripe, a scarlet tunic with brass buttons, and a peaked cap of dark blue. Sev knew how smart he looked when wearing his 'best kit'. Sometimes he would dream that he was marching up Middle Street, Montacute. He would see pride in his mother's eyes, the astonishment of his father. But he knew in his heart that this would never happen.

They walked out into the November evening, he and Taffy Richards. 'Mild for the time of year,' Taf said. 'Be plenty of targets out and about on a night like this, pretending to look at the fashions in the shop windows.' They came out of Mount Street, passed the gates of Vivary Park, and wheeled smartly into High Street.

Sev said enviously, 'You been out wi' a lot of women, eh Taff?'

'Oh well – one or two – nothing special mind you.' He glanced at Sev. 'I heard as how you had a bit of bother yourself when we was in Belfast.'

Sev halted; he turned his full gaze onto Taffy Richards. The Welshman took a step backwards. 'No need to look at me like that, mun! You know what barracks-rooms is like. They knows better than to say anything to your face, but there was a lot of talk behind your back.'

Sev marched on: Taffy fell into step beside him. 'No offence, mun!'

Sev's voice was raw. 'I'll tell thee the truth o' it,' he said, 'I don't know what you heard, but this is what happened. You know how I like a smoke. Well, the fags in the Wet Canteen was never very good in Ireland, sort of mangled in their packets. There was this sweet-shop near the Barracks, I began to go there for my Wild Woodbines. Nice little girl served behind the counter. Sort of friendly she was – well you know how the most of 'em hated our guts. I got talking to her. We met a few times in a kind of alleyway behind the shop. There was this lamp-post. We used to stand under it and talk – only talk, you understand me! She had these brothers, eight of 'em, the maddest bunch of Micks you ever heard of. She told me about 'em, two was boxers; they 'ud kill me, she said, if they ever caught us out together.' Sev sighed. 'Well they never caught us, but they must have heard about me. The next time I went to meet her she was in the usual place underneath the lamp-post. My God, Taff! I shall never forget it. They had tied her to it, wi' thick rope. They'd daubed her clothes wi' tar and stuck chicken feathers on 'em. Worst of all, they'd cut off all her long hair – shaved her head closer than a sergeant's chin.'

Taffy said, 'Bloody hell mun! Whatever did you do?'

'Nothin'. Just stood there, lookin' at her. They was all close-by. I could sense that they was near – you got to feel like that in Ireland. They'd made a decoy of her, Taff. They'd staked her out! I started to run. My God, I'd never shifted so fast in all my born days. Good job I was close to Barracks. I was in through the gates wi' all eight of the brothers pounding close behind me. I very near forgot the Password that night!'

Taffy said admiringly, 'You're a funny bastard, Carew, and no mistake! Always been so close-mouthed have you? If that had been me, I'd have told that yarn all about the Barracks.'

Sev grinned. 'Shut up, you gabby Welshman. Look at these two, just ahead! Now idden that a pretty picture?'

The girls wore identical costumes of powder-blue; their stockings were of pure silk. Their shoes made of crocodile skin, had high heels which clicked as they walked. They paused to look into a shop window. Sev and Taffy idled on the corner of Hammet Street; the clock on St Mary's Tower struck seven times.

'I'm taller than you,' Sev told Taffy. 'You can have the small one.'

The girls began to move away. The soldiers followed close behind them. As they drew level, Sev said, 'Excuse me, miss. You wudden happen to have a light, I s'pose?' He held out an unlit Woodbine, and grinned. 'Come out without my matches,' he explained, 'and I'm jus' dying for a fag!'

It was the smaller of the two who opened her handbag and produced a box of Swan Vestas. 'Take them all,' she said, in a ladylike tone that made Sev feel uneasy, 'I've got plenty more at home.' She turned to the younger girl and took her by the arm. 'Come along, Eve,' said the 'posh' voice, 'time we were getting home. Mother will be getting frantic about us.'

The girl called Eve made no move. She gazed at Sev's face as if she recognised him.

'Not yet, Abi,' she said absently. 'It's only seven o'clock. Even mother would look a bit surprised if we came home this early.'

Sev smiled his crooked, three-cornered smile, and watched her eyes change expression. 'It's a very nice evening, miss. Warm for the time of year. I shan't be in England for much longer. I don't know Taunton very well. P'raps we could take a walk together?'

He took several steps away from Taffy Richards. He had not dared to imagine that such a girl would follow, but there she was, at his side, and moving down the pavement. She said, across her shoulder, 'I'll meet you outside the Tipperary Club, Abi. I'll be there about half-past nine so that we can arrive home together.'

They walked for some time without speaking. Sev glanced down at the girl's neat profile and wondered at his own daring. He knew what Taffy had been thinking, what he would have said, given the chance. He could almost hear the little Welshman's warning. 'Classy birds, these is boyo! We is out of our league here. Let's get the hell away from these two.'

Sev spoke at last because he could no longer bear the silence.

'I don't know how you walk in them high-heeled shoes,' he said gruffly. 'These boots give me bloo – give me proper gyp, when I first started to wear 'em.'

'Oh, I manage. My heels arn't all that high, and anyway, it's the fashion.'

Sev said, 'Who's your friend?'

'You mean Abigail? She's my sister.'

'Older than you by quite a bit?'

'Abi's twenty-six. I shall be nineteen in a few weeks.'

'What do you do?'

'You mean work? Well, Abi stays at home with Mother. I'm an examiner in a place that makes gloves.' She halted, and turned to face him. 'You ask a lot of questions, don't you?'

They had reached the steps that led into the Lyceum Theatre. Light poured out from the illuminated foyer, and Sev saw the girl clearly for the first time.

'Them as don't ask questions never get any answers,' he said smartly, but even as he spoke his mind was overwhelmed by the loveliness of her. He had read about girls like this in the books he had borrowed from Llewelyn Powys. His gaze still upon her face, Sev fumbled for the Woodbine packet and the box of Swan Vestas. He made lighting the cigarette an awkward and drawn-out performance. She turned away and began to study the theatre billboards. He moved with her, and remembered phrases from a printed page read long ago danced across his vision, the words a strangely apt description of the girl at his side.

Her hair was a silky nut-brown; it curled softly back from her forehead, and was drawn into a French pleat at the nape of her neck. Her skin was fine and soft, and what the novelist had described as 'peach-bloom'. The match, held too long against the cigarette, began to burn his fingers. He cursed, quietly, and saw her smile. He saw then that she had small white teeth, and a hint of dimples. It was, he thought, a comely face, full of sweetness. As she turned to look at him he realised, with a sense of shock, that her eyes were the colour of a laurel leaf, and so deeply green as to be opaque.

They moved away into Station Road and began to walk slowly towards Rowbarton.

'Where do you come from?' she asked.

He drew hard on the cigarette before answering. 'A long way from here,' he said briefly, 'somewhere up the country.'

'Have you got a family?'

'Nobody that counts.'

She accepted his words like someone unused to demanding explicit answers to her questions. Or perhaps she just wasn't interested in him? He rushed into speech, determined to impress her.

'My Battalion's just back from Belfast. Ireland's a bloo – a dreadful place. I don't never want to go back there.'

'What happened to you?'

'Well – nothing to me – not personal-like.' He was tempted to tell her about the shorn head of the little Irish girl called Mary, but could not bring himself to repeat that tale.

'We had to search cars and vans, and wagons. They was said to be gun-running on the Border. The Micks,' he said reflectively, 'the Micks really hate us soldiers.'

'My father,' the girl said, unexpectedly, 'my father foretold all this Irish trouble in 1919 when the Sinn Feiner De Valera was allowed to escape from Lincoln Gaol. To think,' she cried passionately, 'that we actually had him, locked away in England.'

'De Valera?' Sev asked, bemused. When the politics of their mission had been discussed in the Wet Canteen, Sev had been reading a book or playing the mouth-organ.

'You know!' the girl insisted. 'He's the one who's killing constables and ordering attacks on police barracks. Don't you ever read the newspapers?' She paused, and went on in a committed tone. 'Of course, Lloyd George is doing his best, but Home Rule for Ireland won't work, not according to Father.' Sev had heard of Lloyd George, but he had no inkling of Home Rule. He switched rapidly to safer subjects.

'We're off to India next week,' he told her.

'My father was there when he was a young man. He said it's a very hot place.'

There was, it seemed, no area that he could mention of which her father did not possess some superior knowledge.

'What,' he said, 'what's the Tipperary Club when it's at home?'

The girl, for some reason, seemed to lose her air of self-assurance.

'It's – well, it's a place where people go to meet each other – you know!'

'Like a pub?'

'No, no. Not like a pub. They don't serve drinks. You can have whisky or gin in your tea or coffee if you want to. There's dancing to a little band. It's all sort of secret.'

'You don't dance do you?' All at once he was jealous, imagining her clasped in some man's arms. He hadn't known until now how deeply he disapproved of dancing.

The tone of her voice told him she was smiling. 'I only go there to please my sister. She's pretty sweet on a fellow who works there. When we dance, we dance together.'

Sev sighed. 'Well that's alright then. I wudden want you to come to no grief,' he explained. 'I've heard funny things about girls what go dancing.' They had walked a long way. Sev counted nine chimes from a nearby church steeple. 'I better be getting back,' he told her, 'or the bugler u'll be blowing "lights out".' He said, as they walked back into Taunton, 'I don't know your name.'

Again the smile was in her voice. 'I was registered as Blanche,' she told him, 'but my uncle wanted Claire, and my grandmother Nevill said I was to be Evangeline.'

'Cripes! What a mouthful!'

My father called me Eve when I was little. That's what everybody calls me, these days.'

'I was christened David John,' said Sev, 'but 'tis only my – well – not many people ever uses they names. People generally call me Sev.'

'Were you going to say "only my mother"?'

'No I wasn't,' he said fiercely, 'so don't you put no words into my mouth!'

'Alright. Don't come off your trolley.' They walked into Taunton in an awkward silence. They came into the main street. Eve said, 'This is Bath Place.' She pointed into the darkness. 'The Tipperary Club is down there. I have to go in and wait for my sister.'

'I'll see you to the door.'

He watched as she knocked four times on the door; he heard her ask for someone called Joey. As she stepped inside, Sev grabbed her hand.

'Can I see you again?'

She paused, and peered back at him through the dark night.

'Tomorrow,' she said. 'Be waiting at seven, on the corner of Hammet Street.'

*

Five evenings had passed in the company of Eve Nevill, and Sev had not known until now that time could pass so happily and quickly. He would be waiting each evening on the corner of Hammet Street, and was every time astounded when he saw her slender fashionable figure come towards him. Her attraction grew more painful with every meeting. She had qualities that made it seem unlikely that she would allow herself to be picked up by a common soldier from the Barracks. He had asked her about it on their final meeting and been surprised at the purpose in her face. A deep crease had appeared between her eyebrows; the soft mouth took on a stubborn line, and a brief rebellion flashed in her green eyes.

'My mother,' she said, 'finds fault with every fella's name I ever mention. She broke off my sister's engagement. Abi's never been the same since that happened. I choose my own friends,' she said quietly. 'I live my own life in spite of Mother.'

They parted with the hesitant, unsure emotion of people just met who are separated too soon. They made promises they would not keep: she said she would give him her address and he vowed to write to her from India. He longed to tell her how pretty she was and how much he liked her; he had paid many empty compliments to Jane and Mary, but he was shy with Eve Nevill. He said, instead, at the moment of leaving, 'That's a nice necklace you're wearing. Pretty, that is!'

'My mother gave it to me on my birthday. It's supposed to be lucky for the one who wears it.'

He said, 'What's it made of?'

'Silver and coral. They tell stories about it in my family. Some say it's a gypsy-piece, others say it came from India in a pedlar's suitcase.'

He had walked with her to the terrace of bay-windowed villas, and been impressed by the size of her house, and its appearance. He had taken the slip of paper that bore her address, kissed her once, and then strode quickly away in the direction of the Barracks.

*

Sev boarded the troopship with mixed emotions of panic and elation. For this dream of India he had suffered twelve weeks of square-bashing and parades; had endured, without once understanding the purpose of his mission, sixteen months of horror among the lunatics of Belfast. But the camaraderie of barrack life in Ireland had taught him to value his fellow soldiers. He, who had always been a loner, now began to learn that it was good and often necessary to have at least one 'acker' on whom he could rely. He noticed, as the military train approached Southampton, a cessation of the leg pulling and joking. A silence fell in the compartment as they first glimpsed the ship; elation changed to apprehension as the inevitability of their journey was confirmed. Sev began to feel queasy as he drew his hammock from the Stores, his discomfort grew acute as he attached its loops to hooks slung below the decks. While the ship still rocked gently at anchor in Southampton Water, Sev Carew was already prostrated with sea sickness.

The horrors of the overnight trip from Holyhead to Belfast could not begin to be compared with the prospect of twenty-one days and nights spent aboard this bucking, rolling steamship. In the Bay of Biscay he prayed to die; he sweated and shivered, his head ached. Most of the Battalion were laid low, but sea sickness they were told was no excuse for dereliction of duty. Groaning, retching men were still obliged to stand sentry in the night hours; giddy heaving soldiers were forced to scrub and hose down the decks they had just fouled. Time had no meaning for them; Sev had looked at Gibraltar but retained no memory of it; and then he woke up one morning to find that his body had adjusted, he felt weak but normal. As they passed through the Suez Canal he lay above decks in the December sunshine. He began to think that he might, after all, live to see the Taj Mahal.

*

Because of the near-blindness of his left eye, Sev's first clear sight of India was not to be from the tender that took them ashore in Bombay, but as he marched from the docks to the railway station. The sepia-tinted pictures in Lord Curzon's books had not prepared him for the strangeness; the combination of riotous colour and dazzling whiteness, the contrast between imposing buildings and emaciated beggars. The Battalion was taken by the train from Bombay to the reception camp of Deolalie, where they were issued with blankets and new kitbags, and had rumours confirmed that their destination was to be Lucknow. The journey, they were told, would take six nights and days; the nights to be spent in the slow train that travelled north; the days in rest camps along the route.

The December days were pleasantly warm, the stays in the rest camps allowing officers and men a chance to acclimatise gradually to changes of temperature and diet. It was at this time that Sev first tasted curry and developed a life-long passion for it; and since the thirst caused by curry could only, according to the 'old sweats', be slaked by beer, he developed an equal liking for that, also. Their days were passed in games of housey-housey, brag and pontoon. Once aboard the train Sev would bargain his winnings for a window seat, so that he might see the sun rise on the following morning. After three nights of uneasy sleep, in which they cursed and moaned and dragged the inadequate issue blankets tight around them, most men were suffering the effects of the unaccustomed diet, and the bitter coldness of the Indian nights. Sev alone seemed to find the travel exhilarating. There was a magical quality about the slow winding route of the train through invisible country. Many stops were made along the route to take on coal and water; he would doze and wake to the hiss of steam and a rattle of strange tongues. Sunrise was abrupt; a sudden flooding of light across a landscape of harsh browns and faded pinks; the dusty dryness of it all never seemed to become familiar to him. Morning after chilly morning, he would gaze at it as if for the first time, and his initial thought was always the same. I'll bet no roses ever grow here.

This compulsion to be the first person in the whole world to see the sun rise, was an old, half forgotten habit of his childhood. Sev sat, huddled in his blue, army-issue blankets in the jolting carriage of an ancient steam-train, and remembered, unwillingly, the break of day over Montacute Park. The charm of the morning was Granfer's description of it; Sev closed his eyes against the thin, sharp sunlight of an Indian daybreak, and quite deliberately called up the misty greenness of Somerset in April. He had meant only to test his ability for total recall of colours and places, but the ache in his throat confirmed his mistake. He looked around the compartment to check that his companions were still sleeping; he smiled, and wiped his eyes on the edge of the woollen blanket. He had forgotten how one incautious memory could give rise to others. To remember Montacute was to bring back Granfer; to give life to Granfer was to admit to the existence of his mother and father. A sudden hollowness in the rumble of the train's wheels made him look again towards the window. Taffy Richards, who had stolen a map from a drunken sailor on the troopship, was awake now and airing his superior knowledge.

'That's the River Jumna, that is! We is coming close to Cawnpore; this is called the North-West Provinces. We should be in Lucknow by tomorrow evening.'

Sev pulled a mangled Woodbine from its flimsy green packet. He placed the cigarette between his lips and lit it. He screwed the packet into a ball, and threw it at Taffy. He said, from the corner of his mouth. 'You Welshmen is all the same. Bunch of bloody know-alls idden you!'

Taffy grinned. 'You'd better learn how to read a map, you ignorant swede-basher, if you ever want to win a promotion.' He leaned forward, no longer smiling. 'You got a good brain in that red head of yours. You could do something better than tipping Brown Windsor soup down a General's shirtfront. We is bound to be here for at least six years. I've seen the books you read. I know you isn't no clod-hopping farmboy, even though you'd have us think so.'

*

The city of Lucknow, out of bounds to soldiers, and seen

only from a distance, seemed to float between earth and sky, a mirage of coloured domes in white and rose and gold. The Fort lay some distance from the city limits. Sev had imagined, because it was British, that this foreign garrison would at least bear some resemblance to the Barracks of Taunton and Belfast. There seemed at first sight to be something less than military about the thick walls of ochre-tinted sandstone, the whitewashed buildings, and the long lines of tents, which at their perimeter reached the sinister edge of jungle territory.

Reason had told him that soldiering in India would be different, but for Sev, the transition from one country to another had been too abrupt. His was a mind that acclimatised only slowly to change; the blood of generations of Particular Baptists was in his veins, warning him that here was the possibility of laxness, the danger of temptation. Instinct warned him to hold fast to what was known and trusted. He used, with reluctance, the new words that were now foisted upon him; viewed with suspicion the nappi-wallah who shaved him while he still slept. Felt guilty about the tiny payment made to the dhobi, who took away his dirty clothing and returned it within hours, spotlessly clean, and beautifully pressed. He had wondered, when in London, how it felt to be Lord Curzon, waited upon and deferred to by menials. It would take time before Sev accepted as his right the salaams of native-servants, and the soldiers' creed that what had been won by the sword must be kept by the sword.

A private soldier's home was his bed and the wooden kit box that stood at its head. For Sev, as for many others who had grown up in overcrowded cottages, the single bed with its rough cotton sheet and dark blue blankets, had a significance that was unique. The large wooden kit box held brushes and cleaning materials, spare underwear and towels, and the new lightweight uniforms of cotton khaki that had been issued to them on their arrival at Lucknow. Most kit boxes contained a few

treasured personal possessions; the penny whistle and
the mouth-organ were wrapped carefully in a piece of
tissue paper, together with the address of the girl called
Eve.

Sev had quite fancied the novelty of sleeping under
canvas, but the Battalion was to be housed in bungalows, in the garrison at Lucknow. These bungalows,
which were designed for coolness, had high vaulted
ceilings, white-washed walls and flagged stone floors.
Each building held sixteen beds, with separate sleeping
compartments for duty corporals. Within hours of
settling in, Sev's name appeared on the list for kitchen
detail. He was put in charge of the boiling up of
Christmas puddings, a task which in view of the outdoor
temperature of seventy-five degrees, struck him as
ludicrous, but was strangely reassuring. He could almost
believe that he was back in Carleton House Terrace, and
stoking the boiler that had caused his downfall. A few
old soldiers were employed in the cook house; men who
had seen it all, and took pleasure in handing out good
advice to the newcomers. The Army cantonments, Sev
learned, were always placed well beyond the nearest
town or city.

'Never even think of sloping off to Lucknow,' warned
his informant. 'This was the fort where the Mutiny
happened! We was hanging rebel natives from the trees
hereabouts, some sixty-odd years ago, and the black
sods have got long memories. Always bear in mind that
we is outnumbered in this God-forsaken country by odds
of ten-million to one. Since Curzon's time we is not
supposed to put the boot in to 'em. But there's other
ways my son, to keep the bastards down. Always
remember, no matter how many times they salaam,
they're only waiting their chance to slip a knife in your
back. Stay inside the Fort! We got our own Bazaar.
There's Army shops that sell everything you need.' The
man paused to stir a huge pot of simmering curry. 'And
whatever you do, don't ever go anywhere near any of

their women. If you doubt what I'm telling you, take a walk to the hospital compound. Put your head around the door of the venereal ward. One sight of those poor devils'll be enough to cool your natural urges!'

On Christmas morning the Battalion paraded to the garrison church; they went, as was their custom, armed to quell rebellion, carrying a rifle and side-arms, and sufficient ammunition to put down a mass uprising. As a Baptist, Sev could have been excused this duty, since there was no provision made at Lucknow for those of his particular persuasion. That he actually chose to attend the Church of England service caused hilarity among his Section, and dismay to Taffy Richards.

'My God, mun! Don't tell me you is a secret Bible-Puncher, after all!'

Sev denied the accusation. 'Don't much fancy sitting here on my bed,' he muttered, 'while the rest of you is away swigging the Communion wine.' Truth to tell, he could not have explained what it was that drew him out in full kit to parade to church on a hot Sunday morning. It had much to do with music; with marching behind the Regimental Band; singing hymns to the accompaniment of the garrison's slightly out-of-tune organ. On this Christmas day they sang 'Once in Royal David's City' and 'While Shepherds Watched Their Flocks'. Sev fixed his gaze on the rifle he had hooked onto the pew's candle holder. He forced his eyelids to remain wide open, in an effort to hold back tears. Every man in the bungalow, save himself and Taffy, had received mail from home. He had watched their faces as they read letters and cards, and stripped the wrapping from their mothers' parcels. He tried to sing – 'watched their flocks by night, all seated on the ground', but his voice cracked upon the words. Ah, he too had sat once, long ago, in the winter hut with Granfer. They had watched the folded flock, together underneath the stars. He had thought, for a long time, that Granfer was God. In a way, he still believed it.

*

Sev had never written to a girl; had never in fact written any kind of letter. He had once received one, in his time in London. He sat on his bed, chewed upon the pencil, and tried to remember the appearance of it. His mother's letter had begun with the words 'Dear David'. Sev wiped his sweating palms on his khaki-covered knees and wrote 'Dear Eve' at the top of the note sheet; starting was the difficult part; since leaving school he had done no more than sign his name on a few forms for the army. His handwriting shamed him. He would, he decided, write a rough draft to begin with, and then, as the writing improved, he would make a fair copy of it.

A week had passed, and many note sheets spoiled before Sev was ready to address an envelope with ink and seal his first letter to Eve Nevill. Taffy Richards, who had witnessed his agonised efforts with the pencil, said that night, in the Wet Canteen, 'They is starting classes next week. Major Bennet says that we can try for our Certificate of Education. I've already put my name down – what about you?' Sev stared moodily into his beer mug. 'Waste of time,' he muttered. 'They 'ont never make scholars out of us. All we need to know is how to blanco webbing, and polish our brass buttons. If you can wind your puttees on right, and keep your rifle clean, then they reckon you're a good soldier. In any case, I don't have the sort of brains that take easy to learnin'.'

Taffy grinned. 'That letter you was writing,' he said slyly, 'it give you one hell of a lot of trouble, you must have gone through a whole pad before you got it right. If you was writing to that classy bird you met in Taunton, she'll laugh her bloody head off when she gets it!'

Sev said, without enthusiasm, 'Come outside you Welsh bastard, and I'll beat your head in.'

'No you won't, mun. I was champion boxer in my valley.'

'Lyin' toad.' Sev's reply was automatic; his mind was busy with the thought of education. Taff was right. He had made a dreadful fist at letter-writing.

369

Taffy said, 'Joining classes will give you a leg-up, get you out of the cook-house. What do you say?'

*

The letter was lying halfway between her plate and Abi's on that Friday evening. Mother's face lacked all expression as she handed bread and butter and poured tea. Eve exchanged a glance with Abi. Her sister's raised eyebrows and wry mouth passed a silent message. Don't let her lack of interest fool you, Abi signalled. She'll start on you as soon as you begin to read it!

Eve allowed the letter to lie unopened; she ate the thin bread and butter, and studied the envelope from beneath half-closed eyelids. The stamp had a picture of an elephant printed on it, and the word India appeared twice, in clear block capitals. Her address and name had been printed carefully in capitals.

'That's a foreign stamp!' Mother's challenge came as Eve was biting into a slice of Aunt Madelina's seed cake. She choked involuntarily upon the dry crumbs, but gained time with an extended fit of coughing, and the need to drink half a cup of tea.

Mother's inability to read made her overly suspicious. She would never ask the outright question, and by the rules of the convoluted game they played, Eve and Abigail were not obliged to tell her. Revelation, as always in this household, must have a quality of drama. To watch and then pounce on the owner of the hand that reached out to claim the letter, was Mother's way. But on this occasion her attention was drawn elsewhere; the arrival of Aunt Candace, bearing a pound of best butcher's brawn, had Annis rushing to lay an extra place at the table, cut more bread and butter and refill the teapot.

'I had hoped,' said Aunt Candace, 'to get here before you'd begun your tea. I had a nice little win on that horse at Wincanton. You know the one I mean Frank – '

The brawn was shared out equally between them. As

the slice of jellied meat slithered onto Abi's plate, Mother noticed the empty space where the letter had lain. She gazed helplessly, from one blank face to the other.

'Lovely bit of brawn, Aunty Can,' Abi said. 'How nice of you to treat us!'

'Well to tell 'ee the truth, my dears,' Candace confided, 'it gets a bit lonely sitting all by yourself out in Rowbarton.'

Annis gazed around the table, counting heads. The satisfaction in her voice had a hint of threat behind it. 'I don't never believe,' she said, 'that young people should be in too much of a hurry to leave home. As for going abroad to foreign parts, I can't understand why any-body – least of all your Billy – '

'My Billy,' Candace said, defensively, 'is doing very well in America. In fact, he's a big word now in the moving pictures. According to his latest letter he's become what they call a film star!'

Abi said, 'Are you sure? Our Billy – a film star?'

Candace reached for her handbag and withdrew a letter.

'Don't you girls never go to the picture-shows? If you did, why you'd see your cousin up there on the screen with all the big names!'

Annis said, 'Oh they got no time for the pictures, Can. Too busy picking up common soldiers on street corners they are!'

Eve willed herself not to look at Abi. She said swiftly, in a high voice, 'Fancy that, now! Cousin Billy come to be a famous person! Oh, do read his letter to us!'

Candace began to read in flat tones, and Eve, conscious of the soldier's letter in the pocket of her skirt, longed to leave the table so that she might open it; she heard nothing of the first and second pages. It was the name of Chaplin that at last caught her attention. ' – Charlie has brought his mother over from England. How I wish I could afford to bring you, Ma, but you have to be a main attraction to make that kind of money. I spend a lot of time with Doug and Mary. They have built a house on Summit Drive in Beverley Hills. They have called it PICKFAIR which is pretty cute since their last names are *Fair*banks and *Pick*ford. You would never believe what a time we have after filming is finished. I am a real actor now, Ma. I got photos of myself in company with all the top names.'

Eve leaned forward, her full attention now upon her cousin's letter. The unemotional tones of Aunt Candace seemed only to enhance the romance and glamour implicit in Billy's words. 'You should just see their furs and jewellery, Ma, and their cars and houses. Doug and Mary have got 15 servants, all living-in. Chaplin has bought a piece of land close beside them and is making the drawings for a house of his own. It's wonderful, for me to be "in" with such as them. There's nothing I wouldn't do for Doug and Mary.'

Eve filled the stone jar with hot water, and slipped it between the sheets. She undressed and put on the thick flannel nightgown that Mother considered essential for winter wear. She moved, absent-mindedly, about the bedroom, hardly noticing the coldness of her feet on the lino. She pulled the hairpins from the French pleat and allowed her hair to fall about her shoulders.

'Do you think,' she asked Abi, 'do you think I look a bit like Mary Pickford?'

'If you don't get into bed my girl, you'll be down with pneumonia by morning. Do stop mooning about. Blow out the candle and get to sleep.'

It was after she had doused the candle and snuggled down beneath the feather quilt, that Eve remembered the letter from India, still folded in the pocket of her skirt. She sat up, abruptly, and fumbled for the matches.

'Oh my dear Lord,' Abi cried, 'whatever is it now? We'll have Mother knocking on the bedroom wall at any minute.'

'I forgot my letter,' Eve whispered. 'It's from India, from that red-haired soldier. You remember, we met them on the corner of Hammet Street – '

'Remember,' Abi interrupted, 'I'm never likely to forget that know-it-all Welshman. I got rid of him pretty smartly I can tell you!' She paused, blinking against the candle's sudden light. 'You don't mean to tell me you gave that cheeky one your name and address?'

'He's no cheekier than Joey Santini, and anyway,' Eve said, 'I sort of liked him.' She gazed wistfully at the unopened letter. 'I can hardly believe he's all those thousands of miles away.'

'Just as well for you that he is!' Abi grinned. 'There'll be hell to pay if Mother finds out that you're writing to a private. Well go on then – open it! I'm thoroughly awake now, so you'd better read it to me.'

Eve began to read aloud from the carefully pencilled pages; Sev described the voyage, the arrival at Bombay, the journey up to Lucknow. He told about the loneliness, the strangeness of a foreign land. Eve paused at the final page.

'Well, I'll say this much for him,' Abi yawned, 'he writes a jolly good letter. Well, go on then – let's hear the rest.'

'He's not much good at spelling.' Eve smiled. 'You can't hear the end bit. That's meant for my eyes alone.'

Abi punched her pillow, and turned her face away from the light. 'Alright then, Mary Pickford – keep your little secrets! But for God's sake hurry up, and put that damned light out!'

Eve said, before they slept, 'What's going on between you and Joey? Mother's getting suspicious. Several people have told her that you and him have been seen together.'

Abi said in a low voice, 'I'm crazy about him, Eve. I'll die if he doesn't ask me to get married.'

'He's a bad lot, Abi. He's got a string of girls all over Taunton.'

'No worse than your Ben Treherne! You've kept very quiet about him, haven't you, my lady! But I saw you with him on Friday night kissing under French's arch-way.'

'Perhaps,' Eve said cautiously, 'perhaps we should all four of us go to see one of cousin Billy's performances. It's nice and dark in the picture house. There'd be less chance there of being spotted by Mother's cronies. Do you think,' she said drowsily, 'do you think I should answer that soldier's letter? It wouldn't do any harm would it, just to write to him – there was something about him, you know Abi –'

*

Soldiering in a hot land, far from England, might, Sev had thought, see a lowering of military standards, a slackening of discipline and 'bull'. There were differ-ences; the very isolation of the Army cantonments caused a better relationship to grow up between officers and 'other ranks'. Captains and Majors who in England and Ireland had been aloof and short with words, became paternalistic and almost chatty in the family atmosphere that developed in this closed community of white men. The discipline, however, was, if anything, more severe. In an under-employed army, the most important function of which was its presence in an occupied country, there was an excessive insistence on smartness of turn-out, on sportsmanship and fitness; and as Taffy Richards observed, 'Them officers probably lie awake at night working out new ways for us to pass the time, so as to keep us out of mischief.'

'Passing the time' had not yet become a burden for Sev and Taffy. A year had passed since their arrival in Lucknow. They attended classes, and within three months had gained their Certificates of Education, 3rd Class, and started to study for a higher Grade. In India, they discovered, the year for the British had only two seasons. There was the Hot Weather, and the Cold Weather. They had sweated and groaned in tempera-tures, that according to the officers, reached 115 degrees

Fahrenheit. Sev, because of his fair skin and red hair, suffered more from the sun that the dark-haired and swarthy Welshman. The pitch helmets and mosquito nets that had caused them amusement on their arrival, had now become their most important items of equipment.

Small events had built confidence in Sev. The Certificate of Education lay in his kit box beside the mouthorgan and the penny whistle, and beneath the letters from the girl met in Taunton. Four times in that year he had come back from Sunday morning Church Parade to hear his name announced at Mail Call. The sight of her strong, backward sloping handwriting had on each occasion almst stopped his heartbeat. Other men often read aloud the more interesting or amusing items in their letters from home. Sev's habit of scanning his letter twice through, and then locking it, without comment, into his kit box caused yells of anger and dismay.

'What's up then Chippy? Can't you make out her writing?' was a favourite jibe. Even Taffy Richards, who had come to respect Sev's withdrawals into silence, his desire for privacy in a style of life that offered none, was sufficiently curious to ask, 'What have she got to say then, mun? Do she ever mention that stuck-up sister, the one what gave me the slip when we was in Taunton?' Taffy, who had never in his life received a letter, looked longingly at the two closely written pages in Sev's hand.

Sev said, awkwardly, 'Oh – she don't have much to tell – not really. She've just bought a new coat. The rain in Taunton have never stopped in the past fortnight. She goes on a lot about some cousin of hers called Billy, what acts in America wi' Charlie Chaplin.'

'A film star you mean?'

Sev tapped the letter, 'So it says here.'

Taffy brightened. 'I heard tell that there's some sort of picture house in the Fort at Agra. Maybe we could spot this cousin of hers. Now that 'ud be a lark mun!'

On the first day of February, 1922, the 2nd Battalion of the Somerset Light Infantry was moved from Lucknow to the Fort of Agra. The approach to the city was through a flat and colourless wasteland. Sev closed his eyes against disappointment and was almost asleep when the train wheels changed rhythm. He looked out onto the stanchions of an iron bridge, and across flights of broad stone steps that led down to an emerald-coloured river. He lifted his gaze, and there was the scene he had studied so often in Lord Curzon's library. The white marble palace called Taj Mahal seemed to float in the thin winter sunshine. He had never quite believed in those pictures; he closed his eyes and then opened them wide, he placed a hand across the weakness of his left eye but still the miracle remained. A silence had fallen in the compartment, men crowded to the window but only Taffy spoke.

'Cripes!' he muttered. 'I never believed what they said about it – but there it is!'

A bend in the track brought into view another monument, and this was a building that had more reality for them; Sev viewed almost with relief the sheer walls and red sandstone battlements of the Fort of Agra. Loud conversation broke out around him to cover the embarrassment of their previous silence. Speculation began about the size and quality of the Garrison's Bazaar, the strength of the canteen beer, and the possibility of 'going over the wall' to sample the out-of-bounds delights of the adjacent city. It was almost dark when they marched into the Fort's approaches, past guard houses that resembled caves hewn into the sandstone, and in through the great gates. Sev felt the excitement that comes only from incredible achievement. He breathed in, with delight, the sharp and bitter night air of the Indian winter. From Montacute to Agra had seemed an impossible dream, but here he was, on the banks of the Jumna, with the Taj Mahal within spitting distance.

The bungalows of 'other ranks' at Agra Barracks were the size and shape of small cathedrals; each one large enough to sleep and house a platoon of fifty men. With their high vaulted ceilings, waving punkahs, and mosquito nets draped over beds, they afforded the coolest and healthiest accommodation available in the fierce heat of the Plains.

For the first weeks of their new posting the days were comfortably warm, the nights very cold, and life was lived in a relaxed and normal fashion. In the months spent at Lucknow, Sev's platoon had already begun to separate out into friendly groups of six or eight. Sev and Taffy were joined by four others who were also moderate drinkers and heavy smokers; young men who enjoyed a bet, a joke, and who were keen on all the forms of sport encouraged by the Army. No man was ever called by his baptismal name. Sev's mention in Taunton that he had once worked for a firm of carpenters and joiners had earned him the nickname of 'Chippy'. Every Welshman in the platoon was known as Taffy. The posting to Agra, it was rumoured, was to be one of years rather than months. Friendships made now were likely to be of long duration, and Sev valued the camaraderie and laughter. But still, there were those times when his need to be solitary was overpowering. Too much talk distressed him; he would feel the onset of the childish irritation at excessive sound and annoying habits. He had learned, in the Army, to accept without comment the snoring and muttering at night, the mealtime torture of men who ate noisily, those who coughed incessantly; the nervous foot tappers and the finger drummers. When the company of others became more than he could bear, he would acknowledge, with a pang of shame, his inner boredom, the conviction that his own thoughts were of more interest and significance than all the spoken words of the combined Battalion. He could no longer escape onto Miles Hill or St James's Park. Sanctuary in the Agra Barracks was found only in the Library, or high on the battlements that overlooked the Bazaars.

At times when the bungalow was empty, he would sit on his bed and play the mouth-organ repeating, until he was note perfect, the musical comedy tunes, and ballads played by the Regimental Band at their evening concerts. The warnings of the 'old sweats' that danger and death lay in wait for any soldier rash enough to walk alone beyond the cantonment were still fresh in his mind. He joined the football team and the boxing team; he put in a request that he might be allowed to own a dog; and returned to the Army classroom, so that he might work for his Certificate of Education 2nd Class.

Punkahing began on the 1st of April. The khaki uniform of winter was laid aside for the white drill of summer. Some men began to suffer early. The monsoon, they were told, did not appear regularly at Agra. Sev's moods of irritation and his need for solitude grew stronger with the increasing heat. He had hurried back from Church Parade every Sunday morning since coming to Agra, but his name had never been mentioned in his bungalow's Mail Call. He wrote one more letter, repeating the news of his move, and his new address. He felt abandoned, and the strength of the feeling surprised and depressed him. The girl's neglect of him seemed to have a dimension that went far beyond that of mere letter writing. On those Sunday afternoons, after Mail Call, and before the opening of the Wet Canteen, Sev would lie on his bed and watch the flapping punkah. All around him men moaned and sweated in uneasy sleep; even Taffy who had withstood the heat of Lucknow, looked pale and drawn, and disinclined to talk. It was at times like these that Sev was most vulnerable; when the facility for total recall held more of agony for him than advantage. No matter how hard he tried to think of other places and people, the image of his mother, seated by the window, head bent to her gloving, was lodged in his mind, and would not go away.

It was on a Monday morning towards noon that the order came for him to appear before Lt. Colonel Paterson. Sev, dressed only in underpants, was checking on the state of neatness of his kit box since random inspections had lately been added to the sufferings of the Platoon.

'Get yourself dressed, and quick!' the Corporal shouted. 'The old man's waiting for you.'

Sev put on a fresh set of white drill trousers and tunic, and carried his cap. Every man in the Platoon turned to watch as he was marched away between four guards who held open bayonets trained upon him. So great was his fear that he actually shivered in the fierce heat. He came into the Orderly Room amid a din of stamping boots and shouted orders; he was referred to as 'the prisoner'. He halted on the order and stood stiffly at attention before the Colonel. He looked at the grim face and knew that whatever his crime, it must be a big one.

The Colonel began in a reasonable tone. 'I've been studying your record, Carew. Your military conduct is exemplary, so your officer tells me. You take part in all games in a sportsmanlike fashion. You are moderate in your habits. Why then,' and now the quiet voice rose to a roar, 'why then should an otherwise good soldier behave like a coward?'

Sev reeled momentarily, as if from a physical blow. The lowest epithet ever used to describe a soldier was that single word 'coward'. Bad enough when it came from your mates in the squad. To have it applied by the Regiment's Colonel was sufficient reason for a ranker to take his rifle into a quiet place and blow his brains out. Sev had never, in his three years as a soldier, come face to face with an officer of this rank. He remembered the charge of insolence put upon him by Lord Curzon at their first confrontation, and kept his gaze lowered to a study of the Colonel's middle jacket button. A single sheet of paper was held out towards him, and then lowered gently to the desk.

'Do you know what this is, Carew?'

The voice was quiet again, almost reverential. Sev, unsure as to whether an answer was expected, began frantically to review his possible misdemeanours. He had heeded the advice of the old soldiers of the Platoon; had kept out of debt, always wore his solar topee and had stayed well away from the native women. He swallowed hard and said hoarsely, 'No, sir.'

'This is a letter, Carew. It is, in fact, the most touching and pathetic letter it has ever been my misfortune to receive in all my years as a serving officer. Perhaps,' said his tormentor, 'perhaps you would care to hazard a guess as to the identity of the writer of this letter?'

Sev glanced down at the sheet of paper and even at a distance there was something familiar about the stiff and upright handwriting. The coldness of his stomach spread up to touch his heart. He felt the blood drain from his face.

The Colonel began to nod his head; he said, with satisfaction, 'Oh yes. I can see from your expression that I hardly need to tell you that my correspondent is your mother.' He paused, 'You left home in January 1919?'

'Yes, sir.'

'It is now July, 1922. For three years your family has had no knowledge of you. For two of those years your mother has mourned you as dead.' The Colonel waited. 'Well, man – what have you to say for yourself? How can you justify such cowardly behaviour?'

Sev asked, 'How – how did she know that I was here, sir?'

The Colonel said, heavily, 'Three Companies came out from Taunton last October. Among them was a young man from your village – one who writes regularly to his family. He recognised you, Carew.'

Sev said, 'I meant to write, sir – '

'And you will! Every Sunday morning! You will present yourself in my office after Church Parade with a letter of not less than two pages. I shall read your letter, and see to it personally that it is stamped and posted, and sent off to England. You will return to your bungalow now, I want your first effort on my desk within two hours. You will apologise to your mother for your disgraceful behaviour and bear this in mind, Carew. If your letter is inadequate in any way, you will continue to rewrite it until it meets with my approval.'

He was marched back to his bungalow, like a criminal, between the unsheathed bayonets of the guards. But for the creaking of the punkahs the room was silent. Of the fifty men in his Platoon, Taffy Richards and Dusty Millar were the only ones still awake and waiting for him.

'What the hell have you been up to, boyo?'

Sev said nothing. He stripped off the damp tunic and trousers and placed them in his laundry bag, ready for the dhobi. He drank water from the chattie beside his bed, and fetched pencil and paper from his kit box.

Dusty said, 'Well come on then, you bastard! Don't keep us waiting! It must be something bad to get you brought before the Colonel?'

'Not all that bad. I shan't be court-martialled if that's what you was thinking.' Sev tried to grin. 'Shove-off will you! I got two hours to write a letter and get it back on the Colonel's desk.'

There was, he thought, a lot to be said for the discipline of the Army. Writing under orders would be so much easier than any voluntary attempt he might have made towards a reconciliation. The words he would use were not his own, but those that the Colonel would have him say. Now, under threat from four exposed bayonets, Sev could write unembarrassed. 'Dear Mother, I am sorry for all the worry I have caused you. I will write regular, every week, in the future, I am fit and well in India. Hope you and father is the same. I have got my Cert. of Education, 3rd Class, and is now working for my 2nd Class. It is very hot here. I have some good mates.'

He laid down the pencil and wiped his sweating hands upon a towel. He read over the first sentence, and imagined his mother opening the letter. 'Dear Mother, I am sorry for all the worry I have caused you – ' He felt weak and empty, and close to tears; he despised himself for this sudden change of mind. He watched new words grow underneath the pencil, and was surprised to see them. 'My pay,' he wrote, 'is now Top Rate since I passed my Examination. I get three shillings and sixpence per day which is One Pound four shillings per week. I shall be making you an Allotment of half my Pay as I know you can do with the money.'

He made a fair copy of the letter, spreading out his hand-writing so that it covered the required two pages. At the very bottom of the second page he wrote, 'From your loving son David.'

*

The temperature had risen steadily since April. In August it stood at 120 degrees in the shade. The monsoon had come late and was of short duration. Parades were held only before the hour of noon; all classes of instruction were suspended. Between midday and sunset Sev moved at regular intervals from swimming pool to library. When the shadows lengthened in the white sand that surrounded the cantonments, he would go back to his bungalow and join the card school. Time passed slowly. The quality of a man, both physical and mental, was tested severely in the Hot Season. Several men went sick; many died of heatstroke and malarial fever. Two NCOs, men who had been mates since the day of their enlistment, quarrelled bitterly over the favours of a native girl; they shot and wounded one another, and were promptly court martialled.

Tedium was rated as great an enemy as heatstroke. They drank beer and sweated, and made plans for the coming of the Cold Season. The Taj Mahal and the Fort lay tantalisingly near, but still unexplored. Sev's application to own a dog had been granted, but no suitable puppy had yet appeared.

His name was shouted regularly now at every Mail Call. The letters came mostly in his mother's stiff upright script. There would be the occasional note added on in his father's small, rounded hand. They told about the English weather, the state of the garden; included bits of village gossip about people he had long forgotten or never known. The letters from Montacute were a burden to him; the very simplicity of them touched a tender place, the existence of which he had only, until now, suspected. He reported to the colonel every Sunday morning, reply in hand, and was acutely conscious of the concealed grins of the guards who were detailed to escort him. The Colonel would read every word and then nod his approval. He said on one occasion, and grudgingly, 'You write a good letter, Carew. They tell me you are working for your 2nd Class Certificate of Education.' He folded the pages back into the envelope. 'A few more weeks and I think we shall be able to dispense with this Sunday attendance. I believe you've learned an important lesson here in Agra.'

The letters from home had piled up like drifted snow in the corner of his kit box, concealing those first few treasured notes from Taunton. Sev tried to pretend that the girl called Eve had never written to him, that he had never walked and talked with her by the high red brick walls of Jellalabad Barracks. But his feelings for her, he now discovered, lived in that same deep and vulnerable place that held memories of his father and mother.

*

In India a soldier could be laughing and ribbing with his mates at breakfast, and by nightfall be in his coffin, awaiting burial. Sev's Company had come through the summer without losing a man. There had been the usual number of hospital cases, men who suffered mental break-down, prickly heat and various fevers. But it was not only the white man who was affected by the excessive heat; if trouble was going to break out among the many native sects, the old soldiers warned, then look out for it towards the end of August.

In September the thermometer still stood at 114 degrees. On the second day of the month news came to the Barracks that communal riots had broken out in Agra; Mohammedan was fighting Hindu. The serious nature of the disturbances could be judged, said the Sergeant, by the fact that the military were never called out until the police had lost control.

The Battalion marched into the city to find that whole sections were burning; looters moved silently about their business. Sev stood fifth in a line of marksmen and awaited the order to fire. The command, when it came was that they should 'fire wide'. Since the massacre of thousands of women and children at Amritsar in the April of 1919, British officers were cautious when called upon to deal with civil disturbance. On this occasion the warning shots were sufficient to clear the area of people. Sev felt ashamed of his lack of stomach for the use of bullets. Booting an idle punkah wallah was one thing; shooting into a crowd which contained women and children, was he hoped, something he would never be called upon to do.

The Agra city riots were quelled with such efficiency and speed by the Battalion, that a party of wealthy Hindu and Mohammedan gentlemen, approached their Colonel, promising to provide an evening of entertainment for the troops involved.

The onset of the Cold Season cooled tempers and bodies. Parades were resumed, classes re-started, route marches were undertaken. Reason returned along with energy and purpose; white drills were laid aside for warmer khaki, men dared to walk out with heads bared to the sun. Sev had longed for the cooler weather, longed for the time when his body would, once again, feel as if it fitted inside his skin; when his head would no longer ache or his eyes smart. What he had not expected was the deep nostalgia brought on by the change of season. In the frost of early evening, and just before sunset, he would see smoke from native fires hanging low across the plains. Several evenings passed before he pinned down the exact source of his heartache and then he remembered the smoke from the shepherd's hut on Ham Hill. He saw Granfer, warming his hands at the blaze; heard the dark woman's gruff voice. 'When the smoke goes so far up and then spreads out, boy, why thass a sign for cold weather comin'.' The dark woman, he thought, had a look of the Hindu about her; she possessed the same loose and easy stride, the same head of black hair, the air of aloof pride. He had feared her; had felt a kind of dread at her intuitive knowledge of him. He looked down at the cigarette that smouldered between his nicotine-stained fingers and remembered her long-ago gift of clay pipe and thick twist tobacco. The allotment of half his pay, made to his mother, had severely curtailed his beer drinking habit. But now, when it came to a straight choice between cigarettes and extra food, his hunger was for Woodbines or Gold Flake. How well she had gauged his nature in childhood; how clever to have given him an addiction that would draw him back to her again and again.

The night came down swiftly, hiding the flat pall of smoke, the hillocks of dry turf and pale sand. Sev began to stroll back from the perimeter of the cantonment; he could just make out the low bulk of the bungalows; the card school would have begun without him. The temperature dropped sharply after sunset; he shivered in the bitter air and began to walk fast towards the lighted windows. His conviction that the dark woman walked beside him did not disappear until he stumbled across the low steps that led up to the verandah. Even then he could hear her voice. 'You'll go to a far land, and bide away from us for many a long year – '

*

Since that January morning when he had followed them, almost barefoot, towards Jellalabad barracks, Sev had been drawn towards the Regimental Band, whenever and wherever they happened to be playing. Every note of every ballad, each excerpt from operetta, all their marches, had become familiar to him. He stayed, whenever possible, within earshot of the Bandroom at practice time. He learned to identify each instrument by sound. It was on a Sunday evening in November, when he was working out a recently heard rendition of the Overture from *Iolanthe*, that he looked up to see the Bandmaster standing by the bungalow door. The man walked towards Sev. He paused before the kit box, and looked at the mouth-organ and the penny whistle. Sev, unsure of the protocol in such a situation, remained seated, cross-legged on his bed. The Bandmaster, who was said to be a martinet, spoke quietly.

'Your name?'

'Carew, sir.'

'You were wrong on that opening passage.'

'I know, sir.'

'You read music, of course.'

Sev looked surprised. 'Why no, sir. Don't know that I ever saw music written down on paper.'

'Are you willing to learn?'

'Well – well yes sir.'

'I'll speak to your Duty Sergeant. Report to the Bandroom at ten o'clock tomorrow morning.'

On any other morning Sev would wake to find his face already shaved, the nappi-wallah absent, and the char-wallah setting down a chattie of hot sweet tea beside his bed. On this Monday morning he saw the dawn come up with the Fort. He commanded the nappi-wallah to shave his face with extra care; he sought out the dhobi and offered him a special rate of three annas if he could produce a set of uniform, freshly washed and ironed before the hour of ten. He polished his boots and buttons; cleaned his teeth with salt on forefinger, and trimmed his fingernails.

'Bloody hell,' cried Dusty Miller, 'it's the Bandroom you've got to report to – not the Delhi Durbar!'

Of all the Platoon it was Taffy Richards who alone seemed to appreciate the full significance of Sev's call.

'Could mean a lot to you, mun – if he takes you on. He got a dreadful reputation, but they do say that he's a fine musician.' Taffy grew thoughtful. 'Them bandsmen got it easy. Special uniforms, excused Parades; they plays at all important functions. You'd still have to go on Route Marches, of course.' He grinned. 'You'd be up at the front of the column, blowing away fit to bust your gut!'

Sev said in a tight voice. 'Don't know for sure if I want to join the Band. 'Twas him what asked me. I never went looking for it.'

He looked up into the faces of his room-mates, and every man in that company knew that he was lying.

The Bandroom was furnished with several metal-framed chairs, a cluster of music-stands and a piano, the legs of which stood in tins of water in an effort to deter the white ants which devoured every piece of wooden furniture that touched the floor. A note on the door said that practice would commence at ten-thirty. Sev waited, at attention, his forehead hot, his palms clammy.

The quiet voice said, 'At ease, Carew.' The Bandmaster held what appeared to be an outsized violin. 'We'll try you with the double-bass. Now you take your bow in your right hand, and place your fingers so upon the strings –' He paused. 'How old are you?'

'I'm twenty-two, sir.'

'And you've never had a music lesson?'

'Never needed one sir. Play anything you like to mention when I've heard it once or twice. Always could, sir.'

'That's a handy trick, Carew, but I'm afraid it won't do for the Regimental Band. Have you the concentration necessary to learn and read music?'

'I got my 3rd Class Certificate of Education in Lucknow. I'm studying for my 2nd here in Agra.'

'So they tell me.' The Bandmaster sighed. 'Well, see how you get on with the double-bass. You'll find the sheet music in the cupboard.' He waved towards the musicians who were now assembling for practice. 'They're not a bad set of chaps. Any one of them will help you out.'

*

Music for Sev had always been a partnership between lips and fingers. He viewed the unwieldy double-bass with a mistrust that deepened daily. He spent hours in the Bandroom wrestling with bow and strings. He disliked the melancholy tone of the thing, was frustrated and angry at his rare inability to produce a recognisable tune. Pride would not let him ask for help. He studied the sheet music until dots and squiggles blurred together. After two weeks of bleeding fingers and sleepless nights, it was the band's first clarionetist who approached him.

'Having trouble, young 'un?'

Sev looked up to see a sympathetic grin.

'I hate the bloody double-bass,' he confided, 'as for reading that stuff,' he pointed to the Army's Manual of Music, 'it might as well be written in Hindi as far as I'm concerned.'

The clarinet player unlatched a small black case. From it he lifted the parts of a clarinet and fitted them together. He held out the instrument to Sev.

'Try that one! From hearing your harmonica playing I'd judge you to be a wind man.'

Sev's hands curled around the familiar shape; it was the penny whistle, only bigger. His fingers settled of their own volition on the silver keys. He placed the reeded mouthpiece to his lips and began to blow, very gently. The sound, still imperfect in his unskilled hands, was for him like liquid gold; like the Indian night sky. Every lovely image ever seen now came out from this magical fusion of lips and fingers. He handed the instrument back; he said unsteadily, 'That one's for me. I'll never play that bloody fiddle if I live to be a hundred!'

'Have a word wi' the Bandmaster. He's a reasonable

man. Tell him you got a strong fancy for the liquorice stick.'

Sev watched as the dismantled clarinet was placed in its velvet-lined case.

'Would you – would you give me a hand wi' the music reading?'

''Course I will, mate. You only had to ask.'

*

'Keeping up appearances' was Annis Nevill's watchword in a world of changing standards. Pride in her attractive daughters was constantly eroded by her fears for their safety. Convention required that in order to prove themselves successful as females, they should marry. But since they were Greypaulls by blood if not by name, tradition required that they should marry well. It was always at this point in her reasoning that confusion overcame Annis.

Eve and Abigail had lately become increasingly aware of Mother's double standards. Hard words had been uttered on Abi's twenty-ninth birthday.

'You might as well stop counting now,' said Mother. 'No man will look at you with a view to marriage if he thinks you're in your thirties.'

Abi said, 'Ah – well you'd know all about the problems of catching a husband wouldn't you, Mother? You were already twenty-seven when Father came back from India. Let me see now – '

Annis interrupted in a tone made sharp by fear.

'It's not me we're talking about. According to what I'm told, you're still hanging about with that Joey Santini. He'll never marry you; you know that, don't you? I can't understand why you don't find some respectable young man.'

'Nick Greypaull was respectable,' said Abi. 'He had a farm in Canada. I could have been a farmer's wife – '

'You could have been dead from the hard life, Abigail. In any case, that's all over and done with.'

'Well what do you suggest then, Mother? Perhaps I should wait beside the Bandstand in Vivary Park on a Sunday morning? Or hang around the Barrack gates in case some respectable young officer takes a fancy to me?'

Eve watched the colour drain away from her mother's face; she saw the hard, unforgiving set of Abi's delicate features, and felt afraid.

Something terrible was going on between these two, some secret agony from which Eve preferred to be excluded. Strong emotions disturbed her and made her want to cry. She dreaded these Sunday evenings spent at home, with Father uncomfortable in a stiff-backed parlour chair, his pipe laid aside, in case the tobacco smoke should turn Mother's best lace curtains yellow. Sunday evening had become Mother's special time for feeling proud. Here they sat on the blue brocade chairs and sofa, posed like people in a picture around a hissing gas fire, and overshadowed by a mahogany chiffonier loaded down with painted vases and ornaments in blue glass. Everything was done in some shade of blue in Mother's parlour. It was, Eve decided, the colour she most hated in all the world. When she got married, her home would be furnished in warm and glowing shades; reds and golds, pinks and yellows, sunshine colours. She looked up towards the overhanging mantel mirror. She could not decide which star of the silver screen she most resembled. Ben said that she was the living image of Mary Pickford, if only she would allow her brown hair to hang down in ringlets. She touched a hand to the thick French pleat in the nape of her neck and studied her reflection. To be shingled and Marcel-waved was of course, the latest fashion; but Eve could not bring herself to disappoint Father. 'You look,' he had once told her, 'a lot like my mother. Ah, she was such a pretty thing, Eve! So soft and gentle, and that nut-brown hair was her crowning glory!' Eve's love for Father was so vast and strong that she could never bear to think too much about it. He was the standard against which she had always measured the rest of the world; and found it wanting. How handsome he was in his brown suit, the thick white hair waving back from his forehead, the white moustaches curling up so nicely at the corners of his long and sensitive upper lip. He always sat, on these Sunday evenings, directly underneath the gaslit bracket, the chain of his silver watch hooked across its copper arm. The silver watch swayed hypnotically in the fire's heat; Eve gazed at it and thought about the black lace evening gown at present to be seen in Hatcher's shop window. It was sleeveless and low-cut, back and front; it had one perfect silver rose on the shoulder's narrow strap. Even Mother had once admitted, reluctantly, that Eve's neck and shoulders were almost as fine as those of the Aunty Blanche, now dead, who had once been an artist's model up in London. Father moved in his chair, he reached up for the watch and nodded towards Mother. He said, as he always did on these Sunday evenings, 'Half past eight, Anni. Time I was getting across to the Half Moon. I always sleep better for having my half-pint of supper cider.'

The closing of the front door seemed to have a curious effect upon Abigail and Mother. It was only now, with Father absent, that they seemed to become more intensely themselves; whatever tensions lay between them were heightened on these Sunday evenings. Eve began to rise from the uncomfortable sofa. She looked from Abigail to Mother.

'I think,' she said, 'that I'll wash my hair; it'll save me doing it tomorrow evening – '

'You washed it on Friday. Too much water on the head is bad for you. It can lead to all sorts of illnesses and complications.' Mother frowned. 'Sit down, miss. It's high time that you and I had words about a certain waster, name of Treherne. Since your father and me have been walking out a bit more in the evenings, we have seen you with our own eyes, going arm in arm with that Ben, along the Praed.'

Eve cried, with a rare flash of spirit, 'Don't bring Father into it. He never complains about my friends.'

Mother's face was triumphant. 'All the more reason for me to be double watchful, then!' All the threat in the whole world seemed to be contained in Mother's next words. 'You're to stay away from that yokel in Rowbarton. Ben Treherne is no good! He comes from a family of drunkards. I don't know how you can bring yourself to consort with such as him. Your own father is a decent man. You don't know what it's like to live in a house where the husband is always the worse for drink.'

The intensity of Mother's look was directed equally now upon both Abigail and Eve.

'We should not, by rights, be living in a villa in Taunton town. Me and Abi should never have to work at the gloving, nor you Eve, go out each day to French's Tannery. There's a little village up in the Blackdowns; a place called Buckland St Mary.' The harshness went out of Mother's features, her voice became soft, almost childlike. The tale, familiar since childhood, sounded new and magical when told to them by Mother. 'There's this farm called Larksleve; the house where I was born. It was painted white, and it had blue shutters at the windows. It had a thatched roof, and a porch. My Mother made a garden. She spelled out the name of Larksleve in white and yellow flowers. I remember how I was holding her hand, looking at the flowers when the bailiffs came riding up to tell us that everything was lost. My father was a drunkard and a gambler. He lost us our birthright and our fortune.' Mother sighed. 'Them that can read and write, have told me how the farm waggons still come down to Taunton market on a Friday with the name of Greypaull painted on 'em.'

Abigail said, 'Aunt Mina tells a different story. She says that Grandfather Philip was cheated out of Larksleve. That he signed a paper to help out a friend, and the friend let him down.'

'That's the very thing that I was pointing out,' cried

Mother. 'He kept bad company. He was muddled from the drink. Never properly knew what he was about. 'Tis very easy, you know,' and now Mother's voice was hardly louder than a whisper "tis very easy to lose your senses when you have drink taken. You can be persuaded to do things you never would when sober.'

Abi said, 'But we don't drink, Mother.'

'You consort with them as do! You go into pubs. You needn't deny it. Your father and me have seen you wi' our own eyes. That Santini is a rotter! Oh, he's handsome, I know. But then so was Philip Greypaull. I just can't understand the two of you. You've been told your family's history, time and time again.'

'Perhaps,' Abi said, 'it's all a waste of breath for you to warn us. You never know what's in the blood, do you, Mother? Most especially in mine.'

Mother leaned towards Abi. Eve saw the hand that was poised to slap her sister's face and the effort with which it was withdrawn.

'Don't talk to me about bad blood, my lady! Your father was no Italian organ grinder. Don't you have any pride at all? How can you be seen around the streets of Taunton, walking hand in hand wi' old Santini's monkey of a son?' She turned upon Eve.

'As for you, miss. I never thought that you, wi' all your pretty looks, would be seen cuddling up to that low-born gardener's boy. Don't ever let me hear that you've been seen with him again!'

*

They had longed, on that Sunday evening, to talk over the latest warnings from Mother. But a rap on the wall, from the adjoining bedroom, had commanded that they at once blow out the candle, and go straight to sleep. It was not until the following evening, when they were seated at their usual table in the Tipperary Club, that Abi said, 'Mother's not speaking to me. We worked all day in the most awful silence. Perhaps it's just as well, though.'

Eve said, 'What do you mean?' But even as she spoke her sister's left hand was laid upon the white cloth of the table. The ring on Abigail's third finger was so broad it reached from one knuckle to another.

'You're engaged!'

'I'm engaged. He gave me the ring on Friday night, but I was too frightened to tell about it. Last night's little exhibition and Mother's day-long sulking has made up my mind. I intend to wear Joey's ring from this minute on!'

'Oh Abi – she'll kill you stone dead! She'll make your life a misery. However shall we bear it? She's always going on about how he stole from that sweet shop when he was a boy, and the time he robbed the Devon and Somerset Stores' van. She'll never see any good in him. She won't have him in the house. She said so.'

'Oh yes she will, Eve. Just you wait and see. As soon as she spots my ring, she'll be issuing the invitation. I've been through all this once before, don't forget, with cousin Nick. I know her little tricks, but they won't work this time.'

*

Eve had sought to conceal the great love of her life among a host of lesser suitors. She had connived and manoeuvred so that Mother should see her, underneath the lamp-post at the end of the terrace, in earnest conversation with Georgie Kennet and Harold Judd. She had dropped various names across the thin bread and butter and apple jelly of Sunday tea times. She had hinted at possible liaisons with the kind of young men approved by Mother; bank clerks or ticket sellers in the railway station office, who displayed half an inch of white shirt cuff, even on a weekday, and wore steel-rimmed spectacles and brown boots.

Directly or indirectly, Abi never lied to mother. Eve envied her sister's courage but could not emulate it. Eve, like Frank her father, believed in the soft answer that turned wrath away. But avoidance of confrontation, once an entertaining game, had become in the past year a dangerous necessity if her passion for Ben Treherne was to remain concealed.

Ben was not the simple gardener's boy of Mother's description. He had recently gained promotion and was now second only to his uncle, who was Head Gardener on a large estate just beyond Rowbarton. Ben's especial skill lay in the propagation of new strains of roses. He exhibited regularly, in the name of his employer, at Taunton's annual flower show that was held in August. Eve had, on two occasions, received the full-blown but still beautiful blooms that had won for Ben several silver trophies. It had been the last gift of so many perfect flowers that had brought Mother's gimlet gaze to bear once more on Eve.

Abi had reported several probing conversations in which Mother had guessed at the possible donors of such expensive bouquets; like owners of flower shops, or wealthy gentlemen of unspecified age. It had, in the end, been an innocent remark from Aunt Candace that revealed the extent and wickedness of Eve's deception.

The clatter of dishes that came from the kitchen on that Friday evening was a familiar signal of coming trouble. Eve was met by Abi in the narrow hallway.

'Look out,' she whispered, 'be ready with some sort of explanation about Ben Treherne. Aunty Can was here this morning. She just dropped into the conversation that you come over to Rowbarton almost every evening. Oh Eve, how could you have been so careless? You know Aunty's garden butts onto Lord Stanley's estate. You can see the gardeners' cottages from her bedroom window. She didn't mean to make trouble for you, but oh my Lord, I've heard about nothing else for the rest of this day!'

Eve said, 'Is Father home yet?'

'No, of course he's not. He said that he'd be working

late – a special job – don't you remember?'

Eve began to rebutton her coat. 'I'm going back to French's. I shan't come home until Father can come with me.'

'He won't help you. He never does. He's no more capable of standing up to Mother than you are. It's too late to run, anyway. She heard you come in. You might as well face her now, as later on.'

❊

Mother sat at the circular table, looking regal behind the teapot. Eve took her place at Mother's left hand; the starched folds of the tablecloth fell in knifepoints on her silk-clad knees, but so great was her terror that she endured the irritation. Mother poured tea. Eve counted the sprigs of forget-me-nots on her flowered tea-plate and felt vague regret that the tension in her stomach muscles would almost certainly prevent her from eating her share of the fruit cake and hot, buttered toast. She looked across at Abi, at her sister's left hand held deliberately angled so that the broad gypsy ring set with sapphires and diamonds might catch the firelight. Mother handed filled teacups. She smiled.

'Well now,' she said, ''idden this a nice change, just the three of us sitting down to tea together. I've been thinking. Now that Abi's got herself engaged, and you Eve, so I'm told by your Aunty Candace, goes courting in Rowbarton every evening; well – 'tis about time your father and me met these two young fellahs, face to face.'

Abi said, at once, 'Joey's always busy. In any case, I wouldn't want you to go to any special trouble.'

'No trouble, Abigail. You know how I enjoy a party.'

Eve knew that some answer was expected from her. She moved, involuntarily, and the sharp points of starched linen tablecloth stabbed her knees. She remembered the rickety table, spread with sheets of newsprint, that she had once glimpsed through Ben Treherne's kitchen window; she said, 'Ben's not really the party going kind. He's very shy.'

'All the more reason for him to come and meet your family! It's all arranged. Dinner and tea, this coming Sunday. I've got a nice crown of lamb ordered from the butcher. Our Mina's promised one of her special cakes. I shall expect you both to stay home on Saturday evening. I can't be expected to do everything by myself.'

✳

The sideboard cupboard held treasures that had once belonged to wealthy Aunty Blanche. There was a set of table linen, with cloth of heavy satin damask and matching napkins. A whole canteen of silver that bore the monogram of the Fitzgeralds. There was a wine cooler of silver gilt with matching napkin rings and flower vase. There were finger bowls and wine glasses of lead-cut crystal. Abi polished silver while Eve washed glass and china. A complete dinner service of fine bone china had been borrowed from Aunt Mina. Between Friday evening and Saturday tea time, the house and all its contents had been scoured and polished. Even the aspidistra leaves in father's conservatory had been wiped with milk so that they shone.

Abi said to Mother, in a concerned voice, 'You and Father usually step out together on a Saturday evening. There's no need for you to stay at home on our account. There's a new film showing at the Empire. According to Aunt Candace, her Billy plays the part of the man who robs the bank.'

Mother hesitated. 'What will you girls be up to while I'm gone?'

Abi pointed to her untidy head and held out her stained hands. 'We both need to wash our hair, and get ready for tomorrow. We shall have an early night. We're both worn out with all this cleaning.'

Eve heated the water and mixed shampoo. As the front door closed behind them she said to Abi, 'You were in a hurry to get rid of Mother and Father.'

'I've got things to do.'

'What things? We've polished everything except the ceilings!'

Abi said, in a strange tone, 'That lino in the hall – it's coming loose. I really ought to nail it down.'

'But that's a job for Father. I've never noticed any loose lino.'

'Well you wouldn't, would you!'

Abigail, Eve thought, always grew irritable when she was overtired and worried.

'It'll be alright; tomorrow I mean. Father'll be there, at the dinner table, and in any case – what harm can Mother really do?'

'It's not Mother I'm worried about.'

Abi went into the kitchen; she returned carrying Father's tool box.

Eve said, 'That's a heavy hammer and a lot of nails to mend a bit of loose lino? There's no gaslight in the hall, you'll have to light a candle. Why can't it wait until the morning?'

Abi said nothing; Eve towelled her wet hair, and began to brush it out before the fire's warmth. She waited to hear the sound of hammering, but there was none. The door that led into the hall was not quite closed. She could see her sister, kneeling down beside the front door; the candle light cast shadows over walls and ceiling. It seemed almost as though Abigail was praying. Eve moved on tiptoe into the hall; she peered across her sister's shoulder and saw six iron nails and Father's hammer laid out carefully in a crescent pattern.

'Don't do it, Abi. It's black magic, and it's dangerous, not to say wicked!'

'I've got to. He'll be coming here tomorrow. It's the only chance I'll ever have to make sure of him – '

'That chap up in London never married Aunty Blanche!'

'I'll take the risk. I'm thirty years old, Eve. Joey Santini must be my last chance of getting married.'

Abi picked up a nail and hammered it into the lino; she continued to hammer until the threshold was lined with spaced out nail heads. Eve shivered; she said, 'What you've just done – it won't have any effect on Ben Treherne, will it?'

Abi turned; her face, in the candlelight, looked drawn and frightened. 'I don't know,' she whispered, 'oh, my God, Eve. I'd forgotten all about him.'

*

The mahogany dining table had once been a gift from Uncle Hugh Fitzgerald to Granny Greypaull. Eve smoothed the damask cloth across its gleaming surface and placed finger bowls at every setting, while Abi laid out rows of silver cutlery, and folded napkins into rings. The silver vase held asters picked from Father's garden. The wine cooler held cider, in a whisky decanter. The smells of beeswax and silver polish mingled oddly with those of roasting lamb, mint sauce and apple pie. It had been arranged that Ben and Joey should arrive together. At a double rap upon the front door, Abi dropped a knife. 'They've come too early,' she said. 'Mother won't like that.' Eve leaned for support upon the half-laid table. 'You'll have to let them in. My legs won't carry me to the front door. Just make sure that Joey Santini steps first across those nails.'

All the dramas of their lives, Eve thought, were played out in this room, and around this circular table. The brown panelled walls reflected the fire's glow; brown chenille curtains hung at the window. The gloving-table, empty now, was pushed back into a corner. The seating arrangements had been decided by Mother; Joe and Ben sat together, facing Abigail and Eve. Mother wore her best black dress and cameo brooch. Father, who usually ate dinner in his shirt sleeves and waistcoat, looked stiff and uneasy in collar and tie, and brown suit. Eve felt the laughter of hysteria bubble in her throat. She saw the exchange of bewildered glances between Ben and Joey, as the crown roast with its many cuffs of frilled white paper was set down in the middle of the table. She watched Ben's fingers as they curled around his knife and fork. He had cleaned the nails of his left hand, but a quantity of garden soil still remained beneath the finger nails of his right. His thick fair hair that looked so boyish when ruffled by the wind, had been slicked down with water for this important occasion, giving his face a sharp and unfamiliar expression. As the hair dried in the room's heat, one lock fell untidily across his forehead. Eve saw Ben as her Mother must see him. His wrists, red and sore from exposure to the weather, jutted awkwardly from jacket sleeves that were too short. The collar of his shirt was limp and not quite white; his tie was knotted clumsily, and was not much wider than a bootlace. While Mother offered gravy and potatoes, Eve glanced sideways at her sister. Abi sat, her food untouched, her gaze transfixed by Joey Santini.

Joey, in an effort to impress, had chosen to wear the unmatched dinner jacket and trousers of his bouncer's outfit. The glossy curls and olive skin that looked so much like those of Rudolph Valentino in the dim lighting of the Tipperary Club, had a cheap almost degenerate air, when viewed by daylight and at Annis Nevill's dinner table. The bright green satin cummerbund was as out of place as the deep yellow watered silk of the bow tie. While Ben Treherne picked unhappily among the crown roast and mint sauce, Joey Santini was eating with all the nervous speed of a frightened man. Eve could feel the movement of Abi's arm, saw her flinch and then look towards Mother, as Joey balanced peas on the blade of his knife, and scooped gravy up with his dessert spoon.

Conversation at the dinner table was limited by the obvious need of the guests to concentrate on the unfamiliar items of cutlery and trappings. While Annis and her daughters cleared the table and washed the dishes, Father followed orders by inviting Joey and Ben to join him in the front parlour. He talked to Ben about gardening; asked about the health of Joey's mother. Abigail and Eve packed Aunt Mina's dinner service back into its box.

'That,' muttered Eve, 'was the very worst meal of my whole life. Thank heavens it's over!'

'Over? She's not even begun yet. You mark my words – the worst is yet to come!'

*

If the appointments of Annis Nevill's dinner table had confused her daughter's suitors, the elegance of her parlour now caused a glazed expression to settle over both sets of features. There they sat, side by side, on the blue brocade sofa; the ebony protuberances of its intricate carving making it impossible for them to lean back and relax. Eve, who spent every Sunday evening trying to accommodate her spine to the awful sofa, knew exactly how they felt.

Father sat in his usual place beneath the gaslight bracket; his silver pocket-watch suspended by its chain, swayed gently above his head. Abigail and Mother perched in separate armchairs; Eve crouched on a footstall, her skirts wrapped around her legs, her right arm resting reassuringly against Father's knee. The gas fire hissed. Ben Treherne hunched his shoulders and seemed transfixed by a painting of Aunty Blanche, dressed in flowing robes, with a Greek urn on her head. Joey Santini stared openly about him. Eve followed his gaze from vase-laden chiffonier to photograph-laden table; from deep-pile carpet to lace-draped window. Joey lived with his mother in a little house behind the Pig Market. Ben lived a rough and ready kind of life with his bachelor uncle, the head gardener.

Mother's face, Eve thought, had on its most snooty Greypaull expression, what Abi described as her 'Queen Victoria look'. She inclined her head towards Joey Santini. 'Tell me Mr Santini, does your mother still take in washing?'

Joey said, 'No, Mrs Nevill. She don't need to do that any more. I got several good jobs on the go – '

'Yes – I've heard a lot about your jobs. Such a shame you got rid of the barrel organ. What happened? Did the monkey die?'

Eve longed to study Abigail's expression, but already the big guns were trained on Ben Treherne.

'I hear that you live with your uncle?'

'Thass quite right,' mumbled Ben. 'He took me in when my mother passed away. He've been good to me, have Uncle.'

'Pity that he drinks.' If Eve had not known her mother, she would have sworn the sympathy genuine, the concern heartfelt.

'Oh – he idden so bad, these days. Well see – the cider do upset his stomach. Now there was a time – '

Eve saw Father's fingers tighten around the cold bowl of his pipe; she felt the twitch of his knee against her shoulder. She closed her eyes, and willed Ben to be silent.

Tea was, if possible, a more testing meal than dinner. Ben used a pastry fork to spread jam on bread and butter. Joey, his temper now held down by an obvious effort of will, seemed determined to clear every slice of cake and bowl of jelly set upon the table.

Mother, equally determined to reminisce, could not be diverted from memory lane. She recalled the arrival of the destitute Santini family in Taunton. She hinted broadly at the sadness of Joey's misspent youth, the trial he had been to his poor widowed mother. She commiserated once more with Ben Treherne about the shame he must feel on account of his drunken uncle. She sketched, with a light hand, her own superior origins; the steadfast and sober nature of Frank. When the last cup of tea had been drunk, and the final piece of bread and butter eaten, Mother rose from the table. Her gaze moved from Ben's fair flushed face, to the dark and mutinous features of Joey Santini.

'Well,' she smiled, 'it's been a proper revelation for me to meet you.' She waved a vague hand towards Father. 'We'd heard such a lot about both of you.' She paused, and braced her shoulders, like a woman threatened. 'Now, I expect you'll both want to be getting off home.' She turned towards Eve and Abigail. 'Well – come on you two! Say goodnight to your friends!'

✻

Abi closed the bedroom door and leaned against it.

'I'd like to kill her. I'd like to to push her in the Tone!' Tears streamed down Abigail's face. 'You know what she's done, don't you?'

Eve nodded. 'We'll be lucky if we ever see them again. Whatever must they be thinking? Oh Abi, why does Mother do this to us?'

✻

The Band, Sev had been told, was the Battalion's showpiece; the faintest tarnish on the smallest of brass buttons would bring his Regiment into disrepute. The uniform of Bandsman was more ornamental than that of ranker. The contrasting white and gold of epaulettes and cording seemed to make the tunic appear more richly scarlet; the crease in a Bandman's trousers was expected to be of a knife edged standard.

The first twenty years of Sev Carew's life had been lived without any knowledge of his own worth; his sense of achievement on gaining the Army's Certificate of Education was diminished by his private conviction that, given time, any fool could do it. The circumstances of his life, and a certain darkness in his nature, had bred cynicism in him. He looked always for the snags and catches of a situation.

Pride had been first aroused by his wearing of the Bandsman's tunic. Achievement was confirmed by his ability to read sheet music. This particular skill, even he was bound to admit, could not, given time, be mastered.

by any fool. Drills and parades had straightened his shoulders, and yet, far back in his mind there remained that old defeated stoop of the child who believed himself to be unloved. Sev did not recognise respect when it was first shown towards him.

*

Time in India, for the ordinary soldier, was an enemy that could be out-witted but never conquered. Sev's greatest fear since coming to Agra had been that some day he would join the pathetic number who lay down on their beds at the onset of hot weather, and for the next six months were content only to observe the swaying of the punkah. The heat did strange things to a man's mind. Small irritations assumed the proportions of major disasters; and Sev's was a nature that had little tolerance for pinpricks. He needed the discipline demanded by total involvement, and that involvement had now come to him through music. The generosity of other Bandsmen still surprised him. The oboe player and the second trumpeter had, between them, taught him to read notation, but a clarinet player, he discovered, needed more than dedication; a wind instrument demanded good lungs, and several years of smoking had impaired his breathing. With the principals of musical notation set firmly in his brain, Sev now turned to the problem of his addiction to tobacco.

His obsession with the clarinet had caused him to lengthen his periods of practice until exhaustion overcame him.

'Kill yourself, you will!' Taffy Richards told him. 'Time you knocked off smoking them old Woodbines, and sitting in the Library, reading books. We got our Second Class Certificates. I reckon we done enough in the cause of education. I've entered my name for the Boxing Championships in March. How 'ud you like to be my trainer?'

Sev looked doubtful. 'I got band practice every

morning – '

Taffy grinned. 'And then you comes back to the bungalow puffing like some old rhino, your face all red, and your temper to match!'

'What would I have to do?'

'Go running with me every evening. The trainer always goes running with his champion.'

'You sound pretty sure of yourself.'

'I've won every heat in the competition, so far!' Taffy paused.

'Be good for them gasping lungs of yours. Make you a better clarinet player, I shouldn't wonder! I got a feeling that 1925 is going to be our best year since we joined this bloody army!'

'Would I have to be your sparring partner?'

'Not if you don't want to. What's your trouble then? Frightened to spoil your looks in case that snooty girl in Taunton don't fancy you no more?'

'She was nice,' Sev said quietly. 'I've tried to forget about her – '

'She don't write to you then?'

'Can't really expect her to, can I? India's a long way off, and we shall be stuck here for a long time yet.'

Taffy grinned. 'She's probably married by now; got a couple of kids and a husband what beats her.' Taffy pointed to the row of dogs who sat patiently on the verandah.

'You'd be better off with one of them, mun!'

*

The dog Nipper had belonged to a Colour Sergeant from another Company, a man who on receiving bad news from home had drowned himself in the River Jumna. Sev rescued the pup within minutes of its execution, waving his written permission to own a pet in the face of the marksman who took care of such matters.

'He's a vicious little tike. He bit me twice before I got him chained up. Take him if you want him – but mind your fingers!'

Responsibility for a living creature was a new experience for Sev. He went down to the Bazaar and bargained for a leather collar. He visited a tinsmith and had Nipper's name and his own Army Service number engraved on a disc. Several hours of careful handling were to pass before collar and disc could be buckled into place. Sev began to doubt the wisdom of taking on another man's dog. Never get attached to nothing or nobody, was Taffy Richards' maxim, but still Sev watched for some sign of devotion once shown by the sheepdog Ruff towards himself and Granfer. Nipper's period of mourning lasted three weeks; and then there came an evening when Sev, still braced against indifference, saw the faintest twitch in the stumpy tail, a look of trust in the yellow eyes. Devotion, it seemed, could now be transferred from one person to another without any loss of face.

Sev no longer feared the slide into apathy that ruined so many men in the Battalion. His mornings were occupied with band practice; his afternoons spent in the Library. He went running almost every evening with Taffy Richards, and always on his return, Nipper sat in the shade of the verandah, waiting for him. The boxing championships were held in early March, and Taffy defeated every single contender. He and Sev were photographed together, Sev on one knee beside the trophy table, Taffy posed in a pugnacious stance.

Music became daily more important and invasive, until it seemed that his whole life was lived with the theme of some great composer throbbing in his head. He developed a passion for the marches of John Philip Sousa; he played the music of Glinka and Tchaikovsky at evening concerts. He was moved to tears by Amy Woodford Finden's 'Indian Love Lyrics'; the words of her 'Kashmiri Song', sung by Taffy at a Regimental dinner, were to stay forever in his mind.

Pale hands I loved, beside the Shalimar,
Where are you now, who lies beneath your spell?

Sev found himself thinking about the girl in Taunton.
Without wanting to he called up her face, so that a
picture of the green eyes and sweet mouth floated
suddenly across his view of the sheet music. He missed
his cue, came in one bar late for the clarinet part, and
earned a look of reproof from the bandmaster. Days
later, Taffy overheard him, still humming the emotive
tune.

Taffy grinned and clapped him on the shoulder.

'Brace up, mun! No use you feeling all romantic in this
godforsaken hole! Proper soft you've got, ever since you
took on that old dog.'

It was true. The dog Nipper had found the soft place in
his heart. 'Leave the door open just a crack,' his Granny
used to say, 'and you might just as well throw up all the
window-sashes.' All his cultivated hardness, his deliberate avoidance of contact with his family; the barriers
with which he had protected the damaged places in his
soul, all had been infiltrated by a black and white
mongrel dog with yellow eyes.

*

Of their Platoon, Sev and Taffy were the only men who
had yet to explore the Taj Mahal. Since their arrival in
Agra, the Welshman had adopted an attitude of censure
towards India's monuments and temples.

'Indecent, I calls it, them old Princes spending all that
money on fancy buildings when the ordinary people was
dying of starvation.'

Sev said, 'My father's job is to do with carving stone
for churches. I could never see what was so important
about it; to hear him droning on you'd have thought
such work was something special.' Sev grinned. 'Spose
we ought to take a look at it before we go home. Can't
very well admit, back in Blighty, that we never got close

to the Taj Mahal.'

They were acutely conscious of the presence of this wonder of the world. It was impossible to ignore since route marches and exercises took them close to and around it. There was, Sev admitted to himself, something childish in their refusal to be impressed by a mere building.

The officers of the Battalion took pleasure in gratuitous instruction on the subject of the Taj, pointing out the cadre of cypress trees that had been planted by the Ex-Viceroy Lord Curzon, and giving lectures on its history. Sev had learned in his first year in Agra how Shah Jehan, grandson of the great warrior Akbar, had mourned so deeply on the death of his favourite wife Mumtaz, that he had built a shrine to her memory and called it Taj Mahal. He had yawned and dozed through the telling of this story, but lately he had remembered and been oddly touched by it. It was in March, in the final weeks of the Cold Season, that news came of the impending visit of minor Royalty to Agra. The Regimental Band, posed dramatically before the Taj, was to give a concert for the Royal party. Band practice was increased, new pieces learned and old ones polished. A special arrangement by the Bandmaster of the 'Indian Love Lyrics' was to be included in the programme.

Sev had been aware for some time of changes within himself. 'Going soft' was how he privately described the new awareness that had come upon him since his mastery of music, and his ownership of Nipper. He continued to do all the manly things, like playing centre forward for his team in games of football against barefoot Hindus, and running several miles each week in his role as trainer to the Regiment's Champion Boxer. This was no time for him to revert to the defenceless child that he had once been. To cover an embarrassment of which he alone was aware, he would push Taffy Richards to ever greater feats of physical endurance, and speak roughly to the adoring mongrel dogs. But nothing could prevent the tears that welled up in his throat when he played certain passages of music; and nothing could overcome his reluctance to gaze too closely at the Taj Mahal.

*

They marched to the Fort of Agra in the cool of early morning. Sev, who had played the marches of John Philip Sousa with his fellow bandsmen, left the head of the column and sought out Dusty and Taffy on their arrival. Refreshments had been laid on at the Fort; and the Battalion's char-wallahs and sandwich sellers had trundled their wagons and urns in the rear of the march. A canteen was set up beneath the sheer walls of ochre sandstone and orders given that men should re-assemble at the hour of four that afternoon. A guard had been mounted, and sentries posted to ensure the safety of the Royal party, but none of Sev's Platoon had been included in their number. Taffy looked towards the domes and minarets.

'No excuse not to look at the bloody thing now, boyos! We is on our own till four o' clock.'

Sev looked down at his clarinet case.

'You lot go on ahead. I'll stow my case and catch you up.'

He had known, from the moment of entering the Fort, that he could never approach the monument to Mumtaz Mahal in the company of others. To be seen to show emotion was his greatest dread. He strolled, hands in pockets, beneath the great gateway of marble-ribbed sandstone, and there it was, filling all his vision; arches and domes, latticed screens and minarets. He moved closer; here there were scrolls and sculptures inlaid with precious stones; he moved back a step, and the whole wonder of the thing was suddenly too much to bear. Sev closed his eyes and the creamy white image hung just behind his eyelids. He opened his eyes and began to move slowly towards the gardens. The officer had said that there were twenty fountains which fed a pool filled with goldfish. English flowers grew here. He saw roses and was reminded of Montacute. He began to think about Jye, his father; the man who had lived and worked in London, and looked only at churches. Sev gazed back towards the Taj; seen from every angle it was perfect. He felt a sudden sharpening of insight, and in that moment Sev knew himself to be his father's son. He experienced that tingling in the blood that Jye himself must have felt on first seeing the Abbey of Westminster. Sev had heard that story, but not understood it. To share an emotion with so unlikely a person surprised other memories in him; he recalled the tall, stooping figure, the head of black curls; the broad and capable hands, so unlike his own; the look of puzzlement in the brown eyes. It occurred to Sev now, as he stood by the marble pool of Shah Jehan's Taj Mahal, that his father had, on occasion, tried to help and understand him.

The thought was so strange that he could not pursue it; he turned away from the pool, and heard Dusty Miller's voice beyond the cypress trees. Sev listened briefly to the laughter of his friends, and then began to walk, swiftly away, in the opposite direction.

The Regimental Band played that evening before an audience of minor British royals, and the Indian Princes who had come to Agra to pay them homage. Sev began to worry, towards the end of the performance, about his inability to read notation in the fading light. He needed spectacles and would not admit it; but every note of the 'Kashmiri Song' was so clear in his mind that he could close his eyes and still be note-perfect.

It was in April, when photographs of the great occasion were distributed among the bandsmen, that he realised fully how significant and strange had been that day. His memories of the Royal party, and the entourage of Indian Princes were already dim. Reality was in the photograph. He found a quiet corner in the library, and sat there for a long time; the picture was better than any he had found in Lord Curzon's books, in London. Here was the Band, posed immediately before the Taj, their mirror-image reflected in the pool. There were the cypress trees, the domes and minarets. Sev was seated at the very end of the front row of bandsmen, the clarinet sloped across his left arm, a serious expression on his face. He thought about the day he had tramped to Taunton; the old woman who had given him bread and jam and hot tea; the man who had given him a lift to Bridgwater. He recalled his rag-bound feet and the way he had tricked the Army doctor.

'I'll remember thee,' he had told those two who had helped him then. But for them he might never have reached Taunton, or lived to see the Wonder of the World.

*

The Hot Weather came in early that year, the temperature climbing by twenty-five degrees within a space of hours. The punkah-wallahs were re-employed on the first day of April. Straw mats were nailed across the open doorways and tatie-wallahs paid to throw water on them so that the little air which came into the bungalows was at least cool.

Sev had withstood the heat of four summers lived on the Indian Plains. So good was his health, so sound his mind, that he believed himself to be immune from the ills that troubled most of the Platoon.

In May, a tattooist appeared in the cantonment. He opened up his wooden case of coloured inks and needles, squatted in a shady corner behind the cookhouse, and announced that he was ready for business. Sev had seen samples of the man's art. The experience would, he knew, be painful, but the results gratifying. He chose a design of entwined snakes, interspersed with hearts and roses. The usual warnings were issued by the Medical Officer, that any man who submitted his skin to the tattooist, risked blood poisoning and possible death.

411

Within three days Sev had acquired his chosen tattoos on both forearms and across his chest.

The trouble began with a swelling on his right forearm.

'You've been bitten by a mosquito,' a fellow bandsman told him.

'I never get mosquito bites.'

'Then it's a dirty needle,' said the timpany player, 'that lousy tattooist needs booting from the Barracks!'

'Better see a Medic,' was the advice of his room mates. Sev covered the swollen arm with a long-sleeved shirt. At morning band practice he found it painful to lift the clarinet, or concentrate upon the music. By mid-afternoon his temperature had risen. He stripped the sheets from his bed, took them to the wash house and soaked them in water. With the old and dripping sheets wrapped closely around him he lay down on his bed. At six in the evening he began to shiver, his ague so violent that it shook the bed frame. Within the hour he was in the hospital ward, a Colonel and a Major disagreeing, one either side of the bed, as to whether his illness was malarial fever, or tetanus induced by the tattooist's needle. Orders were given that he should be rubbed down with ice and given quinine. An incision was made in his upper arm to prevent the spread of possible poison. When he suffered a further bout of shivering at six o'clock precisely on the following evening, a diagnosis of malaria was confirmed. The rash called prickly heat now covered most of his body. He lay for two weeks in the hospital bed. The bouts of fever and shivering grew less; the snakes, and the hearts-and-roses design on his right forearm began, gradually, to assume more normal proportions. Taffy and Dusty brought Nipper in to see him. Dusty said, 'He hardly ate a bloody morsel while you was in here! We was wondering who would be the first to kick the bucket – you or the mongrel!'

Sev grinned. 'Take more than a mosquito bite to finish me off.'

'So it was malaria after all?'

'Don't know. They're still arguing the toss about it.' Sev leaned back against his pillows. 'They're putting me in the convalescent ward tomorrow. Special food in there, so I'm told, and a pint of beer every night with your supper!' He fondled the dog's ears. 'Thanks for looking after him. Now I got another favour to ask. Can you bring me writing paper and pencil. 'Tis weeks past, since I wrote home to my mother. The Medic is talking about sending eight of us sick-bay scroungers up into the Hills for the rest of the summer. We can go to the soldiers' rest home at Naina Tal – but only if we can afford it.'

'And can you afford it? Most of your pay goes on fags and extra bits of food for Nipper.'

Sev said, 'I made an allotment of half my pay to my mother. That was four years ago. I'll write home and ask if she can send me a few quid, on account of I need to convalesce.' He paused. 'Ask the Bandmaster for me, if I can have my clarinet and sheet music. I'm the sort that needs to practice reg'lar every day.'

*

To be invalided to the Hills was the ambition of every soldier who ever served his time on the Plains. Sev travelled with his fellow convalescents by train and horse-drawn covered cart to the hill station at Naina Tal. The batch of forty men, most of them as thin as scarecrows, had the yellowed skin and dulled eyes of malaria victims, but even as they moved upwards from the scorching plains and towards the snows, a visible change overcame them.

They arrived in darkness. The bungalows were smaller than those in Agra, and instead of punkahs and straw taties over open doorways, each room had a fireplace in which logs were burned. There was a feeling of English-ness about this Station; the air was fresh and bracing; it reminded Sev of Montacute on an October evening. He slept long and deeply.

The money from England, wired by his mother, was sufficient to pay for a stay of six weeks in the Hills. The monsoon was over, the weather cold and sunny. Within hours of his arrival the blistery rash of prickly heat had started to heal. Within days, the lassitude and lack of appetite caused by illness, were replaced by a hunger and vitality he had not experienced since leaving England. He and his five room mates were checked daily by the doctor, who warned that they should take only short walks to begin with, since the thin air at these altitudes could do damage to their hearts. He had asked for, and been granted, permission to bring Nipper with him. Sev heard the names of mountains spoken for the first time. They were, he discovered, perched among the very foothills of the Himalayas. There were times on a clear day when Mount Anapurna looked close enough to touch; and the highest peak of all, the one called Everest, could be seen, hanging like the dome of the Taj Mahal in the eastern sky.

The men who shared his room had come from various stations on the Plains. There were two Scotsmen from the Fort at Meerut. A Lancashire youth from the Barracks at Delhi; an Irish fusilier from Lucknow; and a fast-talking Cockney corporal who had promised them all, on that first evening in Naina Tal, that he would not dream of pulling rank. A common bond of malaria and prickly heat had at first kept them together. They took short walks, never venturing too far from the Rest Home. They viewed the English-looking houses and bungalows which belonged to British officials. Here it was that the memsahib and her children sought refuge from the heat of the Plains. But as they grew stronger the two Scotsmen sought the company of their compatriots who occupied an adjoining room. The Lancashire youth developed a heart murmur and was confined to bed. Sev was left with the Irish fusilier and the Cockney corporal.

Every day they ventured further, climbed higher, and grew more daring. Sev, who had no head for heights, soon learned to keep his gaze on distant peaks, and never to look down. The corporal Alfie, who boasted an ability to go sick every summer, was a regular visitor to the Rest Home. He had become acquainted with certain of the hill people, and learned a little of their language.

'They believe,' he told Sev and Paddy, 'that all these parts is haunted by spirits. They reckon that the Gods live in them mountains.' They were walking in an area of rocky outcrops, tender greenery, and waterfalls. As they came around a bend in the track, Sev saw the special place to which he knew he would return alone.

It was in the fourth week of his convalescence that the malaria returned. He and Alfie had gone climbing; they were resting in a high place when Sev's first bout of shivering occurred. They came down to the Rest Home as fast as Sev's condition would allow. For five days he sweated and shivered; the weight he had gained dropped away. He was visited daily by the doctor, an elderly ex-Major, who upon retirement from the Army had chosen to remain in India. On the evening of the fifth day, when his temperature was normal, Sev asked, 'Well doctor, how many times is this likely to happen? I thought it was all finished with, that being in a colder climate was all I needed to put me right?'

The doctor pulled a chair up to the bedside and sat down.

'Malarial fever,' he explained, 'has nothing at all to do with climate. The infection is in your bloodstream. You will suffer recurring attacks in the middle of an English winter. How long is your period of service?'

Sev said, 'I'm on a five and two. I've done six years already, more than four of them down on the Plains.'

'Too long!' The doctor shook his head. 'The Army never changes. They still keep the fittest of their young men for far too long in that intolerable heat.' He consulted Sev's records. 'You are due to leave us in a fortnight. I rather doubt that you will be recovered sufficiently in that time, to make the journey back to

Agra.'

'But I must, sir. It took every penny I've got to pay for my six weeks' convalescence.'

'You have drawn no pay since you arrived here, so you are in credit with your Paymaster. In any case, the Army owes you an extra month to recover your health, and I shall put in a report to that effect.'

Sev lay back on his pillows. 'Do you mean to tell me that I've got this bloody fever for the rest of my life?'

The doctor shrugged. 'It will grow less as you get older. If you're lucky, by middle-age, it might have disappeared altogether.' He paused and smiled. 'It's not just malarial fever, Carew. Look at me! I could be retired in England, growing roses and playing golf. India gets in the blood.'

✻

Sev was granted an extended sick leave. He regained his lost weight; the mountain hikes with Alfie and Paddy were resumed, but sometimes he preferred to walk alone.

The people of this region were taller and more impressive than those of the Plains. Their yellowish skins had a flush of pink across the cheekbones; their eyes were narrow and slanted. There were many goat-herders and shepherds among them; the tinkling of sheepbells a frequent sound along the mountain paths.

By September the British memsahibs and their servants had started to leave their comfortable houses and begun the journey back to their officer husbands at Agra and Meerut. Sev and Alfie watched them go in rickshaws and mounted on fine bay horses. Alfie spat across his shoulder. 'Parasites,' he muttered. 'They don't have to find their own expenses to come up here. They don't even need to be sick in the first place!'

Sev had rarely mentioned his brief time in London. Now, he felt a sudden need to talk about it.

'I worked for Curzon once. I lived at Number 1

Carleton House Terrace; just off the Mall. I was only a green kid, just up from the country. The bastard sacked me.'

'What for?'

Sev grinned. 'It was Armistice Day. I went out with the crowds and forgot to stoke the boiler. God's Butler was to dine that night with the King and Queen at Buckingham Palace. I took cold bath water to his room. My God, Alf – you should just have seen his face!'

Alfie laughed. 'Is that how you came to join up?'

'More or less. I was sent home, in disgrace. I took a load of his Lordship's silver with me in my suitcase. My mother damn near died of shame when she saw it. She sent it all back.' He paused. 'There was nothing but farm labouring to be had in Montacute. I was never trained for anything – '

'And we ain't trained for nothing now, matey! 'Ave you ever thought about what's waiting for us back in Blighty? How old are you?'

Sev said, 'Coming twenty-five next April. Another year and I'll have done my five and two.'

'And what then? You'll go home and join the bloody dole queue!'

'But there must be plenty that we can do.'

'You give me a for instance, then.'

Sev said, with pride, 'I'm a musician. Clarinettist. Regimental Band. Somerset Light Infantry.'

Alfie spat again. 'Oh well, in that case you'll probably be alright. You can always find yourself a spot in one of these new-fangled dance bands.'

Alf and Paddy left Naina Tal at the end of that week. There was a space of days before the arrival of the new intake. Sev suffered a reversal of spirits; he felt depression settle on him. He remembered the rocky outcrop, the green ferns and waterfalls where he had once walked. He went back to that place and thought how like it was to Miles Hill. He sat by a waterfall and looked down on the tea plantations that marched clear across the valley. He heard the tinkling of sheepbells on the upper slopes, and the sound of pan pipes, played by the boy whose job it was to mind them. He lay down on the short turf, and perhaps it was his weakened condition that caused him to turn his face into the grass and sob. He wept, mindlessly, and for a long time. He mourned for Granfer and Ham Hill; for the desolation of his childhood. He grieved for all his disappointments; the agonies suffered but never truly acknowledged, until this moment. He remembered his mother, who had once assumed him dead, and who had sent, without question, the money which had enabled him to convalesce. Twenty-five years old come next April, and here he was wailing like an infant. He sat up, blew his nose and wiped his face. He felt eased and peaceful in himself. He recalled Alfie's words, and grinned. If all else failed on his return to England, he could always try for a job in a new-fangled dance band.

He gazed out across the valley. In the eastern sky Mount Anapurna stood like a giant; beyond was the peak of Everest which never quite managed to look real. All at once he was back again on Miles Hill, and this time in the company of Llewelyn Powys.

'Stay away from mountains,' the poet had told him. 'That silence is designed to shrivel a man's soul.'

The man was wrong. Here he sat, among the highest peaks in the whole world, and felt his soul expand until it touched these mountains called Himalayas. The natives believed that their gods dwelt in the Hills. Sev remembered Granfer, and this time it was without pain. Sev's God had always dwelt in the high places of the world.

He returned to Agra at the end of November, to find his Platoon in a state of keen anticipation. 'We is off to the Sudan, boyo,' Taffy told him. 'We sets sail for Port Sudan in three weeks time!'

*

It was over a year since Joey Santini and Ben Treherne

had visited Number 5, The Terrace. The sisters had spoken often of that disastrous Sunday. Abi had, at first, said brave things.

'It makes no difference at all to my feelings for him. Mother had no right to show Joey up, like that. So what if he does eat peas from his knife and wear bright colours? He's got spirit and he's stylish. Have you noticed Eve? We have no strong men in our family.'

Eve said, 'There's Uncle David. Now he won't stand for any nonsense from Aunt Mina. Have you noticed how, whenever she starts to lay down the law, he only needs to look sort of gently at her and she goes quiet.'

Abi frowned. 'It's a pity that Father hasn't got the same power over Mother. Joey says he'll never come to this house again, and who can blame him!'

Eve said, tentatively, 'He stepped over your six iron nails. Surely that must make a difference?'

Abi sighed. 'I don't know. We quarrel such a lot. He says that I'm too domineering; that I try to run his life. We have dreadful rows, Eve. Well, you know my temper, don't you? It's his Italian blood I suppose that makes him so swaggering and bombastic. We went for a walk down Tangier the other night, and he made me so mad I tried to push him in the river!'

Eve looked shocked. 'Oh Abi, that's hardly a nice thing to do to the man you mean to marry!'

'I don't think I ever will – marry, I mean. I shall be thirty-two years old this year, and Joey shows no sign of wanting to settle down.'

'You don't look that old! You're so slim and smart, why anyone would take you for no more than twenty-five. Anyway, there's other fish in the sea besides Joey Santini!'

In the months that followed, they continued to say the same things but with less assurance. Abigail lost heart; she continued to wear Joey's ring, but more from a feeling of bravado than any conviction that she would ever achieve the plain gold band that should be its companion. She and Eve still left the house together every weekday evening. The large iron doorkey was left by Mother underneath a flat stone, near to the doorstep; but on their strict promise to be home by half past nine. The first to arrive would open the front door, and then replace the key beneath the stone. Mother still believed that they came home as they went out; together. But Eve was always in bed and asleep when Abi climbed the stairs.

*

Eve enjoyed the admiration of young men; she saw no point in discouraging their attentions. There was always a limit, of course, beyond which a nice girl did not go. But that went without saying! She had never needed to labour the point; she was, after all, Annis Nevill's daughter. The young men of Taunton, if not personally acquainted with Eve's mother, were acutely aware of that lady's reputation. She had, in years past, boxed the ears of several hopeful swains who had come to her door in search of Eve.

Ben Treherne meant more to Eve than she was willing to admit. The fact that he was one of many admirers did not make his changed attitude towards her less poignant or disturbing. He was first among equals, she told herself; but nothing more.

They never spoke about that dreadful Sunday, but continued to meet at least three times in every week. Eve no longer walked to Rowbarton, but waited for Ben on the steps of the Empire cinema, or in the Lyceum foyer. They walked in places where Mother's relatives and friends were unlikely to go. Ben had, in the summer months, grown quiet and less attentive. Eve had not received a single rose from his triumph at the Flower Show in August. She continued, secretly, to meet Georgie Kennet and Harold Judd on the nights when she was not with Ben. She met them in a vain hope of better things; hardly listened to their conversations; answered their questions in an abstracted fashion. When Georgie asked when was her birthday, she said vaguely, 'Oh, next week, I think.' Five days later an urchin appeared at Annis Nevill's door, carrying a parcel.

''Tis from him down there, standing underneath the lamp-post. 'Un never dared to come hisself. He've paid me a penny to tell you that this box holds a birthday present for your youngest daughter.'

Mother's anger was terrifying. She stood over Eve while the wrappings were removed. Georgie had paid a great deal of money for the tortoiseshell-backed brush and mirror, and the matching comb.

'And why would that grinning fool be buying you such expensive presents?'

'I – I don't really know, Mother. He asked me when was my birthday, and I wasn't listening properly. I think I said next week.'

'But your birthday's not till January! You must give it all back to him, this instant!'

'But I can't,' Eve wailed, 'he'll take me for a liar!'

'And so you are. Why, when I was a girl, we knew better than to take presents from young men. I don't know what your father will have to say about all this!'

The threat was an empty one. Frank was never told and the tortoiseshell set looked very nice on the dressing table. Eve thanked Georgie, and said he should not have spent his money on her. It was at about this time that Ben Treherne failed to arrive for their Wednesday cinema outing.

Eve waited for twenty minutes in the rain before joining Abi in the Tipperary Club. She dabbed at the muddy splashes on her silk clad legs. 'Well, that settles it! If he thinks I'll wait for him on any other evening he's very much mistaken.'

Abi said thoughtfully, 'Now don't be too hasty. I've got a feeling that Mother's up to something. She was saying only yesterday that she hoped you would see more of Harold Judd. She'd walked up to Haines Hill with Aunt Mina. They'd been viewing the Judds' farm. I think Mother sees you as a farmer's wife.'

'Well I don't!' Eve paused. 'I wonder what makes her so dead set against Ben? He's never done her any harm.'

'Neither has Joey, but she can't abide him either. She said once that fair-haired men were never to be trusted and that Ben Treherne reminded her of someone.'

Eve recalled Ben's impressive height, his well-set shoulders, the thatch of blond hair that was always falling forward. 'He's such a lovely-looking fella, Abi. He's quiet and gentle. He's not much for talking but it's nice, somehow, just to be in his company.'

'Has he ever let you down before?'

'Never! Ah, but wait. He did say when we parted on Saturday that he'd be writing me a letter. I wondered at the time if he meant to propose by post.'

Abi drained her teacup of the tea-and-gin mixture; she gestured towards the dancing couples. 'There's a new chap in tonight. He's so ugly as to be quite fascinating. He says that he's a White Russian, whatever that is! He was asking after you. Seems that he's the new projectionist at the Empire. Play your cards right, Evie, and we could be given free tickets for the best seats in the house.'

Eve said, 'Are you sure that no letter came for me?'

'None that I saw. Oh, don't worry about it. Look out – here's that Boris what's his name. He's coming over to be introduced to you.'

*

It had, Annis thought, been a satisfying year in many ways. The front door and window frames of Number 5, The Terrace had that autumn received a fresh coat of green paint. New lace curtains hung at all the windows. The aspidistras flourished in Frank's conservatory; the beds in the tiny walled garden had been filled with flowers that summer. Annis paused in her polishing of the brass bedstead and considered the bedroom shared by her daughters. It was, as far as she was able, a faithful reproduction of the room she had once shared with her sister, Blanche, in the Larksleve farmhouse. The wallpaper matched its design of pink moss roses with the flowered toilet set on the marble topped washstand. Fresh white towels hung across the towel rail; jars of rose-scented pot pourri stood on the mantel shelf. A honeycomb bedspread of dazzling whiteness was reflected in the polished bedrails. Annis moved to the cluttered dressing table; she fingered the bottles and jars and the bits of jewellery strewn across its surface. This room had refinements never seen in the Larksleve farmhouse. She had, that summer, bought carpet for all three bedrooms; a good plain drugget in a beige colour, one that Mina had assured her would never wear out. She had also bought an expensive gas fire and had it fitted in the little fireplace. Her girls would be cosy in the coming winter; they would never want to leave her. She sat down on the dressing table stool and was careful not to study too closely her own reflected image. She opened drawers and inspected their contents; found clean hand-kerchiefs and underwear, neatly folded blouses and rolled silk stockings. She slid a hand beneath the lining paper in each drawer, and found nothing but two safety pins and a hair grip. Annis stood up, and as she moved, the letter in her apron pocket crackled loudly; she had studied the envelope many times in the past week. It had arrived unstamped. She went into her own bedroom and opened the top drawer of her dressing table. She lifted up the lining paper and laid the little brown envelope down among a dozen others.

*

In December, Annis gave a party for Eve's twenty-fifth birthday. Harold Judd and his older sister were invited. They came in a dog cart pulled by a pony, both of which they parked in the yard of the Half Moon pub. Annis reminisced at length about the dog cart in which she had ridden with her grandmother, when a child on Larksleve

Farm. Harold's sister had been impressed.

'I never knew you was a Greypaull before marriage, Mrs Nevill! Well I never! I must remember to tell my father about that.'

Eve had waited for a sign from Ben, but there was none.

'That settles it,' she said to Abi. 'If he can let my birthday pass without a word then I shan't give him another thought.' But she did think about him. Every time she looked at Harold's broad brown face, or saw shy and stammering Georgie Kennet, she ached for a sight of Ben; but pride would not permit her to walk over to Rowbarton. Even the incredible ugliness of the White Russian, Boris, could turn her thoughts back to Ben's fair and open features.

At Christmas, a card came from Charlie Nevill, Frank's nephew. Frank read aloud the accompanying letter.

Dear Uncle and Aunt, Abigail and Eve,

As you will see from the stamp I am now in the Sudan. Arrived last week after a dreadful voyage out, but settled in Khartoum. Very hot here. Get fed up at times. Would love to have a letter from you. Perhaps Abi and Eve could drop me a line, when they find time from courting. Hope you are well, as it leaves me at present.

Your loving nephew, Charlie.

Frank turned to his daughters.

'He sounds pretty lonely, and I know that feeling! I was once a young soldier, thousands of miles from home. Why don't you drop him a line? He would appreciate it!'

Eve had always been the family scribe. She it was, who on that Monday evening sat down at the circular table and wrote a letter to her cousin Charlie. She was about to seal the envelope when Abi said, 'Send him your photograph, why don't you? According to Father, soldiers love to pin photos up above their beds.'

The head and shoulders study was post-card size; in it Eve wore a white blouse; she was smiling her soft, enigmatic smile. She wrote, in her strong, backward sloping sript, across the bottom left hand corner, 'love and best wishes, from Eve.'

She studied her likeness with a smile of satisfaction. Every coral bead in the silver necklace stood out clearly against the creamy column of her throat. She was not beautiful like Aunty Blanche; she lacked Abigail's confidence and sophistication. Ben Treherne had abandoned her completely. Her hair, she thought, looked quite lovely in the photo, thanks to Amami shampoo.

*

Sev came back to Agra with his body weight regained, and his skin healed of the lesions made by prickly heat. The bouts of malaria had not recurred; he felt strong and unusually optimistic. The hours spent alone in high and mystic places had affected him deeply. It was as if he had gone to the hills as a child, and returned a man.

Rumours had reached him in Naina Tal that the Battalion was likely to be posted elsewhere. His dismay on having those rumours confirmed was not something he could confess to his friends. He said, offhandedly, to Taffy, 'We had better see as much of this place as we can, I reckon. After all, we shall never be coming back here.'

Taffy said, 'Not me, mun! They've excused us route-marches and parades for these last few weeks, while the Battalion is making ready to shift. A new card school started up while you was away, and I'm on a winning streak.'

Sev went alone into the Bazaar. He bargained for a model of the Taj Mahal, made of pure white marble. He bought a shawl of pink, fringed silk for his mother. The December days were pleasantly warm; Sev noticed for the first time how radiant the light was at this time of year. He wandered aimlessly, the model Taj growing heavier with every step. He walked beyond the Bazaar towards a shady tree. He would never, when in the company of Taffy, have sat down beneath a banyan tree and spoken to a native. But the old man who leaned against the tree's trunk had the neck of a sitar fitted closely to his shoulder. Sev set down his parcels, and sat cross-legged on the parched grass. He studied the sitar, counted its many strings, and could not decide if there were twenty-five or thirty. He remembered his own agony when trying to play the double bass, the raw state of his fingertips. The old man's hands were scored from a lifetime of contact with the sitar strings. He stared long and hard at Sev.

'You want music, Sahib?'

Sev nodded, never taking his gaze from the plectrum in the long, brown fingers. The music, when it came, had none of the plaintive quality of the pan pipes heard in the Hills. These were sounds unlike any other; he had an urgent desire to rise and run, but the melody would not let him go. This man played as Sev himself had played since childhood; without sheet music, or a bandmaster's guidance. The notes rose and swelled, to an unbearable tension, and then died away to an unexpected whisper. Sev stood up. He felt shaken and uncertain. It was his duty to despise these people, every decent soldier did so. He felt the old man's keen gaze on him, sensed his contemptuous appraisal of pale skin, blue eyes, and red hair. Sev took from his tunic pocket the last two annas that remained from his shopping, and dropped them awkwardly before the silent sitar.

'Acha, Sahib,' the musician murmured, 'most good of you, I am sure.'

He grinned, revealing pink gums. 'You will not forget India, I think, Sahib.'

His mood, as he walked back to the cantonment, was receptive to every sight and sound. He noticed, as if for the first time, the poverty and thinness of the dhobis and camp followers who lived in hovels just beyond the barrack walls. To feel shame, however faintly, was not required of a serving soldier. They would, Sev told himself, all have died of starvation without the presence of the British; or have slaughtered one another.

His last task, before boarding the train that was to take them to Bombay, was the clearing out and repacking of his kit box. Nothing could be packed that was not approved by the Duty Sergeant. Souvenirs of India were permitted; most men had purchased a model of the Taj, and a few yards of Indian Silk. Old letters were considered to be excess baggage. Sev tore into tiny pieces the many pages of his mother's writing. It was when he reached the very bottom of the kitbox that he found the four envelopes which bore a Taunton postmark. Just to see again her handwriting, was enough to resurrect the girl called Eve. He glanced quickly around him and finding himself unobserved he slipped the four letters into his tunic pocket. They travelled with him on the long haul down to Bombay. He held on to them as a talisman when he boarded the HT *Derbyshire* for the queasy voyage to Port Sudan. Taffy Richards stood beside him at the rails, as he watched Bombay recede and grow unimportant. The phlegmatic little Welshman brushed his hands together.

'Well, that's India done with! Next stop Khartoum and the bloody desert. Then comes the big decision, boyo! Does we stay in this rotten Army, or do we kiss it goodbye?'

Sev looked back towards Bombay. He could just make out The Gates of India which lay beyond the quayside.

'Good question, matey. Do you know what day this is? It's Boxing Day back in England. We spent Christmas Day in that lousy embarkation shed in Deolalie.' The words were spoken absent mindedly; they covered the thought that burned in his mind. India, he suspected, was never done with by the white men who experienced its magic. He could still hear the voice of the old sitar player. 'You will not forget India, I think, Sahib.'

A lecture on the subject of their destination was delivered by an officer on the night before they disembarked. They sat, cross-legged, on the upper deck of the HT *Derbyshire*. Taffy pointed upwards towards the stars.

'That's the Southern Cross,' he informed Sev.

'I'll have silence in the ranks!' the officer barked. Sev saw, in the lantern light, the indulgent smile that accompanied the order. They treat us, he thought, as if we were naughty ten-year-olds, out on a Sunday school picnic. They never see us as grown men. Perhaps nobody does. He began to think about going home to England; civilian life was not an experience he recalled with pleasure. He looked around him at the tanned and inattentive faces of the seated men. He grew sick sometimes of taking orders; the music alone had made bearable the last few years in Agra – and yet, there was safety to be found in numbers.

'We have recently sailed,' the officer said, 'across the Arabian Sea, through the gulf of Aden, and are now in the Red Sea. Tomorrow we land at Port Sudan; we travel by camel train across the desert to Berber. From thence we proceed by dhow and steamer up the River Nile to Khartoum.'

Faint groans were heard among the seated men. 'Come along now, chaps! Where's your spirit of adventure? There are wealthy men who pay a fortune to see what you are about to witness.' The officer looked stern. 'Now, there are certain warnings I must issue. This month of January will be the most comfortable for which we can possibly hope. By March the temperature will have increased to degrees we have never known on the Indian Plains. Salt tablets will be issued to prevent cramp. Your heads and spines must be protected at all times from direct sunlight.' He paused. 'There is one other danger I should mention. The Sudan is, in many ways, more dangerous than India. The British Government maintains a presence in the Sudan in conjunction with Egypt. But these are nomadic peoples. They wander about – they have no respect for the forces of Order. Slavery is rife among them. Soldiers have been known to disappear from Omdurman and Khartoum.'

Dusty Miller sniggered behind his cupped hand. 'I'm ready to be kidnapped any old time by some desert princess,' he whispered.

The officer, who according to Taffy, had ears like a kitehawk, said wryly, 'You're more likely to be picked up by the Dervishes, Miller. Not an experience to be recommended. We must always remember that it was in Khartoum that General Gordon met his death at the hands of the Mad Mahdi!'

They arrived bone-weary from the most extraordinary journey they had ever known; the regimental Band leading the column of men through the broad avenues of Khartoum. They were given a meal of fried eggs and chipped potatoes on their arrival at the Barracks. Thick walls and high, vaulted ceilings kept their quarters reasonably cool. The change of station had put Sev among strangers. His new bed stood in a corner and beneath a window. He had expected to sleep at once, but could not. Sev's sense of place had always been acute; he thought about the Blue Nile which turned out to be a greenish-grey; the silence of the yellow desert which had been terrifying. Palm trees made a change from banyan and cypress; camels were the most unpleasant animals that walked the earth. He had become accustomed to the golden bronze of Indian skins; the Sudanese were the blue-black colour of good Welsh coal. He slept at last on the uneasy thought that Sudan was a cruel place.

The diversions promised by the officer did not happen. Nobody was kidnapped; the people of the country were unusually friendly to the soldiers. Army life in Khartoum seemed likely to be even more tedious than in Agra. As Dusty Miller said, 'When you've seen one bloody palm tree, you've seen 'em all.'

A corner bed meant that Sev had only one neighbour, a very young infantry man who introduced himself as Charlie. The boy had come out recently from England; he was a pleasant and cheerful fellow, always whistling the latest dance tunes. The first mail call in a new Station was an event that caused disappointment to many. There was the inevitable lapse of time in which letters were re-routed, and relatives informed of the new address. Sev's name was not called on that Sunday morning. He straightened his kit box in case of random inspection; made sure that the precious four letters, yellow and curled at the edges from India's heat, were safely concealed beneath the tray that held his boot cleaning equipment. He looked to the next bed where Charlie was brandishing a fistful of letters.

'You done well, young 'un. Seems like there was none for me.'

Charlie grinned. 'You'll no doubt do better next time. I got a lot of sisters, see. They all promised to write – look at this! I even got a letter from my cousin!'

Sev sat on his bed and remembered himself at the age of eighteen. Seven years of Army discipline had changed him in every way. His own mother would never recognise him now. He glanced idly across to where the boy was busy pinning photographs above his bed.

As he drove in the final pin, Charlie's top lip trembled. Sev at once crossed the short space between beds and proffered a crumpled packet of Woodbines.

'Here,' he said roughly, 'have a fag. You'll feel better in a – '

His gaze, as he spoke, was on the photographs just come from England. He pointed his cigarette towards a head and shoulders study.

'I – I know that girl. She lives in Taunton. Her name's Eve Nevill.' He rounded on the young soldier. 'So what is she to you, eh?'

Charlie grinned again, and blew smoke towards the ceiling.

'Keep your hair on, matey! She's my cousin, if you must know. I'll ask you the same question – what's my cousin Eve to do with you, eh?'

Sev crossed to his kit box and pulled out the four letters.

'I met her years ago, in Taunton. She wrote to me when I was first in India. Then the letters stopped.'

'That's her handwriting,' Charlie admitted, 'I'd know it anywhere. Best scholar of us all was Evie!' He looked keenly at Sev. 'Sweet on her was you? Shouldn't blame you for that! Prettiest maid in all of Taunton town, my cousin is!'

Sev said, unable to conceal anxiety, 'She's – she's not married is she?'

Charlie laughed. 'You never met my Aunt Annis did you? She've already broke up two engagements for her other daughter, and from what I heard before we sailed, she've just parted Evie from her best-beloved!' He paused. 'Why did you stop writing to her?'

Sev coloured. 'She never wrote back to me. I got some pride left, you know.'

'Then you're a bloody fool, mate! Try again, why don't you? You might get an answer this time.'

He took the photograph down from the wall.

'Here take it. Pin it over your bed. You never know – it might change your luck.'

*

Eve came fully awake on that February morning to find Mother standing at the bedside; two cups of steaming tea stood on the night table; the gas fire hissed and popped and filled the room with bluish light.

'Drink your tea while it's still hot,' Mother's tone was indulgent.

'I've lit the fire so that it's warm for you to get dressed by – we had a hard frost in the night – your Aunt Mina thinks we shall have snow'. Mother went away, closing the door quietly behind her. Abi sat up, rubbed her eyes, and leaned back against her pillows. She said, through yawns, 'What was all that about?'

'Aunt Mina says we shall have snow.' Eve struck a match and lit the candle.

Abi smiled. 'So! Mother's turned on the gas fire for us! Have you noticed how she spoils us lately? Carpet on the floor, early morning tea – whatever can we have done to deserve such treatment?'

Eve sipped her tea. She said thoughtfully, 'Mary from the sweetshop came into the Tipperary Club last night. She said that Mother goes out around the town at night, looking for me.'

'Looking for you?'

'Seems that somebody told her I was still seeing Ben Treherne, and she's determined to catch me with him.'

'And are you seeing him?'

'Of course I'm not! He's courting a Rowbarton girl. I saw them together. I wouldn't have minded quite so much if he'd explained; if he'd at least written me a letter.'

Abi said, 'Don't think too badly of him.' She hesitated. 'I don't know if I should tell you this, but I think he may have written to you, and more than once!'

'What do you mean?'

'It was just before Christmas, I came in early that night and found Mother burning envelopes in the living-room firegrate.'

'Where was Father?'

'He had a cold coming on; he'd gone to bed early.' Abi moved uneasily against her pillows.

'I said to her, what's that you're burning? Oh she said, just a few old letters.'

'But nobody ever writes to Mother. Why should they when she can't read. They could have been letters sent to Father I suppose –'

'No!' Abi's tone was certain.

'I can always tell when Mother's lying. Her neck goes all red, and she won't look directly at me. I can't believe that Ben would have given you up without a word. Why don't you face her out for once? Ask her if she burns your letters?'

Eve said, 'You know I could never do that. Anyway, Ben Treherne is already engaged to the Rowbarton girl, so I could never – '

All at once the bedroom door came open and there was Mother, a letter in her hand. She waved the envelope as if it were a flag of truce.

'Post for one of you,' she said brightly. 'The stamp's got a camel pictured on it.'

Abi took the letter and passed it on to Eve.

Mother said, 'It'll be from your cousin Charlie. You wrote to him didn't you?' She smiled. 'You'd better get up now, Evie. Time's getting on.'

Once again the door closed quietly behind her. Eve allowed the letter to lie unopened on the bedspread.

'Do you think she heard what we were saying?'

'Shouldn't be at all surprised. Oh for heaven's sake open your letter. Let's hear what's been happening to Charlie.'

Eve drew out the single page of flimsy paper and began to read.

'It's not from Charlie. Do you remember that red-haired soldier we met all those years ago on the corner of Hammet Street?'

'The one with the Welsh friend?'

'That's him! It says here that he's in Khartoum. That his bed stands next to Charlie's. That he saw my photo pinned above cousin Charlie's bed and recognised me straight away! He says he's glad that I'm not married; that he's often thought about me and the walks and talks we had together. He wants me to write to him.'

'What will you tell Mother?'

'I'll say that he's a friend of Charlie's – a lonely fellah who never gets a letter.

*

Khartoum in April was already hotter than Agra had ever been. Band practice and parades ended promptly at noon and within minutes of dismissal almost every soldier in the Garrison lay exhausted on his bed. Ten salt tablets were issued daily to every man, with predictable results.

'We all drinks too much beer as it is,' grumbled Taffy. 'All that salt is like to turn us into raving dipsos.' Sev crumbled his salt tablets into the sand, but could not avoid the doses of quinine that were said to keep malaria at bay. It was a life of idleness, enlivened only by their small personal dramas. The surrounding desert deepened Sev's sense of isolation; he felt the slow drift into depression that had been his dread, lifelong. The girl in Taunton would never write to him. Why should she? Eve Nevill was popular and lively, according to her cousin Charlie. But for her watchful mother, she would have been married, long since.

Sunday Mail Call brought him a letter, the envelope black-edged. It lay on his bed for several hours, unopened. The address had been written by his mother; the relief he felt at this realisation had surprised and embarrassed him, but still he was reluctant even to touch it. It was not until evening, when men were drinking in the Wet Canteen, and the barrack room deserted, that he tore open the awful envelope and read its contents.

His grandmother Honeybone, so his mother said, had died quite peacefully in her seventy-eighth year. Her body had been brought back from Yeovil, for burial in Montacute, beside Granfer. Sev read no further. He crumpled the letter into a tight wad, and threw it into his kit box. He began to walk through deepening shadows to the place where the blue and white rivers of the Nile converge. He walked for a long time. Granny had been the first, the only woman who had ever shown him love. She had washed and dressed him, ruffled his hair and made things right for him with Granfer. She had tucked him up in the box-bed beside the firegrate; tended him in sickness, understood the wild and restless nature of him. It had all ended years ago with the death of Granfer, but still, he had always known that she was there, in Yeovil, living in her son's house. A memory of the dark woman flickered briefly at his mind's edge, and was dismissed; with her it had been different; he had sensed her deep need to possess him; she, he thought bitterly, would be bound to live forever. All his childish love had been for Granfer and Granny. He recalled her small stooped figure, the wisps of white hair curling from beneath her widow's cap. He had never thought about her dying, had never written to her in all the years of his absence from England. Sev walked to the place of dangerous currents, where great rivers meet. The ache in his chest rose into his throat, and he could no longer contain it.

Sev Carew sat down by the waters of the Blue Nile and wept for the lost years; for the opportunities wasted, the times when he might have returned the devotion that Granny had shown to him. The bad feeling stayed with him for a long time. It would go away, only to return at certain moments. A passage of music, a chance remark, and sometimes his own urgent need to go back and relive misery. He wept silently at night, his gaze fixed on the stars of the Southern Cross as it marched beyond his window; the tears running hot into his ears and neck. It happened to most of them, on these tours of foreign service; the bad news from home, the black-edged envelope, and their feeling of impotence in the face of far-away disaster. He hated Khartoum in the month of April; detested the yellow sands which marked out their isolation, the angled palm trees and sluggish river. He loathed ungainly camels, the craft and greed that showed in Arab faces. He had no wish to stay in this cruel and alien country; but neither had he any inclination to return to England.

At the end of April he was promoted to Lance-Corporal. He stitched the stripes onto his sleeves in a mood of bored abstraction. The advancement meant little to him; he had never wanted to become a Lance-Jack. With the wearing of a stripe came responsibility; the need to give orders would lose him friends. The key of the broom cupboard was now in his charge. The Indian cleaners had been left back in Agra. In Sudan a non-commissioned soldier did his own washing and cleaned his own quarters. Sev handed out buckets and brooms to Dusty and Taffy, and counted them in on their return. He felt awkward and guilty, as if in some way he had betrayed them. Taffy Richards, for all his book learning, had never earned a single stripe. When the Duty Sergeant called Carew on that first Sunday of May, Sev did not at first hear him. He took the envelope, without enthusiasm, expecting further unhappy news from Montacute.

The first glance revealed a Taunton postmark. There was no mistaking that strong, individual hand. He felt the heart move within him. She had written! She had answered to him! In the time it took for him to scan her letter, the whole aspect of his world had changed. He wandered, bemused, out into the dangerous sunlight of midday, and was shouted at by a Corporal. 'Where's your pith helmet, soldier? Gone bloody crazy have you?'

The letter had taken two months to reach him. She wrote about snow, and the films she had seen at the picture house in Taunton. She said that she remembered him well; had never really forgotten him. Her sister, she said, had told her to enquire about his Welsh friend.

His grief at the loss of Granny still hung about him; it made him vulnerable to other losses. He put a new nib in the army-issue pen, assembled ink and writing paper; he unpinned her photograph from the wall above his bed, and took it to a quiet corner in the Garrison Library. His answer to her letter was, he thought, the most important reply he might ever make. He had lost her seven years ago. He suspected that he could not easily endure another rejection.

*

Sev's name was shouted up regularly at Mail Call. Eve's letters were written every Sunday afternoon. His replies were penned every Sunday evening. The square white envelope, still faintly scented even after its long journey across sea and desert, soon became a target for the ribaldry of the Duty Sergeant.

'Got a secret admirer, have we, Lance-Corporal? Wrote and told her you'd got yourself a stripe, did you?'

Charlie Nevill declared himself to be 'tickled pink' about the whole affair. He assumed full responsibility for the resumed romance.

Sev endured the severe heat of Khartoum's summer with only a token grumble. He took the quinine doses, but continued to crumble his salt tablets into the sand. He still grieved for his grandmother Honeybone but not with the scouring intensity that he had at first felt. Writing to Eve, telling her about his situation, attempting for the first time in his life to convey his feelings to another person, had confirmed the maturity found in Naina Tal. He had not felt small among the mountains, it was here in this endless desert with its terrifying sandstorms, that a man might feel diminished. By September, he knew without a doubt, that all he wanted for the future was a life in England, with Eve Nevill. He began to save money, avoided all visits to the Wet Canteen, and drank only cold tea or ginger ale. His sole expenditure was on Woodbines and writing paper. He kept well away from the card schools and games of chance. The Garrison Library was well stocked. He read Sapper's 'Bulldog Drummond' stories; the complete works of Edgar Allan Poe and H.G. Wells. He discovered Sexton Blake and the humorous character of Bindle, the Cockney furniture remover, created by Herbert Jenkins. There were weightier volumes written by Llewelyn and John Cowper Powys, passages of which brought Somerset and Montacute painfully to mind. He knew now that he would be going home at the end of his five-and-two. Nothing, save death, could keep him from

Taunton and Eve. That he would have to face his mother, be judged by his father, was the penance he must do for past sins of omission; and he would do it.

Unlike the Plains of India, the heat of Khartoum was still fierce into October. The Garrison had no swimming pool, but, as Taffy said, they had the Blue Nile on their very doorstep. Sev was not a strong swimmer; he was careful always to stay within his depth and never to attempt the tests of endurance invented by the officer in charge of sports. It was while he was floating on the green-grey water, looking up at the luminosity of blue sky, that leg cramps struck, rendering him helpless. He cried out but the swimmers could not hear him. The muscles of his calves and thighs contracted in an agonising spasm; twice he went under. It was Taffy Richards who, from the river bank, saw his waving arm, and dived in to save him.

'Recognised them bloody old snakes tattooed on your arm, mun! Knew it must be you!' Taffy was a hero; his name was to be put forward for a life saving medal. Sev, when he had recovered, was severely reprimanded.

If he had died, the Major told him, it would have been his own fault, entirely. Salt tablets were issued for the express purpose of preventing cramps. For a man to even enter the water without his daily ration of salt, was tantamount to suicide. Was that, perhaps, what the Lance-Corporal had intended? He could thank Private Richards for his life. If he had not been present, had not noticed – as it was the Private had been almost too late! Seven days confined to Barracks for neglecting to eat your salt – and let that be a salutory lesson! The Major grinned. It would be a shame to cut short the career of a good clarinettist, and surely he wanted to see England again?

*

Boris Doctorow was chief projectionist at the cinema which frequently showed films in which their cousin Billy featured. Abigail and Eve were careful to limit their visits to the Empire, to those nights when they could be absolutely sure that Mother and Father would not be occupying seats in the front stalls. The appearance of Boris in the Tipperary Club had been a rare event, arranged for the sole purpose of gaining an introduction to Eve Nevill. But White Russians, Eve now discovered, were a passionate and unbalanced kind of people. Boris frightened and at the same time intrigued her. Part of his fascination lay in the thick and pitted skin of his face, the largeness of his features, and the unnerving degree of slant in which one small black eye seemed determined to escape from the other. He was a tall man, heavily built, and inclined to bow from the waist at unexpected moments. His English, strongly accented, and learned mainly from the Jewish jeweller with whom he lodged, was incomprehensible to Eve. In the moments when she was obliged to halt before him and accept his gifts, she was aware of an intensity of passion in him that was barely controlled.

It was Abigail who first accepted the present of the cinema tickets and Eve who was forced to say thank you for the expensive casket of chocolates presented by Boris on their entrance to the picture house. The time must come, Eve feared, when Boris would expect some return for these tokens of devotion. Meanwhile, as Abi pointed out, the job of projectionist kept him occupied for six nights out of seven, and Mother did not allow her daughters to go out on the Sabbath evening; and the chocolates were delicious!

The letters from Khartoum had at first soothed the hurt caused by Ben Treherne's defection. To be remembered so clearly, and with such enthusiasm after a lapse of seven years, was to say the least, flattering. But as the summer progressed, a new note had come into the accounts of army life; she detected a serious intent, an invitation to commit herself to a more lasting relationship. She talked to Abi about it.

'But I don't know him,' she wailed. 'He's sort of hinting-on, about wanting to settle down when he comes home in February. I knew him for just a week – and that was seven years ago!'

'But it's very romantic,' Abi said. 'Like a fairy tale, really. Just think, Eve. If cousin Charlie had been posted to another barracks – if you had never sent your picture to him – it almost seems as if it's meant to be!'

Eve had thought that Ben Treherne was meant to be. According to Aunt Candace, he had married the Rowbarton girl. They were living together in the little gardener's cottage. Eve wondered if the sheets of newspaper on the kitchen table had been replaced by a proper cloth.

In December a Christmas card arrived from Khartoum. It showed a picture of the Regimental Bandmaster; the inscription beneath the Army crest read, 'From your loving sweetheart, Sev'. She truly did not know how matters had progressed so far, so quickly. He would soon be home, he told her. It was wonderful to see the barrack room filled with packing cases. He would bring her a model of the Taj Mahal made of pure white marble. They were due to sail from Port Sudan on January 12th, in the HT *Assaye*.

*

Sev's vocabulary was wide and varied. He was articulate, he wrote an interesting letter, was not easily bested in argument, could be very persuasive when the need arose. But there were certain words he never used, not even in his mind. Emotion was a dangerous and painful indulgence; so great was his aversion that he avoided the actual terms by which feelings were described. The most dangerous word of all was love; the second was grief.

There is a particular poignancy about remembered love; a child who has experienced its warmth, however briefly, will carry it always in some deep place of the heart. Sev might yet have remained safe in his life if he had never been shown love. But for Granfer and Granny, and their devotion to him, grief could have been sidestepped, sorrow outwitted. His defence had been first breached by the dog, Nipper. Concern for the condemned pup had turned to rough affection; but his sadness on leaving the dog had opened his heart to admit the devastation of Granny's dying. He had thought that there was still time, that she would be there, in Yeovil, on his return. He had not known how deep were his feelings for her until it was too late.

*

Charlie Nevill had brought a new song out from England; the kind of melody that Sev thought cheap, but which caught in the mind and would not be dislodged. Charlie sang his song amid the packing cases and brown paper that littered the barrack room floor, and the words had a peculiar aptness for these men, the majority of whom had been absent from England and home for many years.

> Pack up all my cares and woe,
> Here I go, swinging low,
> Bye bye, blackbird.
> Where somebody waits for me,
> Sugar's sweet, so is she,
> Bye bye, blackbird.

Sev sat on his bed and wrapped the tiny white minarets of the model Taj Mahal in cotton wool. He laid the Indian silks and the dyed ostrich feathers between sheets of tissue paper. Charlie's tune had a certain haunting quality; it could not, of course, be compared to the 'Indian Love Lyrics' or the aching beauty of the sitar music, played by the old man beneath the banyan tree. Sev could not decide between tune and words; would the one have been as effective without the other? He paused in his wrapping of the mouth-organ, placed it to his lips

441

and played a few bars of Charlie's song. A cry went up from adjacent beds.

'That's right then Chippy! Give us a tune! You never play to us anymore since you got made up to Lance-Jack!'

Sev looked around at the familiar faces. There was Taffy who had saved his life; Dusty and Charlie, and all those others with whom he had sat in at housey-housey, and the card schools; with whom he had suffered the endless parades, the mindless brutality of certain sergeants, the sickness and tedium of India's Plains. He would miss them! With the thought came the knowledge that, all unconsciously, his mind had been made up; any final doubts he might have had, dispelled by the silly song. He breathed into the mouth-organ, and Charlie Nevill sang – 'Where somebody waits for me – sugar's sweet, so is she – bye bye, blackbird.' Oh yes, she was waiting for him. She said so in every letter. He could hardly believe in the miracle of it. He looked up to where her photograph was pinned above the bed rails; the likeness was a good one; why she even wore the coral necklace that he had admired at their last meeting.

The month of December in Sudan was like a warm summer's day in England. Sev walked in Khartoum as he had done in Agra; knowing that he would never return, feeling the fine balance between his love and hatred of these alien places.

> Pack up all my cares and woe –
> Here I go – swinging – low
> Bye bye, blackbird.

The Somerset name for the blackbird was colley-bird; it was, he remembered used especially among travelling people. He walked down to the banks of the Blue Nile, and looked out across the yellow desert. He studied the plaque which marked the place where General Gordon had been murdered. A short walk away, in Omdurman, the remains of the Mad Mahdi lay entombed in a silver palace. He wandered along the river bank to the place where the White and Blue Niles came together. On the far banks a company of Bedouin lay encamped. He watched the blue smoke curl up from their fires; studied the brown tents, the tethered sheep and goats, the resting camels. Substitute horses for camels he thought; replace sand with green grass, and here was the exact scene he had so often witnessed in the Montacute lanes, and beside the copse in Norton. He began to watch the Bedouin; he walked to the half-way point of an iron bridge, which was as close to them as he dared to go. A man, dressed in white shirt and shorts, and solar topee, turned to face him as he paused beside a stanchion. Sev realised, too late, that the man was Major Stanley, the Battalion doctor. He saluted, and the Major returned the gesture. Sev hesitated, uncertain as to whether he should go or stay. The Major nodded towards the encampment.

'Interested in them are you? So am I. Full of disease you know! It is one of their men who will act as our guide when we cross the desert. He's a malaria victim like yourself. Better keep him fit eh, until we reach Port Sudan?' The Major turned. 'Still taking your salt tablets are you?'

'Yes sir.'

'Thought you were a goner, that day they pulled you from the river.' The Major looked back towards the encampment. 'Strange people, the Bedouin. The young man Nuri, who will be our guide, speaks a little English. They have the damndest customs. Completely nomadic of course; never stay longer than a week in any one place.' The Major struck the iron rail with the flat of his hand. 'They fascinate me, Carew! By George, they fascinate me!'

Sev murmured, 'Yes sir.' The Major, he thought, would never have spoken to him at all, but for the fact that he was a doctor and Sev his patient. The near-drowning had brought them into closer contact of course. The

Major was a good sort.

'They tell me you're a Bandsman.'

'Clarinettist, sir.'

'Well done!' The officer's gaze was still fixed upon the brown tents. 'They're as superstitious as hell. They believe that all sickness comes from ill-wishing; the "evil eye" and all that rubbish! The women wear amber and coral necklets as talismans. I've given Nuri a supply of quinine for his malaria, but I suspect he never takes it. Their pride is astounding. They never bathe – hardly ever wash – and yet they believe that it is we who are unclean. They despise us, Carew.'

'Is that a fact, sir?'

'And perhaps they are right to do so?' The Major waved a hand at the bulk of Government House, and the Garrison that lay beyond it. 'This has been my final tour of duty. I shall be a free man when we get back to England. But what to do with freedom?' He smiled. 'Perhaps I'll buy myself a tent, take up the gypsy way of life, eh?'

Sev did not smile.

'You could do worse, sir. I saw a lot of the travelling people when I was a young 'un. I've always had itchy feet myself, but – well – there's this girl back in Taunton. She's waiting for me. I shall be twenty-six in April. Time I was married, I reckon.'

The Major said, 'Itchy feet and marriage don't go well together.'

'Ah, but you should see my girl, sir! Any gypsy chal would settle down for the sake of her!'

They boarded the HT *Assaye* in Port Sudan on the fourth day of January, 1927. Sev lay in his hammock, already sea-sick before the ship had raised its anchor. Up on deck the Regimental Band played without him; he heard them strike up a familiar tune.

'Pack up all my cares and woe,' sang the men of the Battalion. 'Here I go, swinging low, bye bye blackbird.'

*

Whenever Damaris remembered Sev it was always in the same way; sometimes she dreamed about him, and it was always the same dream. She could never see his face, whether waking or sleeping, but only his thin shoulders, deliberately squared beneath the shabby jacket, and the set of his bright head which told her that he would not look back. He had walked away from her on a January morning, and for three years she had mourned him, believing that he must be dead. Now, he was coming home. She sat in her corner, close beside the window, and re-read the letter that told of the heat of India's Plains, the unimaginable vastness of the Nubian desert, the fine buildings of Khartoum and Agra, the waters of the River Nile. His last letter, posted in Port Sudan before the ship sailed, spoke of his weariness of army life, his intention of settling down when back in England. She looked up at his photo, framed, and standing beside the clock on the mantelshelf. It might have been anybody; but for the fierce and penetrating gaze she could not recognise a single feature. She looked down at her own wasted frame; she too had changed in the past years. The long black skirts hung slack about her waist; the winter had seemed longer this year. She pulled the shawl tight across her shoulders; she was always cold, the pain in her side a nagging torment.

The doctor had been kind. 'You'll feel better when your son comes home. I know that you have fretted for him. Meanwhile, Mrs Carew, I have written a letter to the big hospital in Bristol. I want you to go there, to see another doctor.'

Her daughters were married, with small children, or far away in domestic service. She had gone alone to the city of Bristol, telling no one but Jye about her journey and the reason for it. She had been frightened and confused. Somewhere, between changing trains and among so many strangers, she had lost the letter. The hospital doctor had not been pleased.

'I cannot possibly treat you,' he said, 'or examine you

without your doctor's letter!'

She told Jye on her return. 'It makes no difference. There's nothing they can do for me. 'Tis but a matter of time, and just as well I lost that letter.'

He looked suspiciously at her. He said, in his slow way, ''Twill all get better when the boy comes back. Seven years you've fretted for 'un. Wore yourself to a shadow on account of him.'

'He's no more a boy, Jye! He's a man now, coming twenty-six this April.'

'Well let's hope the Army have managed to get him quieted-down.'

Maris said, 'They made him a Lance-Corporal. Look see! He got a stripe on his tunic in the latest photo.'

*

Southampton in February, in the pouring rain, must be, said Taffy, the most beautiful place they had seen in seven years of foreign service. They were to stay overnight in an army reception centre. In the morning they would transfer to Tidworth where their release would be accomplished. That night, in a dockside pub, they drank good beer from pint mugs; from their seats at the fireside they could see the bar and the shelf that stood behind it. Dusty Miller nudged Sev.

'Don't let on that you've noticed anything funny,' he whispered, 'but there's something rum going on in this place! Take a look at that wooden box on the bar shelf. There's music coming out of it, and people's voices.'

Taffy laughed. 'That'a a gramophone you fool! Surely you've seen one of them before?'

'No,' said Dusty, 'I've been watching for the last ten minutes. You has to put records on a gramophone, and wind it up. But nobody have gone anywhere near to that wooden box!'

Sev's gaze followed Dusty's pointing finger. 'Bloody magic, that is,' he murmured. He studied the landlord. 'I wonder how the hell he manages to do it?'

Taffy stood up. He collected the three empty tankards and walked to the bar. 'Hey, landlord,' he shouted, 'who've you got nailed up in the little coffin, eh? And where's the music come from?'

The landlord grinned. 'Been away a long time, have you, soldier?'

'Seven years in India and Sudan.'

'Ah well, that explains it.' The man leaned confidentially across the bar. 'We've had a few changes since you went away.' He turned and pointed to the polished cabinet. 'This is what you calls a wireless set. I can't tell you how it works because I don't understand it. All I know is that you turns a little knob and you can hear people talking up in London.'

Taffy went back to fireside. 'Now listen boyos – you aren't never going to believe what that publican just told me!'

The officer in Tidworth was especially persuasive. He studied Sev's army records. 'I see here that your initial intention was to remain in the service. You were measured in Khartoum for a complete set of uniform for the English climate. You were made up to Lance-Corporal. You do understand that as a Bandsman you have a certain standing? Your officers say that you could still make Sergeant – ' he paused, 'what changed your mind, man?'

'I want to settle down, sir. Get married. Have a home of my own.'

'You can do that in the Army.'

'No sir. I've seen married quarters – that's no life for a woman.'

'Have you a job to go to?'

'No sir.'

'Well, I will tell you now that unemployment in England is higher than it has ever been. It is most unlikely that you will find work.'

'I'll take my chance, sir.'

The officer said, 'You have a month's leave owing to

you. Go home and think carefully about our conversation.'

He came back to Montacute on a Sunday morning, wearing his best walking-out uniform of scarlet and navy, and carrying two kitbags. He was the only passenger to step down from the train; he walked up through the village, and people stared curiously at him, but nobody spoke. He came into Middle Street, and there it was, the view he had carried over continents and oceans. The tender haze of spring green already covered Miles Hill. The church, and the little houses lay golden and unchanged in the grey, February morning. He had, throughout the journey up from Tidworth, refused to think about this moment. He had gone away, intending never to return, but his mother had found him, there had been the letters. More written words had passed between them in the past four years, than they had spoken one to the other in all his lifetime. His hand found the familiar door latch; he hesitated, shouldered the kitbags, and went in.

The room was dim and very quiet. The man who sat before the range fire did not turn at his entrance. He put down the kitbags and moved into the firelight. They gazed at one another, and Sev, who had long since learned how to be easy in the company of others, had no words for Jye, his father. He returned to the kitbags, lifted them and leaned them against the far wall. His shoulders moved uneasily inside the scarlet tunic; he removed his cap and laid it on the gloving-table.

He said when he could no longer bear the silence, ' – Where's my mother, then?'

His sudden words had caught his father's full attention, and Sev remembered with a sense of shock, the total deafness of this man. Two attempts at speech were made before the reply came.

'Her's – her's not been any too well jus' lately. Stomach trouble. She've watched out every day since the letter came. When she see'd you coming up from station she run and hid herself.'

'Why?'

Jye stood up; as they faced one another Sev saw that his father was quite unchanged. There was no touch of grey in the black curls, the brown face was almost unlined; but something in the eyes alarmed him.

'What is it? What's happened? Where's the rest of them – the baby?'

'Your sisters is all growed up and left us. The youngest have gone to stay wi' her aunty, in Yeovil.' Jye unhitched his jacket from the doorpeg; he shrugged the garment on, pulling it hastily across his shoulders. He opened the door and left the house, without giving Sev another word or glance.

Sev sat down in his father's chair; he stared into the fire and waited. The beat of his heart was so loud in his ears that he did not at first hear her.

She came up to him slowly, her long black skirts whispering across the coconut-matting. He turned at the sound, and his first thought was that if he had met her in the street he would not have recognised her. She had never been plump, but her thinness had been of the vital kind, every movement energetic and quick. Now she was so thin as to be almost transparent. He had the crazy thought that if she stood against bright sunlight he would be able to see right through her. The red-gold hair was grey and dulled; only her smile had the old, three-cornered charm. She sat down in the facing chair.

'You've come back, then.'

'I've come back.'

''Tiv been a long time.'

'I know.'

'I was worried about you.'

'You shudden never have worried. I was alright.'

'Be you here to stay? We got room now for you.'

The tightness in his throat would hardly let him speak. He unbuttoned his jacket, held his hands out to the fire's blaze.

She said, 'You've altered. I wudden never have know'd it was you, but for the uniform. You've grow'd very handsome. You take after my side for your colouring – how proud your Granfer would have been to see you now.'

He did not dare to weep; to show emotion was to admit that she was dying. He rose abruptly, dragged the kitbags into the firelight. He began to pull the strings. There was so much that he should say to her. He dragged out the big square box and began to tear at the brown paper wrapping.

'I brought you a model of the Taj Mahal. I packed it in cotton wool. I hope that none of it got broken on the voyage home.'

He watched her delight as she unwrapped each tiny marble minaret and placed it carefully in position. He held the model on his knees, leg muscles aching from its weight, the emotion draining from him, leaving him cold. He shivered and she said, 'Well, whatever am I thinking of? I should have made some tea for you straightaway.' She stirred the fire and put the kettle on the hob, and he could see that every movement caused her pain.

He said, 'Have you seen the doctor?'

'Nothing to be done. Just a matter of time.' She turned a smile of aching brilliance upon him. 'I'll be right as rain now that you be home.'

The words seemed to ease the awful tension that had lain between them. They drank their tea, and she asked him many questions.

'Be you finished with the Army?'

'Not yet, I got a month's furlough. Then I go back to get my discharge papers.'

'There's no work in these parts.'

'I'll find something.'

'You mentioned,' she said shyly, 'you mentioned in your letters that you've been writing to a maid in Taunton.' She folded her hands across her waist, as if to keep pain at bay. 'I'd like to see you settled down. I'd like to think that you had somebody – '

'Oh, I will,' his tone was rough-edged. 'I've known her for years. It's all settled between us. Just a matter now of naming the happy day.'

'That's good, then. You must bring her up to meet me.' She paused. 'You turned out to be musical then?'

'I can play clarinet good enough for the Regimental Band; I play saxophone at the officers' dances. I learned to read sheet music soon after I got to Agra.'

Damaris smiled. 'I always knowed that you was clever. Trouble was, you never could find which way best to go.'

'The Army was the saving of me! But for this uniform and badge, I'd have ended up on the gallows.'

They talked for a long time, and the rough edges of his voice became soft. In the days that followed he found ways to be tender with her that did not commit him to any display of overt emotion. As he prepared to leave for Taunton, she heard him singing,

> Make my bed and light the light
> I'll be home late tonight,
> Blackbird – bye, bye.

She had never heard a dance tune; she knew about wireless, but had never seen the actual contraption. She believed that Sev, in his role of musician, had composed the song especially for her. He allowed her to believe it; sang the words a dozen times in every day, and saw her smile. He bought an overcoat in Yeovil; navy blue, double-breasted, with a blue velvet collar.

'Are you well-off for money?' she asked.

'Well enough.'

She went to a dresser-drawer; she handed him a thick brown envelope; inside it he found a small blue bank book.

'The allotment that you made me,' she said, 'I never spent any of it. There's but the one withdrawal, made

when you asked me to send you money to convalesce.'
She touched his hand, uncertainly, 'I saved it for you.
You'll need it now that you're getting wed.'

*

The dress was displayed on a wax model which stood
behind the plate-glass of Hatcher's shop window. Eve
had visited High Street many times in the past week. The
dress was smart but demure, made in fine grey wool with
broad bands of lilac-coloured satin at wrists and
neckline. It was fashionable, of exactly knee-length and
with the new dropped waist-line; her grey shoes with
their bar strap fastenings and pointed toes would go
perfectly with it. First impressions were important. The
letter had said that he would be coming to Taunton on
Sunday morning and that he would be staying at the
Soldiers' Home in High Street; that he would come to see
her at seven o'clock on Monday evening. She ordered her
thoughts to stay solely on the dress, but the stray pangs
of worry were becoming harder to suppress. She had
taken his letters from beneath the lining paper of her
dressing-table drawer and re-read them on a wet Sunday
afternoon. She had studied the many photographs he
sent her; there was Sev, stern and military-looking in his
best dress tunic, the stripe of Lance-Corporal showing on
his sleeve. There was Sev, pictured with a boxer, beside a
table full of trophies. There were other photos in which
he sat on rocks, among trees and waterfalls, his hand
placed fondly on the head of a black and white dog. The
face in the photographs bore no resemblance to that of
the youth she had met all those years ago on the corner
of Hammet Street. She touched her finger to the deep-set
eyes, the high cheekbones and strong jawline. She
recalled Ben Treherne's soft and pleasant features;
smiled briefly at the memory of brown and stolid
Harold; the pleading eyes of Georgie Kennet; the
fascinating ugliness of Boris. It was then, with the letter
and photographs spread around her that the first

stirrings of anxiety had begun. The fierce eyes that looked out from each photo, would not, she thought, see life as she and Abi saw it. Everything for them was great fun! The sisters had together broken the Greypaull spell of gloom, and anticipation of disaster; and this was the nineteen-twenties, when young people were lighthearted.

Eve bought the grey and lilac dress; it cost twenty-seven shillings and sixpence, which was expensive, even for a shop like Hatchers's. But as she said to Abi, that evening's entertainment would at least cost her nothing, since she was meeting Harold for the last time. Harold did not yet know that this would be their final meeting; she would break it to him at the last possible moment. Eve could not bear the thought of his inevitable reproaches. She and Abi had walked one Sunday afternoon to the brow of Haines Hill. They had looked down upon the Judds' farm, had seen Harold and his mother in the farmyard, feeding chickens from a pail. Abi had said, 'You could be the next Mrs Judd if you play your cards right. You could be there with him, feeding the stock.' Eve had glanced down at her fur-trimmed coat, silk-stockinged legs and narrow, pointed shoes. 'Can you see me? Can you really see me in gumboots and flowered pinny, mixing mash for hens?' They had started to laugh, had clung to each other in paroxysms of helpless mirth on the windy top of Haines Hill. As they walked home Abi said, 'Now you let him down gently, mind Eve! Start discouraging him now. That soldier will be coming home soon from the Sudan, and you don't want too many complications.'

Eve had not needed to rebuff Georgie Kennet. They met on a Tuesday in the Tipperary Club, and she had managed to introduce him to a predatory girl friend who had vowed that she would never let him go. The problem of Boris Doctorow was less complicated but more alarming. They had never actually walked out together, but there was the matter of the free cinema tickets and the caskets of handmade chocolate. Cinema projectionists were well paid but worked long hours, and Boris, penned up in his little dark box every evening, could only dream of Eve, seated in the front stalls and eating his Vanilla Creams. He had presented her at Christmas with a large package, tied up with tinsel. She had viewed with delight the knee-high leather boots, the hat and muff of pale grey astrakhan.

'He's determined to make you look like a Russian.' Abi had grinned encouragingly.

'People say that he comes from a very aristocratic family.'

The hat and boots and muff still lay at the bottom of the wardrobe in their Christmas wrappings. She had not yet dared to wear them lest Boris should interpret this as a sign of her affection. Not that she had found it easy to allow such fashionable gifts to remain unworn. But there were the letters, coming twice and often three times weekly from Khartoum, and if his photographs were any clue by which he might be judged, Sev Carew would not be the tolerant kind.

*

Sev put on the white shirt and dark blue suit that had been the Army's parting gift; over it he wore the expensive navy blue overcoat with the velvet collar that had been his own choice. His hair was still close-cropped from its final cutting by the Battalion's barber. He hid it beneath a trilby hat of soft blue felt, one with a snap brim which shadowed his face and gave him a slightly sinister appearance. He grinned at his reflection in the square of mirror which stood on the kitchen window sill.

'Her won't never recognise 'ee,' Maris murmured, 'not after all this long time away.'

'Hardly recognise myself in all this fancy clobber.'

'You'm a handsome feller, David.' She moved closer to the fire, both hands pressed against her side.

'Sing the song!' Her voice was urgent. 'The one you made up 'specially for me, about the blackbird.'

He began to sing, and the sound of his pleasant baritone voice filled the cottage.

> Make my bed and light the light,
> I'll be home late tonight,
> Blackbird, bye bye.

Maris sat down. She closed her eyes until the song was ended. She said, 'How long will you be gone, boy?'

'A few days. Long enough to find out if she'll still have me.'

'She'll have you.'

His mother's face was white against the cushions of her chair.

He said, awkwardly, 'Will 'ee be alright? I got to catch the Taunton train now.'

'I'll be alright. Your father'll be coming back any time.'

Sev passed his father in the street. They nodded briefly but did not speak. So, Sev thought, he still visits the dark woman on a Sunday morning! No matter how ill my mother is, no matter how much it upsets her to know about it; he still has to go there!

In the train, between Montacute and Taunton, Sev thought about his situation. He had forgotten how daunting was his father's silence; had not expected to witness his mother's suffering. The meeting with Eve was still thirty-six hours away, but he preferred the roughness of the Soldiers' Home to the claustrophobic atmosphere of the Middle Street cottage.

He was shown his bed in the Soldiers' Home, deposited his luggage with an elderly ex-sergeant, drank a mug of stewed tea and went out into the town. He strolled along High Street, passed Vivary Park and came into Mount Street. He stood beneath the red walls of the Barracks, and read the word JELLALABAD inscribed above the main gates. He walked down to Hammet Street and stood on the corner; he sought and found the

455

spot where he and Eve had first spoken together. He looked at cinemas and shops and was constantly surprised at his own civilian reflection in plate-glass windows. He watched the new recruits as they came from the Barracks, treading gingerly in the agony of new boots, and on the look-out for likely targets among the girls of Taunton. He remembered himself and Taffy Richards, and thought how young he had been then; for all his army years, and the confidence bestowed by new clothes, he was still unsure when it came to the conquest of a girl like Eve. He went into a pub, drank a half of bitter beer that he did not really want. The clock on St Mary's church struck nine as he left the bar. He would walk to the terrace where she lived! He would stand underneath the lamp-post, for old times' sake!

*

Mother's disinclination to allow her daughter's freedom on that Sunday evening was overcome when she learned Eve's companion was to be Harold Judd.

'You'll have to tell him,' Abigail insisted. 'If you're serious about this soldier –?'

'I'm not sure,' wailed Eve. 'How can I be?' Even so, she was bound to admit that she had, in the circumstances, a superfluity of male friends. She and Harold strolled around the town. He brought her a port and lemon in The Four-Alls. He told her of the prices made by his father's fat-stock in last Friday's market. He said that his mother's arthritis was worsening; that she found it increasingly difficult to work around the farm. That his parents were always hinting-on that it was time he found a nice girl and got married to her. They walked back towards the terrace, past the lamp-post, and into the shadow of a high wall. The evening was cold. Eve was greatful for the warmth of her close-fitted cloche hat, and the wide furry collar of her beige coat. She barely noticed the man who stood underneath the lamp-post.

456

'I can't meet you anymore,' she told Harold. 'Well – at least – not for a bit. I'm giving up my job at French's. I shall work at home at the gloving with Abigail and Mother. I can make more money that way.'

Harold said, 'But surely –!'

She laid her hand upon his sleeve. 'Now don't be upset. I shall still see you from time to time. I might be bringing work from French's at about the time you come into market in your dog trap. You never know when we may run into one another.'

Later on, as they drank their supper cocoa, Eve said to Abi, 'I thought I'd never get rid of that Harold! I don't know how I could ever have got involved with him in the first place.'

Abi twitched aside the bedroom curtain.

'That fellow's still standing underneath the lamp-post. He's been there for hours. I don't recognise him. He's not another one of your secret admirers is he?'

*

The door of Number 5, The Terrace was opened on that February evening by a silver-haired man who said quietly, 'You must be Sev. Come you in, boy. You must be feeling the cold, having just come home from Sudan.' They walked through a narrow brown hallway into a room that was crowded with ornaments and vases, and in which everything was blue.

She was standing on a sheepskin hearthrug, the gaslight shining directly down onto her soft brown hair. She was exactly as he had remembered, but with the subtle differences which turned a pretty girl into a lovely woman.

The silver-haired man introduced Sev with an almost proprietary air.

'This is the young man from Sudan. He's feeling the change of climate, so find him a chair close to the fire.'

He turned to Sev. 'Mother's in the kitchen making supper. I'll leave you with Evie. You two 'ull have plenty to say to one another.' They shook hands, because to kiss would have been impossible with Eve's father standing by. Sev sat down on a blue-brocaded armchair. Eve perched nervously on an uncomfortable sofa. They were unaware of the closing door, so fierce was their concentration upon the other.

Sev said, 'into a lengthening silence, 'It's – it's nice to see you again, after so long.'

She sat absolutely still, that amazing jade-green gaze fixed upon his face. She said, 'I'm so glad you wrote to me – so glad you came to see me – wasn't that a funny thing – you seeing my photo pinned up over cousin Charlie's bed?'

Her words meant little to him; he was achingly aware of the soft, slightly breathless quality of her voice; the promise in it. He spoke random words, agreeing with all she said, and all the time his mind was mesmerised by the strange quality of her. He was not experienced with women; how could he be after seven years of army life, most of which had been spent among plains and desert? But he was a man who had always known exactly what it was he wanted at the moment of first seeing; and he was looking at her now as if for the first time.

'Father,' she was saying, 'served nine years with the Somerset Light Infantry in India and Burma. He's looking forward to talking to you about the Army – he hardly ever gets the chance these days –'

She sat absolutely still, her hands folded one across the other. She had a way of tilting her head a little to one side as she spoke. He found her self-possession daunting. He said, abruptly, 'I came down to Taunton yesterday. I spent the evening walking around town. I wanted to make sure that I remembered where you live.' He paused. 'I was standing at the bottom of the street, underneath the lamp-post. I thought I saw you with a fellah?'

She said 'You must have been mistaken. I never go out on Sunday evenings.'

'I watched the girl. It was this house that she came into.'

'You'll have seen my sister, but please don't mention it in front of Mother. There's been a lot of trouble over Abi's engagement to Joey Santini. Mother doesn't know that they still meet.'

He felt the sharp edge of jealousy recede. He said, 'Your letters meant a lot to me. Not many soldiers are lucky enough to have a girl to come home to.'

'So what will you do?' she asked. 'Will you stay in the Army?'

'No, I've had enough of taking orders. I want to settle down, have my own home,' he grinned, 'I want to see more of you –'

She said swiftly, 'But what about your family, and there's not much work to be had in these parts?'

'My mother's very ill. It was a bit of a shock to see her, I can tell you! My father and me don't have much to say to one another. Never did have. I'll get a job. There's plenty of things that I can do.'

The front door opened and closed. Eve said, 'That'll be Abigail – you remember my sister, don't you?'

Sev stood up as Abi entered the room. They shook hands. She said, 'How you've changed! Well, I'd never have recognised you!'

He laughed. 'That's what everybody says.'

Abi turned to Eve. 'He's still wearing his overcoat – and sitting with his hat on his knee!' To Sev she said, 'You must have made a big impression on her, she's not usually so forgetful of her manners.'

*

If it was possible, Sev thought, to sit at the head of a circular table, then Annis Nevill had achieved that position. It was to the mother that respect was shown in this family. Sev was conscious of being tested, but for what he could not be certain.

The table was set with an array of china and silver, the

459

quality of which would not have disgraced an Officers' Mess. He sat very straight in his chair, was careful to hand dishes and condiments to the three ladies; he complimented Eve's mother on her cooking, enquired abut her father's garden. He was careful when answering Mrs Nevill's questions, sensing traps beneath the pleasant words. Yes, he had reached the rank of Lance-Corporal; yes, he was a military Bandsman. No, he did not drink or gamble. He smoked, but then so did most men. No, he did not intend to stay in the Army; yes, he supposed that his Bounty money, after seven years service with the Colours, would be quite a good sum. He was staying at the Soldiers' Home which was lacking in home comforts, but he was used to that.

'If you intend to come again,' Mrs Nevill said, 'you must stay with us, of course. I wouldn't hear of you going to that rough place up in High Street.'

The astonishment of the assembled faces told Sev that this was a unique invitation.

'Well – thank you,' he murmured, 'I should like to come back again – if you'll have me.'

They said goodnight in the shadows cast by the open front door. He kissed her, inexpertly at first, and then with increased assuredness.

'My mother likes you,' she whispered.

'I haven't come courting your mother. It's what you think about me that really matters.'

'I'll tell you that tomorrow night. Call for me at seven. We'll go for a long walk.'

*

Several pots of tea were brewed in Annis Nevill's kitchen in that spring of 1927, and many teacups filled and passed across her gloving-table. Eve had given up her job at French's, which was never well paid, to work at home with Abigail and Mother. Working at home required industry and discipline, but the money was better. There were also the diversions provided by visiting aunts; it was at Number 5, The Terrace that the Greypaulls gathered. When subjects unsuitable for her daughters' hearing were to be discussed, Annis swiftly despatched them to the Tanyard with orders to collect a further batch of work. It was in the absence of Eve and Abi that Sev Carew was talked over and grudgingly approved.

'He's only a Lance-Corporal, of course. But he is a Bandsman, we mustn't forget that.' Annis leaned forward across the table and rapped sharply with her gloving-stick.

'He's a gentleman, Mina. He know'd his manners, at the table, and towards me. He sat bolt upright and always used the proper knives and forks. He made nice conversation; he spoke very touchingly about his poor sick mother back in Montacute.' Annis smiled. 'He's proper moonstruck by our Evie. Couldn't take his eyes off her for more than a second.'

Candace said, 'And what about Eve? How does she feel about him?'

'Oh you know my Eve.' Annis's tone was indulgent. 'She's a fickly liddle minx if ever I saw one! She've got a string of admirers from here to Bishop's Hull.'

'Watch your step this time, Anni,' Madelina warned. 'You interfered between her and Ben Treherne. Eve took that very badly.'

'But I was proved right in the end! He went off and married another girl in no time at all. He was never right for my maid.'

'You seem very sure of this one, Anni?'

'Oh I am, Mina. 'Tis the way a family behaves, one towards the other, that really tells! He was all set to stop the week in Taunton, but a telegram came from his mother. It seems there's the chance of a job for him in Yeovil, if he goes after it straight away.' Annis sipped her tea and set the cup down. 'Now that's what I call proper family feeling. A mother what spends money on telegrams to make sure of her son's job, must be one of our sort of people. That woman's heart is in the right place!'

Candace said, 'So he's gone back home then?'

Annis looked triumphant. 'Only till Friday. He's coming back for the weekend. I said that he could bide here with us. They say that there's fleas and worse in that Soldiers' Home.'

※

Sev came back to Taunton; he arrived in the terrace in late afternoon, carrying a duck, plucked and dressed, ready for the oven, a dozen oranges, and a bunch of daffodils for Mother.

Annis said, 'Oh, you shouldn't have!' But Eve could tell that Mother was both charmed and gratified that her assessment of Sev had been a true one. She looked from her mother's flushed and smiling face, to the handsome young man who was so unlike all her former suitors, and felt a tiny pang of fear. He must be alright if Mother liked him; Father also spoke well of him. Sev and Father had gone together to the Half Moon Inn; they had talked about India and army life. Father, who rarely voiced an opinion in Mother's presence, had declared Sev to be 'the right sort'. It was only when Sev turned that brilliant blue gaze towards Eve that she felt unsure. There was something about his eyes; a piercing significant stare that held a hint of boldness. He was so sure of himself and she was not accustomed to the ways of confident men. Eve's pace of life was gentle; she made her mind up only slowly, especially about people, and this was a young man in a hurry.

The weekend passed quickly. They walked to Rowbarton and had tea with Aunt Candace. Eve averted her gaze from the gardener's cottage where Ben Treherne was living with his new wife. Sev's kisses in the darkness were increasingly passionate; he was the first of her beaux not to feel inhibited by Mother's strict views.

Eve came home from Rowbarton looking flushed and faintly guilty, but Mother seemed not to notice. All her attention was on the jeweller's sizing-card which Sev had produced, magician-like, from his jacket pocket. He slipped the cardboard rings across Eve's engagement finger until he found the one which fitted. He pushed the sizing-card back into his pocket, nodded mysteriously and grinned.

'Next weekend,' he whispered, 'I'll have a little surprise for you.'

The job, Sev told Father, was in an engineering factory; and no, he knew less than nothing about the working of a lathe, but he was nobody's fool and very quick to learn. It had, he said, been his ability to play the clarinet that had assured his employment. The factory band had needed a musician, and good liquorice-stick players were hard to come by around Yeovil. Sev had a turn of phrase that made both Father and Mother laugh; Eve noticed how people, even the staid and buttoned-up ones like her Aunt Mina, seemed to come alive when in his company. She too was aware of stirrings and expansions in her own heart since his arrival. She wondered if this was what the singers of romantic songs meant when they crooned about love.

The engagement ring was quite lovely, and in perfect taste; three large and brilliant diamonds encircled by a band of gold. He slipped it without a word across the third finger of her left hand. He had, she thought contentedly, not even asked if she wanted to get married to him. She thought about the ways of Rudolph Valentino and Ramon Navarro with Greta Garbo and Pola Negri. Masterful men were like that; and she was beginning now to love the ways of Sev Carew.

*

Meridiana Carew had achieved the respect that is given to great age. They said that she was probably the oldest woman still living in the village, although no records existed by which this could be proved. She had simply outlived all the people who remembered her arrival there with Luke, all those years ago. She was, thanks to Jye's many daughters, a great-grandmother several times over. Jye came to see her every day now, on his way home from the Hill.

News of Sev had come to her without surprise. She had foretold that he would wander; had known about the music in him, the gift that lay within his fingers. Jye had read aloud the letters that came from Agra and Khartoum. Sev had passed her house on his way up from the station; she had watched him go by in his scarlet-and-navy, had observed with wry amusement his determination to look anywhere at all save towards her window. She was not upset by his neglect, did not need the proof of his physical presence to reinforce her total possession of him. He was hers by blood, always had been, always would be. Proof lay in all his actions, in the letters that he wrote, in the direct and unmistakable look of menace that showed up in his photographed eyes.

There were many things no longed needed by Meridiana. The old urge to roam would never quite go away; but infirmity had taken care of that. In her mind she ranged far and wide, back and forth across time and space, and always in the company of travellers long dead.

Jye brought her a photograph of Sev's future wife; she gazed for a long time at Eve Nevill's lovely face; her recognition of the features had been instant; here at last was the nut-brown girl of her prediction. Engaged, Jye said; plans made for a wedding in early August; a girl of good family. Meri grinned, and kept her secrets close. There was much she could have told him about Eve Nevill's family. Her thoughts drifted off towards Eliza Greypaull; she came back to hear Jye say, 'And he've got hisself a good job in Yeovil, in the engineering. He plays the clarinet in the Works' Band. He found an evening job too, playing saxophone in a dance-band. You'd never believe how the Army have changed 'un. He'm all for work these days, and getting money. He bought a motorbike last week, he needs it to get about the country.'

'I know,' she said, 'I see'd 'un go roaring up the street.'
She laughed. 'He raised a fine cloud o' dust! Chickens
and people was scattered in all directions! Ah, they
knows in Montacute that Sev Carew is home again!'

'He never come to see you?'

'No, Jye; and you's'll say no word to 'un on that
subject. Him and me understands one another. He've
done all I wanted 'un to do. Very soon he'll bring me the
nut-brown girl. I been waiting for her these many-a-long
years.' She tapped Eve's photograph and chuckled softly.
'You reckons I be crazy, don't you? But hear me Jye!
That maid got property o' mine, and I want it back!'

Jye was proud of Sev, glad of his changed ways, his
long years of soldiering in far lands, his talent for music.
That Sev would never know of his father's pride in him,
Meri was certain; the boy's affection was all for his
mother. The mother whom he had allowed to presume
his death, and who was herself now close to dying.

'What news of *her*?' Meri asked in a gruff tone.

'Her's hanging-on. Struggles up each morning to get
dressed and get his breakfast. Won't let 'un see how bad
she really is. He sings her this daft song, "Bye bye,
blackbird". She says he made it up especially for her. I
can't bide in the same room when the two of 'em is there
together. They be so like to one another – and yet there's
something "other" in him.'

Meri said, 'You recalls the patteran left by the
roadside? The sign that one travelling family leaves
behind, to guide the ones what follow? Well, that's how
'tis wi' men and women. We all leaves a bit of ourselves
behind to guide the ones what come after.' She sighed.
'Your Sev got a quick mind. He'll read all the signs I've
left him.' Her lips curved up with sly amusement. 'He'll
pass on my father's music, and my own gift for fortune-
telling. I intend to live long enough to see Sev's children.'

*

Dramatic events would never come singly in the Greypaull family. Disasters and joys had a way of spilling over from one sister to another. Eve's re-union with her long-lost soldier sweetheart had proceeded to the enchantment of a swift engagement, and the plans for a wedding in early August. The morning gathering around the gloving-table was still deep in romantic speculation, when Candace arrived with bad news of Billy.

The letter had been written in Mary Pickford's own hand. It told of an accident while filming. A car crash on the 'set', in which Billy had volunteered to take the place of an absent stuntman. His injuries were severe. He had been taken to a hospital in Los Angeles, all expenses paid for by Douglas Fairbanks. The doctors were confident that Billy would live, but it seemed unlikely that he would ever work again.

Annis wept while Candace remained dry-eyed.

'Well at least,' Abi said, 'he's among wealthy people. They're looking after him. He'll be getting good treatment.'

Candace said, 'Perhaps he'll come home when he's feeling better. Perhaps he'll have got all that acting business out of his system.' She sighed. 'Poor Billy. He never seemed to know where acting ended, and real life began.'

*

Sev's release from the Army had been completed; he received his Bounty money and an 'Assessment of Conduct and Character on Leaving the Colours' in which his military conduct was described as Exemplary. It was testified by his Lieutenant Colonel that he was a 'sober, honest and thoroughly reliable worker. Fit to take his place in any Band as a clarinet player. Has been employed in the Officers' Mess. Holds a 2nd Class Certificate of Education. Plays all games.'

For the first time in his life Sev was almost happy. He

travelled the lovely uphill-and-downdale road from Montacute to Taunton on an ancient two-stroke Norton motorbike that trailed smoke and made strange noises. He arrived in Taunton on a Saturday afternoon and left on a Sunday evening. The weekdays were spent in an engineering works in Yeovil, and on Friday nights he played in the Imps Dance Band. It was a full life, but unsettled. His confident manner concealed a dozen fears. He refused to acknowledge his mother's illness; would not allow Eve to speak upon the subject. He had lately detected a change in Mrs Nevill's manner towards him. His mention of new houses being built in Montacute, and his intention of making a down-payment on the one that was closest to completion, had seemed to upset her even more than his plans for an August wedding. Eve had tried to reassure him that all was as before, but he was sensitive to atmosphere, and this was a family in which the bizarre and unusual was rendered commonplace and hardly commented upon. He remarked upon the fineness of the Nevill's cutlery and china; he had worked in the Officers' Mess and for Lord Curzon. He knew about such things. Eve had said vaguely that the expensive items had once belonged to an aunt who was a close friend of the Prince of Wales; she mentioned, in the same bored tones, a cousin who was a film-star in Hollywood; a young man whose recent accident had brought a letter to Taunton, written by Mary Pickford. Sev's sense of unreality when in the Nevill household was only heightened by the familiar gloving-table set beneath the window, and the curious incidents which happened in his presence, but were never satisfactorily explained.

They had eaten the roast chicken that was Sev's contribution to the weekend, and enjoyed Mrs Nevill's apple-pie. Eve's father dozed in his chair beneath the gas-bracket; her mother rattled dishes in the kitchen. Sev sat with Abigail and Eve on the uncomfortable sofa; they talked about the new house, and when the Banns should be called in Trinity Church. The knock on the door brought Abi to her feet; she peered out through the thick lace curtain. She turned to Eve.

'It's that Boris!'

Eve said, 'See what it is he wants, Abi! Go quickly, he's trying to knock the door down!' She spoke anxiously. Sev noted her sudden pallor.

'Who is it?' he asked. 'Who is Boris?'

Eve smiled. 'Oh it's nothing to worry about. He's an old flame of Abi's.'

Sev said, 'He sounds annoyed about something.'

The voice of Boris Doctorow came clearly from the hallway. 'And I want my presents back – all of them – and you can –'

'Stay there!' ordered Abi. 'I'll go upstairs and fetch them for you.'

From the room above, Sev could hear the sounds of cupboard doors opening and closing. He heard Abi's quick steps on the staircase. He shook off Eve's detaining hand and went towards the window. Through the side pane of the bay he could see a man, his arms outstretched to receive a pair of high leather boots, a hat and muffs of curly grey fur. He heard Abi say, 'Now go away and don't come back here, you understand! Nobody asked you for free cinema tickets, or boxes of chocolates. You gave them of your own free will!'

Sev watched as the man walked away, his shoulders bowed, his head bent across the peculiar burden of fur and leather. He felt sorry for him, sensed his misery and anger. The colour came back slowly to Eve's face. Abi closed the front door; she came back into the room, and sat down upon the sofa as if nothing remarkable had happened. She grinned at Eve, and brushed her palms together.

'That's settled him,' she said with satisfaction. 'Pity though! He did provide such lovely chocolates.'

It was later that evening, when they were walking out along the Staplegrove Road that Sev said, 'I don't think much of the way your sister treated that poor chap. He looked ready to cut his throat as he walked away down the street. I've got no time for fickle-minded girls. I'd better tell you now, Eve. I've got a very jealous nature. I can't help it, it's the way I am.' His step slowed, his voice became dangerously quiet.

'You know that I love you, don't you? More than I ever loved any living soul. But if you ever let me down, then God help you, Eve Nevill!'

He looked down and saw her stricken face, and was at once contrite.

'I never meant to frighten you. It was just seeing the way your sister got rid of that poor devil.' He halted and took both her hands in his. 'Tell you what,' he laughed, 'let's make the whole thing final. Let's put up the Banns! Say you'll come and live with me in Montacute!'

She smiled and sighed, and just for a moment he thought she looked relieved.

'Oh yes, Sev! Let's do that. I think it's high time I got away from Taunton.'

They had talked all summer about an August wedding, but no date had yet been set. Before his departure for Montacute that night, Sev spoke to Mother. Eve was almost deluded by the helpfulness of Annis; her enthusiasm, the clarity with which she gave Sev instructions as to where the Vicarage was to be found. An appointment with the Vicar of Holy Trinity was to be made for the following weekend. The Banns would be called on the next three Sundays, which would bring them neatly up to their chosen date of August 6th.

A deposit of twenty-five pounds had been paid down on the new house, and weekly repayments of twenty-two shillings and sixpence agreed. Eve and Abi stole a day off from the gloving; they took the train to Montacute on a July morning, telling no one of their intentions. They found the almost completed house that Sev had described. It stood on high ground, and could be approached only by a flight of steps. Eve loved the newness of it; the absence of dark-green paint and lived-in gloom that characterised the villas of Taunton. It had a large living-room and kitchen, three bedrooms, and a tiny bathroom and garden.

Abi gazed from the window which gave a view of towering Miles Hill.

'It's very quiet here,' she said uneasily, 'not many shops. Did you notice how the women stared at us as we came through the village?'

Eve said, 'I don't suppose they see many strangers, especially ones who wear snakeskin shoes and silk-stockings.'

'Do you think you'll like it here?'

'Oh, I'll be alright! I can always go shopping into Yeovil. There must be a bus or something.' Eve studied the empty rooms. 'I'll have plenty to do – curtains to hang – furniture to buy; and you'll visit me, won't you?'

'Every week.'

*

Happiness and anguish became inextricably mixed in that month of July. Every pleasure it seemed, had an undertow of sadness, a hint of fearful things yet to be revealed. Eve was not quite sure how she had arrived at this irrevocable point; her growing indecision was laughed at by Abigail, but deepened by every word that Mother uttered.

Sev introduced her to his mother and father; he met her at the village station, and they walked arm-in-arm through deserted Sunday afternoon lanes, Eve's fashionable snakeskin shoes growing dusty on the country paths. She felt loved and happy in the little room which held a familiar gloving-table, a dark Welsh dresser filled with flowered china, and a fire beside which Sev's mother sat, wrapped in shawls although the day was warm. Eve drank tea and ate scones; on her way back to the station she and Sev viewed the almost completed house. He stood at the living-room window which looked directly up towards Miles Hill. He said in a curious tone, 'They liked you. They liked you very much. My father talked to you. He hardly ever talks to anybody. He never speaks to me.'

She said, 'I'm glad they liked me. I shall grow very fond of them; in fact I already am. They're lovely people, they made me feel as if I belong to them, and we're not even married yet.'

She looked at his profile, saw the muscles tighten in his jaw, heard the pain in his voice. He pointed to the hills ranged across the horizon.

'I never really belonged at home. I was always happiest up there – alongside my grandfather. He was the Good Shepherd. I was my Granfer's sonner.'

Eve said, 'Your mother's very ill.'

'She's getting better. Gets stronger every day. 'Twas just the doctor getting over-anxious about her. She was always thin. I don't see any change in her. No change at all.'

'They won't be coming to the wedding. Your mother's not strong enough, and your father won't leave her. I promised to show them my gown and head-dress, and tell them about it.'

He repeated, in the same ambiguous tone, 'They liked you. Well, I'm glad about that. It'll make things much easier when you come to live here.'

Annis said on Eve's return, 'You'll go mad in that village! You've never been on your own, not for a single day in your whole life. I don't see why you can't bide in Taunton.'

'Sev's job is in Yeovil.'

'He could find work here.'

'I don't think he wants to. He needs to stay close to his mother.'

'And what about me? Don't I count for nothing in your life?'

'I'm getting married, Mother. A wife goes where her husband's job is.'

'So that's what he says to you behind my back! I knew

from the very first that he'd be up to no good. Well, let me tell you, my girl, I never did like men who was easy talkers. You've made fools of half the young men who live in this town, but you won't wind this one around your liddle finger! Oh no, Eve! I've seen this sort before. He'll be the master in his house, and you'll do exactly as he tells you!'

Eve walked away from the bitter words. She went into her father's conservatory and stood among the aspidistras. She thought about Sev's fierce gaze and the warnings he had issued.

'If you ever let me down,' he had said, 'then God help you, Eve Nevill.' She twisted his engagement ring around her finger and recalled the almost completed house with its fourteen steps that led up to the front door. They had come, hand-in-hand down those steps, just a few hours ago, laughing and counting at the same time.

*

Annis now practised the brand of silence that spoke volumes.

'Ignore her,' was Abigail's advice. 'We've got less than three weeks to organise this wedding, and if Mother won't help us then we'll go to see Aunt Mina.'

It was Abi who found the length of wild-silk that was hare-bell blue in colour; she who searched in Taunton's most exclusive milliners for the picture-hat of pale blue lace and matching gloves. A dressmaker who lived in Trinity Street was recommended by Aunt Candace. A simple but fashionable wedding-dress was Eve's choice; knee-length and dropped-waisted, with a square neckline, and long sleeves that flared towards the wrists. Shoes were bought of a toning deep-blue satin. Sev brought her a gift of sheer silk stockings. He went with her to Sunday morning Service; they sat in a rear pew, shoulders touching, and heard their Banns called for the first time, and then the second.

Eve had wondered how Mother would behave towards

Sev, but such was her state of mind that she had moved far beyond worry. He was confident in her mother's kitchen; a towel looped about his waist, he dried dishes and cutlery, and put things away in their proper places. Eve heard him say, 'and I'm having a suit tailor-made in Bond Street, Yeovil. A neat brown pin-stripe.'

'You'll need a nice white shirt, Sev, and white gloves of course! Now what colour tie was you thinking of wearing? I've got a lovely gold tie-pin if you'd care to use it?' Mother's tone was light and sweet. It held no hint of her true feelings.

Eve kissed Sev goodbye in the shadow of the front door. The green motorcycle roared out of the terrace in a cloud of black smoke. She went upstairs to the room she shared with Abi. She said, 'Mother's up to something. She's being over-nice to him. I don't understand it.'

'Oh, I do!' Abi smiled. 'If you were not so frightened of her – but who am I to criticise you – she had me in the same state when I was courting Nicholas and Joey. Oh yes, I understand our mother very well. Sit down and I'll explain it to you.'

Abi settled herself against the pillows. 'Poor Mother,' she said, 'has never met a man like Sev Carew. He's a fellah in a hurry. He knows what he wants and he'll brook no interference. He takes for granted all those things that you and I hesitate about. He's so sure of himself – why, between February and July he's found himself two jobs, got engaged to you, bought a motorbike and a house, and is to be married next Saturday morning!' Abi smiled. 'Chaps like Nick Greypaull and Ben Treherne were easy meat for Mother. Sev Carew is from a different breed of people. There's something in his nature that will not be gainsaid.'

Eve thought about Sev's gentle mother, his soft-voice father, their kindness towards her. She told Abi, 'You're right of course. There is something a bit – a bit wild about him. He's nothing like his parents.'

'He'll be a throw-back.' Abi nodded wisely. 'Ah but

he's handsome, Eve, especially now that his hair has grown longer. How I envy him those thick waves and curls.' She touched the paper curlers in her own hair. 'It's not fair, is it?'

Eve did not return her sister's smile. She moved restlessly about the bedroom.

Abi said, 'Mother's problem is that she respects Sev; against her will she's obliged to admire him. He's nice-mannered, he's a hard worker, he laughs and jokes with her. His only fault is that he's not frightened of her. So all her spite is turned on you. She'll change your mind if she can, and make the whole sad business appear to be your fault.'

Eve said, 'She's already made me doubtful. Whatever will I do all day on my own in that little village? Oh Abi, I can't bear it when Mother won't speak to me. Whatever shall I do?'

Abigail pointed to the wedding dress on its padded hanger; to the hat and shoes that lay beside it.

'Tomorrow,' she said firmly, 'we shall go out and buy your going-away outfit. The bouquet must be ordered; now let's decide on your flowers. Sweetpeas I think, and carnations –'

All Eve's attempts to tell Mother about the new house and its furnishings were met by indifference. Eve went to see Aunt Madelina who was sympathetic and attentive.

'Now don't you worry about a thing, my dear. We all know what Anni is. She'll come round in the end, you mark my words. Meanwhile, I'll do all I can to help you. Sev can sleep here, in my house, on the night before the wedding. I'll come to the Terrace and help you prepare the wedding breakfast.'

Eve told her aunt about the seven-piece suite of sofa and armchairs, made of golden brown hide-leather, that had been their choice.

' – and oh, Aunty, I did so fancy a Turkey carpet for it to stand on, but Sev said no, we can't afford it. But we found a cork-linoleum in a similar red Turkey-pattern, and Father's present to us is several lovely sheepskin rugs, cured specially for me in the Tanyard.'

Mina said, 'So the house is all furnished and ready for you to move into?'

'Yes – yes, we intend to go back there straight after the wedding. We can't afford to go away.'

'It'll be nice for you, Evie, to have your own home, to be independent.'

'I suppose so,' Eve's tone was doubtful. 'I suppose I'll get used to it, in time.'

*

Mother said things to Father in a hurt tone, as if Eve was not present and within her hearing.

'I shan't go to this wedding, of course. They've made it quite clear that they' don't want me in church. Our Candace is doing the flowers, and the reception is all down to Madelina. The best man is to be an old friend from Sev's army days. I wonder who will give the bride away?' Mother paused to gaze significantly at Father. 'You can't be expected to do it, Frank. You've always said that you could never give your Evie away to any man, be he commoner or Prince! No, no, Frank I won't hear of your being persuaded against your will to do anything that would upset you. There's plenty of cousins on the Nevill side who'd be only too delighted to get a party invitation; any one of them will fill the bill.'

The tension in the house was tinder-dry, needing only an unwise word from Eve to set off a conflagration that would destroy them all. So she crouched low within herself, said no word to Father on the subject, and arranged that a Nevill cousin should 'give her away'. Admiration for the wedding presents came from everyone save Mother. The Nevill kitchen was taken over by Aunt Madelina and Sev on the day before the wedding. Eve could hear his laughter as he filled jelly-moulds on her aunt's instructions, and poured coloured blancmange into fancy glass dishes. He arranged iced cakes onto paper doilies, and was complimented on his deftness. He was, Eve thought, too happy to sense the undercurrents; and it needed practice to read the subtle danger-signals now being flown by Mother. The explosion was imminent. The rictus of her mother's smile, the hunched misery of her father's shoulders, Abi's brittle attempts to avert disaster, could no longer be ignored.

Eve awoke on her wedding morning to a perfect August day of hot sunshine and blue skies. Everything was ready; she would be married at two that afternoon; the taxi that was to take them to the station had been ordered for six o'clock. The train that would take them to Montacute and their new home, was due to leave Taunton at six-thirty. The hours spun around in her brain; she sat up, abruptly. To the already wakeful Abigail, Eve said, 'I can't go through with it. I can't marry him. I shall cancel it all.'

Abi said, 'He's not the sort of fellah you can jilt. But you already know that.'

'I'll – I'll go to Rowbarton and stay with Aunt Candace. Mother can tell him that it's all off –'

Abi spoke in different voice, one that Eve had never heard her use. 'Listen to me, Evie. You have this one chance to live your own life – to break away from Mother. Take it, for God's sake! Don't let her do to you what she's done to me! I'm thirty-three years old. Oh, I know I look younger. But Joey won't ever marry me now. I shall go to my grave with his engagement ring on my finger. We shall keep company, go on walking-out together. We shall be a joke. The oldest courting-couple ever seen in Taunton, that's how people will describe us.' She paused. 'You will put Mother and all her tricks right out of your mind. You will go to church this afternoon, Eve Nevill, marry Sev Carew, and live happily ever after.'

Eve said, 'He wants me to wear that old coral pendant with my wedding-gown. He says it's a lucky piece, a sort of amulet. Oh, Abigail, I think I'm going to need it!'

476

It was a lovely wedding; everybody said so. The church was filled with people. As Eve walked down the aisle on Sev's arm, she saw a shimmer of grey silk in a rear pew, and knew that her Mother, after all her hard words, had at least come to see her married. Out in Trinity Street a crowd of neighbours waited to see the happy couple. Sev and Eve posed on the church steps; while photographs were taken Eve heard a neighbour say, 'Nice day for a wedding, Mrs Nevill. Is this Frank's adopted daughter, or is it his own child that's just got married?'

Eve looked towards Abi, who had also heard the jibe.

'That woman knows very well who you are, and who I am,' Abigail whispered. 'But they have long memories round here. Poor old Mother! She won't forget this day in a hurry!'

They sat down at three o'clock to the wedding-breakfast prepared by Sev and Aunt Mina. They drank wine with the meal, and kegs of cider were on tap in the kitchen. The party became merry, and then rowdy. The parlour furniture was pushed back to make a space for dancing. Eve saw Sev's face, his lips thinned in disapproval; she sensed his anger.

'It's alright,' she said lightly, 'my relatives always get like this when they've had a few drinks.'

'Well I'm just thankful that my mother and father couldn't come. They're Particular Baptists. I can't think what they'd make of this lot!' Sev watched a young man who was hauling a girl up to dance beside him on the circular table. 'I've had enough of this, Eve. I'm going round to see the taxi driver. We'll go straightaway to the station. I'd sooner sit and watch the trains than witness this sort of behaviour.'

Eve said to Abi, 'Change of plan. Sev wants to leave early. Can you make some excuse to Mother for me. I would never have guessed he was so prim and proper.'

Her going-away outfit was in shell-pink wool, trimmed with brown. A pink dress and matching coat, and a toque hat of pink silk, trimmed with a long brown tassle. Eve said, as Abi helped her to dress, 'Is it alright? Is Mother angry with me for leaving early?'

'Mother,' said Abi, 'is dancing with the butcher. To judge by her colour she has already drunk her share of cider, and Father's too!'

Eve smiled. The expected explosion had, after all, been averted. The taxi came; Father held her close and whispered, 'Be happy, Evie.' Even Mother kissed her, and waved goodbye.

Sev and Eve Carew sat for two hours on a bench on Taunton station, and watched the trains come and go. They held hands, and stole shy glances at each other. In Montacute the new house waited; soon they would climb the fourteen steps that led up to their own front door. Alighting passengers smiled fondly at them, they were so obviously newly-wed; so absorbed in one another. On Platform Two a ganger tapped train-wheels with an iron mallet. The bridegroom seated on the far bench was a stranger to him; but he recognised the bride as Annis Nevill's daughter.

٭

Eve went back to Taunton on a Friday morning. She carried with her an empty suitcase. Her wedding dress and hat, her shoes and veil were still in Number 5, The Terrace. She twirled the wedding ring around her finger, and smiled at the memory of Sev as he had looked that morning, riding off on the old green motorbike, on his way to the engineering works in Yeovil. She looked forward to a long and cosy chat with Abi and Mother. There were wedding gifts still to be collected. The suitcase would be full and heavy on her return to Montacute.

Eve walked up the familiar incline and along the yellow pavement. The front door was on the latch, which meant that Abi was at the Tanyard, delivering finished gloves and collecting new works. She went into the dim brown hallway and looked upwards. Mother's white face seemed to hang, as if disembodied across the banister-rails.

'And what do you want here?' Mother's tone was bitter. 'I'm surprised that you have the nerve to come back after what you did!'

Eve tried to speak, but could not.

'Oh don't bother to lie about it, Eve. Your father's brother is a railway ganger. You were seen – you and the bossy chap you've married. Preferred to sit on a bench on Taunton station for more than two whole hours didn't you, rather than stay at the wedding breakfast it took me so many hours of work to provide for you!'

Mother's face leaned out further, until it seemed that she might be in danger of falling into the stairwell.

'I – I've just come for my dress and veil,' stammered Eve.

'You couldn't wait to get away from me,' screamed Mother, 'that husband of yours changed the time of the taxi. Oh yes. I found out what he'd been up to. Who does he think he is, anyway? Just a common soldier from the Barracks – a tyrant – that's what you've married my girl. Your soul will never be your own with a man of his sort. Ah, you'll have to toe the line with him. Just you wait until the honeymoon days is over!'

Eve took one step forward towards the stairs.

'Get out!' shouted Mother. 'Get out of my house and never set foot in here again. I never want to see your face for the rest of my days.'

*

Eve went sobbing down the street, the empty suitcase in her hand. The explosion had not, after all, been averted. Mother had needed a grudge on which to hang her malice, and Sev had, all unwittingly, provided it for her. The slight had been a very small one, and accidental. Eve walked, without thinking, up to Tancred Street and Father. The dinner-time whistle had blown in French's

479

Tanyard. Eve waited beneath the archway until Father came out from the Fleshers' shed. Trolleys, piled high with uncured sheepskins, lined the yard. She looked up towards the examiner's window where she had once worked. Life had been so simple at the age of fifteen.

Father came slowly down the yard, unaware that Eve stood in the shadows. He looked old and tired. The work of a flesher demanded great skill and dexterity; the curved, double-edged knife used to scrape away the particles, required careful handling. He came up to the cool shadows of the gateway, and it was the sight of his hands, scarred with old cuts, and sore from new ones, that caused her tears to flow again.

He said, 'You've been home?'

She nodded. 'And told to get out, and never come back.'

Frank sighed. He put his arm about Eve's shoulders. 'It's been a bad week. We've heard nothing else, night and day. You know how she is, how she've always been. Her temper 'ull have to run its course, Evie. There's nothing I can do about it.'

Eve sobbed. 'I know – I know how it is for you. Better that I never come back again to Taunton.'

He said, in a quiet voice, 'I can't bear that either.'

They gazed helplessly at one another. Frank said at last, 'Leave her to me, maid. Time usually works wonders wi' your mother.'

Eve shook her head. 'No, no I'll never come back here. You and Abi shall come to visit me, in Montacute?'

Frank nodded his agreement, but they both knew that he would never come to Montacute unless Mother came with him.

He picked up the empty suitcase. They stepped out into hot sunshine.

'Where will you go now, maid? What time does your train leave?'

'Not until four o'clock. I'll go round to Aunt Mina.'

Frank looked relieved. 'That's right. You go to see

your aunty.'

Eve went with him to the end of the terrace. A brief pressure of hands was all they could manage on parting. She knew as she walked away that he still watched her, but did not trust herself to look back.

Madelina was both angry and sympathetic. She sat Eve down at the kitchen table, gave her strong sweet tea, and rock cakes still warm from the oven.

'Well,' she declared, 'I always knew our Anni for a silly woman, but this time she's gone too far! Just you wait till I go round there! She'll get a piece of my mind that she won't relish! To turn you out of the house like that – what ever can she be thinking of? Of course,' Mina grew thoughtful, 'she has been building up trouble for some months past. I held my breath for you Eve, all through the wedding. I know my sister's temper. She wants you to be happy and married – but at the same time she can't bear to let you go. She'll regret it. Just you wait a week or two and you'll see how sorry she can be.' Eve said dully, 'I don't care anymore. I'll never feel the same about her. Abi is the one I feel really sorry for. I've escaped – but she can't.'

Sev put the empty suitcase into the boxroom. He comforted Eve. 'Go and see my mother. Spend some time with her. She's very fond of you. She'll be glad of your company.'

He went out on a Sunday morning; he came back carrying a puppy. He handed her the squirming white and brown spaniel.

'A late wedding present,' he grinned, 'just so's you don't get too lonely.'

*

To have Sev in England, living in his own house in the village, and married to a girl like Eve, was a miracle, the scope of which gave Damaris hope that she might live to see her grandchild. The baby, Eve had told her, was expected at the end of May. Maris managed, on an afternoon in late October, to climb the fourteen stone steps that led up to the house on the hill. She admired the brown leather armchairs, the Turkey-patterned linoleum, and delicately-tinted sheepskin rugs that had been Frank's present. She approved the positioning of her own wedding gift; smiled to see the two large gilt-framed pictures of the Scottish Highlands hung above Sev's fireplace; and at Eve's concern.

'You should have sent word that you were coming. I would have met you and walked with you.'

'I'm feeling better lately, my dear.' Maris took from her bag a ball of pink wool and a crochet hook. 'I've made a start on some baby clothes for you.' She sipped her tea, and admired the china tea-set. 'You've got nice things. You keep the house lookin' lovely, everything neat as a new pin.'

'There's nothing else for me to do. Sev won't hear of me taking any gloving even though we need the money. That job in the engineering pays only twenty-eight shillings. The mortgage uses most of his wages, and now, with the baby coming – well he's taken on evening jobs. I hardly ever see him.'

'Evening jobs?'

'He's out evernight, save Sunday. He plays five nights a week at the Palace Cinema in Yeovil. On Saturday nights he plays saxophone with the Imps' Dance Band at the Yeovil Assembly Rooms. The cinema pays seven shillings and sixpence for a single night's work, and the Imps pay ten shillings for a Saturday performance. Of course,' Eve said carefully, 'I know that you don't approve of dancing – well neither does Sev. But we need the money so very badly, and music is the only skill he has.'

Maris said, 'I never know'd that being a musician brought in so much money.' She paused. 'The dancing is sinful of course, but Sev'll be safe enough, while he's busy with his music. What I don't understand is this cinema business, and why shud they need music for it?'

'Did you never go to the pictures?'

'No my dear, I never didden.'

'Well – well you know what a photograph looks like? In the cinema you see a sort of moving photo. You can see the actors' lips move but there's no sound. The musicians play according to what's happening on the screen. If it's a sad tale, then they play sad tunes, and so on – There's usually a pianist, a clarinettist, and a trombone player. Sev reckons it to be hard work. They make up the music, mostly as they go along. He's worn out when he comes home, but we do so need the money.'

Maris said, 'Well I never! He was always clever o' course, always making up tunes when 'un was a liddle boy. I once bought 'un a penny-whistle.' Eve smiled. 'Yes I know. He told me about that.'

'He made up a special song for me when he came back from the Army. All about blackbirds – going away – and coming back – just like Sev himself. Such a pretty tune.' Maris looked keenly at Eve. 'He'm not an easy feller to get on with. He'm many-minded; all sharp edges and dark moods. It do all come from hurt feelings, long time ago. Mistakes was made – times was hard, Eve. Sev can't never trust, can't believe that people care about him. He was over-devoted to his Granfer. He was never the same boy after my father passed on.'

Eve said, 'He'll soon have his own child. He's making plans already, how he'll teach her early, to read books and listen to music.'

'Her?' Maris looked at the pink wool wound around her fingers, and smiled. 'You'm quite right, maid. The same thought was in my own mind.'

※

Jye took cuttings from his roses and planted them in Eve's garden. He made a trellis of wood against which, he told her, sweet-peas would climb in the summer days. He found her gentle and good-tempered. He said, 'Had you ever been to Montacute before you knew my son?'

'No. No I had never been in this part of the country.'

Jye sighed. 'You remind me of somebody. Not so much in looks, but in the way you smile. The way you hold your head a bit to one side when you'm listening to something.' He hesitated. 'Your mother's maiden name, what was it?'

Eve looked surprised. 'Greypaull,' she said, 'my mother's name was Annis Greypaull before she married.'

*

Jye sawed logs and put them in a sack; he filled a bag with potatoes and winter cabbage, wrapped brown eggs in straw and took a loaf from Maris's baking. He left the cottage, saying nothing to Damaris about his destination. He did not need to.

Meridiana had aged in the past months. There was, at last, a hint of silver among the black plaits. She found walking difficult, spent many hours alone, her gaze fixed upon the glowing embers of the wood fire. Jye sat down, and she turned her face towards him.

She said, in her abrupt way, 'Spit it out, then! You'm bustin' to tell I something! Let's be hearing!' She reached for her clay pipe and tobacco, and began to roll the thick-twist between her fingers. Jye said, 'Our Sev – the girl he married – her's from the Greypaull family. The mother's name is Annis.'

'I already know'd that.'

'How cud you? You've never met her.'

'Her passes by my window. I see her and Sev walking out together.'

Meri turned upon Jye the black gaze that confused his soul. 'I don't always need to be told things. You knows that. The power in me grows stronger as I gets older. That maid was promised to me years ago, by Eliza Greypaull. "If I can't bring your necklace myself," Liza said, "it shall be brought to 'ee by another."' Meri drew hard on the clay pipe and blew smoke out through her nostrils. 'Sev found the nut-brown maid down to

Taunton. Her do wear my coral.' She chuckled deep in her throat. 'My legs might not carry me so good anymore, but there's nothing wrong wi' my eyesight.'

Jye said, 'You leave Sev's wife alone, do you hear me? Don't you start your meddling in their lives. You done enough harm already.'

'I don't meddle, Jye. The path is laid down at birth, what we poor mortals is bound to follow.' Meri turned her gaze towards the fire. 'I sees clearer than most, what lies ahead on the big drom. There's a new child comin'. Sev's child. A great-grand-daughter of Eliza Greypaull.' Meri sighed. 'Ah dordi, but the drom'll wind uphill for that one!'

Jye stood up. 'Stop it! Don't say another word. You leave 'em be – you hear me?'

Meri grinned. 'Don't excite yourself, boy. Annis Greypaull's daughter'ull be good for Sev. He'm in right hands now. You can stop your worrittin' about him. Go home Jye. Your wife is mortal sick. She'm only hangin' on to see the new child what's coming.'

*

Annis had known from the moment the hard words were spoken that she had lost Eve. This conviction had been reinforced by Madelina, and confirmed by Frank.

Mina had said, 'I always knew that temper of yours would be your downfall in the end.'

Frank had said, in tones of disbelief, 'You turned her from the house? You told her never to come back here? All she did was to leave the wedding reception a bit earlier than planned!'

Abigail, when angry, sounded more than ever like her Aunty Blanche Fitzgerald. 'Oh no, Father! Eve's leaving early was only the peg on which Mother hung her disappointment. She never really believed that Eve would go through with this wedding.' Abi turned to Annis, 'You thought that the same tricks you had once worked on me would force Eve to break off her engagement; and you almost succeeded. But Sev Carew was too much for you, eh Mother? He's a strong man, and you don't like strong men, do you?

The memory of Eve's stricken face, as she had last seen it, was like an illness for which Annis could find no cure. Abigail was right; they were all correct in their reading of her nature; Annis knew now how protected and indulged she had always been by her husband and family. But this dreadful and singular act of rejection had been hers alone and she must pay the price. Getting Eve back became her sole preoccupation. Abi visited Montacute every Friday. She took, on her return, the very keenest pleasure in telling Annis about Eve's happiness with Sev. Abigail told her mother all about the house on the hill, with the fourteen steps that led up to the front door; the garden, dug by Sev's father and planted with roses.

'– And of course, as you might have expected, Eve's grown very close to Sev's mother – such a lovely little woman – very quiet-voiced – never loses her temper with anybody. Mrs Carew comes to tea with Evie.' Abi's tone was purposefully offhand. 'She's doing the most beautiful crochet work for Eve's baby. All in pink and white –'

'Eve's baby?'

'Ah yes. I must have forgotten to mention it to you. Old Mrs Carew will have a grandchild come next May. She's ever so happy about it – her being so ill – she says it has given her something to live for.' Abi smiled. 'Isn't it lucky for Evie, to have Sev's mother living close by, and her such a *pleasant* woman?'

Annis had never, in all her life, regretted her inability to read and write, but she regretted it now. 'Actions speak louder than words,' was one of Madelina's favourite sayings, and so Annis tried by the means of gifts to win back the love of her younger daughter. There was an evening in November when Abi returned from Montacute to report that Sev was laid low with malarial fever. Frank, who knew about such matters, said, 'He must be kept warm. Have they got enough blankets?'

Abi said, 'I don't think so. He was lying on the sofa beside the fire. Eve had piled every available cover on him, even his best overcoat, but his shivering and shaking was terrible to watch.'

Annis went upstairs; she returned carrying blankets. 'Tomorrow morning,' she said, 'you'll catch the first train up to Montacute, our Abi.' She hesitated and glanced at Frank. 'While you're up there you might ask your sister if there's anything else she's short of. You might mention that I'd like to see her – when she can spare the time.'

Abi delivered the blankets and the message. 'You can thank her for me,' Eve said slowly, 'and tell her I'll pay her back when I can afford it. As for going to see her – I was banished from that house you might remind her – I have no intention of crawling back!'

Abi saw with surprise the resolution of her sister's features. The flirtatious girl, for whom most troubles in life could be dispelled by laughter, had changed in the past months into a mature woman. The hint of stubbornness that had once been latent about the soft mouth and chin was now pronounced. 'No,' said Eve, 'even though it breaks my heart to stay away from Father, I will not set foot across that threshold, I have my own home now. I have Sev, and next year I shall have my baby. I don't need Mother any longer.'

Abi passed on the message, word for bitter word, and watched her Mother's features crumple into weeping. Abi offered no consolation. Annis said, at last, ''Tis nearly Christmas. Surely she won't bide away from us at Christmas.'

'You could,' Abi said, 'go to Montacute and see Eve. Tell her that you're sorry.'

'I can't do that! After all, I am the mother – I've got my pride!'

'Your pride,' Abi said, 'has ruined my life, and come very close to spoiling Eve's. No man was ever good enough for us! You found fault with every friend we ever had. You are a spoiled and selfish woman, Mother! The only good thing you ever did for me was to marry Frank Nevill.' Abi's laugh was bitter. 'You brought me up to believe that I was something special; that money would come to me from the Castlemain family. That I was, in fact, although base-born, some kind of heiress.'

Annis said, 'They will acknowledge you. I know they will!'

'No Mother. I'll tell you what will happen to me. I shall be the daughter who never marries. The one who stays at home to look after her parents in their old age. In the end, I shall be alone in this house. I shall remember then that I am Jeremy Castlemain's daughter – and almost a lady.'

A silence fell between them in which neither woman dared to look directly at the other. Annis said at last, 'I'll go to Montacute if you think I ought to. Ask your sister if – if she'll let me come to see her. Tell her that I'm sorry.'

*

Miles Hill had a way of advancing or receding according to the weather. On a December morning of hard frost and brilliant sunshine it seemed very distant. Eve's depression lightened; she dreaded the wet days when the surrounding hilltops seemed to lean inwards to enclose the village. Then it was that she felt the agony of her separation from Father; the sorrow of Damaris Carew's advancing illness; the growing awareness of Sev's reluctance to remain in Montacute. He had started, very gradually, to tell her his secret thoughts and feelings. The deepness and strangeness of his nature was, she found, distressing to witness. There were many things she did not understand. He had walked with her to the little village school. 'How I hated that place,' he told her. 'I played truant whenever I could. They called me carrot-head and diddecoi. I was always running off; up-in-ground with my Granfer was where I loved most to be.

My child shall never go to that school!'

He talked at other times about his childhood, about lambing-time, the loss of Granfer; the encounters with the famous Powys brothers. 'Imagine my surprise,' he said, 'when I found their novels in the Army Library in Agra! I felt proud then. I thought to myself – I once walked and talked on Ham Hill with John Cowper Powys!'

Of their love for one another there was no doubt. He worked long hours to provide for her and the coming baby. 'You and the British Army,' he told her, 'are the two best things that ever happened to me.' She was proud of his good looks, of his musical talent; loved him for the inexperience that so often showed through his assumed airs of sophistication.

'I've knocked about the wide world!' he was fond of saying. 'There's not much I don't know about life and people.' But for all his dark moods and infectious laughter, Eve knew that Sev could not bear to contemplate his mother's increasing weakness.

'You should visit her more often. She wants to see you!'

'I will – I will! Just don't nag at me about it. Can't you see how tired I am? I was playing in the Assembly Rooms until two o'clock this morning, then I had a five-mile drive back from Yeovil!'

It was all true. He fell asleep across the table, the knife and fork still in his hand, the Sunday dinner half consumed. It was Eve who sat by his mother's bed, held her hand, and told her about events in Taunton.

Damaris said, ''Tis nearly Christmas, maid, and she is your mother when all's said and done! She must be feeling true regrets now, specially with a grandchild coming! There's your father too. Think how he must be feeling!'

Eve thought about Father. She sent a letter to Abi. 'Sev,' she wrote, 'will be coming to Taunton on Christmas Eve. The Imps' Dance Band has got evening engagements in the town for the whole of the Christmas season. I have decided to come with him.'

*

Coming back to the Terrace on that Christmas Eve was the hardest move that she had ever made. It was Abigail who opened the front door; she whispered anxiously, 'Mother's truly sorry, Eve. She is really sorry this time. Please try to smooth things over – if only for Father's sake!'

'Smoothing things over' was a Greypaull euphemism for forgiveness. It required that Eve should sit quietly, sip her tea, admire the Christmas decorations, and smile and nod as if the quarrel, in which she had been forbidden to enter this house, had never happened.

Mother played her part; she was effusive in her welcome, smiled and smiled, and made clear in her conversation that there was no aspect of Eve's new life that had not been relayed to her by Abi. She spoke familiarly of Montacute although she had never been there; expressed doubts about the fourteen steps that led up to Sev's front door, and Eve's ability to manoeuvre a pram up and down with a baby inside it. Mother would, so she said, come to stay in Montacute for at least a week before the birth was expected, and remain for a month or even longer until Eve had regained her strength. Mother talked and talked, until the smell of Christmas puddings, boiling dry in the kitchen, claimed her attention.

Abi sighed her relief. 'Well that went better than I expected!'

Father sighed. ''Tis so good to have you back, maid! Now everything can go on nicely, just like it used to be.'

Eve smiled back. 'Yes,' she said, 'now everything can go on nicely.'

She thought about Sev, playing clarinet in a dance band on this Christmas Eve to earn money for a cradle and a pram. She studied Abigail and Father, trapped endlessly in the bonds of Mother's love. She remembered

Damaris Carew, who was hanging on to life so that she might hold Sev's child; Maris, who would never see another Christmas. Everything had changed, and she herself was in a state of wonderful transition. Of one thing only could she be certain; that her feelings towards Mother would never be the same.

*

Sev had almost forgotten how subtle and sweet were the seasons of England. In April his whole attention had been directed towards Eve and Taunton, his romantic mood intensified by blackthorn flowers and birdsong.

Summer had passed on the vague thought that this warmth was a pleasure when compared to the fierce heat of Agra and Khartoum. But his mind had been busy with wedding plans, the purchase and furnishing of the new house. The need to earn sufficient money to support a wife.

October brought a stillness. The cider apples were gathered-in from Mr Coles's orchard. Sev became aware of the slowing of the year's pulse. The recent momentum of his own life was no longer sufficient to enable him to evade thought. There were days when his need to be alone in a high place became acute. He went out from the house on a Sunday morning with a murmured excuse to Eve that he needed cigarettes. He climbed up to the outcrop of stone from which he could see the rich fields of Long Load and High Ham. He walked downwards from Jack o'Beards to Tinker's Spring, and caught the soft sheen of the River Parrett, low now between its banks because of the long dry summer.

As he walked, the shadow of the dark woman walked with him. Sev knew that he had, all unwittingly, strayed onto her set route, and into her own footfalls. He passed through dingles filled with the mist of autumn; came up again into the hazy gold of October sunshine. There was a smell of ash-smoke in the lanes. He began to run. He looked out across Norton, and there were the painted waggons, and the little brown bender tents, erected in a long line down the length of the hedge. He felt the old restlessness come upon him, and now, for the first time he experienced fear of a truly terrifying nature.

Sev came to the hollow place in the hillside that had once been Granfer's winter hut. He sat down in a sheltered spot, and spread out below him, as if arranged for his direct evaluation, were the two symbols of his divided nature.

The white sheep made a pattern against the green turf. They cropped slowly, moving ever forward, their faces turned towards the sun. The shepherd who had taken Granfer's place was grown old before his time. He stood, stoop-shouldered, crook in hand, and studying his flock. This man, Sev thought, was more strongly rooted in the soil than the elder-tree beneath which he stood. A man was born to shepherding, Granfer had said. It was something of the blood, an ability to cherish and protect; to remain in the one place, to be accountable and steady.

Sev turned his gaze away towards the gypsy waggons; he noted the signs of their imminent departure. He remembered that this was the season of horse-fairs. Even at this distance he could sense excitement among the travellers. He felt the itch in his own feet. He recalled the words of Major Stanley, the Battalion doctor. 'Itchy feet and marriage don't go well together.' 'Ah,' Sev had said, 'but you should see my girl, sir! Any gypsy-chal would settle down for the sake of her!'

He thought about Eve and knew that he had chosen well. There was the house, purchased and not rented, the brown leather armchairs, the china tea-set; the child she would bear him in the coming summer. Granfer would be proud if he could see Sev now.

He had not visited the dark woman since his return to England. He had passed by her window, head deliberately averted, his mind closed against her. But there had never been a need for him to see her face, hear her voice, cross her curious threshold. The link between them was of the spirit, and there was nothing he could do to change it. The waggons pulled out of the lane. Sev watched them go, saw the coloured concourse wind around the Hill, and pass out of sight. He felt suddenly older, like a child who has outgrown a favourite toy. He would never again see the dark woman, hear her gruff voice, and her dangerous predictions. He looked back towards the grazing sheep and the observant shepherd. The choice was made. There would be dreams, small excursions into waywardness and fancy. But the Lord was still his Shepherd; his Shepherd was the Lord; and Sev was, as he had always been, his Granfer's sonner.

※

Sev's daughter was born on a Thursday afternoon in late May, with a midwife and doctor in attendance. Annis, wilfully misinformed by Eve of the expected date of the confinement, was still safely unaware in Taunton. Sev sent a telegram to Number 5, The Terrace, and Annis arrived on the evening train. Her first move was to lift the infant from the cradle, carry her towards the window and study her colouring and features. The silence was prolonged. Annis said at last, 'Well – I wouldn't say that she've exactly got red hair, would you Eve? No, I don't think we need to worry on that count.' Even as she spoke a shaft of evening sunlight shone across the baby's head, turning to flame the thick soft hair. Annis moved swiftly back into the shadow. 'That's better,' she whispered, 'you could almost call it brown in a poor light.' She turned to Eve. 'We don't need no more unlucky redheads in the family! Remember what happened to your Granny Greypaull!'

Eve called her daughter Victoria Abigail. The christening was performed at Trinity church by the Vicar who had married Sev and Eve. Abigail was godmother. Annis had prepared a special tea; the front parlour was filled with aunts and cousins. Billy, just returned from Hollywood, looking older and very frail, was seated in a blue brocade armchair. He told Eve about his life among the film stars; the kindness of Mary Pickford and Douglas Fairbanks; the money that had been collected among his fellow actors so that he might return and live comfortably in England. Abigail, proud and happy in her role of aunt, showed the baby to Billy. He stared at the infant. 'My God, Eve!' he said at last. 'I'm sorry to have to say it – but it's got ginger hair!'

*

Victoria Abigail. The names seemed too long for so small a creature. Sev searched for signs of Greypaull in her, and found none. Already, at the age of only three months, the baby looked exactly like himself, and Damaris, his mother. Sev turned the apple-wood logs brought by Jye, his father. He gazed into the heart of the fire and foretold a thin-boned child, blue-eyed and tiny, reddish of hair, and many-minded. He saw pictures in the fire. When his child was grown he would show her those pictures; they would sit together on wild winter days and read the message of the flames. She was so like him in every way that already he felt frightened for her. She cried with such intensity, the almost-adult sobs shuddering through her frail body, until he thought that she might die of weeping. After long hours spent in the Palace Cinema in Yeovil, playing music which was meant to enhance the antics of Charlie Chaplin and Greta Garbo, Sev would come home to find Eve awake and exhausted, and close to tears. He would take the baby from her, hold the creature against his shoulder, pace the room with her when all he craved was sleep.

In the month of October the crying ceased. The baby grew plump and rosy-cheeked; she sat up, unaided; smiled whenever he approached her. He dared to believe that she would live.

Eve dressed her daughter in the pink-crocheted dresses made by Maris. Sev's mother clung to life with a tenacity that amazed her doctor; she had taken to her bed in early June, and was tended by a cousin. Eve brought the baby to her every afternoon. In the month of November a change came over Maris; she grew weaker. She said to Eve, 'He never comes to see me anymore. I lie awake at night. I hear his motorbike go by when he comes back from Yeovil.'

Eve said, 'I'll speak to him about it.' She paused. 'It's not that he stays away on purpose. Those Saturday-night dances go on until all hours, and then there's his regular job, and the evenings in the Palace cinema in Yeovil.'

Damaris said, 'Will you kiss me, Eve, before you go?'

✱

Sev stood at the window on that Sunday morning. Miles Hill looked so close beneath the rain clouds, almost within touching distance. His mind strayed from one restless thought to another. He was hampered in his unease by a need for silence in the house while the baby slept. He put a new reed into the clarinet, fitting it with care, loving the smooth feel of the ebony and silver beneath his fingers. He thought about the sitar player beneath the banyan tree; the waterfalls in Nai Natel where he had laid down and wept. India was still with him, in his blood like a recurring fever, like the malarial attacks that still came upon him without warning. He looked to the corner of the room where his child lay sleeping in her pram. He would tell her about the sitar player, and the Taj Mahal seen by moonlight, just as soon as she was old enough to understand. Since leaving the Army, the only music he had played was dance tunes. He hated syncopation, but there was money in it. He would explain to his child about music; how to listen to it – but she would have the right ear – for she was his daughter. He would give her titles, and names. Amy Woodford Finden. 'The Indian Love Lyrics'. He began to list them in his mind. There was 'Kashmiri Song', and

'Less Than the Dust'; 'Temple bells' and 'Until I Awake'. To remember the music he had played in Agra was all that it needed to transport him; he was back there, under the luminous sky and brilliant light, with the Taj and its minarets, the red-sandstone Fort and its sheer walls; and he and Taffy running together in the cool air of the evening. There were other things that must be passed on, for this child must know from whence she came; what blood had gone into the making of her; it would be his duty to tell her about patteran. She must know about Granfer Honeybone and how Sev had felt about him; about London and Lord Curzon; about Bristol and the long tramp through the frozen lanes to Jellalabad Barracks and the salvation he had found there. He would never lie to her. These were my mistakes, he would tell her, and these were my glories. He hoped that she might understand and be lenient with him. He would tell her that in school he had been called carrot-head and diddecoi. He would protect her from all hurt; all danger. The baby whimpered in her sleep. In the kitchen, Eve peeled potatoes. Sev looked up towards Miles Hill; he felt the itch in his feet, the need to be up and moving on. Next year, he thought; next year or maybe sooner, they would move to Yeovil. Eve loved to live in towns, she needed shops and traffic, and the company of people. They would find a house close to a school. He would teach his child to read just as soon as her eye could follow his pointing finger across a printed page.

Down the village street came Jye; he walked slowly, his shoulders bowed, his head bent. Sev wanted to run; up to Miles Hill, to London, back to the Army. He stood, rooted by the window, and watched as his father climbed the fourteen steps. It was Eve who opened the front door; Eve who was first to receive the news that Damaris was dead.

*

Abi visited Montacute every Monday morning. On

Fridays Eve took the early train to Taunton, the baby shawled thickly against the morning chill, the pram travelling in the guard's van. In between, Eve walked the lanes of Montacute that seemed to lead nowhere, and told the wakeful child that they must consider themselves lucky to be spending two days out of every seven among their own sort of people.

Eve and Abi could only afford to window shop these days. They no longer entered emporiums like Chapman's and Hatcher's. Eve wore the pink dress and coat that had been her going-away outfit. Abigail, aunt and godmother, spent all of her money on baby clothes; could not be persuaded from the purchase of a little blue-satin coat and bonnet trimmed with white swansdown, frilled white dresses, and shoes of soft red leather. The baby, while in Taunton, was handed from one pair of loving hands to another; carried everywhere by Abigail and Mother; seated on Father's knee and allowed to play with the precious silver pocket watch. The child, Eve thought, was like a magic wand, in spite of the hair that Billy had called 'ginger'; she had brought happiness and peace into Number 5, The Terrace.

There had been other changes. Billy, who talked like a film-star, said 'You've lost your pretty-little-girl looks, Evie!' He regarded her thoughtfully. 'What you have now is the face of a dreaming Madonna – much more beautiful and permanent. Prettiness never did last long.'

Mother said meaningly, 'You've lost weight, my girl. You must know now what big responsibilities we mothers have to carry.' But what Mother said no longer seemed important. Sev's voice was stronger and more insistent.

Abi said, 'You're happy, aren't you: you have a husband, home and child. It's what every woman longs for.'

'And what about you?'

Abi twisted the engagement ring around her finger, and smiled. 'The six iron nails are still there, across the

497

threshold. No matter what Joey does, he'll never really get away.'

Eve laughed. 'Why, you're as superstitious as the rest of the Greypaulls.'

'What about you then? I see you're still wearing Mother's lucky pendant.'

'Oh, I don't believe in charms, Abi. I only wear it because Sev likes it. These heavy silver pieces are so old-fashioned. I like my string of artificial pearls much better!'

On a cold afternoon in late March Eve pushed the pram to Odcombe. The winter days were almost ended, there were primroses in the hedgerows; the latest spring fashions were displayed in Hatcher's windows. She remembered her wedding-dress of blue silk. There was said to be a dressmaker in Yeovil who was good at renovations. She leaned over the pram towards the solemn baby. 'You're the fashionable one in the family these days! The lucky girl who gets all the new clothes!' The baby smiled back as if she understood. She did not smile at many people; she had an alarming way of crying out at the approach of strangers, and hiding her face from them. Eve feared that her daughter would turn out to be a shy child; she tucked strands of the rust-coloured hair beneath the pink-crocheted bonnet, and wished with all her heart that Damaris had lived just a little longer.

Sev and his father had endured solitary grief; they might well, Eve thought, have lived a thousand miles apart, so wide was their division. When the initial agony had passed, Jye talked to Eve as he could never talk to his only son. He sat in the brown leather armchair, he told her about his roses; he said that Sev was too impatient, that he would never make a gardener; he promised to bring plants and cuttings when they moved to their new home in Yeovil. Jye no longer looked at Eve as though hers was a face to which he could put a name. To begin with, she had sensed a certain puzzlement, had read confusion in his eyes. He had on two occasions called her 'Blanche'. 'No,' she had laughed, 'Not Blanche – I'm Eve! Blanche was my aunty, but you could never have known her!'

The isolation of his deafness was more pronounced since Maris's death. Eve promised to visit often; she saw how Sev's baby was already very special to his father. Victoria was the first blue-eyed girl child to be born into this family; Jye often looked at her and said, 'Why, her's the living image of my Maris.'

The house on the hill was strewn with half-packed boxes; the move to Yeovil would be made on the fifth of April. Eve turned the pram back towards Montacute; she thought about the new house which stood directly opposite a school. The view from the upper windows was of steep and dangerous Babylon Hill. Sev had warned her to beware of gypsies. 'That's the way they always come,' he explained, 'when they ride into Somerset from Dorset.' He had grinned as he spoke. 'Clever they are; and persuasive. They'll talk the money from your pocket, and the good coat from your shoulders.'

Eve came into Montacute; she crossed the green grass of the Borough; a woman stood waiting at a cottage doorway. She said, 'Pardon me, my dear, but be I right in thinking that you'm the wife of Sev Carew?'

Eve said, 'Yes – yes I'm Sev's wife.'

The woman bent towards the pram, and Victoria began at once to cry and hide her face against the pillows. 'She's shy,' Eve said quickly. 'She's not used to strangers.'

The woman said, 'There's an old lady who's very keen to see both you, and Sev's baby. Won't you come inside for just a minute. You can't think how happy that 'ud make her. She'm very old. She don't get many visitors these days. She sees you passing by her window. Bring that pretty maid in to see me! That's what she keeps on saying.' Eve glanced towards the cottage window; a sudden terror seized her.

'Tomorrow,' she promised, 'in the afternoon. I can't really stop now. Sev comes back from Yeovil about six – he'll expect his dinner to be ready.'

The woman nodded her relief. 'Tomorrow,' she said. 'Yes, I'll tell her you'll be round tomorrow. She've got a strong will, I can tell you – she've talked of nothing else since word got round the village that you and Sev is off to live in Yeovil.'

Eve walked swiftly away; she regretted the promise as soon as it was given. Victoria always screamed at the sight of a new face. The old lady would be upset. They would both of them feel embarrassed. She would make the visit a very short one; she would not mention it to Sev.

*

Meridiana sat upright against spotless pillows, and covered by the dazzling whiteness of a honeycomb bedspread. Her greying hair was braided and coiled, she wore her golden earrings and her amber necklets. To the woman who tended her she said, 'You can go home now. Leave the door on the latch. I can manage for myself till tomorrow morning.' The silence of the house had that special quality of waiting; she had known it so often in her long life, that hush that came before a significant happening. She had experienced it on the brow of Babylon Hill, when she had paused there as a young girl and looked out towards Yeovil, and beyond, to Montacute where Luke dwelt. She recalled the stillness of the blackthorn hedges, where she had waited for that final meeting with Eliza Greypaull. 'Yes,' Eliza had said, ''tis your coral beads what my Annis do wear. But you shall have 'em back, I promise. If I can't bring your necklace myself, it shall be brought to 'ee by another!'

This day, the first of April, was the time when prophecy would be fulfilled, and promises honoured. Annis Greypaull's daughter would bring the coral pendant; Meri would gaze for the first and last time on

Sev Carew's baby daughter. A light step in the porch, a hesitant tapping on the door, and Eve was with her, the pendant gleaming against her white throat, the red-haired infant in her arms.

Meri sensed the young woman's terror of her. She studied the lovely face, the slender figure, the long and shapely legs in pale silk-stockings, the pointed snakeskin shoes; the fashionable style of Sev's wife. The girl came on tiptoe towards the bed, the baby clutched hard against her shoulder.

Meri said, 'I know'd that you'd be something extra-special. He was always a partikler sort of feller!' The dimples came and went in the girl's flushed cheeks; tendrils of nut-brown hair curled softly from beneath the pink hat with its tassel of brown. Meri pointed to the chair that stood close beside the bed.

'Sit down,' she commanded. 'Put the child on the bed, sit her on my lap. I wants to look at her.' Meri gazed into Eve's green eyes, and beyond, into her soul. She saw at first outright refusal; and then gradually, an unwilling compliance. The girl came towards her; she lowered the baby very slowly. She said, 'Don't mind too much if she cries. She's not used to strangers.'

Meri said, 'What makes you think that her and me be strangers to one another? Just see the way her's looking at me. Ah dordi, but I've see'd that look before! This chavvie do already recognise me.'

The baby sat, wide-eyed and solemn. She seemed to be studying the seamed face, the dark eyes, and the golden earrings. She did not smile, neither did she cry. Meri took the child's hand into her own; she unfurled the plump pink fingers and then quickly closed them. 'No,' she muttered, 'let come what will to this one. I got no need to know about it.'

The mother's face grew anxious, she reached her arms towards her baby. 'Let her bide,' said Meri, ''tis on'y for a short time. I hears tell that you be off to Yeovil?'

'We move at the weekend. It'll be better, you see, for

Victoria to grow up in the town.'

'You don't like this village? Well, no more did I when I first came here.' An awkward silence fell between them, broken only when Meri said, abruptly, 'Give me the pendant then! After all, 'tis what you've come here for – no need to make me wait any longer, for it, is there?'

'You – you want my necklace? It's not worth much, just a cheap trinket that once belonged to my mother.' The young woman's voice was hesitant and nervous. 'You can have it if you like, if it would make you happy? I'll tell my husband that I lost it, though he probably won't notice.' She laughed. 'I'll wear my pearls instead.'

Meri watched as the young woman raised her hands to unclasp the pendant. Beyond them the applewood fire burned red and blue about its edges, the heart of it fallen into valleys and plains of white ash.

Meri sat immobile and willed Eve to come towards her. Other figures rose up from among the ashes. She saw Eliza, red-haired and tiny. Annis, tall and fair, and indecisive. Even as she watched, the vision blurred and shifted. The image of Eliza faded quite suddenly and was gone. The figure of Annis retreated and grew pale. It was the nut-brown girl who came smiling towards Meri, both hands outstretched. Neat hands they were, square-fingered and compact. Those fingers advanced until they filled all of Meri's vision.

Her heartbeat slowed so that her breath was almost stilled. Linked between those hands, and glowing like a live thing in the firelight, swung the necklace of heavy silver and carved coral.

Eve said, 'The catch is very stiff. Here – let me fasten it for you.'

Meri leaned forward; as the silver and coral settled around her throat, she smiled at Eve for the first time; she laid both hands across the pendant and leaned back against her pillows. She spoke with dignity and in a quiet voice.

'You 'ont ever know how much I have waited for this

day. Must be goin' on seventy years since I parted company wi' this necklace.'

Even as Meridiana spoke, the sun moved across the heavens; the world turned, letting sunlight into the room, it touched the baby, turning to flame the fine straight hair. Meri spoke, in a voice so absent and strange that it confirmed for Eve the craziness of this unknown and aged woman. The words, addressed to a corner of the room where a blue bowl stood on a table, were preceded by a chuckle.

'I got the best of the chop after all – eh, Liza!'